David Peace grew up in Yorkshire  remembers listening to the hoax tape of way home from school. He was selected ... ... Young British Novelists 2003. In 2007, he was named GQ Writer of the Year. He lives in Japan.

Serpent's Tail publishes the four volumes of his Red Riding Quartet, *Nineteen Seventy Four*, *Nineteen Seventy Seven*, *Nineteen Eighty*, *Nineteen Eighty Three*.

Praise for the Quartet

Nineteen Seventy Four

'Peace's stunning debut has done for the county what Raymond Chandler and James Ellroy did for LA...a brilliant first novel, written with tremendous pace and passion' *Yorkshire Post*

'Peace's pump-action prose propels the book's narrative with a scorching turn-of-speed to an apocalyptic denouement...One hell of a read' *Crime Time*

'This breathless, extravagant, ultra-violent debut thriller reads like it was written by a man with one hand down his pants and the other on a shotgun. Vinnie Jones should buy the film rights fast' *Independent on Sunday*

'*Nineteen Seventy Four* takes the direct approach: straight to the heart of Ellroy-land, turning his native Yorkshire of the early seventies into a pustulant, cancerous core of complete corruption' *Uncut*

Nineteen Seventy Seven

'Simply superb...Peace is a masterful storyteller, and *Nineteen Seventy Seven* is impossible to put down...Peace has single-handedly established the genre of Yorkshire Noir, and mightily satisfying it is. *Nineteen Seventy Seven* is a must-read thriller' *Yorkshire Post*

'Peace's policemen rape prostitutes they are meant to be protecting, torture suspects they know cannot be guilty and reap the profits of organised vice. Peace's powerful novel exposes a side of life which most of us would prefer to ignore' *Daily Mail*

Nineteen
Seventy Four

David Peace

A complete catalogue record for this book can be obtained from the British Library on request

The right of David Peace to be identified as the author of this work has been asserted by him in accordance with the Copyright, Designs and Patents Act 1988

First published in 1999 by Serpent's Tail

First published in this edition in 2008 by Serpent's Tail,
an imprint of Profile Books Ltd
3A Exmouth House
Pine Street
London EC1R 0JH
website: www.serpentstail.com

ISBN 978 1 84668 705 1

Printed and bound by CPI Group (UK) Ltd, Croydon, CR0 4YY

10   9   8   7   6

This book is printed on FSC certified paper

For Izumi

In memory of Michael and Eiki

With thanks to my family and friends, home and away

*'The only thing new in this world is the
history you don't know.'*

– Harry S. Truman

Beg

Christmas bombs and Lucky on the run, Leeds United and the Bay City Rollers, The Exorcist *and* It Ain't Half Hot Mum.

Yorkshire, Christmas 1974.

I keep it close.

I wrote lies as truth and truth as lies, believing it all.

I fucked women I didn't love and the one I did, I fucked forever.

I killed a bad man but let others live.

I killed a child.

Yorkshire, Christmas 1974.

I keep it close.

Part 1
Yorkshire wants me

Chapter 1

'All we ever get is Lord fucking Lucan and wingless bloody crows,' smiled Gilman, like this was the best day of our lives:

Friday 13 December 1974.

Waiting for my first Front Page, the Byline Boy at last: Edward Dunford, North of England Crime Correspondent; two days too fucking late.

I looked at my father's watch.

9 a.m. and no bugger had been to bed; straight from the Press Club, still stinking of ale, into this hell:

The Conference Room, Millgarth Police Station, Leeds.

The whole bloody pack sat waiting for the main attraction, pens poised and tapes paused; hot TV lights and cigarette smoke lighting up the windowless room like a Town Hall boxing ring on a Late Night Fight Night; the paper boys taking it out on the TV set, the radios static and playing it deaf:

'They got sweet FA.'

'A quid says she's dead if they got George on it.'

Khalid Aziz at the back, no sign of Jack.

I felt a nudge. It was Gilman again, Gilman from the *Manchester Evening News* and before.

'Sorry to hear about your old man, Eddie.'

'Yeah, thanks,' I said, thinking news really did travel fucking fast.

'When's the funeral?'

I looked at my father's watch again. 'In about two hours.'

'Jesus. Hadden still taking his pound of bloody flesh then.'

'Yeah,' I said, knowing, funeral or no funeral, no way I'm letting Jack fucking Whitehead back in on this one.

'I'm sorry, like.'

'Yeah,' I said.

Seconds out:

A side door opens, everything goes quiet, everything goes slow. First a detective and the father, then Detective Chief Superintendent George Oldman, last a policewoman with the mother.

I pressed record on the Philips Pocket Memo as they took their seats behind the plastic-topped tables at the front, shuffling papers, touching glasses of water, looking anywhere but up.

In the blue corner:

Detective Chief Superintendent George Oldman, a face from before, a big man amongst big men, thick black hair plastered back to look like less, a pale face streaked beneath the lights with a thousand burst blood vessels, the purple footprints of tiny spiders running across his bleached white cheeks to the slopes of his drunken nose.

Me thinking, *his face, his people, his times*.

And in the red corner:

The mother and the father in their crumpled clothes and greasy hair, him flicking at the dandruff on his collar, her fiddling with her wedding ring, both twitching at the bang and the wail of a microphone being switched on, looking for all the world more the sinners than the sinned against.

Me thinking, did you do your own daughter?

The policewoman put her hand upon the mother's arm, the mother turned, staring at her until the policewoman looked away.

Round One:

Oldman tapped on the microphone and coughed:

'Thank you for coming gentlemen. It's been a long night for everyone, especially Mr and Mrs Kemplay, and it's going to be a long day. So we'll keep this brief.'

Oldman took a sip from a glass of water.

'At about 4 p.m. yesterday evening, 12 December, Clare Kemplay disappeared on her way home from Morley Grange Junior and Infants, Morley. Clare left school with two classmates at a quarter to four. At the junction of Rooms Lane and Victoria Road, Clare said goodbye to her friends and was last seen walking down Victoria Road towards her home at approximately four o'clock. This was the last time anyone saw Clare.'

The father was looking at Oldman.

'When Clare failed to return home, a search was launched early yesterday evening by the Morley Police, along with the help of Mr and Mrs Kemplay's friends and neighbours, however, as yet, no clue has been found as to the nature of Clare's disappearance. Clare has never gone missing before and we are obviously very concerned as to her whereabouts and safety.'

Oldman touched the glass again but let it go.

'Clare is ten years old. She is fair and has blue eyes and long straight hair. Last night Clare was wearing an orange waterproof kagool, a dark blue turtleneck sweater, pale blue denim trousers with a distinctive eagle motif on the back left pocket and red Wellington boots. When Clare left school, she was carrying a plastic Co-op carrier bag containing a pair of black gym shoes.'

Oldman held up an enlarged photograph of a smiling girl, saying, 'Copies of this recent school photograph will be distributed at the end.'

Oldman took another sip of water.

Chairs scraped, papers rustled, the mother sniffed, the father stared.

'Mrs Kemplay would now like to read a short statement in the hope that any member of the public who may have seen Clare after four o'clock yesterday evening, or who may have any information regarding Clare's whereabouts or her disappearance, will come forward to assist us in our investigation. Thank you.'

Detective Chief Superintendent Oldman gently turned the microphone towards Mrs Kemplay.

Camera flashes exploded across the Conference Room, startling the mother and leaving her blinking into our faces.

I looked down at my notebook and the wheels turning the tape inside the Philips Pocket Memo.

'I would like to appeal to anybody who knows where my Clare is or who saw her after yesterday teatime to please telephone the police. Clare is a very happy girl and I know she would never just run off without telling me. Please, if you know where she is or if you've seen her, please telephone the police.'

A strangled cough, then silence.

I looked up.

Mrs Kemplay had her hands to her mouth, her eyes closed.

Mr Kemplay stood up and then sat back down, as Oldman said:

'Gentlemen, I have given you all the information we have at the moment and I'm afraid we haven't got time to take any questions right now. We've scheduled another press conference for five, unless there are any developments before then. Thank you gentlemen.'

Chairs scraped, papers rustled, murmurs became mutters, whispers words.

Any developments, fuck.

'Thank you, gentlemen. That'll be all for now.'

Detective Chief Superintendent Oldman stood up and turned to go but no-one else at the table moved. He turned back into the glare of the TV lights, nodding at journalists he couldn't see.

'Thank you, lads.'

I looked down at the notebook again, the wheels still turning the tape, seeing any developments face down in a ditch in an orange waterproof kagool.

I looked back up, the other detective was lifting Mr Kemplay up by his elbow and Oldman was holding open the side door for Mrs Kemplay, whispering something to her, making her blink.

'Here you go.' A heavy detective in a good suit was passing along copies of the school photograph.

I felt a nudge. It was Gilman again.

'Doesn't look so fucking good does it?'

'No,' I said, Clare Kemplay's face smiling up at me.

'Poor cow. What must she be going through, eh?'

'Yeah,' I said, looking at my father's watch, my wrist cold.

'Here, you'd better fuck off hadn't you.'

'Yeah.'

The M1, Motorway One, South from Leeds to Ossett.

Pushing my father's Viva a fast sixty in the rain, the radio rocking to the Rollers' *Shang-a-lang*.

Seven odd miles, chanting the copy like a mantra:

A mother made an emotional plea.

The mother of missing ten-year-old Clare Kemplay made an emotional plea.

Mrs Sandra Kemplay made an emotional plea as fears grew.

Emotional pleas, growing fears.

I pulled up outside my mother's house on Wesley Street,

Ossett, at ten to ten, wondering why the Rollers hadn't covered *The Little Drummer Boy*, thinking get it done and done right.

Into the phone:

'OK, sorry. Do the lead paragraph again and then it's done. Right then: Mrs Sandra Kemplay made an emotional plea this morning for the safe return of her daughter, Clare, as fears grew for the missing Morley ten-year-old.

'New para: Clare went missing on her way home from school in Morley early yesterday evening and an intensive police search throughout the night has so far failed to yield any clue as to Clare's whereabouts.

'OK. Then it's as it was before . . .

'Thanks, love . . .

'No, I'll be through by then and it'll take my mind off things . . .

'See you Kath, bye.'

I replaced the receiver and checked my father's watch:

Ten past ten.

I walked down the hall to the back room, thinking it's done and done right.

Susan, my sister, was standing by the window with a cup of tea, looking out on the back garden and the drizzle. My Aunty Margaret was sat at the table, a cup of tea in front of her. Aunty Madge was in the rocking chair, balancing a cup of tea in her lap. No-one sat in my father's chair by the cupboard.

'You all done then?' said Susan, not turning round.

'Yeah. Where's Mum?'

'She's upstairs, love, getting ready,' said Aunty Margaret standing up, picking up her cup and saucer. 'Can I get you a fresh cup?'

'No, I'm OK thanks.'

'The cars'll be here soon,' said Aunty Madge to no-one.

I said, 'I best go and get ready.'

'All right, love. You go on then. I'll have a nice cup of tea for you when you come down.' Aunty Margaret went through into the kitchen.

'Do you think Mum's finished in the bathroom?'

'Why don't you ask her,' said my sister to the garden and
the rain.

Up the stairs, two at a time like before; a shit, a shave, and
a shower and I'd be set, thinking a quick wank and a wash'd
be better, suddenly wondering if my father could read my
thoughts now.

The bathroom door was open, my mother's door closed. In
my room a clean white shirt lay freshly ironed on the bed, my
father's black tie next to it. I switched on the radio in the shape
of a ship, David Essex promising to make me a star. I looked at
my face in the wardrobe mirror and saw my mother standing
in the doorway in a pink slip.

'I put a clean shirt and a tie on the bed for you.'

'Yeah, thanks Mum.'

'How'd it go this morning?'

'All right, you know.'

'It was on the radio first thing.'

'Yeah?' I said, fighting back the questions.

'Doesn't sound so good does it?'

'No,' I said, wanting to lie.

'Did you see the mother?'

'Yeah.'

'Poor thing,' said my mother, closing the door behind her.

I sat down on the bed and the shirt, staring at the poster of
Peter Lorimer on the back of the door.

Me thinking, ninety miles an hour.

The three car procession crawled down the Dewsbury Cutting,
through the unlit Christmas lights in the centre of the town, and
slowly back up the other side of the valley.

My father took the first car. My mother, my sister, and me
were in the next, the last car jammed full of aunties, blood and
fake. No-one was saying much in the first two cars.

The rain had eased by the time we reached the crematorium,
though the wind still whipped me raw as I stood at the door,
juggling handshakes and a cigarette that had been a fucker to
light.

Inside, a stand-in delivered the eulogy, the family vicar too
busy fighting his own battle with cancer on the very ward my

father had vacated early Wednesday morning. So Super Sub gave us a eulogy to a man neither he nor we ever knew, mistaking my father for a joiner, not a tailor. And I sat there, outraged by the journalistic licence of it all, thinking these people had carpenters on the bloody brain.

Eyes front, I stared at the box just three steps from me, imagining a smaller white box and the Kemplays in black, wondering if the vicar would fuck that up too when they finally found her.

I looked down at my knuckles turning from red to white as they gripped the cold wooden pew, catching a glimpse of my father's watch beneath my cuff, and felt a hand on my sleeve.

In the silence of the crematorium my mother's eyes asked for some calm, saying at least that man is trying, that the details aren't always so important. Next to her my sister, her make-up smudged and almost gone.

And then he was gone too.

I bent down to put the prayer book on the ground, thinking of Kathryn and that maybe I'd suggest a drink after I'd written up the afternoon press conference. Maybe we'd go back to hers again. Anyway, there was no way we could back to mine, not tonight at any rate. Then thinking, there's no fucking way the dead can read your thoughts.

Outside, I stood about juggling another set of handshakes and a cigarette, making sure the cars all knew the way back to my mother's.

I got in the very last car and sat in more silence, unable to place any of the faces, or name any of the names. There was a moment's panic as the driver took a different route back to Ossett, convincing me I'd joined the wrong fucking party. But then we were heading back up the Dewsbury Cutting, all the other passengers suddenly smiling at me like they'd all thought the exact same thing.

Back at the house, first things first:
  Phone the office.
  Nothing.
  No news being bad news for the Kemplays and Clare, good news for me.

Twenty-four hours coming up, tick-tock.

Twenty-four hours meaning Clare dead.

I hung up, glanced at my father's watch and wondered how long I'd have to stay amongst his kith and kin.

Give it an hour.

I walked back down the hall, the Byline Boy at last, bringing more death to the house of the dead.

'So this Southern bloke, his car breaks down up on Moors. He walks back to farm down road and knocks on door. Old farmer opens door and Southerner says, do you know where nearest garage is? Old farmer says no. So Southerner asks him if he knows way to town. Farmer says he don't know. How about nearest telephone? Farmer says he don't know. So Southerner says, you don't know bloody much do you. Old farmer says that's as may be, but am not one that's lost.'

Uncle Eric holding court, proud the only time he ever left Yorkshire was to kill Germans. Uncle Eric, who I'd seen kill a fox with a spade when I was ten.

I sat down on the arm of my father's empty chair, thinking of seaview flats in Brighton, of Southern girls called Anna or Sophie, and of a misplaced sense of filial duty now half redundant.

'Bet you're glad you came back, aren't you lad?' winked Aunty Margaret, pushing another cup of tea into my palms.

I sat there in the middle of the crowded back room, my tongue on the roof of my mouth, trying to move the stuck white bread, glad of something to clear out the taste of warm and salty ham, wishing for a whisky and thinking of my father yet again; a man who'd signed the Pledge on his eighteenth birthday for no other reason than they asked.

'Well now, would you look at this.'

I was miles and years away and then suddenly aware my hour was at hand, feeling all their eyes on me.

My Aunty Madge was waving a paper around like she was after some bluebottle.

Me sat on the arm of that chair, feeling like the fly.

Some of my younger cousins had been out for sweets and had brought back the paper, my paper.

My mother grabbed the paper from Aunty Madge, turning the inside pages until she came to the Births and Deaths.

Shit, shit, shit.

'Is Dad in?' said Susan.

'No. Must be tomorrow,' replied my mother, looking at me with those sad, sad eyes.

'*Mrs Sandra Kemplay made an emotional plea this morning for the safe return of her daughter.*' My Aunt Edie from Altrincham had the paper now.

Emotional fucking pleas.

'*By Edward Dunford, North of England Crime Correspondent.* Well I say,' read Aunty Margaret over my Aunt Edie's shoulder.

All around the room everyone began assuring me how proud my father would have been and how it was just such a pity he wasn't here now to witness this great day, my great day.

'I read all stuff you did on that Ratcatcher bloke,' Uncle Eric was saying. 'Strange one that one.'

The Ratcatcher, inside pages, crumbs from Jack fucking Whitehead's table.

'Yeah,' I said, smiling and nodding my head this way and that, picturing my father sat in this empty chair by the cupboard reading the back page first.

There were pats on the back and then, for one brief moment, the paper was there in my hands and I looked down:

Edward Dunford, North of England Crime Correspondent.

I didn't read another line.

Off the paper went again round the room.

I saw my sister across the room sat on the windowsill, her eyes closed, her hands to her mouth.

She opened her eyes and stared back at me. I tried to stand, to go over to her, but she stood up and left the room.

I wanted to follow her, to say:

I'm sorry, I'm sorry; I'm sorry that it had to happen today of all days.

'We'll be asking him for his autograph soon, won't we,' laughed Aunty Madge, passing me a fresh cup.

'He'll always be Little Eddie to me,' said Aunt Edie from Altrincham.

'Thanks,' I said.

'Doesn't look so good though does it?' said Aunty Madge.

'No,' I lied.

'There's been a couple now, haven't there?' said Aunt Edie, a cup of tea in one hand, my hand in the other.

'Aye, going back a few years now. That little lass over in Castleford,' said my Aunty Madge.

'That is going back a bit, aye. There was that one not so long ago mind, over our way,' said Aunt Edie, taking a mouthful of tea.

'Aye, in Rochdale. I remember that one,' said Aunty Madge, tightening her grip on her saucer.

'Never found her,' sighed Aunt Edie.

'Really?' I said.

'Never caught no-one either.'

'Never do though, do they,' said Aunty Madge to the whole room.

'I can remember a time when these sorts of things never happened.'

'Thems in Manchester were the first.'

'Aye,' muttered Aunt Edie, letting go of my hand.

'Evil they were, just plain bloody evil,' whispered Aunty Madge.

'And to think there's them that'd have her walking about like nowt was wrong.'

'Some folk are just plain daft.'

'Short memories an' all,' said Aunt Edie, looking out at the garden and the rain.

Edward Dunford, North of England Crime Correspondent, out the door.

Cats and bloody dogs.

Motorway One back to Leeds, lorry-thick and the going slow. Pushing the Viva a hard sixty-five in the rain, as good as it got.

Local radio:

'The search continues for missing Morley schoolgirl Clare Kemplay, as fears grow . . .'

A glance at the clock told me what I already knew:

4 p.m. meant time was against me, meant time was against

her, meant no time to do background checks on missing kids, meant no questions at the five o'clock press conference.

Shit, shit, shit.

Coming off the motorway fast, I weighed up the pros and cons of asking my questions blind, right there and then at the five o'clock, with nothing but two old ladies behind me.

Two kids missing, Castleford and Rochdale, no dates, only maybes.

Long shots in the dark.

Punch a button, national radio: sixty-seven dismissed from the *Kentish Times* and the *Slough Evening Mail*, NUJ Provincial Journalists set to strike from 1 January.

Edward Dunford, Provincial Journalist.

Long shots kick de bucket.

I saw Detective Chief Superintendent Oldman's face, I saw my editor's face, and I saw a Chelsea flat with a beautiful Southern girl called Sophie or Anna closing the door.

You might be balding but it's not fucking Kojak.

I parked behind Millgarth Police Station as they were packing up the market, gutters full of cabbage leaves and rotten fruit, thinking play it safe or play it scoop?

I squeezed the steering wheel, offering up a prayer:

LET NO OTHER FUCKER ASK THE QUESTION.

I knew it for what it was, a prayer.

The engine dead, another prayer from the steering wheel:

DON'T FUCK UP.

Up the steps and through the double doors, back into Millgarth Police Station.

Muddy floors and yellow lights, drunken songs and short fuses.

I flashed my Press Card at the desk, the Sergeant flashed back a mustard smile:

'Cancelled. Press Office rang round.'

'You're joking? Why?'

'No news. Nine o'clock tomorrow morning.'

'Good,' I grinned, thinking no questions asked.

The Sergeant winced.

I glanced around, opened my wallet. 'What's the SP?'

He took the wallet out of my hand, plucked out a fiver, and handed it back. 'That'll do nicely, sir.'

'So?'

'Nowt.'

'That was a fucking fiver.'

'So a fiver says she's dead.'

'Hold the fucking Front Page,' I said, walking back out.

'Give my best to Jack.'

'Fuck off.'

'Who loves you baby?'

5.30 p.m.

Back in the office.

Barry Gannon behind his boxes, George Greaves face down on his desk, Gaz from Sport talking shit.

No sign of Jack fucking Whitehead.

Thank Christ.

Shit, so where the fuck was he?

Paranoid:

I'm Edward Dunford, North of England Crime Correspondent and it says so on every fucking *Evening Post*.

'How did it go?' Kathryn Taylor, fresh curls to her fringe and an ugly cream sweater, standing up behind her desk and then sitting straight back down.

'Like a dream.'

'Like a dream?'

'Yeah. Perfect.' I couldn't keep the grin off my face.

She was frowning. 'What happened?'

'Nothing.'

'Nothing?' She looked utterly lost.

'It was cancelled. They're still searching. Got nothing,' I said, emptying my pockets on to her desk.

'I meant the funeral.'

'Oh.' I picked up my cigarettes.

Telephones were ringing, typewriters clattering.

Kathryn was looking at my notebook on her desk. 'So what do they think?'

I took off my jacket and picked up her coffee and lit a

cigarette, all in one move. 'She's dead. Listen, is the boss in a meeting?'

'I don't know. I don't think so. Why?'

'I want him to get me an interview with George Oldman. Tomorrow morning, before the press conference.'

Kathryn picked up my notebook and began spinning it between her fingers. 'You'll be lucky.'

'Will you speak to Hadden. He likes you,' I said, taking the notebook from her.

'You're joking?'

I needed facts, hard fucking facts.

'Barry!' I shouted over the telephones, the typewriters, and Kathryn's head. 'When you've got a minute, can I have a quick word?'

Barry Gannon from behind his fortress of files, 'If I must.'

'Cheers.' I was suddenly aware of Kathryn's eyes on me.

She looked angry. 'She's dead?'

'If it bleeds, it leads,' I said, walking over to Barry's desk and hating myself.

I turned back. 'Please, Kath?'

She stood up and left the room.

Fuck.

Tip to tip, I lit another cigarette.

Barry Gannon, skinny, single, and obsessed, papers everywhere, covered in figures.

I crouched down beside his desk.

Barry Gannon was chewing his pen. 'So?'

'Unsolved missing kids. One in Castleford and one in Rochdale? Maybe.'

'Yeah. Rochdale I'd have to check, but the one in Castleford was 1969. Moon landings. Jeanette Garland.'

Bells ringing. 'And they never found her?'

'No.' Barry took the end of the pen from his mouth, staring at me.

'Police have anything at all?'

'Doubt it.'

'Cheers. I'd better get to it then.'

'Mention it,' he winked.

I stood up. 'How's Dawsongate?'

'Fuck knows.' Barry Gannon, not smiling, looking back down at the papers and the figures, chewing the end of his pen.

Fuck.

I took the hint. 'Cheers, Barry.'

I was halfway back to my desk, Kathryn coming into the office hiding a smile, when Barry shouted, 'You going to the Press Club later?'

'If I get through all this.'

'If I think of anything else, I'll see you there.'

More surprised than grateful. 'Cheers Barry. Appreciate it.'

Kathryn Taylor, no trace of a smile. 'Mr Hadden will see his North of England Crime Correspondent at seven sharp.'

'And when do you want to see your North of England Crime Correspondent?'

'In the Press Club, I suppose. If I must.' She smiled.

'You must,' I winked.

Down the corridor, into records.

Yesterday's news.

Through the metal drawers, into the boxes.

A thousand Ruby Tuesdays.

I grabbed the reels, took a seat at a screen, and threaded through the microfilm.

July 1969.

I let the film fly by:

B Specials, Bernadette Devlin, Wallace Lawler, and *In Place of Strife*.

Wilson, Wilson, Wilson; like Ted had never been.

The Moon and Jack fucking Whitehead were everywhere.

Me in Brighton, two thousand light years from home.

Missing.

Bingo.

I started to write.

'So I went back through all the files, spoke to a couple of the lads, rang Manchester, and I think we've got something,' I said, wishing my editor would look up from the pile of Spot the bloody Ball photos on his desk.

Bill Hadden picked up a magnifying glass and asked, 'Did you talk to Jack?'

'He's not been in.' Thank Christ.

I shifted in my seat and stared out of the window, ten floors up, across a black Leeds.

'So what exactly have you got?' Hadden was stroking his silver beard, peering through the magnifying glass at the photographs.

'Three very similar cases . . .'

'In a nutshell?'

'Three missing girls. One aged eight, the others both ten. 1969, 1972, yesterday. All of them went missing within yards of their homes, within miles of each other. It's Cannock Chase all over again.'

'Let's hope so.'

'Fingers crossed.'

'I was being sarcastic. Sorry.'

'Oh.' I shifted in my seat again.

Hadden continued to peer through the glass at the black and white photographs.

I looked at my father's watch; eight bleeding thirty.

'So what do you think?' Not hiding my irritation.

Hadden held up a black and white photograph of some footballers, one of them Gordon McQueen, going up for a cross. There was no ball. 'Do you ever do these things?'

'No,' I lied, disliking the game we were about to play.

'Spot the Ball,' Bill Hadden, editor, said, 'is the reason thirty-nine per cent of working-class males buy this paper. What do you think of that?'

Say yes, say no, but spare me this.

'Interesting,' I lied again, thinking the exact fucking opposite, thinking thirty-nine per cent of working-class males have been having some fun with your researchers.

'So what do you honestly think?' Hadden was looking back down at some other photographs.

Caught off guard, genuinely dumb. 'About what?'

Hadden looked up again. 'Do you seriously think it could be the same man?'

'Yeah. Yes, I do.'

'All right,' said Hadden and put down the magnifying glass. 'Chief Superintendent Oldman will see you tomorrow. He won't thank you for any of this. The last thing he wants is some bloody Kiddie-Catcher scare. He'll ask you not to write the story, you'll agree, and he'll appear grateful. And a grateful Detective Chief Superintendent is something every North of England Crime Correspondent should have.'

'But . . .' My hand was up in the air and it felt stupid there.

'But then you'll go ahead and prepare all the background on the two Rochdale and Castleford girls. Interview the families, if they'll see you.'

'But why, if . . .'

Bill Hadden smiled. 'Human interest, five years on or whatever. And so then, if you are right about all this, we won't be left back in the starting stalls.'

'I see,' I said with the Christmas present I'd always wanted, but in the wrong size and colour.

'But don't push George Oldman tomorrow,' said Hadden, edging his glasses back up the bridge of his nose. 'This paper has an excellent relationship with our new West Yorkshire Metropolitan Police Force. I'd like to keep it that way, especially now.'

'Of course.' Thinking, *especially now?*

Bill Hadden leant back in his big leather chair, arms behind his head. 'You know as well as I do that this whole thing could blow over tomorrow and, even if it doesn't, it'll be buried by Christmas anyway.'

I stood up, reading my cue, thinking you're so wrong.

My editor picked up his magnifying glass again. 'Still getting letters on the Ratcatcher. Good stuff.'

'Thank you, Mr Hadden.' I opened the door.

'You really ought to have a go at one of these,' said Hadden, tapping a photograph. 'Right up your street.'

'Thank you, I will.' I closed the door.

From behind the door, 'And don't forget to talk to Jack.'

One two three four, down the stairs and through the door:

The Press Club, in the sights of the two stone lions, Leeds City Centre.

The Press Club, gone eleven, Christmas busy from here on in.

The Press Club, members only.

Edward Dunford, member, down the stairs and through the door. Kathryn at the bar, an unknown drunk at her ear, her eyes on me.

The drunk slurs, 'And one lion says to other, fucking quiet isn't it?'

I looked to the real stage and a woman in a feather dress belting out *We've Only Just Begun*. Two steps this way, two steps that way, the world's smallest stage.

Excitement shrinking my stomach, swelling my chest, a Scotch and water in my hand beneath the tinsel and the fairy lights, a pocketful of notes, thinking THIS IS IT.

From out of the reds and the black, Barry Gannon raised a fag hand. Taking my drink and leaving Kathryn, I went over to Barry's table.

'First Wilson gets burgled then, two days later, John fucking Stonehouse vanishes.' Barry Gannon decrees to the dumb, holding court.

'Don't forget Lucky either,' smirked George Greaves, old hand.

'And what about bloody Watergate?' laughed Gaz from Sport, bored of Barry.

I stole a seat. Nods all round: Barry, George, Gaz and Paul Kelly. Fat Bernard and Tom from Bradford two tables down, Jack's mates.

Barry finished his pint. 'Everything's linked. Show me two things that aren't connected.'

'Stoke City and the League fucking Championship,' laughed Gaz again, Mr Sport, lighting up another.

'Big match tomorrow, eh?' I said, part-time football fan.

Gaz, real anger in his eyes. 'Be a right fucking shambles if it's owt like last week.'

Barry stood up. 'Anyone want anything from the bar?'

Nods and grunts all round, Gaz and George up for another night talking Leeds United, Paul Kelly looking at his watch, shaking his head.

I stood up, downing my Scotch. 'I'll give you a hand.'

Back at the bar, Kathryn down the other end talking to the barman and Steph the typist.

Barry Gannon, straight out of nowhere, 'What's your plan then?'

'Hadden's fixed me up an interview with George Oldman for tomorrow morning.'

'So why aren't you smiling?'

'He doesn't want me to push the unsolveds with Oldman, just get some background shit together, try and interview the families, if they'll see me.'

'Merry Christmas Mr and Mrs Parents of the Missing, Presumed Dead. Santa Eddie, bringing it all back home.'

Down pat: 'They'll be following Clare Kemplay. Be right back there anyway.'

'In fact you'll be helping them. Catharsis.' Barry smiled for a second, looking round the room.

'They're linked, I know it.'

'But to what? Three pints and a . . .'

Not following, catching up late, 'A Scotch and water.'

'And a Scotch and water.' Barry Gannon was looking down the bar at Kathryn. 'You're a lucky man, Dunford.'

Me, guilt and nerves jangling, too much Scotch, too little Scotch, the conversation strange. 'What do you mean? What do you think?'

'How long you got?'

Fuck you, too tired to play the game. 'Yeah. I know what you mean.'

But Barry had turned his back to talk to some kid at the bar, pencil thin in a fat maroon suit with an orange feather cut; nervous black eyes darted my way over Barry's left shoulder.

Bad fucking Bowie.

I tried to listen in but the Feather Dress upon the small stage lurched into *Don't Forget to Remember.*

I looked to the ceiling, I looked to the floor, and back to the bar.

'Having a nice time?' Kathryn's eyes were tired.

Me thinking, here it comes. 'You know Barry. Gets a bit obtuse,' I whispered.

'Obtuse? There's a big word for you.'

Ignoring one piece of bait, falling for another, 'How about you?'

'How about me what?'

'Having a good time?'

'Oh I love standing alone at a bar twelve days before Christmas.'

'You're not alone.'

'Was until Steph came.'

'You could've come over.'

'I wasn't invited.'

'That's pathetic.' I smiled.

'Go on then, since you're asking. I'll have a vodka.'

'Think I'll join you.'

The cold air didn't help much.

'I love you,' I was saying, unable to stay upright.

'Come on love, taxi's here.' A woman's voice, Kathryn's.

The pine-scented air-freshener didn't help much either.

'I love you,' I was saying.

'He better not puke,' shouted the Paki driver over his shoulder.

I could smell his sweat amongst the pine.

'I love you,' I was saying.

Her mother was sleeping, her father was snoring, and I was on my knees on their toilet floor.

Kathryn opened the door and switched on the light and bought another piece of me.

It hurt and it burned as it all came up, but I didn't want it to ever stop. And, when it finally did, I stared a long time at the whisky and the ham, at the bits in the bog and the bits on the floor.

Kathryn put her hands on my shoulders.

I tried to place the voice in my head saying, *you've actually got people feeling sorry for him, I never thought that was possible.*

Kathryn moved her hands into my armpits.

I didn't want to ever stand again. And, when I finally did, I started to cry.

'Come on love,' she whispered.

I awoke three times in the night from the same dream.

Each time thinking, I'm safe now, I'm safe now, go back to sleep.

Each time the same dream: a woman on a terraced street, clutching a red cardigan tight around her, screaming ten years of noise into my face.

Each time a crow, or some such big black bird, came out of a sky a thousand shades of grey and clawed through her pretty blonde hair.

Each time chasing her down the street, after her eyes.

Each time frozen, waking cold, tears on the pillow.

Each time, Clare Kemplay smiling down from the dark ceiling.

Chapter 2

7.55 a.m.

Saturday 14 December 1974.

I was sitting in the Millgarth office of Detective Chief Superintendent George Oldman, feeling like dogshit.

It was a bare room. No photographs, no certificates, no trophies.

The door opened. The black hair, the white face, the hand outstretched, the grip tight.

'Pleased to meet you, Mr Dunford. How's Jack Whitehead and that boss of yours?'

'Fine, thank you,' I said, sitting back down.

No smile. 'Sit down, son. Cup of tea?'

I swallowed and said, 'Please. Thank you.'

Detective Chief Superintendent George Oldman sat down, flipped a switch on his desk and breathed into the intercom: 'Julie, love. Two cups of tea when you're ready.'

That face and that hair, up close and near, a melted black plastic bag dripped over a bowl of flour and lard.

I ground my back teeth down tight together.

Behind him, through the grey windows of Millgarth Police Station, a weak sun caught on the oil in his hair.

I felt sick.

'Sir,' I swallowed again. 'Chief Superintendent . . .'

His tiny shark eyes were all over me. 'Go on, son,' he winked.

'I was wondering if, well if there was any news?'

'Nothing,' he boomed. 'Thirty-six hours and fuck all. Hundred bloody uniforms, relatives and locals. Nothing.'

'What's your personal . . .'

'Dead, Mr Dunford. That poor little lass is dead.'

'I was wondering what you . . .'

'These are violent bloody times, son.'

'Yes,' I said weakly, thinking, so how come you only ever arrest gyppos, nutters, and Paddies.

'Best result now is to find the body quick.'

My guts coming back, 'What do you think . . .'

'Can't do bugger all without a body. Helps the family too, in long road.'

'So what will . . .'

'Check the bins, see who's got themselves an early away day.' He was almost smiling, thinking about winking again.

I fought for my breath. 'What about Jeanette Garland and Susan Ridyard?'

Detective Chief Superintendent George Oldman half opened his mouth, running a fat, wet, purple and yellow tongue along his thin lower lip.

I thought I was going to shit myself right there and then in the middle of his office.

George Oldman reeled in his tongue and closed his mouth, the tiny black eyes staring into my own.

There was a soft knock at the door and Julie brought in two cups of tea on a cheap floral tray.

George Oldman, eyes on me, smiled and said, 'Thank you, Julie love.'

Julie closed the door on her way out.

Unsure I still had the power of speech, I began to mutter, 'Jeanette Garland and Susan Ridyard both went . . .'

'I know what bloody happened, Mr Dunston.'

'Well, I was just wondering, thinking back to Cannock Chase . . .'

'What the fuck do you know about Cannock Chase?'

'The similarity . . .'

Oldman brought his fist down on to the desk. 'Raymond Morris has been under lock and fucking key since nineteen bloody sixty-eight.'

I was staring at the two small white cups on the desk, watching them rattle. As calmly and as evenly as I could, I said, 'I'm sorry. What I'm trying to say is that, in that case, three little girls were murdered and it turned out to be the work of one man.'

George Oldman leant forward, his arms on the desk, and sneered, 'Those little lasses were raped and murdered, God help them. And their bodies were found.'

'But, you said . . .'

'I don't have any bodies, Mr Dunfield.'

Again, I swallowed and said, 'But Jeanette Garland and Susan Ridyard have been missing for over . . .'

'You think you're the only cunt putting that together, you vain little twat,' said Oldman quietly, taking a mouthful of tea, eyes on me. 'My senile bloody mother could.'

'I was only wondering what you thought . . .'

Detective Chief Superintendent Oldman slapped his thighs and sat back. 'So what have we got, according to you?' he smiled. 'Three missing girls. Same age, or near enough. No bodies. Castleford and . . .'

'Rochdale,' I whispered.

'Rochdale, and now Morley. About three years between each disappearance?' he said, raising a thin eyebrow my way.

I nodded.

Oldman picked up a typed sheet of paper from his desk. 'Well, how about these?' he said and tossed the paper over the desk on to the floor by my feet, reciting by heart: 'Helen Shore, Samantha Davis, Jackie Morris, Lisa Langley, Nichola Hale, Louise Walker, Karen Anderson.'

I picked up the list.

'Missing, the bloody lot of them. And that's just since the start of '73,' said Oldman. 'A little bit older, I'll grant you. But they were all under fifteen when they went missing.'

'I'm sorry,' I mumbled, holding out the paper across the desk.

'Keep it. Write a bloody story about them.'

A telephone buzzed on the desk, a light flashed. Oldman sighed and pushed one of the white cups across the desk towards me. 'Drink up 'fore it gets cold.'

I did as I was told and picked up the cup, drinking it down in one cold mouthful.

'To be blunt son, I don't like inexactitudes and I don't like newspapers. You've got your job to do . . .'

Edward Dunford, North of England Crime Correspondent, off the ropes with a second wind. 'I don't think you're going to find a body.'

Detective Chief Superintendent George Oldman smiled. I looked down into my empty teacup.

Oldman stood up, laughing, 'See that in your bleeding tea-leaves do you?'

I put the cup and saucer on the desk, folded up the typed list of names.

The telephone buzzed again.

Oldman walked over to the door and opened it. 'You do your digging and I'll do mine.'

I was standing up, legs and stomach weak. 'Thank you for your time.'

He gripped my shoulder hard at the door. 'You know, Bismarck said a journalist was a man who'd missed his calling. Maybe you should have been a copper, Dunston.'

'Thank you,' I said with all the courage I could muster, thinking, at least then one of us would be.

Oldman suddenly tightened his grip, reading my thoughts. 'Have we met before son?'

'A long time ago,' I said, loose with a struggle.

The telephone on the desk buzzed and flashed again, long and hard.

'Not a word,' said Oldman, ushering me through the door. 'Not a bloody word.'

'They'd hacked the wings off. Fucking swan was still alive an' all,' smiled Gilman from the *Manchester Evening News* as I took my seat downstairs.

'You're fucking joking?' said Tom from Bradford, leaning over from the row behind.

'No. Took the wings clean off and left the poor bastard just lying there.'

'Fuck,' whistled Tom from Bradford.

I glanced round the Conference Room, boxing thoughts hitting me all over again, but this time no TV, no radio. The hot lights were off, allcomers welcome.

Only the Paper Lads here.

I felt a nudge to the ribs. It was Gilman again.

'How was yesterday?'

'Oh, you know . . .'

'Fuck, yeah.'

I looked at my father's watch, thinking about Henry Cooper and my Aunty Anne's husband Dave, who looked like Henry, and how Uncle Dave hadn't been there yesterday, thinking about the great smell of Brut.

'You see that piece Barry did on that kid from Dewsbury?' It was Tom from Bradford, Scotch breath in my ear, hoping my own wasn't as bad.

Me, all ears, 'What kid?'

'Thalidomide Kid?' laughed Gilman.

'The one that got into bloody Oxford. Eight years old or something.'

'Yeah, yeah,' I laughed.

'Sounded a right little cow.'

'Barry said her father was worse.' Still laughing, everyone laughing with me.

'Father's going down with her an' all, isn't he?' said Gilman.

A New Face behind us, next to Tom, laughing along, 'Lucky bastard. All them student birds.'

'Don't reckon so,' I whispered. 'Barry said father had only got eyes for one little lady. His Ruthie.'

'If it's young enough to bleed,' said two of us at once.

Everybody laughed.

'You're bloody joking?' Tom from Bradford, not laughing very much. 'He's a dirty git, Barry.'

'Dirty Barry,' I laughed.

New Face said, 'Barry who?'

'Backdoor Barry. Fucking puff,' spat Gilman.

'Barry Gannon. He's at the *Post* with Eddie here,' said Tom from Bradford to New Face. 'He's the bloke I was telling you about.'

'The John Dawson thing?' said New Face, looking at his watch.

'Yep. Here, talking of dirty bastards, hear about Kelly?' It was Tom's turn to whisper. 'Saw Gaz last night and he was saying he didn't turn up for training yesterday and he wouldn't be laking tomorrow.'

'Kelly?' New Face again. National, not local. Lucky bastard. My nerves kicking in, the story going national, my story.

'Rugby,' said Tom from Bradford.

'Union or League?' said New Face, fucking Fleet Street for sure.

'Fuck off,' said Tom. 'We're talking about the Great White Hope of Wakefield Trinity.'

I said, 'Saw his Paul last night. Didn't say owt.'

'Cunt just ups and does a runner, what Gaz said.'

'Be some bird again,' said Gilman from the *Manchester Evening News*, not interested.

'Here we go,' whispered New Face.

Round Two:

The side door opens, everything quiet and slow again.

Detective Chief Superintendent George Oldman, some plain-clothes, and a uniform.

No relatives.

The Pack smelling Clare dead.

The Pack thinking no body.

The Pack thinking no news.

The Pack smelling a story dead.

Detective Chief Superintendent Oldman straight into my eyes with hate, daring me.

Me smelling the great smell of Brut, thinking, SPLASH IT ALL OVER.

The first spits of a hard rain.

Crawling west out of Leeds, Rochdale way, my notes on my knees, my eyes on the walls of dark factories and silent mills:

Election posters, mush and glue.

A circus here, a circus there; here today, gone tomorrow.

Big Brother watching you.

Fear eats the soul.

I switched on the Philips Pocket Memo, playing back the press conference as I drove, searching for details.

It had been a waste of everybody's time but mine, no news being good news for Edward Dunford, North of England Crime Correspondent, playing hunches.

'Concern is obviously mounting . . .'

Oldman had stuck to his story: bugger all despite all the best efforts of all his best men.

The Public had come forward with information and possible sightings but, as yet, all the best men had nothing substantial to go on.

'We'd like to stress that any member of the public who may have any information, no matter how trivial, should contact their nearest Police Station as a matter of some urgency, or telephone . . .'

Then there had been a spot of fruitless Q&A.

I kept it shut, *not a bloody word.*

Oldman, each of his answers straight back to me, eyes locked, never blinking.

'*Thank you, gentlemen. That'll be all for now . . .*'

And, as he stood up, Detective Chief Superintendent Oldman winked the Big Wink my way.

Gilman's voice at the end of the tape: '*What the fuck's with you two?*'

Foot down with Leeds behind me, I switched off the tape, turned on the heater and the radio, and listened in as fears continued to grow on the local stations and a story grew on the nationals.

Every fucker biting, the story refusing to lie down and die.

I gave them one more day without a body before it went inside to Page Two, then a police reconstruction next Friday marking the one week anniversary and a brief return to the Front Page.

Then it was Saturday afternoon sport all the way.

One arm on the wheel, I killed the radio as I flipped through Kathryn's precise typed A4 on my lap. I pressed record on the Pocket Memo, and began to chant:

'Susan Louise Ridyard. Missing since 20 March 1972, aged ten years old. Last seen outside Holy Trinity Junior and Infants School, Rochdale, 3.55 p.m.

'Extensive police search and nationwide publicity spelling zero, nothing, nowt. George Oldman headed the inquiry, despite being a Lancashire job. Asked for it.'

'*Castleford and . . . ?*'

'*Rochdale.*'

Lying bastard.

'Investigation still officially open. Parents solid, two other kids. Parents continue to regularly put up fresh posters across the country. Re-mortgaged house to cover the cost.'

I switched off the tape, smiling a big Fuck You to Barry

Gannon, knowing the Ridyards would be right back there and I'd be bringing them nothing new but fresh publicity.

I pulled up on the outskirts of Rochdale beside a freshly painted bright red phonebox.

Fifteen minutes later I was reversing into the drive of Mr and Mrs Ridyard's semi-detached home in a quiet part of Rochdale.

It was pissing down.

Mr Ridyard was standing in the doorway.

I got out of the car and said, 'Good morning.'

'Nice weather for ducks,' said Mr Ridyard.

We shook hands and he led me through a tiny hall into the dark front room.

Mrs Ridyard was sitting on the sofa wearing slippers, a teenage girl and boy on either side of her. She had her arms round them both.

She glanced at me and whispered, 'Go and tidy your rooms,' squeezing them tight before releasing them.

The children left the room looking at the carpet.

'Please sit down,' said Mr Ridyard. 'Anyone for a cup of tea?'

'Thank you,' I said.

'Love?' he said, turning to his wife as he left the room.

Mrs Ridyard was miles away.

I sat down opposite the sofa and said, 'Nice house.'

Mrs Ridyard blinked through the gloom, pulling at the skin on her cheeks.

'Looks like a nice area,' I added, the words dying but not quick enough.

Mrs Ridyard sat on the edge of the sofa, staring across the room at a school photograph of a little girl poking out between two Christmas cards on top of the TV. 'There was a lovely view before they put them new houses up.'

I looked out of the window, across the road, at the new houses that had spoilt the view and no longer looked so new.

Mr Ridyard came in with the tea on a tray and I took out my notebook. He sat down on the sofa beside his wife and said, 'Shall I be mother?'

Mrs Ridyard stopped staring at the photo and turned to the notebook in my hands.

I leant forward in my seat. 'As I said on the phone, my editor and I thought that now would be a good . . . It'd be interesting to do a follow-up piece and . . .'

'A follow-up piece?' said Mrs Ridyard, still staring at the notebook.

Mr Ridyard handed me a cup of tea. 'This is to do with the little girl over in Morley?'

'No. Well, not in so many words.' The pen felt loose and hot in my hand, the notebook cumbersome and conspicuous.

'Is this about Susan?' A tear fell on to Mrs Ridyard's skirt.

I gathered myself. 'I know it must be difficult but we know how much of your time you've, er, put into this and . . .'

Mr Ridyard put down his cup. 'Our time?'

'You've both done so much to keep Susan in the public's mind, to keep the investigation alive.'

Alive, fuck.

Neither Mr or Mrs Ridyard spoke.

'And I know you must have felt . . .'

'Felt?' said Mrs Ridyard.

'Feel . . .'

'I'm sorry, but you have no idea how we feel.' Mrs Ridyard was shaking her head, her mouth still moving after the words had gone, tears falling fast.

Mr Ridyard looked across the room at me, his eyes full of apologies and shame. 'We were doing so much better until this, weren't we?'

No-one answered him.

I looked out of the window across the road at the new houses with their lights still on at lunchtime.

'She could be home by now,' said Mrs Ridyard softly, rubbing the tears into her skirt.

I stood up. 'I'm sorry. I've taken up enough of your time.'

'I'm sorry,' said Mr Ridyard, walking me out to the door. 'We were doing so well. Really we were. It's just brought it all back, this Morley thing.'

At the door I turned and said, 'I'm sorry but, reading through the papers and my notes, the police don't seem to have had any real leads. I was wondering if there was anything more you felt they could have done?'

'Anything more?' said Mr Ridyard, almost smiling.

'Any lead that . . .'

'They sat in this house for two weeks, George Oldman and his men, using the phone.'

'And there was nothing . . .'

'A white van, that's all they bloody went on about.'

'A white van?'

'How, if they could find this white van, they'd find Susan.'

'And they never paid the bill.' Mrs Ridyard, her face red, was standing at the far end of the hall. 'Phone almost got cut off.'

At the top of the stairs, I could see the heads of the other two children peering over the banister.

'Thank you,' I said, shaking Mr Ridyard's hand.

'Thank you, Mr Dunford.'

I got into the Viva thinking, Jesus fucking Christ.

'Merry Christmas,' called Mr Ridyard.

I leant across to my notebook and scrawled two words only: *White Van.*

I raised a wave to Mr Ridyard standing alone in the doorway, a lid on all my curses.

One thought: Call Kathryn.

'It was a fucking nightmare.' Back in the bright red phonebox, I dropped in another coin, hopping from foot to foot, freezing my balls off. 'Anyway, then he says well there was this white van, but I don't remember reading anything about a white van, do you?'

Kathryn was flicking through her own notes on the other end, agreeing.

'Wasn't in any of the appeals for information?'

Kathryn said, 'No, not that I remember.' I could hear the buzz of the office from her end. I felt too far away. I wanted to be back there.

'Any messages?' I asked, juggling the phone, a notebook, a pen, and a cigarette.

'Just two. Barry and . . .'

'Barry? Say what it was about? Is he there now?'

'No, no. And a Sergeant Craven . . .'

'Sergeant who?'

'Craven.'

'Fuck, no idea. Craven? Did he leave a message?'

'No, but he said it was urgent.' Kathryn sounded pissed off.

'If it was that fucking urgent I'd know him. Calls again, ask him to leave a message, will you?' I let the cigarette fall into the pool of water on the floor of the phonebox.

'Where you going now?'

'The pub, where else? Bit of the old local colour. Then I'm coming straight back. Bye.'

I hung up, feeling fucked off.

She was staring at me from across the bar of the Huntsman.

I froze, then picked up my pint and walked towards her, drawn by her eyes, tacked up by the toilets, above a cigarette machine, at the far end of the bar.

Susan Louise Ridyard was smiling big white teeth for her school portrait, though her eyes said her fringe was a little too long, making her appear awkward and sad, *like she knew what was coming next.*

Above her the biggest word was in red and said: MISSING.

Below her was a summary of her life and last day, both so brief.

Finally, there was an appeal for information and three telephone numbers.

'Do you want another?'

With a jolt, back to an empty glass. 'Yeah. Just the one.'

'Reporter are you?' said the barman, pulling the pint.

'That obvious is it?'

'We've had a fair few of your lot in here, aye.'

I handed over thirty-six pence exactly. 'Thanks.'

'Who you with?'

'*Post.*'

'Owt fresh?'

'Just trying to keep the story alive, you know? We don't want people forgetting.'

'That's commendable that is.'

'Just been to see Mr and Mrs Ridyard,' I said, making a pal.

'Right. Derek pops in every once in a while. Folk say she's not too good like.'

'Yeah,' I nodded. 'Police don't seem to have had a right lot to go on?'

'Lot of them used to sup in here while it was all going on.' The barman, probably the landlord, turned away to serve a customer.

I played my only card. 'There was something about a van though. A white van?'

The barman slowly closed the till drawer, frowning. 'A white van?'

'Yeah. Police told the Ridyards they were looking for a white van.'

'Don't remember owt about that,' he said, pulling another pint, the pub now Saturday lunchtime busy. He rang up another sale and said, 'Feeling I got was they all thought it were gypsies.'

'Gypsies,' I muttered, thinking here we fucking go.

'Aye. They'd been through here week before with the Feast. Maybes one of them had a white van.'

'Maybe,' I said.

'Get you another?'

I turned back to the poster and the eyes that knew. 'No, you're all right.'

'What do you think?'

I didn't turn around. My chest and my stomach ached, the beer making them worse, telling me I should have eaten something.

'I don't think they'll ever find a body,' I whispered.

I wanted to go back to the Ridyards and apologise. I thought of Kathryn.

The barman said, 'You what?'

'You got a phone?'

'There,' smiled the fat barman, pointing to my elbow.

I didn't fucking care. I turned my back again.

She picked up on the second ring.

'Look. About last night, I . . .'

'Eddie, thank God. There's a press conference at Wakefield Police Station at three.'

'You're fucking joking? Why?'

'They've found her.'

'Shit.'

'Hadden's been looking . . .'

'Fuck!'

Edward Dunford, North of England Crime Correspondent, out the door of the Huntsman.

Wakefield Police Station, Wood Street, Wakefield.

2.59 p.m.

One minute to kick-off.

Me, up the stairs and through the one door, Detective Chief Superintendent Oldman through the other.

The Conference Room horror-show quiet.

Oldman, flanked by two plainclothes, sitting down behind a table and a microphone.

Down the front, Gilman, Tom, New Face, and JACK FUCKING WHITEHEAD.

Eddie Dunford, North of England Crime Correspondent, at the back, behind the TV lights and cameras, technicians whispering about bloody fucking cables.

Jack fucking Whitehead on my fucking story.

Cameras flashed.

Detective Chief Superintendent Oldman, looking lost, a stranger in this station, in these times:

But these were his people, his times.

He swallowed and began:

'Gentlemen. At approximately nine thirty this morning, the body of a young girl was discovered by workmen in Devil's Ditch here in Wakefield.'

He took a sip of water.

'The body has been identified as that of Clare Kemplay, who went missing on her way home from school in Morley on Thursday night.'

Notes, take fucking notes.

'At the present time, the actual cause of death has not been determined. However, a full scale murder investigation has been launched. This investigation is being led by myself from here at Wood Street.'

Another sip of water.

'A preliminary medical examination has been conducted and Dr Alan Coutts, the Home Office pathologist, will conduct the post-mortem later tonight at Pinderfields Hospital.'

People checking spelling, glances at their neighbour's notes.

'At this stage in the investigation that is all the information I am able to give you. However, on behalf of the Kemplay family and the entire West Yorkshire Metropolitan force, I would like to renew our appeal for any member of the public who might have any information to please contact your nearest police station.

'We would particularly like to speak to anyone who was in the vicinity of Devil's Ditch between midnight Friday and 6 a.m. this morning and who saw anything at all, particularly any parked vehicles. We have also set up a hot-line so members of the public can telephone the Murder Room direct on Wakefield 3838. All calls will be treated in the strictest confidence. Thank you gentlemen.'

Oldman stood, his hands already up in the face of a barrage of questions and flashes. He shook his head slowly from side to side, mouthing apologies he didn't mean, excuses he couldn't use, trapped like King fucking Kong on top of the Empire State.

I watched him, watched his eyes search the room, my heart pounding, my stomach aching, reading those eyes:

SEE ME NOW.

A shove in the shoulder, smoke in my face. 'Glad you could join us, Scoop. Boss wants to see you a.s.a.p.'

Face to face with the slicked-back ratface of my fucking nightmares, Jack fucking Whitehead; whisky on his breath, a smile on his chops.

The Pack pushing past us, running for their phones and their cars, cursing the timing.

Jack fucking Whitehead, giving me the big wink, a mock punch to the jaw. 'Early bird and all that.'

Fuck.

Fuck, fuck, fuck.

The M1 back into Leeds.

Fuck, fuck, fuck.

Fat grey slabs of Saturday afternoon skies turning to night on either side of me.

Fuck, fuck, fuck.

Eyes out for Jack fucking Whitehead's Rover.

Fuck, fuck, fuck.

Hitting the dial for Radio Leeds:

'The body of missing Morley schoolgirl Clare Kemplay was discovered on wasteland in Wakefield's Devil's Ditch by workmen early this morning. At a press conference at Wakefield's Wood Street Police Station, Detective Chief Superintendent George Oldman launched a murder hunt, appealing for witnesses to come forward:

"On behalf of the Kemplay family and the entire West Yorkshire Metropolitan force, I would like to renew our appeal . . ."'

Fuck.

'Someone's got to you. Someone's fucking got to you!'

'You are very wrong and I'd thank you to watch your language.'

'I'm sorry, but you know how close I am . . .'

The words became inaudible again and I gave up trying to hear what was being said. Hadden's door was thicker than it looked and Fat Steph the Secretary's typing wasn't helping.

I looked at my father's watch.

Dawsongate: Local Government money for private housing; substandard materials for council housing; back-handers all round.

Barry Gannon's baby, his obsession.

Fat Steph looked up from her work again and smiled sympathetically, thinking You're Next.

I smiled back wondering if she really did like it up Trap Two from Jack.

Barry Gannon's voice rose again from within Hadden's office. 'I just want to go out to the house. She wouldn't have bloody phoned back if she didn't want to talk.'

'She's not a well woman, you know that. It's not ethical. It's not right.'

'Ethical!'

Fuck. This was going to take all bloody night.

I stood up, lit another cigarette, and began to pace again, muttering, 'Fuck, fuck, fuck.'

Fat Steph looked up again, pissed off, but not half as much as I was. Our eyes met, she went back to her typing.

I looked at my father's watch again.

Gannon arguing the toss with Hadden over bloody Dawson-gate, crap that no-one but Barry gave a fuck about or wanted to read, while downstairs Jack fucking Whitehead wrote up the biggest story of the bloody year.

A story everyone wanted to read.

My story.

Suddenly the door opened and out came Barry Gannon smiling. He closed the door softly behind him and winked at me. 'You owe me.'

I opened my mouth but he put a finger to his lips and was away down the corridor, whistling.

The door opened again. 'Sorry to keep you waiting. Come in,' said Hadden in his shirtsleeves, the skin beneath his silver beard shining red.

I followed him inside, closing the door and taking a seat. 'You wanted to see me?'

Bill Hadden sat down behind his desk and smiled like Father bloody Christmas. 'I wanted to make sure there was no bad feeling over this afternoon.' He held up a copy of the *Sunday Post* to emphasise his point.

MURDERED.

I glanced at the thick black bold headline and then stared at the byline beneath, thicker, blacker, and bolder still:

BY JACK WHITEHEAD, CRIME REPORTER OF THE YEAR.

'Bad feeling?' I said, unable to tell if I was being goaded or placated, hounded or hugged.

'Well I hope you don't feel that you were in any way bumped off the story.' Hadden's smile was somewhat wan.

I felt totally fucking paranoid, like Barry had left all his own paranoia dripping off the bleeding walls of the office. I had no idea why we were having this conversation.

'So I'm off the story?'

'No. Not at all.'

'I see. But then I don't understand what happened this afternoon.'

Hadden wasn't smiling. 'You weren't about.'

'Kathryn Taylor knew where I was.'

'You couldn't be reached. So I sent Jack.'

'I understand that. So now it's Jack's story?'

Hadden started smiling again. 'No. You'll be covering it together. Don't forget, Jack was this paper's . . .'

'North of England Crime Correspondent for twenty years. I know. He tells me every other bloody day.' I felt sunk with despair and dread.

Hadden stood up, looking out over a black Leeds, his back to me. 'Well, perhaps you ought to listen more carefully to what Jack has to say.'

'What do you mean?'

'Well, after all, Jack has developed an excellent working relationship with a certain Detective Chief Superintendent.'

Riled, I said, 'Well, maybe we should have done with it and just make Jack the bloody editor while we're at it.'

Hadden turned back from the window and smiled, almost letting it go. 'Doesn't sound like you're managing to form very many healthy relationships, does it?'

My chest was tight and thumping. 'George Oldman's spoken with you?'

'No. But Jack has.'

'I see. That's that then,' I said, feeling less in the dark, more in the cold.

Hadden sat back down. 'Look, let's just forget about it. It's as much my fault as anyone's. I have a number of other things I want you to follow up.'

'But . . .'

Hadden held up his hand. 'Look, I think we'd both agree that your little theory seems to have been somewhat disproved by the events of today so . . .'

Farewell Jeanette. Farewell Susan.

I mumbled, 'But . . .'

'Please,' smiled Hadden, his hand back up. 'We can drop the missing angle.'

'I agree. But what about this?' I said, pointing at the headline on his desk. 'What about Clare?'

Hadden was shaking his head, staring at his paper. 'Appalling.'

I nodded, knowing I'd lost.

He said, 'But it's Christmas and it'll either be solved tomorrow or never. Either way it's going to die a death.'

'Die a death?'

'So we'll let Jack handle it for the most part.'

'But . . .'

Hadden's smile was fading. 'Anyway, I have a couple of other things for you. Tomorrow, as a favour to me, I want you to go out to Castleford with Barry Gannon.'

'Castleford?' My stomach hollow, my feet searching for the floor, unable to fathom the depth.

'Barry's got this notion that Marjorie Dawson, John Dawson's wife, will actually see him and provide him with corroboration on everything he's dug up on her husband. I think it's somewhat unlikely, given the woman's mental history, but he'll go anyway. So I've asked him to take you along.'

I said, 'Why me?' Playing it dumber than dumb, thinking Barry was right and just because you're paranoid doesn't mean you don't have every bloody reason to be.

'Well, if it ever did come to anything there would be arrests and prosecutions and what-have-you and you, as this paper's North of England Crime Correspondent,' smiled Hadden. 'You would obviously be up to your neck in it. And, as a favour to me, I want you to make sure that Barry doesn't go off the bloody deep end.'

'The deep end?'

Hadden looked at his watch and sighed, 'What do you know about what Barry's been doing?'

'Dawsongate? Just what everyone knows, I suppose.'

'And what do you think? Just between you and me?' He was leading me, but I'd no idea where we were going or why.

I let myself be led. 'Between you and me? I think there's definitely a story there. I just think it's more up *Construction Weekly*'s street than ours.'

'Then we think alike,' grinned Hadden, picking up a thick manila envelope and handing it across the desk to me. 'This is all the work that Barry's done so far and submitted to the legal department.'

'The legal department?' I felt like fucking Polly the bleeding Parrot.

'Yeah. And, frankly, the legal boys reckon we'd be lucky to print one single bloody sentence of it.'

'Right.'

'I don't expect you to read it all, but Barry doesn't tolerate fools so . . .'

'I see,' I said, patting the fat envelope on my knee, eager to please if it meant . . .

'And finally, while you're out that way, I want you to do another piece on the Ratcatcher.'

Fuck.

'Another piece?' New depths, my heart on the floor.

'Very popular. Your best piece. Lots of letters. And now that neighbour . . .'

'Mrs Sheard?' I said, against my will.

'Yep, that's her. Mrs Enid Sheard. She phoned and said she wants to talk.'

'For a price.'

Hadden was frowning. 'Yeah.'

'Miserable bitch.'

Hadden looked mildly annoyed, but pressed on. 'So I thought, after you've been over to Castleford, you could pop in and see her. It'd be just right for Tuesday's supplement.'

'Yeah. OK. But, I'm sorry, but what about Clare Kemplay?' It came from despair and the pit of my belly, from a man seeing only building sites and rats.

Bill Hadden looked momentarily taken aback by the pitiful whine of my question, before he remembered to stand up and say, 'Don't worry. As I say, Jack'll hold the fort and he's promised me he'll work as a team with you. Just talk to him.'

'He hates my guts,' I said, refusing to move or hum along.

'Jack Whitehead hates everybody,' said Bill Hadden, opening the door.

*

Saturday teatime, downstairs the office thankfully quiet, mercifully devoid of Jack fucking Whitehead, the *Sunday Post* already in bed.

Leeds United must have won, but I didn't give a fuck.

I'd lost.

'Have you seen Jack?'

Kathryn alone at her desk, waiting. 'He'll be at Pinderfields won't he? For the post-mortem?'

'Fuck.' The story gone, visions of waves upon waves of more and more rats scurrying across mile upon mile of building sites.

I slumped down at my desk.

Someone had left a copy of the *Sunday Post* on top of my typewriter. It didn't take Frank fucking Cannon to work out who.

MURDERED — BY JACK WHITEHEAD, CRIME REPORTER OF THE YEAR.

I picked it up.

The naked body of nine-year-old Clare Kemplay was found early yesterday morning by workmen in Devil's Ditch, Wakefield.

An initial medical examination failed to determine the exact cause of death, however, Detective Chief Superintendent George Oldman, the man who had been leading the search for Clare, immediately launched a murder investigation.

It was expected that Dr Alan Coutts, the Home Office Pathologist, would conduct a post-mortem late Saturday evening.

Clare had not been seen since Thursday teatime when she went missing on her way home from Morley Grange Junior and Infants. Her disappearance sparked one of the biggest police searches seen in the county with hundreds of local people joining police in searches of Morley and nearby open land.

Initial police enquiries are concentrating on anyone who may have been in the vicinity of Devil's Ditch between midnight Friday and six a.m. Saturday morning. Police would particularly like to speak to anyone who may have noticed any vehicles parked near Devil's Ditch between those hours. Anyone with information should contact their nearest police station or the Murder Room direct on Wakefield 3838.

Mr and Mrs Kemplay and their son are being comforted by relatives and neighbours.

If it bleeds, it leads.

'How'd it go with Hadden?' Kathryn was standing over my desk.

'How do you fucking think,' I spat, rubbing my eyes, looking for someone easy.

Kathryn fought back tears. 'Barry says to tell you he'll pick you up at ten tomorrow. At your mother's.'

'Tomorrow's bloody Sunday.'

'Well why don't you go and ask Barry. I'm not your bloody secretary. I'm a fucking journalist too.'

I stood up and left the office, afraid someone would come in.

In the front room, my father's Beethoven as loud as I dared.

My mother in the back room, the TV louder still: ballroom dancing and show jumping.

Fucking horses.

Next door's barking through the Fifth.

Fucking dogs.

I poured the rest of the Scotch into the glass and remembered the time when I'd actually wanted to be a fucking policeman, but was too scared shitless to even try.

Fucking pigs.

I drank half the glass and remembered all the novels I wanted to write, but was too scared shitless to even try.

Fucking bookworm.

I flicked a cat hair off my trousers, trousers my father had made, trousers that would outlast us all. I picked off another hair.

Fucking cats.

I swallowed the last of the Scotch from my glass, unlaced my shoes and stood up. I took off my trousers and then my shirt. I screwed the clothes up into a ball and threw them across the room at fucking Ludwig.

I sat back down in my white underpants and vest and closed my eyes, too scared shitless to face Jack fucking Whitehead.

Too scared shitless to fight for my own story.

Too scared shitless to even try.

Fucking chicken.

I didn't hear my mother come in.

'There's someone on the phone for you love,' she said, drawing the front room curtains.

'Edward Dunford speaking,' I said into the hall phone, doing up my trousers and looking at my father's watch:

11.35 p.m.

A man: 'Saturday night all right for fighting?'

'Who's this?'

Silence.

'Who is it?'

A stifled laugh and then, 'You don't need to know.'

'What do you want?'

'You interested in the Romany Way?'

'What?'

'White vans and gyppos?'

'Where?'

'Hunslet Beeston exit of the M1.'

'When?'

'You're late.'

The line went dead.

Chapter 3

Just gone midnight, Sunday 15 December 1974.

The Hunslet and Beeston exit of the M1.

It came out of the dark at me like I'd been asleep my whole life:

Tall yellows and strange oranges, burning blues and real reds, lighting up the black night to the left of the motorway.

Hunslet Carr ablaze.

I pulled up fast on the hard shoulder, hazard lights on, thinking the whole of fucking Leeds must be able to see this.

I grabbed my notebook and bolted out of the car, scrambling up the embankment at the side of the motorway, crawling through the mud and bushes towards the fire and the noise; the noise, revving engines and the thunderous, continuous, monotonous banging of time itself being beaten out.

At the top of the motorway embankment I pulled myself up on my elbows and lay on my belly staring down into hell. There below me in the basin of Hunslet Carr, just 500 yards beneath me, was my England on the morning of Sunday 15 December, in the year of Our Lord 1974, looking a thousand years younger and none the better.

A gypsy camp on fire, each of the twenty or so caravans and trailers ablaze, each beyond relief; the Hunslet gypsy camp I'd seen out of the corner of my eye every single time I'd driven into work, now one big fat bowl of fire and hate.

Hate, for ringing the burning gypsy camp was a raging metal river of ten blue vans churning seventy miles an hour in one continuous circle, straight out of speedway night at Belle fucking Vue, trapping within the roaring wheels fifty men, women and children in one extended family hanging on to each other for dear life, the intense flames scolding and illuminating the sheer stark fucking terror upon their faces, the children's cries and mothers' howls piercing through the sheets and sheets of noise and heat.

Cowboys and fucking Indians, 1974.

I watched as fathers and sons, brothers and uncles, broke

from their families and tried to charge between the vans, to punch, to kick, to beat on the metal river, screaming up at the night as they fell back into the mud and the tyres.

And then, as the flames rose higher still, I saw who the gypsy men were so desperately trying to reach, whose hearts they had their own so set upon.

Around the entire camp, in the shadows down below me, lay another outer circle beyond the vans, two men deep, beating out time with their truncheons upon their shields:

The new West Yorkshire Metropolitan Police putting in a spot of overtime.

And then the vans stopped.

The gypsy men froze in the firelight, slowly edging back towards their families in the middle, dragging the injured back through the dirt with them.

The banging of the shields intensified and the outer ring of police began to advance, one big fat black snake sliding in single file between the vans, until the outer circle became the inner, the snake facing the families and the flames.

Zulu, Yorkshire style.

And then the banging stopped.

The only sounds were the fire cracking and the children crying.

Nothing moved, 'cept my heart at my ribs.

Then, out of the night and away to the left, I could see a van's headlights approaching, bumping across the wasteground towards the camp. The van, maybe white, suddenly braked hard and three of four men tumbled out. There was some shouting and some police broke off from the circle.

The men tried to get back into the van and the van, definitely white, began to reverse.

The nearest police van jerked into life, churned mud and hit the van full on in the side, nought to seventy in half the metres.

The van stopped dead and the police descended on it, dragging men out through broken windows, exposing flanks of white flesh.

Sticks and stones set about their bones.

Within the circle a man stepped forward, barechested. The man lowered his head and charged, screaming.

Instantaneously the police snake sprang, moving in and swallowing up the families in a sea of black and sticks.

I stood up too quickly and toppled down the banking, back towards my car, the motorway, and out.

I reached the bottom of the banking, puking:

Eddie Dunford, North of England Crime Correspondent, with my hand upon the Viva's door, saw the flames reflected in the glass.

I ran along the hard shoulder to the emergency phone, praying to Christ that it worked and, when it did, beseeching the operator to summon every available emergency service to the Hunslet and Beeston exit of the M1 where, I breathlessly assured her, a ten-car pile-up was fast becoming more, with a petrol tanker ablaze.

That done, I ran back along the motorway and back up the banking, looking down on a battle being lost and a victory that filled my whole body with a rage as impotent as it was engulfing.

The West Yorkshire Metropolitan Police had opened up the backs of their vans and were throwing the bloodied and beaten men inside.

Within the big wheel of fire, officers stripped gypsy women and children of their clothes, throwing the rags into the flames and randomly striking out with their clubs at the naked white skin of the women.

Sudden and deafening shotgun blasts punctuated the horror, as petrol tanks exploded and gypsy dogs were shot, as the police took their shotguns to anything that looked remotely salvageable.

I saw in the midst of this hell, naked and alone, a tiny gypsy girl, ten years old or less, short brown curls and bloody face, standing in that circle of hate, a finger in her mouth, silent and still.

Where the fuck were the fire engines, the ambulances?

My rage became tears; lying at the top of the banking I searched my pockets for my pen, as though writing something, anything, might make it all seem a bit better than it was or a little less real. Too cold to fucking grasp the pen properly, scrawling red biro across dirty paper, hiding there in those skinny bushes, it didn't help at all.

And then he was right there, coming towards me.

Wiping the tears away with mud, I saw a red and black shining face tearing straight out of hell and up the banking towards me.

I half stood to greet it, but fell straight back down into the ground as three black-winged policemen grabbed the man by his feet and greedily took him back down into their boots and clubs.

And then I saw HIM, in the distance, behind it all.

Detective Chief Superintendent George Oldman, illuminated behind the sticks and the bones like some bloody cave painting against the side of a police van, smoking and drinking with some other coppers as the van rocked from side to side.

George Oldman and friends tilted back their heads to the night and laughed loud and long until George stopped dead and stared straight at where I lay 500 yards away.

I threw my face deep down into the mud until it filled my mouth and small stones cut into my face. Suddenly I was ripped free of the mud, pulled up by the roots of my hair, and all I could see was the dark night sky above me before the fat white face of a policeman rose like the moon into my own.

A leather fist went hard into my face, two fingers in my mouth, two blinding my eyes. 'Close your fucking eyes and don't you speak.'

I did as I was told.

'Nod if you know the Redbeck Cafe on the Doncaster Road.' It was a vicious whisper, hot in my ear.

I nodded.

'You want a story, be there at five o'clock this morning.'

Then the glove was gone and I opened my eyes to the black fucking sky and the sound of a thousand screaming sirens.

Welcome home Eddie.

Four hours straight driving, trying to outrun my visions of children.

A four-hour tour of a local hell: Pudsey, Tingley, Hanging Heaton, Shaw Cross, Batley, Dewsbury, Chickenley, Earlsheaton,

Gawthorpe, Horbury, Castleford, Pontefract, Normanton, Hemsworth, Fitzwilliam, Sharlston, and Streethouse.

Hard towns for hard men.

Me, soft; too pussy to drive through Clare's Morley or sneak a peak at Devil's Ditch, too chicken to go back to the gypsy camp or even home to Ossett.

Somewhere in the middle of it all, sleep nailing shut my eyes, I'd drifted into some Cleckheaton lay-by and dreamt of Southern girls called Anna or Sophie and a life before, waking with a hard-on and my father's final rattle:

'The South'll turn you bloody soft, it will.'

Awake to the face of a brown-haired girl ringed in a wheel of fire and school photographs of little girls no longer here.

Fear turned the key as I rubbed my eyes free and drove off through the grey light, everywhere the browns and the greens waking up all damp and dirty, everywhere the hills and the fields, the houses and the factories, everywhere filling me with fear, covering me in clay.

Fear's abroad, home and away.

Dawn on the Doncaster Road.

I pulled the Viva into the car park behind the Redbeck Cafe and Motel. I parked between two lorries and sat listening to Tom Jones sing *I Can't Break the News to Myself* on Radio 2. It was ten to five when I walked across the rough ground to the toilets round the back.

The toilets reeked, the tiled floor covered in black piss. The mud and clay had dried hard on my skin, turning it a pale red beneath the dirt. I ran the hot tap and plunged my hands into the ice-cold water. I brought the water to my face, closing my eyes and running my wet hands through my hair. The brown water trickled down my face and on to my jacket and shirt. Again I brought the water up to my face and closed my eyes.

I heard the door open and felt a blast of colder air.

I started to open my eyes.

My legs went from beneath me, kicked out.

My head hit the edge of the sink, bile filled my mouth.

My knees found the floor, my chin the sink.

Someone grabbed my hair, forcing my face straight back into the sink's dirty water.

'Don't you fucking try to look at me.' That vicious whisper again, bringing me an inch out of the water and holding me there.

Thinking, Fuck You, Fuck You, Fuck You. Saying, 'What do you want?'

'Don't fucking speak.'

I waited, my windpipe crushed against the edge of the sink.

There was a splash and I squinted, making out what looked to be a thin manila envelope lying next to the sink.

The hand on my hair relaxed, then suddenly pulled back my head and casually banged it once into the front of the sink.

I reeled, thrashing out with my arms, and fell back on to my arse. Pain pounded through my forehead, water seeped through the seat of my pants.

I pulled myself up by the sink, stood and turned and fell through the door out into the car park.

Nothing.

Two lorry drivers leaving the cafe pointed at me and shouted, laughing.

I leant against the door to the toilets and fell back through, the two lorry drivers doubling up with laughter.

The A4 manila envelope lay in a pool of water by the sink. I picked it up and shook off brown drops of water, opening and closing my eyes to ease the pain in my head.

I opened the door to the cubicle and grabbed the metal chain, flushing away the long pale yellow shit in the bowl. I closed the cracked plastic lid on the roaring water and sat down and opened the envelope.

Fresh hell.

I pulled out two thin sheets of typed A4 paper and three enlarged photographs.

It was a copy of the post-mortem on Clare Kemplay.

Another horror show.

I couldn't, wouldn't, didn't look at the photographs, I just read as the dread rose.

The post-mortem was conducted at 7.00 p.m. on 14 December 1974 at Pinderfields Hospital, Wakefield by Dr Alan Coutts, with

Chief Superintendent Oldman and Superintendent Noble in attendance.

The body measured four feet three inches and weighed seventy-two pounds.

Facial abrasions, possibly bites, were noted on the right upper cheek, as well as on the chin and on the front and back of the neck. Ligature marks and burns upon the neck indicated strangulation as the cause of death.

Strangulation.

The tongue had been gouged by her own teeth as she died strangling. It was suggested that she was probably not unconscious when the final force was applied.

Probably not unconscious.

The markings 4 LUV had been cut into the victim's chest with a razor blade. Again, it was suggested this wound was not post-mortem.

4 LUV.

Ligature marks were also found on both the ankles and the wrists. Both sets of marks had drawn blood from deep cuts, suggesting that the victim had fought her attacker for a length of time. The palm of each hand had also been pierced through, possibly by a large nail or a similar metal instrument. A similar wound was found on the left foot and it appeared that an unsuccessful attempt had been made to inflict the same injury to the right foot, resulting in only a partial piercing.

The victim had fought her attacker for a length of time.

Further tests would be needed, however an initial examination of particles taken from the victim's skin and nails revealed a strong presence of coal dust.

Coal dust.

I swallowed.

The vagina and anus showed tears and bruising, both internal and external. The internal tears to the vagina had been caused by the stem and thorns of a rose inserted into the vagina and left there. Again, the substantial majority of these wounds were not post-mortem.

The stems and thorns of a rose.

Horror on horror.

I fought hard for my breath.

They must have turned her over then, on to her chest.

Clare Kemplay's back was a different world.

A different hell:

Two swan's wings had been stitched into her back.

'*TOOK THE WINGS CLEAN OFF AND LEFT THE POOR BASTARD JUST LYING THERE.*'

The stitching was irregular and used a thin waxed rope. In places the skin and the muscle had been reduced to pulp and the stitching had broken free. The right wing had become completely detached, the skin and the muscle unable to support the weight of either the wing or the stitching, causing a large tear along the victim's right shoulder blade.

'*THEY'D HACKED THE WINGS OFF. FUCKING SWAN WAS STILL ALIVE.*'

At the conclusion of the report, the pathologist had typed:

Cause of death: ASPHYXIA DUE TO STRANGULATION

Through the thin white paper I could see the outlines and shadows of a black and white hell.

I thrust it all back into the envelope, photographs unseen, dry heaving as I struggled with the toilet lock.

I wrenched open the cubicle door, slipping and falling into another fucking lorry driver, his hot piss hitting my leg.

'Fuck off you bloody puff!'

Out the door, sucking in the Yorkshire air, tears and bile across my face.

None of the injuries were post-mortem.

'I'm talking to you, puff.'

4 LUV.

My mother was sat in her rocking chair in the back room, looking out at the garden in the light drizzle.

I brought her a cup of tea.

'Look at the state of you,' she said, not looking at me.

'Says you, not dressed at this time. Not like you.' I took a big mouthful of hot sweet tea.

'No, love. Not today,' she whispered.

Out in the kitchen the six o'clock news came on the radio:

Eighteen dead in an old people's home in Nottingham, the second such fire in as many days. The Cambridge Rapist had claimed his fifth victim and England were trailing by 171 runs in the Second Test.

My mother sat staring out at the garden, letting her tea go cold.

I put the envelope on top of the chest of drawers and lay on my bed and tried to sleep, but couldn't, and cigarettes didn't help at all and only made things worse and likewise the mouthfuls of whisky which just couldn't or wouldn't go or stay down, and soon I was seeing rats with little wings that looked more like squirrels with their furry faces and kind words but who would, suddenly, again become rats at my ear, whispering harsh words, calling me names, breaking my bones worse than any sticks or stones until I jumped up and put on the light, except it was day and the light was already on, and so off it would go and so on, sending out signals that no-one was receiving, least of all The Sandman.

'Hands off cocks!'

Shit.

'Anybody hurt in this wreck?'

I opened my eyes.

'Looks like you had quite a night.' Barry Gannon surveying the ruin of my room, a cup of tea in his hand.

'Fuck,' I mumbled, no escape at all.

'It lives.'

'Christ.'

'Thanks. And a good morning to you.'

Ten minutes later we were on the road.

Twenty minutes later, headache banging on an empty stomach, I had finished up my story.

'Well, that swan was found up in Bretton.' Barry was taking the scenic route.

'Bretton Park?'

'My father's mates with Arnold Fowler and he told him.'

Blast from the past number ninety-nine; me sat cross-legged on a wooden school floor as Mr Fowler talked birds. The man had been a fanatic, starting a bird-watching club at every school in the West Riding, a column in every local paper.

'He still alive?'

'And still writing for the *Ossett Observer*. Telling me you haven't been reading it?'

Almost laughing, I said, 'So how did Arnold find out?'

'You know Arnold. Owt goes down in the bird world, Arnold's the first to hear.'

Two swan's wings had been stitched into her back.

'Seriously?'

Barry looked bored. 'Well Sherlock, I imagine the good people at Bretton Park'll have told him. Spends every waking hour up there.'

I looked out of the window as another silent Sunday sped by. Barry had seemed neither shocked nor even that interested in either the gypsy camp or the post-mortem.

'Oldman's got a thing about gypsies,' was all Barry had said, before adding, 'and the Irish.'

The post-mortem had gotten even less of a reaction and had had me wishing I'd shown the photographs to Barry or, at the very least, had the bloody guts to have looked at them myself.

'They must be bad,' was all I'd said.

Barry Gannon had said nothing.

I said, 'It must've been a copper at the Redbeck.'

'Yeah,' he said.

'But why?'

'Games, Eddie,' he said. 'They're playing fucking games with you. Watch yourself.'

'I'm a big boy.'

'So I've heard,' he smiled.

'Common knowledge round these parts.'

'Whose parts?'

'Not yours.'

He stopped laughing. 'You still think there's a connection to them other missing girls?'

'I don't know. I mean, yeah. There could be.'

'Good.'

And then Barry began to rattle on about Johnny bloody Kelly

again, the bad boy of Rugby League, and how he wouldn't be playing today and no-one knew where the fuck he was.

I looked out of the window thinking, like who gives a shit?

Barry pulled over on the outskirts of Castleford.

'We here already?' I asked, imagining Dawson's area would be much posher than this.

'You are.'

I didn't follow, turning my head every which way.

'Brunt Street's the first on the left back there.'

'Eh?' Lost, turning my head that way.

Barry Gannon was laughing. 'Who the fuck lives at 11 Brunt Street, Castleford, Sherlock?'

I knew that address, raking through the pain in my brain until it slowly came to me. 'The Garlands?'

Jeanette Garland, eight, missing Castleford, 12 July 1969.

'Give the boy a prize.'

'Fuck off.'

Barry looked at his watch. 'I'll meet you in a couple of hours at the Swan across the road. Swap horror stories.'

I got out of the car, pissed off.

Barry leant over to close the door. 'I told you, you owe me one.'

'Yeah. Cheers.'

And laughing Barry was gone.

Brunt Street, Castleford.

One side pre-war terrace, the other more recent semi-detached.

Number 11 was on the terrace side with a bright red door.

I walked up and down the street three times, wishing I had my notes, wishing I could phone first, wishing I didn't stink of drink, and then rapped quietly and just once upon the red door.

I stood in the quiet street, waited, and then turned away.

The door flew open. 'Look, I don't know where the fuck he is. So will you just piss off!'

The woman paused, about to slam the red door shut. She dragged a hand through her dirty yellow hair and pulled a red cardigan tight around her gaunt frame. 'Who are you?' she whispered.

'Edward Dunford.' My little red ape rattling the bars of his cage.

'You here about Johnny?'

'No.'

'What then?'

'Jeanette.'

She put three thin fingers to her white lips and closed her blue eyes.

There at death's door, with the sky above breaking into a December blue, I took out my pen and some scraps of paper and said, 'I'm a journalist. From the *Post*.'

'Well then, you'd better come in.'

I closed the red door behind me.

'Sit down. I'll put the kettle on.'

I sat down in an off-white leather armchair in a small but well-furnished front room. Most of the stuff was new and expensive, some of it still wrapped in plastic. A colour TV was on with the sound off. An adult literacy programme was just beginning, the title *On the Move* written on the side of a speeding white Ford Transit van.

I closed my eyes for a moment, trying to lose my hangover.

When I opened my eyes, there she was.

On top of the TV was the photograph, the school portrait I'd dreaded.

Jeanette Garland, younger and fairer than Susan and Clare, was smiling at me with the happiest smile I'd ever seen.

Jeanette Garland was mongoloid.

Out in the kitchen the kettle began to scream and then abruptly went dead.

I looked away from the photograph, glancing at a cabinet stuffed with trophies and tankards.

'Here we are,' said Mrs Garland, putting down a tray on the coffee table in front of me. 'Just let it stand a moment.'

'Quite the sportsman, Mr Garland,' I smiled, nodding back at the cabinet.

Mrs Garland pulled her red cardigan tight again around her and sat down on the off-white leather sofa. 'They're my brother's.'

'Oh,' I said, trying to calculate the woman's age: Jeanette had been eight years old in 1969, making her mother maybe twenty-six or twenty-seven then, early thirties now?

She looked like she hadn't slept in days.

She caught me looking. 'What can I do for you, Mr Dunford?'

'I'm doing an article on the parents of children who have gone missing.'

Mrs Garland picked at some flecks on her skirt.

I went on, 'There's always a lot of publicity at the time and then it dies down.'

'Dies down?'

'Yeah. The article is about how the parents have coped, after all the fuss has died down, and . . .'

'About how I've coped?'

'Yeah. For example, at the time, do you think the police could've done anything more to have helped you?'

'There was one thing.' Mrs Garland was staring straight at me, waiting.

I said, 'And what was that?'

'They could have found my bloody daughter, you ignorant, heartless, fucking bastard!' She closed her eyes, her whole body shaking.

I stood up, my mouth dry. 'I'm sorry, I didn't . . .'

'Get out!'

'I'm sorry.'

Mrs Garland opened her eyes and looked up at me. 'You're not sorry. If you were capable of feeling sorry, you wouldn't be here.'

I stood in the centre of her front room, my shins trapped between the coffee table and the armchair, suddenly thinking of my own mother and wanting to go over and hold the mother before me. Awkwardly I tried to stride over the coffee table and the pot of tea, unsure of what to say, saying only, 'Please . . .'

Mrs Paula Garland rose to meet me, her pale blue eyes wide with tears and hate, pushing me back hard against the red door. 'You fucking journalists. You come into my house talking to me about things you know nothing about, like you're discussing the weather or some war in another fucking country.' She was crying huge tears now as she struggled to open the front door.

My face on fire, I stepped backwards into the street.

'*This thing happened to me!*' she screamed, slamming the door in my face.

I stood in the street, in front of the red door, and wished I were anywhere else in the world but Brunt Street, Castleford.

'How'd you get on then?'

'Fuck off.' I'd had an hour and three pints to brood over by the time Barry Gannon showed up. It was now almost last orders and most of the Swan had fucked off home for Sunday lunch.

He sat down with his pint and took a cigarette from my pack. 'Didn't find their Johnny hiding under the bed then?'

I was in no fucking mood. 'What?'

Barry spoke slowly, 'Johnny Kelly. Great White Hope?'

'What about him?' I was on the verge of cracking him.

'Jesus fucking Christ, Eddie.'

The tankards, the trophies, fuck. 'He's related to the Garlands?'

'Give the boy another fucking prize. Paula Garland's bloody brother. Been living there since her husband died and that model left him.'

Face on fire again, blood boiling. 'Husband's dead?'

'Fuck, Dunford. You've got to know these things.'

'Shit.'

'Never got over Jeanette. Ate a shotgun two or three years ago.'

'And you knew this? Why the fuck didn't you say?'

'Fuck off. Do your fucking job or ask.' Barry took a big bite out of his pint to hide his bloody grin.

'All right, I'm asking.'

'The husband topped himself about the same time their Johnny started making a name for himself, on and off the pitch.'

'Bit of a Jack the Lad?'

'Aye, right lad about town. Married Miss Weston-super-Mare 1971 or something. Didn't last. So, when she upped and left him, it was back to his Big Sister's.'

'The Georgie Best of Rugby League?'

'Don't suppose you followed it much down South?'

Salvaging some pride, I said, 'Wasn't exactly Front Page stuff, no.'

'Well it was here and you should've fucking known.'

I lit another cigarette, hating him for rubbing it in and the smile on his cakehole that went with it.

But fuck pride and the fall. I said, 'So Paul Kelly at work, he's what?'

'Some cousin or something. Ask him.'

I swallowed, swearing this would be the last time ever, 'And Kelly didn't show up for the game today?'

'I don't know. You'll have to find out, won't you?'

'Yeah,' I muttered, thinking please God don't let my eyes fill up.

A voice boomed, 'Time gentlemen please.'

We both drained our glasses.

I said, 'How'd you get on with Mrs Dawson?'

'She told me my life was in danger,' smiled Barry as he stood up.

'You're joking? Why?'

'Why not? I know too much.'

We walked out through the double doors to the car park.

'You believe her?'

'They have something on everyone. The question's just when they'll use it.' Barry stubbed out his cigarette in the gravel.

'Who's they?'

Barry was rummaging through his pockets, looking for his car keys. 'They don't have names.'

'Fuck off,' I laughed, the three pints and the fresh air giving me guts.

'There are Death Squads out there. Why not one for Barry Gannon?'

'Death Squads?'

'You think that shit is just for the Yellow Man or the Indian? There are Death Squads in every city, in every country.'

I turned and started to walk away. 'You've fucking lost it.'

Barry caught my arm. 'They train them in Northern Ireland. Give them a taste, then bring them back home hungry.'

'Fuck off,' I said, shaking him loose.

'What? You really think it's gangs of Paddies in donkey

jackets, lugging round big bags of fucking fertiliser, blowing up all these pubs?'

'Yeah,' I smiled.

Barry looked down at the ground, ran his hand through his hair, and said, 'If a man comes up to you in the street and asks you for an address, is he lost or is he interrogating you?'

I smiled, 'Big Brother?'

'He's watching you.'

I glanced up at blue sky turning grey and said, 'If you seriously believe her, you should tell someone.'

'Who am I going to tell? The Law? These people are the fucking Law. Every life is in danger.'

'So why go on? Why not top yourself like Garland?'

'Because I believe in right and wrong. I believe I will be judged and not by them. So fuck them all's what I say.'

I looked at the gravel and wanted a slash.

'You coming or what, you pisshead?' said Barry, unlocking his car door.

'I'm going the other way,' I said.

Barry opened the door. 'See you then.'

'Yeah, see you.' I turned and started to weave across the car park.

'Eddie!'

I turned round and squinted into the fading winter sun.

'You've never had that urge to go and deliver us all from evil then?'

'No,' I shouted across the empty car park.

'Liar,' laughed Barry, pulling shut his car door and starting the engine.

3 p.m. Sunday afternoon, Castleford, waiting for the bus to Pontefract, glad to be out of the madness of Barry Gannon. Three and a half pints and almost glad to be going back to my rats.

The Ratcatcher: a story that had touched the hearts of Yorkshire folk.

The bus was coming up the road. I stuck out my thumb.

The Ratcatcher: Graham Goldthorpe, the disgraced music teacher turned council Rat Man who had strangled his sister

Mary with a stocking and hung her in the fireplace last Mischief Night.

I paid the driver and went to the back of the deserted single-decker to smoke.

The Ratcatcher Graham Goldthorpe, who had then taken a shotgun to his troubled mind and its visions of plague upon plague of dirty brown rats.

Mandy Sucks Paki Cocks, said the back of the seat in front of me.

The Ratcatcher: a story close to the heart of Edward Dunford, North of England Crime Correspondent, the former Fleet Street Hack turned Prodigal Son who had shaken and shocked a county with his troubled tale and its visions of plague upon plague of dirty brown rats.

Yorkshire Whites, said the next seat.

The Ratcatcher: my first story at the *Post* and a Godsend with my father and Jack fucking Whitehead both in hospital.

I rang the bell wishing Jack Whitehead dead.

I stepped off the bus into the end of a Pontefract afternoon. I hid another cigarette inside my father's old coat and beat the whip of a winter wind on the third attempt.

Ratcatcher Country.

It took me the exact length of the JPS to reach Willman Close from the bus stop, nearly treading in some bloody dogshit as I stubbed it out.

Dogshit in Willman Close, that would have really pissed Graham Goldthorpe off.

It was already dark and most of the Close had the lights on their Christmas trees all lit up. Not Enid Sheard though, the miserable bitch.

Not the Goldthorpes either.

I cursed my life and knocked on the glass door of the bungalow, listening to the barking of the huge Alsatian, Hamlet.

I'd seen it a hundred times before during my all-too-brief stint on Fleet Street. The families, the friends, the colleagues, and the neighbours of the dead or the accused, the very people who would act so offended, so appalled, so insulted, and even so angry at the mere mention of cash for their story. The self-same families, friends, colleagues, and neighbours of the dead or the accused, the very people who would telephone a month later, suddenly so eager, so keen, so helpful, and so fucking greedy to mention cash for their story.

'Who is it? Who is it?' The miserable bitch wouldn't even switch on the hall light, let alone open the door.

I hollered through the door, 'It's Edward Dunford, Mrs Sheard. From the *Post*, you remember?'

'Of course I remember. Today's Sunday, Mr Dunford,' she screamed back over the noise of Hamlet the Alsatian.

'My editor, Mr Hadden, said you telephoned and wanted to speak with one of his reporters,' I shouted through the rippled glass.

'I telephoned last Monday, Mr Dunford. I do my business during the working week, not on the Lord's Day. I'd thank you and your Boss to do the same, young man.'

'I'm sorry Mrs Sheard. We've been very busy. I've come a long way and I don't usually work . . .' I was mumbling, wondering whether Hadden had lied to me or just mixed up the dates.

'All I can say is, you better have my money then, Mr Dunford,' said Mrs Enid Sheard as she opened the door.

Nigh on penniless, I stepped into the dark and narrow hall and the stink of Hamlet the Alsatian; a stink I had hoped I would never have to suffer again.

The Widow Sheard, seventy irritable years if she was a day, ushered me through into the front room and once again I found myself sitting in the gloom with Enid Sheard, her memories and her lies, as Hamlet scratched at the foot of the glass kitchen door.

I perched on the edge of the sofa and said, 'Mr Hadden said you wanted to talk . . .'

'I've never spoken with this Mr Hadden of yours . . .'

'But you do have something you want to share with us about the events next door?' I was staring at the blank face of the TV, seeing the dead eyes of Jeanette Garland, Susan Ridyard, and Clare Kemplay.

'I'd thank you not to interrupt when I'm speaking, Mr Dunford.'

'I'm sorry,' I said, my stomach hollowed out at each thought of Mrs Garland.

'You smell of alcohol to me, Mr Dunford. I think I'd prefer to meet with that nice Mr Whitehead of yours. And not on a Sabbath, mind.'

'You spoke to Jack Whitehead?'

She smiled with thin lips. 'I spoke to a Mr Whitehead. He never told me his Christian name and I never asked.'

I was suddenly hot inside her cold black hole of a room. 'What did he say?'

'He said I should speak to you, Mr Dunford. That it wasn't his story.'

'What else? What else did he say?' I was struggling for air.

'If you'd let me finish . . .'

I moved along the sofa towards the Widow's chair. 'What else?'

'Really Mr Dunford. He said I should let you have the key. But I said . . .'

'Key? What key?' I was almost off the sofa and in the Widow's lap.

'The key to next door,' she proudly announced.

Suddenly the kitchen door flew open with a crash and a thunder of barking as Hamlet the Alsatian charged into the room and jumped between us, his tongue hot, loose, and wet on both our faces.

'Really Hamlet, that's quite enough.'

It was night outside and Mrs Enid Sheard was fumbling with the back door key to the Goldthorpes' bungalow. She turned the lock and in I went.

A month ago the police had point blank refused all requests to view the scene of the tragedy and Enid Sheard had not even so much as intimated that she might have had any means of access, but here I stood in the Goldthorpes' kitchen, in the Lair of the Ratcatcher.

I tried the kitchen light.

'They'll have disconnected them, won't they?' whispered Mrs Sheard from the doorstep.

I gave the switch another flick. 'Looks that way.'

'Wouldn't fancy going in there without any light. Gives me the willies just standing here.'

I peered into the kitchen, wondering when Enid Sheard last had any willy. The place smelt stale, like we'd just got back from a week at the caravan.

'You'll have to come back when it's light, won't you? I did tell you you shouldn't work on a Sunday, didn't I?'

'You did indeed,' I mumbled from under the kitchen sink, wondering if Enid Sheard had enjoyed her last willy and if she missed it and how that would explain quite a bit.

'What are you doing down there, Mr Dunford?'

'Hallelujah!' I shouted, coming up from under the sink with a candle, thinking thank fucking Christ for that and the Three Day Week.

Enid Sheard said, 'Well if you will insist on looking around in the pitch dark, I'll see if I can't find you one of Mr Sheard's old torches. He was always a great one for his torches and his candles was Mr Sheard. Be prepared, he always said. And what with all these strikes and what have you.' She was still chundering on as she walked back to her own bungalow.

I closed the back door and took a saucer from a cupboard. I lit the candle and dripped the melting wax on to the saucer, securing the candle to the base with a few drops.

Alone at last in the Lair of the Ratcatcher.

The blood in my feet had run cold.

The candle lit up the walls of the kitchen in reds and yellows, reds and yellows that plucked me up and dropped me back on a hill above a burning gypsy camp, the face of a young girl with brown curls crying out into the night while another little girl lay on a mortuary slab with wings in her back. I swallowed hard, wondered what the fuck I was doing here and pushed open the glass kitchen door.

The bungalow was laid out exactly the same as Mrs Sheard's. A little light coming through the glass front door at the other end of the hall added to the candle, illuminating a thin hall with a couple of drab Scottish landscapes and an etching of a bird. The five other doors off the hall were all closed. I set the candle on the telephone table, rummaging through my pockets for scraps of paper.

In the Lair of the Ratcatcher . . .

I'd have no trouble selling it to the nationals. A few photographs and I'd be set. Maybe a quick paperback after all. Like Kathryn had said, it practically wrote itself:

6 Willman Close, home to Graham and Mary Goldthorpe, brother and sister, killer and prey.

Inside the hall of the Ratcatcher, I took out my pen and picked a door.

The back bedroom had been Mary's. Enid Sheard had said before that Graham had been particular about this, insisting that his big sister have the big bedroom for privacy's sake. The police had also confirmed that Graham had telephoned twice in the twelve months prior to the events of 4 November, complaining of a Peeping Tom at his sister's window. The police had never been able to substantiate his claims, or had never tried. I felt the heavy dark curtains and wondered if they were new, if Graham had bought them for Mary, to keep out Tom and save her from the eyes he saw.

Whose were those eyes that moved across his sister's body? The eyes of a stranger, or the same eyes that now stared back at him in the mirror.

The curtains and all the other furniture seemed too heavy for the room, but the same was true of Enid Sheard's next door and my mother's. There was a single bed, a wardrobe, and a chest of drawers with a mirror on top, all of them big and wooden. I set the candle down by the mirror beside two hairbrushes, a clothes brush, a comb, and a photograph of the Goldthorpes' mother.

Did Graham come into this room while she slept, taking strands of yellow hair from her brush, hair like their mother's, to treasure and to keep?

In the top left-hand drawer was some make-up and some skin creams. In the top right-hand drawer I found Mary Goldthorpe's underwear. It was silk and had been disturbed by the police. I touched a white pair of knickers, remembering the photographs we'd published of a plain but not unattractive woman. She had been forty when she died and neither the police or myself had turned up any boyfriends. It was expensive underwear for a woman with no lover. And a waste.

Graham watched her as she slept, her hair upon the pillow. Quietly he slipped open the top right-hand drawer, burying his hands deep in the silk contents of her most private drawer. Suddenly Mary sat up in bed.

The bathroom and the toilet were together in the one room and smelt of cold pine. I stood on a pink mat and took a quick piss in Graham Goldthorpe's toilet, still thinking of his sister. The sound of the flush filled the bungalow.

'Graham? What are you doing?' she whispered.

Graham's bedroom was next to the bathroom at the front of the house, small and filled with more heavy inherited furniture. On the wall above the head of his single bed were three framed pictures. I rested a knee on Graham's bed and brought the candle up close to three more etchings of birds, similar to the one in the hall. Graham's pyjamas were still under his pillow.

Graham froze, his pyjamas stuck to his body with sweat.

Beside the bed were stacks of magazines and files. I put the candle down on a bedside table and picked up a bunch of magazines. They were all transport magazines, about either trains or buses. I left them on the bedspread and went over to the desk, on top of which was a large reel-to-reel tape recorder. There was a space on the bookcase where the police had removed the spools.

Fuck.

The Ratcatcher Tapes, gone and not for good.

'Tonight she caught me in her room as I watched over her,' whispered Graham underneath the bedcovers as the spools span silently round. 'Tomorrow is Mischief Night and tomorrow they will come.'

I pulled a thick book of old railway timetables from the bookcase, marvelling at the uselessness of the thing. On the inside title page Graham Goldthorpe had stuck a drawing of an owl wearing glasses and written, THIS BOOK BELONGS TO GRAHAM AND MARY GOLDTHORPE. DO NOT STEAL IT OR YOU WILL BE HUNTED DOWN AND KILLED.

Fuck.

I took another book from the shelf and found the same message and in another, and another, and another.

Bloody weirdo.

I began to put the books back, stopping when I came to a

hardback copy of *A Guide to the Canals of the North* which wouldn't shut properly.

I opened up *A Guide to the Canals of the North* and went straight back smack into Hell.

Stuck between the photographs of various canals of the North were the photographs of ten or twelve young girls.

School photographs.

Eyes and smiles shining up in my face.

My mouth dry, heart pounding, I slammed the book shut.

A second later I had it open again, closer to the candle, flying through the photographs.

No Jeanette.

No Susan.

No Clare.

Just ten or so school portraits, six by four inches, of young girls aged ten to twelve.

No names.

No addresses.

No dates.

Just ten pairs of blue eyes and ten white smiles against the same sky-blue background.

Mind and pulse racing, I took another book from the shelf, and another, and another.

Nothing.

Five minutes later I had turned every book and every magazine inside out.

Nothing.

I stood in the middle of Graham Goldthorpe's bedroom clutching *A Guide to the Canals of the North*, the rest of his room at my feet.

'I don't know what's so important that you couldn't come back another day. Oh my! What a mess.' Enid Sheard shone the torch from corner to corner, shaking her head. 'Mr Goldthorpe would have a fit if he saw his room like this.'

'You don't know what the police took away do you?'

She shone the torch in my eyes. 'I mind my own business, Mr Dunford. You know that.'

'I know that.'

'They swore to me mind, swore to me they'd left everything

just as they'd found it. Will you look at this mess. Are the other rooms the same?'

'No. Only this one,' I said.

'Well, I suppose this'd be the one that interested them,' said Enid Sheard, using her torch as a Colditz searchlight to sweep the room from corner to corner.

'Can you tell what's missing?'

'Mr Dunford! I never set foot in Mr Goldthorpe's bedroom before tonight. You journalists. Minds like sewers, the lot of you.'

'I'm sorry. That's not what I meant.'

'They took away all his drawings and his tapes, I do know that.' The beam of white light fixed upon the reel-to-reel. 'Saw them carrying the stuff off myself.'

'Mr Goldthorpe never said what was on the tapes?'

'A couple of years ago Mary did tell me he kept a diary. And I remember I said, he likes writing then Mr Goldthorpe does he? And Mary said, he doesn't write a diary, he tells it to his tape-recorder.'

'Did she say what kind of things he . . .'

The bright beam hit me square in the eyes. 'Mr Dunford, how many times? She didn't say and I didn't ask. I . . .'

'You mind your own business, I know.' With *A Guide to the Canals of the North* half under my shirt, half down my trousers, I awkwardly picked up the candle. 'Thank you, Mrs Sheard.'

Out in the hall Enid Sheard paused by the door to the front room. 'You went in there then?'

I stared at the door. 'No.'

'But that's where . . .'

'I know,' I whispered, picturing Mary Goldthorpe hanging by her stocking in the fireplace, her brother's brains across three walls. I saw Paula Garland's husband in the same room.

'Bit of a wasted journey, if you ask me,' muttered Enid Sheard.

In the kitchen I opened the back door and blew out the candle, leaving the saucer on the draining board.

'Better come back inside for a cup of tea,' said Enid Sheard as she locked the back door and dropped the key in her apron pocket.

'No thank you. I've taken up quite enough of your Sunday.'
The large book was digging into my stomach.

'Mr Dunford, you may conduct your business out in the
street for all to see, but I do not.'

I smiled. 'I'm sorry. I don't quite follow you.'

'My money, Mr Dunford.'

'Oh, of course. I'm sorry. I'll have to come back tomorrow
with a photographer. I'll have a cheque for you then.'

'Cash, Mr Dunford. Mr Sheard never trusted banks and
neither do I. So I'll have one hundred pounds cash.'

I started to walk down the garden path. 'One hundred
pounds cash it is then, Mrs Sheard.'

'And I trust this time you'll have the good manners to telephone and see it's convenient,' shouted Enid Sheard.

'Really Mrs Sheard. How could you think otherwise,' I
shouted, breaking into a run, *A Guide to the Canals of the North*
into my ribs, a bus at the top of the main road.

'One hundred pounds cash, Mr Dunford.'

'Having a nice time?'

8 p.m. The Press Club, in the sights of the two stone lions,
Leeds City Centre.

Kathryn was ordering a half, I was nursing a pint.

'How long have you been here?' she said.

'Since they opened.'

The barmaid smiled at Kathryn, mouthing six as she passed
her the cider.

'How many you had?'

'Not enough.'

The barmaid held up four fingers.

I scowled at the barmaid and said, 'Let's get a fucking table.'

Kathryn ordered two more drinks and followed me to the
darkest corner of the Press Club.

'You don't look so good, love. What you been doing?'

I sighed and took a cigarette from her pack. 'I don't know
where to begin.'

Life on Mars came on the jukebox. 'Take your time. I'm in no
rush,' said Kathryn, putting her hand on mine.

I pulled my hand out from under hers. 'Did you go into the office today?'

'Just for a couple of hours.'

'Who was in?'

'Hadden, Jack, Gaz . . .'

Jack fucking Whitehead. My neck and shoulders ached with tiredness. 'What was he doing in on a Sunday?'

'Jack? The post-mortem. Apparently it was really appalling. Really . . .' Her words fell away.

'I know.'

'You spoke to Jack?'

'No.' I took another cigarette from her pack, lighting it tip to tip.

Bowie gave way to Elton.

Kathryn stood up and went to the bar again.

George Greaves raised a cigarette my way from another table. I nodded back. The place was beginning to fill up.

I leant back and stared up at the tinsel and the fairy lights.

'Mr Gannon been in?'

I leant forward too quickly, my stomach and head spinning. 'What?'

'Barry been in?'

'No,' I said.

A skinny boy in a maroon suit turned and left.

'Who was that?' said Kathryn, setting down the glasses.

'Fuck knows. Mate of Barry's. The post-mortem's the lead then?'

She put her hand on mine again. 'Yeah.'

I moved my hand. 'Fuck. Is it good?'

'Yeah.' Kathryn reached for her cigarettes but her pack was empty.

I took a pack of cigarettes from my pocket. 'Anything else big?'

'Fire at an old folks home killed eighteen.'

'That's not the lead?'

'No. Clare is.'

'Fuck. Anything else?'

'Cambridge Rapist. Cup draw. Leeds have got Cardiff.'

'Nowt about that gypsy camp on the way in, one just off the M1?'

'No. Not that I've heard. Why?'

'Nothing. Heard there'd been a fire or something, that's all.'

I lit another cigarette and sipped at my pint.

Kathryn took another cigarette from my pack.

'What about the white van? Did you turn anything up?' I asked, putting my cigarettes back in my pocket, trying to remember what kind of car Graham Goldthorpe had driven.

'I'm sorry love. I haven't had the time. I don't think there's anything to it though. The police would have mentioned it and I'm sure it's not in any of the reports.'

'Mr Ridyard was pretty fucking sure.'

'Well maybe they were just humouring them.'

'They should fucking burn in hell if they were.'

Kathryn's eyes were shining through the low light, on the verge of tears.

I said, 'I'm sorry.'

'It's OK. Did you meet Barry?' Her voice was shaking.

'Mm. The post-mortem, how much detail did he put in?'

Kathryn downed her drink. 'None. How much do you bloody think?'

'Do you know if Johnny Kelly was playing for Trinity today?'

'No, he wasn't.'

'Gaz say what happened?'

'Nobody knows.'

'Gaz didn't say why?'

'Nobody knows.' Kathryn picked up her empty glass and put it back down again.

'The press conference is tomorrow?'

Kathryn picked up her empty pack of cigarettes. 'Of course.'

'What time?'

'I think they said ten. But I'm not sure.' She pulled out the silver foil from inside the packet.

'What did Hadden say about the post-mortem?'

'I don't know Eddie. I don't bloody know.' Her eyes were full again, her face red. 'Edward, can I please have a cigarette?'

I took out my pack. 'There's only one.'

Kathryn sniffed hard. 'Forget it. I'll get some more.'

'Don't be daft. Take it.'

'Did you go to Castleford?' She was rooting around in her bag.

'Yeah.'

'You saw Marjorie Dawson then? What's she like?'

I lit my last cigarette. 'I didn't see her.'

'Eh?' Kathryn was counting out change for the cigarette machine.

'I saw Paula Garland.'

'Jesus, you never. Fucking hell.'

Her mother was sleeping, her father was snoring, and I was on my knees on her bedroom floor.

Kathryn pulled me up, bringing my mouth up to hers as we toppled back on to her bed.

I was thinking of Southern girls called Sophie or Anna.

Her tongue pushed down harder on mine, the taste of her own cunt in her mouth pushing her harder. I used my left foot to free her legs of her knickers.

I was thinking of Mary Goldthorpe.

She took my cock in her right hand and guided it in. I pulled back, using my own right hand to move my cock clockwise around the lips of her cunt.

I was thinking of Paula Garland.

She dug her nails into my arse, wanting me in deep. I went in hard, my stomach suddenly hollow and sick.

I was thinking of Clare Kemplay.

'Eddie,' she whispered.

I kissed her hard, moving from her mouth to her chin and on to her neck.

'Eddie?' There was a change in her voice.

I kissed her hard, moving from her neck to her chin and back to her mouth.

'Eddie!' A change not for the better.

I stopped kissing her.

'I'm pregnant.'

'What do you mean?' I said, knowing exactly what she fucking meant.

'I'm pregnant.'

I slipped out of her cunt and on to my back.

'What are we going to do?' she whispered, putting her ear to my chest.

'Get rid of it.'

Fuck, I still felt drunk.

It was almost 2 a.m. when the taxi dropped me off.

Fuck, I thought as I turned the key in the back door. There was a light still on in the back room.

Fuck, I needed a cup of tea and a sandwich.

I switched on the kitchen light and began to root through the fridge for some ham.

Fuck, I ought to at least say hello.

My mother was sat in her rocking chair, staring at the black TV.

'Do you want a cup of tea, Mum?'

'Your friend Barry . . .'

'What about him?'

'He's dead, love.'

'Fuck,' I said automatically. 'You're joking.'

'No, I'm not joking.'

'How? What happened?'

'Car crash.'

'Where?'

'Morley.'

'Morley?'

'Police just said Morley.'

'The police?'

'They rang a couple of hours ago.'

'Why'd they ring here?'

'They found your name and address in the car.'

'My name and address?'

She was shaking. 'I've been worried sick, Eddie.' She pulled her dressing gown tight, rubbing her elbow over and over again.

'I'm sorry.'

'Where've you been all this time?' She was shouting. I couldn't remember the last time I'd heard her raise her voice.

'I'm sorry.' I went to put my arms around her just as the kettle in the kitchen began to whistle.

I went out into the kitchen and switched off the electric ring.

I came back with two mugs of tea. 'This'll make you feel better.'

'He's the one who was here this morning isn't he?'

'Yeah.'

'He seemed ever so nice.'

'Yeah.'

Part 2
Whispering grass

Chapter 4

'Brakes went. He goes straight into the back of the van. Bang!' Gilman smashed his fist into his open palm.

'Van was carrying windows wasn't it?' whispered New Face, sitting down next to Tom.

'Aye. I heard one of the panes severed his fucking head,' said Another New Face behind us.

We all said, 'Fuck.'

16 December 1974.

Wakefield Police Station, Wood Street, Wakefield.

Business as usual:

A dead mate and a dead little girl.

I looked at my father's watch on the worst rainy day and Monday of them all.

It was almost ten.

We'd met up in the Parthenon at the top of Westgate, downed coffee and toast and watched the windows steam up and the rain come down.

Talking Barry.

At nine-thirty we'd run through the rain with rival papers on our heads, up to Wood Street Nick and Round 3.

Gilman, Tom, and me; two rows back and not giving a fuck. Nationals down the front. Familiar faces from before giving it to me cold. Me not giving a fuck. Or not much of one, any road.

'What the fuck was he doing in Morley?' said Gilman again, shaking his head from side to side.

'You know Barry, probably looking for Lucky,' smiled Tom from Bradford.

A big hand into my shoulder. 'Drunk as a fucking skunk is what I heard.'

Everyone turning round.

Jack fucking Whitehead sitting directly behind me.

'Fuck off,' I said weakly, not turning round.

'And a good morning to you Scoop.' Whisky breath on the back of my neck.

'Morning Jack,' said Tom from Bradford.

'Missed quite a eulogy this morning. Not a dry pair in the office after Bill had finished. Quite moving it was.'

Tom said, 'Really? That's . . .'

Jack Whitehead leant forward into my ear, but didn't lower his voice. 'Could have saved yourself a journey too, Scoop.'

Me, eyes front. 'What?'

'Mr Hadden wants you back at base, Scoop. Like pronto. Asap. Etc.'

I could feel Jack's smile behind me, boring into the back of my head.

I stood up, not looking at Gilman or Tom. 'I'll go and phone him.'

'You do that. Oh, and Scoop?'

I turned round, looking down at Jack in his seat.

'The police are looking for you.'

'What?'

'You were drinking with Barry, I heard.'

'Piss off.'

'Star witness. How many did you have?'

'Fuck off.'

'Yep,' winked Jack, looking around the crowded room. 'Looks like you're in just the right place at the right time. For once.'

I pushed past Tom, moving as fast as I could to the end of the row.

'Oh, and Scoop?'

I didn't want to turn round. I didn't want to look at that fucking grin again. I didn't want to say, 'What?'

'Congratulations.'

'What?' I said again, trapped against the legs of hacks and chairs.

'What the Lord taketh with one hand, he giveth with the other.'

I was the only person in the room standing who wasn't a technician or a copper, the only one saying, 'What?'

'The pitter-patter of tiny feet and all that?'

'What the fuck are you talking about?'

The whole room was looking from me to Jack and back.

Jack put his hands behind his head and gave the floor his best stage laugh. 'Don't tell me I've scooped Scoop?'

The room was smiling with Jack.

'Your girlfriend, Dunston?'

'Dunford,' I said, involuntarily.

'Whatever,' said Jack.

'What about her?'

'Told Stephanie she's feeling a little under the weather this morning. But that it's just something she'll have to get used to.'

'You're fucking joking?' said Tom from Bradford.

Gilman was looking at the floor, shaking his head from side to side.

I just stood there, Edward Dunford, North of England Red Face, the eyes of the room on me, National and Local.

'So?' I said lamely.

'Going to make an honest woman of her, I hope?'

'Honest! What the fuck would you know about honest?'

'Temper, temper.'

'Fuck off.' I started to edge along the row. It took an age to get there. Just long enough for Jack to get another laugh.

'I don't know, young people these days.'

The whole room was smirking and tittering along.

'I think Mrs Whitehouse has got a point.'

The whole room giggling with Jack.

'The Permissive fucking Society, that's what it is. Me, I'm with Keith Joseph. Sterilise the fucking lot of them!'

The whole room laughed out loud.

One hundred years later I got to the end of the row and the aisle.

Jack Whitehead shouted, 'And don't forget to turn yourself in.'

The whole room erupted.

I pushed past the wink-wink coppers and the nudge-nudge technicians and got to the back of the room.

I wanted to curl up and die.

There was a bang.

The whole room went dead.

The side door down the front slammed shut.

I turned around.

Detective Chief Superintendent George Oldman and two other men in suits entered.

I turned my red face for one last look.

Oldman had aged another hundred years.

'Thank you for coming gentlemen. We're going to keep this very brief as you all know where we'd rather be. The gentleman on my right is Dr Coutts, the Home Office pathologist who conducted the post-mortem. On my left is Detective Superintendent Noble who, along with myself, will be leading the hunt for the killer or killers of little Clare Kemplay.'

Detective Superintendent Noble was looking straight at me.

I knew what was coming and I'd had enough of it to last me a lifetime.

I turned away through the double doors.

'They're saying Barry was drunk?'

Rain ran down the inside of the phonebox making a pool around my shoes. I stared through the dirty glass at the yellow lights of the Wood Street Nick across the road.

Hadden on the other end sounded gutted. 'That's what the police are saying.'

I fumbled through my pockets. 'It's what Jack's saying as well.'

I stood in the puddle, my shoes taking in water, juggling a box of matches, a cigarette, and the receiver.

'When you coming back to the office?'

I got the cigarette lit. 'This afternoon sometime.'

A pause and then, 'I need to speak to you.'

'Of course.'

A longer pause and then, finally, 'What happened yesterday, Eddie?'

'I got to see Enid Sheard. She's only got a bleeding key to Goldthorpe's house.'

Hadden, many more than ten miles away, said, 'Really?'

'Yeah, but I need some photos. Can you get Richard or Norman to meet me there?'

'When?'

I checked my father's watch. 'About twelve. And maybe it'd be best if one of them brought the money.'

'How much?'

I stared down Wood Street, past the Police Station, as black clouds made an evening of the morning.

I inhaled deeply, a small pain in my chest. 'Greedy bitch wants two hundred.'

Silence.

Later, 'Eddie, what happened yesterday?'

'What?'

'With Mrs Dawson? What happened?'

'I never saw her.'

Hadden, anger in his voice, said, 'But I asked you specifically . . .'

'I stayed in the car.'

'But I asked you . . .'

'I know, I know. Barry thought I'd make her too nervous.' I dropped my cigarette in the puddle at my feet and almost believed myself.

Hadden, down the line, suspicious: 'Really?'

The cigarette hissed in the dirty water. 'Yeah.'

'What time will you be back?'

'Sometime between two and three.'

'I need to see you.'

'Yeah, I know.'

I hung up.

I watched as Gilly and Tom and the rest of the pack came running out of the Nick, jackets over their heads, making for their cars and offices with their warm yellow lights.

I pulled my jacket up over my head and got ready to make a run for it.

Thirty minutes later and the Viva stank of bacon.

I wound down the window and stared down Brunt Street, Castleford.

My fingers felt greasy from the sandwich.

The light was on in the front room of number 11, reflecting in the wet black pavement outside.

I took a mouthful of hot sweet tea.

The light went off and the red door opened.

Paula Garland came out of the house under a flowered

umbrella. She locked the door and walked up the street towards
the Viva.

I wound up the window and slid down in my seat. I could
hear her tall brown boots approaching. I closed my eyes and
swallowed and wondered what the fuck I'd say.

The boots came and went on the other side of the street.

I sat up and looked out of the back window.

The brown boots, the beige raincoat, and the flowered
umbrella turned the corner and disappeared.

Barry Gannon had once said something like, 'All great buildings
resemble crimes.'

In 1970, according to the notes Hadden had given me, John
Dawson had designed and built Shangrila to the acclaim of both
the architectural community and the general public. Television,
newspapers, and magazines had all been invited inside to
witness the equally lavish interior in dutiful double-page
spreads. The cost of the enormous bungalow had been estimated
at being in excess of half a million pounds, a present from
Britain's most successful postwar architect to his wife on the
occasion of their Silver Wedding anniversary. Named after
the mythical city in Marjorie Dawson's favourite film, *Lost
Horizon*, Shangrila had captured the imagination of the Great
British Public.

Briefly.

My father used to say, 'If you want to know the artist, look
at the art.'

He was usually talking about Stanley Matthews or Don
Bradman when he said it.

I vaguely recalled my father and mother taking a special
Sunday drive over to Castleford in the Viva. I pictured them
making the run over, talking a little bit but mainly listening to
the radio. They had probably parked at the bottom of the drive,
peering up at Shangrila through the car window. Had they
brought sandwiches and a flask? I hoped to fuck they hadn't.
No, they'd probably popped into Lumbs for an ice-cream on
the way back to Ossett. I saw my parents sitting in their parked
car on the Barnsley Road, eating their ice-creams in silence.

When they got back home my father must have sat down to

write his critique of Shangrila. He'd have been to see Town the day before, if they were at home, and he'd have written about that before giving his two-penneth on Shangrila and Mr John Dawson.

In 1970, Fleet Street still a year off, I was in my seaview flat in Brighton, skimming the weekly letter from up North which Southern girls called Anna or Sophie found so very endearing, throwing the half-read letter in the bin, thanking fuck The Beatles had come from Liverpool and not Lambeth.

In 1974 I sat in the same car at the bottom of the same drive and stared up through the rain at the same big bleached white bungalow, wishing to God I'd read my father's two-penneth on Shangrila and Mr John Dawson.

I opened the door, pulled my jacket over my head, and wondered why the fuck I'd come this way at all.

There were two cars in the drive, a Rover and a Jaguar, but no-one was answering the door.

I pressed the chimes again and looked out over the garden, across the rain on the pond, to the Viva parked back down on the road. I thought I could make out two or three giant bright orange goldfish in the pond. I wondered if they liked the rain, if it made any difference to their lives at all.

I turned back to give the chimes one last go and found myself face to face with the unkind face of a heavy-set man, tanned and dressed for golf.

'Is Mrs Dawson home by any chance?'

'No,' said the man.

'Do you know when she might be back?'

'No.'

'Do you know where I might be able to reach her?'

'No.'

'Is Mr Dawson at home?'

'No.'

I vaguely placed the face. 'Well, I won't keep you then Mr Foster. Thank you for your help.'

I turned and walked away.

Halfway down the drive I looked back and caught the twitch of a curtain. I turned right on to the lawn and walked across the soft grass to the pond. The raindrops were making beautiful patterns on the surface. Down below the bright orange fish were still.

I turned and stared back at Shangrila in the rain. The curved white tiers looked like a rack of oyster shells or the Sydney fucking Opera House. And then I remembered my father's two-penneth about Shangrila and Mr John Dawson:

Shangrila looked like a sleeping swan.

Noon.

Willman Close, Pontefract.

Knuckles rapped on the steamed-up window of the Viva. Back to earth with a bump, I wound down the window.

Paul Kelly leant into the car. 'What about Barry? Fucking hell, eh?' He was out of breath and didn't have an umbrella.

I said, 'Yeah.'

'Heard his head came right off.'

'That's what they're saying.'

'What a way to go. And in fucking Morley, eh?'

'Yeah, I know.'

Paul Kelly grinned, 'It stinks in here, man. What the fuck you been doing?'

'I had a bacon sandwich. Mind yourself,' I said as I wound the window back up, though not all the way, and got out.

Fuck.

Paul Kelly, photographer. Cousin of the more famous John and sister Paula.

The rain was coming down even harder, with it all my fucking paranoia:

Why Kelly and not Dicky or Norm?

Why today?

Coincidence?

'Which one is it?'

'Eh?' I said, locking the car door, pulling my jacket over my head.

'The Goldthorpe's?' Kelly was looking at the bungalows. 'Which one is it?'

'Number 6.' We walked across the Close to the houses at the end.

Kelly took a huge fucking Japanese camera out of his bag. 'The old bag's in 5 then?'

'Yeah. Did Hadden give you the money for her?'

'Yeah,' said Kelly, stuffing the camera inside his jacket.

'How much?'

'Two hundred.'

'Cash?'

'Aye,' grinned Kelly, tapping his jacket pocket.

'Half and half?' I said, knocking on the glass door.

'That'll do nicely, sir,' said Kelly as the door opened.

'Good morning Mrs Sheard.'

'Good afternoon Mr Dunford and. . .'

'Mr Kelly,' said Mr Kelly.

'A much more civilised hour, don't you think Mr Dunford?' Enid Sheard was smiling at Paul Kelly.

'I think so,' said Kelly, smiling back.

'Would you gentlemen care for a cup of tea?'

Quickly I said, 'Thank you but I'm afraid we're a little pushed for time.'

Enid Sheard puckered her lips. 'This way then gentlemen please.'

She led us down the path between the two bungalows. When we reached the back door to Number 6, Kelly jumped at the sudden barking from Number 5 next door.

'Hamlet,' I said.

'My money, Mr Dunford?' said Enid Sheard, clutching the key.

Paul Kelly handed her a plain brown envelope. 'One hundred pounds cash.'

'Thank you, Mr Kelly,' said Enid Sheard and stuffed the money into her apron pocket.

I said, 'Our pleasure.'

She unlocked the back door to Number 6, Willman Close. 'I'll be putting on the kettle, so you gentlemen just knock on the door when you're finished.'

'Thank you. That's very kind,' said Kelly as we went inside.

I shut the door in her face.

'You want to watch yourself there. Get her sexual motor running, you best know how to turn it off,' I laughed.

'You can talk,' said Paul laughing along, his face then suddenly falling.

I stopped laughing, staring at the candle on the draining board, thinking about *A Guide to the Canals of the North*, wondering where the fuck it was.

Kathryn's house.

'The Lair of the Ratcatcher,' whispered Kelly.

'Aye. Not much to it is there?'

'How many do you want?' Kelly was attaching a flash to one of his cameras.

'I reckon a couple of each room and a few more of the front room.'

'A couple of each room?'

'Well, between you and me, I'm thinking of doing a book on it, so I'm going to need a fair few photos. Cut you in if you're interested?'

'Yeah? Cheers Eddie.'

I kept out of the light as Kelly moved from the kitchen into the hall and to the door of Mary Goldthorpe's bedroom.

'This her room then?'

'Yeah,' I said, pushing past Kelly.

I went over to the chest of drawers and opened the top right hand one. I rooted down through the knickers until I found what I was looking for. I draped a single stocking over the edge of the drawer and hated my own fucking guts.

'Magic,' clicked Kelly as I moved out of the way.

I stared out on the back garden and the rain, thinking of my own sister.

'Do you reckon they were at it?'

'Probably.' I put the stocking back and closed the drawer on Mary Goldthorpe's underwear.

'Dirty bastards.'

I led the way into Graham's room. I took a book from the shelf and opened it up. 'Try and get a good one of this,' I said, pointing at the sticker of the owl and the threat it carried.

'This book belongs to Graham and Mary Goldthorpe. Do not steal it or you will be hunted down and killed,' read Kelly. 'Fucking hell.'

'Get one of the bookcase and all.'

'Some real page-turners,' laughed Kelly.

I walked across the small dark hall and opened the door to the front room.

The fireplace was the first thing I saw.

Kelly came up behind me, camera flashes exploding across the dim room. 'This is where he did it then?'

'Yeah.'

Naked and strangled.

'In the fireplace, yeah?'

'Yeah.'

Hung in the fireplace.

'You'll want a few of that then?'

'Yeah.'

The shotgun in his mouth.

'Gives me the fucking creeps, it does.'

'Yeah,' I said into the space above the hearth.

The finger on the trigger.

'Why'd he do it?'

'Fuck knows.'

Kelly snorted, 'You must have some bloody notion, you've been living the thing for God knows how long.'

'Police reckon he hated noise. Wanted silence.'

'Well he's got that all right.'

'Yeah.'

I looked at Kelly clicking away, white stars shooting across the room.

Paula's husband had shot himself too.

'You wonder why they bother with chimneys in this day and age,' said Kelly, still snapping away.

'They have their uses.'

'If you're fucking Santa Claus, aye.'

'Style?' I suggested.

'Well these ones have got that. Remember all the fucking fuss about them?'

'About what?'

'These bungalows?'

'No.'

Kelly began changing films. 'Oh aye, right to-do there was.

I remember because we wanted to get my Nana and Daddy Kelly in one of these or one of them others in Castleford.'

'I'm not with you.'

'They were supposed to be old folks homes, that's why they're all bungalows. But fucking council sold them off. Tell you one thing, they must have had some brass must the Gold-thorpes.'

'How much were they?'

'I can't remember. They weren't bloody cheap, can tell you that. Designed by John fucking Dawson. Ask the old lass next door. Bet she can tell you exactly how much they cost.'

'John Dawson designed these bungalows?'

'Aye, Barry's mate. My father reckons that was what gave council idea to flog them off, all the bloody fuss about his work.'

'Fuck.'

'It was one of the things Barry kept bringing up. It was out of order, everyone knew that at the time.'

'I didn't know.'

'Well it was old news here so I don't suppose it was owt at all down South.'

'No, I don't suppose it was. When were they built?'

'Five, six years ago. About same time . . .' Kelly drifted off. I knew where he was going.

We stood in the cold dark room with its sudden bursts of light and said nothing until he'd finished.

'There, that's your lot, unless there's owt else you can think of,' said Kelly as he sorted through his camera bag.

'A couple of outside do you think?' I said, looking out at the rain.

A car was turning into the Close.

Kelly glanced out of the front window. 'Might have to come back on a better day, but I'll try.'

The car pulled up in front of the house.

'Shit,' I said.

'Fuck,' said Kelly.

'Yeah,' I said as two police officers got out of the blue and white car.

The two policemen were coming up the path as we came out

of the house. One was tall with a beard, the other short with a big nose. They could have been some comedy double act, except no-one was laughing and they looked as mean as fuck.

Hamlet started barking next door, making the short officer curse. Kelly shut the door behind us. There was no sign of Enid Sheard. It was pissing down and we had nowhere to hide.

'What's going on lads?' asked the tall copper with the beard.

'We're with the *Post*,' I said, looking at Kelly.

The short officer was grinning. 'So what the fuck does that mean?'

I fished in my jacket for some credentials. 'We're doing a story.'

'Fuck off,' said the short one again, taking out his notebook and glancing up at the sky.

'It's right,' said Kelly, first with his press pass.

The tall one held the passes as the other copied down the details. 'So how'd you get in the house lads?'

The short one didn't let me answer. 'Aw fuck,' he said. 'Open the door will you. I'm not standing out here in this piss.' He tore out the rain-soaked piece of paper he'd been trying to write on and screwed it up.

I said, 'I can't.'

The tall one had stopped smiling. 'You fucking can and you will.'

'It's a Yale lock. We don't have the key.'

'So you're fucking Father Christmas are you? How the fuck did you get in?'

I gambled and said, 'Somebody let us in.'

'Stop arsing around. Who the fuck let you in?'

'The Goldthorpes' family solicitor,' said Kelly.

'Who is . . .?'

I tried not to look too pleased. 'Edward Clay and Son, Towngate, Pontefract.'

'Fucking smart arse,' spat the tall one.

'Here, you're not related to Johnny Kelly are you?' said the short officer as he handed back the passes.

'He's my second cousin.'

'You fucking Micks breed like bloody rabbits.'

'Done a Lucan hasn't he? Legged it.'

Kelly just said, 'I don't know.'

The taller officer jerked his head towards the road. 'You better fuck off and find him 'fore next Sunday, hadn't you?'

'Not you Santa,' said the short one poking me in the chest.

Kelly turned round. I tossed him the keys to the Viva. He shrugged and jogged off towards the car, leaving the three of us stood there by the back door, the pouring rain running off the roof of the bungalow, listening to Hamlet, waiting for someone to speak.

The short one took his time putting his notebook away. The tall one took off his gloves, stretched his fingers, cracked his knuckles, and then put his gloves back on. I rocked back on my heels, hands in my pockets, rain dripping off my nose.

After a couple of minutes of this shit I said, 'What is it then?'

The taller copper suddenly reached out with both his arms and pushed me back against the door. He gripped one gloved hand around my throat and crushed my face flat against the paint with the other. My feet weren't on the floor.

'Don't go bothering people who don't want bothering,' he whispered into my ear.

'It's not nice,' hissed the short one, an inch from my face on tiptoes.

I waited, stomach taut, expecting the punch.

A hand closed over my balls, gently stroking them.

'You should get yourself a hobby.'

The short one tightened his hand around my balls. 'Bird-watching, that's a nice quiet hobby.'

A finger pressed through my trousers, pushing up into my arsehole.

I wanted to spew.

'Or photography.' He let go of my balls, kissed me on the cheek, and walked off whistling *We Wish You a Merry Christmas and a Happy New Year*. Hamlet began barking again.

The tall copper pushed my face further into the door. 'And remember, Big Brother's watching you.'

A car horn honked.

He dropped me to the ground. 'Always.'

The horn honked again and, coughing on my knees in the

rain, I watched the size eleven steel-toecaps walk down the path and get into the police car.

The tyres turned and then the boots and the police car were gone.

I heard a door open, Hamlet barking louder.

I got to my feet and ran across the Close, rubbing my neck and clutching my balls.

'Mr Dunford! Mr Dunford!' shouted Enid Sheard.

Kelly had the Viva running. I opened the passenger door and jumped in.

'Fuck,' said Kelly, putting his foot down.

I turned round, my balls and face still burning, and saw Enid Sheard screaming bloody hell across Willman Close.

'Don't go bothering people who don't want bothering.'

Kelly had his eyes on the motorway. 'It's not such bad advice, you know.'

'What do you mean?' I said, knowing what he meant.

'Spoke to our Paula last night. She was in a bad way you know.'

'I know. I'm sorry,' I said, my eyes on the car in front, wondering why he'd waited until now.

'You could've asked me first.'

'I didn't know. It was Barry's idea more than mine.'

'Don't say that Eddie. It's not right.'

'No, really. I had no idea she was family. I . . .'

'You're doing your job, I know. But it's just that, you know, none of us have ever really got over it. Then all the stuff with this other lass, it just brings it back.'

'I know.'

'Plus all this shit with our Johnny. It just never seems to stop.'

'You've not heard anything then?'

'No, nothing.'

I said, 'I'm sorry, Paul.'

'I know everyone reckons it'll be some bird or he'll be on one of his benders, but I don't know. I hope he is.'

'But you don't think so?'

'Johnny took it the hardest, you know, after Paula and Geoff.

He loves kids. I mean, he's just a big fucking kid himself. He really doted on our Jeanie.'

'I'm sorry.'

'I know. I wasn't going to mention it, but . . .'

I didn't want to hear it. 'Where do you think he is?'

Kelly looked at me. 'If I knew that I wouldn't be bleeding driving you around like your fucking chauffeur would I?' He tried to smile, but it wouldn't come.

'I'm sorry,' I said for the thousandth time.

I stared out of the window at the brown fields with their single brown trees and bits of brown hedges. We were coming up to the gypsy camp.

Kelly switched on the radio and the Bay City Rollers were briefly singing *All of Me Loves All of You* before he switched them off again.

I stared past Kelly as the burnt-out caravans flew by and tried to think of something to say.

Nobody spoke until we were in Leeds, parking under the arches near the *Post* building.

Kelly switched off the engine and took out his wallet. 'What do you want to do with this?'

'Half and half?'

'Yeah,' said Kelly, counting out the tenners.

He handed me five.

'Thanks,' I said. 'What happened to your car?'

'Hadden said to take the bus. That you'd be coming back here, said you could drive me back.'

Fuck, I thought. I bet he did.

'Why do you ask?'

'Nowt,' I said. 'Just asking.'

'We live in the Great Age of Investigative Journalism and Barry Gannon was one of the men who gave us this age. Where he saw injustice, he asked for justice. Where he saw lies, he asked for truth. Barry Gannon asked big questions of big men because he believed that the Great British Public deserved the Big Picture.

'Barry Gannon once said that the truth can only make us

richer. For all of us who seek that truth, Barry's premature passing has left us all so much the poorer.'

Bill Hadden, looking drained and small behind his desk, took off his glasses and looked up. I nodded, thinking Barry Gannon had so said many things over so many beers, one of them being something he picked up in India about an elephant, three blind men, and the truth.

After a suitable pause, I said, 'Is that in today's?'

'No. We're going to wait until after the inquest.'

'Why?'

'Well, you know how it is. Never know what they might turn up. What do you think?'

'Very good.'

'You don't think it's too overtly panegyric do you?'

'Absolutely not,' I said, absolutely ignorant of what the fuck panegyric meant.

'Good,' said Hadden and put the typed sheet of A4 to one side. 'You met up with Paul Kelly then?'

'Yeah.'

'And you gave Mrs Sheard her money?'

'Yep,' I said much too cheerfully, wondering if the miserable bitch would call Hadden about the police and start talking pennies.

'He got the photos and everything?'

'Yeah.'

'Have you finished the copy?'

'Almost,' I lied.

'What else have you got on?'

'Nothing much,' I lied again, thinking of Jeanette Garland, Susan Ridyard, Clare Kemplay, burning gypsy camps, *The Canals of the North*, Arnold Fowler and his wingless swans, PCs Tweedle Dum and Tweedle Dee, and the last words of Barry Gannon.

'Mmm,' said Hadden, the city dark behind him already.

'I did talk to the parents of Susan Ridyard on Saturday, like we said. You remember, the human interest bit?'

'Forget that,' said Hadden standing up, about to pace. 'I want you to concentrate on the Clare Kemplay story.'

'But I thought you . . .'

Hadden had his hand raised. 'We're going to need a lot more background stuff if we're going to keep this one alive.'

'But I thought you said it was Jack's story now?' The whine was back in my voice.

Hadden's face darkened. 'And I thought we'd agreed you'd be covering it together?'

I pushed on. 'But there doesn't seem to be a right lot of togetherness so far.'

'Mmm,' said Hadden, picking up Barry's obituary. 'This is a very difficult time for all of us. You've had your reasons no doubt, but you haven't always been here when we've needed you.'

'I'm sorry,' I said, thinking what a twat he truly was.

Hadden sat back down. 'As I say, you've had your own losses and problems, I know. The point is Jack's covering the day to day investigation and you're on background.'

'Background?'

'It's what you do best. Jack was only saying today what a great novelist you'd make.' Hadden was smiling.

I could picture the scene. 'And that's supposed to be a compliment is it?'

Hadden was laughing. 'From Jack Whitehead it is.'

'Yeah?' I smiled and began to count backwards from one hundred.

'Anyway, you'll love this. I want you to go and visit this medium . . .'

Eighty-six, eighty-five. 'Medium?'

'Yes, medium, fortune teller,' said Hadden, rooting through one of the drawers of his desk. 'Claims she led the police to Clare's body and that she's been asked to help them find the killer.'

'And you want me to interview her?' I sighed, thirty-nine, thirty-eight.

'Yes. Here we are: Flat 5, 28 Blenheim Road, Wakefield. Behind the Grammar School.'

Hello Memory Lane. Twenty-four, twenty-three. 'What's her name?'

'Mandy Wymer. Calls herself Mystic Mandy.'

I gave up. 'We going to cross her palm with silver?'

'Unfortunately a woman of Mandy's many talents doesn't come cheap.'

'When?'

'Tomorrow. I've made you an appointment for one o'clock.'

'Thank you,' I said, at sixes and sevens, standing up.

Hadden stood up with me. 'You know it's the inquest tomorrow?'

'Which one?'

'Barry's.'

'Tomorrow?'

'Yes. A Sergeant Fraser wants to talk to you.' He looked at his watch. 'In about fifteen minutes, in the lobby.'

More cops. I felt my balls shrink.

'Right.' I opened the door thinking it could have been worse, he could have mentioned Mrs Dawson, the run-in with the two coppers in Ponty, or even Kathryn bloody Taylor.

'And don't forget Mystic Mandy.'

'How could I?' I closed the door.

'Be right up your street.'

'I'm sorry to bother you Mr Dunford at a time like this, but I'm trying to build up an exact picture of Mr Gannon's movements for yesterday.' The Sergeant was young, friendly, and blond.

I thought he was taking the piss and said, 'He picked me up at about ten maybe . . .'

'I'm sorry sir. This would be where?'

'10 Wesley Street, Ossett.'

'Thank you.' He noted it down and looked back up.

'We drove over to Castleford in Barry, er, Mr Gannon's car. I interviewed a Mrs Garland at 11 Brunt Street, Castleford, and . . .'

'Paula Garland?'

'Yeah.'

Sergeant Fraser had stopped writing. 'As in Jeanette Garland?'

'Yeah.'

'I see. And this was with Mr Gannon?'

'No. Mr Gannon met with Mrs Marjorie Dawson at her home. That's Shangrila, Castleford. As in John Dawson.'

'Thank you. And so he dropped you off?'

'Yeah.'

'And that was the last time you saw him?'

I paused and then said, 'No. I met up with Barry in the Swan public house in Castleford, sometime between one and two. I couldn't tell you exactly when.'

'Was Mr Gannon drinking?'

'I think he had a half. Pint at the most.'

'And then?'

'We went our separate ways. He never said where he was going.'

'How about yourself?'

'I got the bus over to Pontefract. I had another interview.'

'So what time would you say it was when you last saw Mr Gannon?'

'It must have been about a quarter to three at the latest,' I said, thinking and he told me Marjorie Dawson had said his life was in danger and I thought nothing of it then and I'm going to say nowt of it now.

'And you've no idea where he went from there?'

'No. I assumed he'd be coming back here.'

'Why did you think that?'

'No reason. I just assumed that's what he'd do. Type up the interview.'

'You've no idea why he might have gone to Morley?'

'None.'

'I see. Thank you. You'll be obliged to attend the inquest tomorrow, you do know that?'

I nodded. 'Bit quick isn't it?'

'We have almost all the details and, between you and me, I think the family are keen to, you know . . . What with Christmas and everything.'

'Where's it at?'

'Morley Town Hall.'

'Right,' I said. I was thinking about Clare Kemplay.

Sergeant Fraser closed his notebook. 'You'll be asked much the same questions. They'll probably be a wee bit more on the drinking, mind. You know how these things are.'

'He was over then?'

'I believe so.'

'What about the brakes?'

Fraser shrugged. 'They failed.'

'And the other vehicle?'

'Stationary.'

'True it was carrying plates of glass?'

'Yes.'

'And one went through the windscreen?'

'Yes.'

'And . . .'

'Yes.'

'So it was instantaneous?'

'I'd say so, yes.'

'Fuck.'

'Yeah.'

We were both white. I stared out of the foyer at the traffic heading home through the rain, the headlights and the brake-lights flashing on and off, yellow and red, yellow and red. Sergeant Fraser flicked through his notebook.

After a while, he stood up. 'You don't know where I could reach Kathryn Taylor do you?'

'If she's not in the building she's probably gone home.'

'No, I've been unable to contact her either here or at home.'

'Well I doubt she knows anything. She was with me most of the evening.'

'So I've been told. But you never know.'

I said nothing.

The Sergeant put on his hat. 'If you do speak with Miss Taylor, please ask her to get in touch. I can be reached any time through the Morley Station.'

'Yeah.'

'Thank you for your time Mr Dunford.'

'Thanks.'

'See you tomorrow then.'

'Yeah.'

I watched him walk over to reception, say something to Lisa behind the desk, and then leave through the revolving doors.

I lit a cigarette, my heart beating ninety miles an hour.

*

Three hours straight I sat at my desk and worked.

There's no quiet time on the only regional newspaper with a morning and an evening edition, but today was as close to the grave as it got, everybody pissing off as early as possible. A goodbye here, a goodbye there, and a few of us'll be down the Press Club later if you fancy it.

No Barry Gannon.

So I typed and typed; the first real work I'd done since my father died and Clare Kemplay disappeared. I struggled to remember the last time I'd sat at this desk and just worked and typed. Joyriders, that would've been it. But I couldn't remember if my father had still been in the hospital or if he'd been moved back home by then.

No Ronald Dunford.

At about six, Kelly brought the photos up and we went through them, putting the best in the drawer. Kelly took my piece and his photos to the Sub, then to Layout. In the process I lost fifty words which, on a good day, would've been cause for a large one in the Press Club with Kathryn.

But this wasn't a good day.

No Kathryn Taylor.

I'd been to see Fat Steph and told her to keep it shut but she didn't know what the fuck I was going on about, except that Jack Whitehead was right about me. We're all upset you know, but I should get a grip. Jack was right about me, Stephanie had said over and over, again and again, to me and everyone else within a ten-mile radius.

No Jack fucking Whitehead?

No such fucking luck.

On every desk were copies of tonight's paper.

CATCH THIS FIEND.

Banner headlines across the Front Page of the *Evening Post*.

BY JACK WHITEHEAD, CHIEF CRIME REPORTER & CRIME REPORTER OF THE YEAR 1968 & 1971.

Fuck.

A post-mortem into the death of ten-year-old Clare Kemplay revealed that she had been tortured, raped, and then strangled. West Yorkshire Police are withholding the exact details of the injuries, but Detective Chief Superintendent George Oldman, speaking at a press conference earlier today, described the extreme nature of the murder as 'defying belief' and as 'by far the most horrific case encountered by myself or any other member of the West Yorkshire Metropolitan Force'.

Home Office pathologist Dr Alan Coutts, who conducted the post-mortem, said, 'There are no words to fully convey the horror visited upon this young girl.' Dr Coutts, a veteran of over fifty murders, looked visibly moved as he spoke, saying he hoped, 'never to have to perform such a duty again'.

Detective Chief Superintendent Oldman spoke of the urgency in finding the killer and announced that Detective Superintendent Peter Noble would be in charge of the day to day hunt for whoever was responsible for Clare's murder.

In 1968, Detective Superintendent Noble, then with the West Midlands Force, gained national recognition as the man chiefly responsible for the arrest of the Cannock Chase Murderer, Raymond Morris. Between 1965 and 1967, Morris had molested and then suffocated three little girls in and around Stafford, before being arrested by then Detective Inspector Noble.

Detective Superintendent Noble spoke of his resolution to find Clare Kemplay's murderer, appealing to members of the public for assistance, saying, 'We must catch this fiend before he takes another young innocent life.'

Detective Chief Superintendent Oldman added that the police are particularly interested in speaking to anyone who was in the vicinity of Devil's Ditch, Wakefield on the night of Friday 13 December or early on the morning of Saturday 14 December.

West Yorkshire Metropolitan Police are appealing for anybody with information to contact the Murder Room direct on Wakefield 3838 or 3839 or to contact their nearest police station. All calls will be treated in the strictest confidence.

The report was accompanied by two photographs: the school photograph of Clare which had accompanied my initial report into her disappearance, and a grainy one of police searching Devil's Ditch in Wakefield, where Clare's body had been found.

Hats off to Jack.

I tore the Front Page off, stuffed it inside my jacket pocket, and walked across to Barry Gannon's desk. I opened the bottom drawer and took out Barry's trusty bottle of Bells, pouring a triple into a half-drunk cup of coffee.

Here's to you Barry Gannon.

It tasted fucking shit, so fucking shit I found another cup of cold coffee on another desk and had another bloody one.

Here's to you Ronald Dunford.

Five minutes later I put my head down on my desk and smelt the wood, the whisky, and the day's work on my sleeves. I thought about phoning Kathryn's house but the whisky must have beaten the coffee and I fell into a crap sleep beneath the bright office lights.

'Wakey-wakey Scoop.'

I opened one eye.

'Rise and shine Mr Sleepyhead. Your boyfriend's on line two.'

I opened the other.

Jack Whitehead was sat in Barry's chair at Barry's desk, waving a telephone receiver across the office at me. The place was no longer dead, gearing up for the next edition. I sat up and nodded at Jack. Jack winked and the phone buzzed on my desk.

I picked up the phone. 'Yeah?'

A young man's voice said, 'Edward Dunford?'

'Yeah?'

There was a pause and a click, Jack having taken his fucking time hanging up. I stared back across the office. Jack Whitehead raised his empty hands in mock surrender.

Everybody laughed.

My breath stank against the phone. 'Who is this?'

'A friend of Barry's. You know the Gaiety pub on Roundhay Road?'

'Yeah.'

'Be at the phonebox outside at ten.'

The line went dead.

I said, 'I'm sorry, I'd have to check with my editor first. However, if you'd like to call back sometime tomorrow . . . I understand, thank you. Bye.'

'Another hot one Scoop?'

'Fucking Ratcatcher. Be the bloody death of me.'

Everybody laughed.

Even Jack.

Nine-thirty on a Monday night, 16 December 1974.

I pulled into the car park in front of the Gaiety Hotel, Roundhay Road, Leeds, and decided to stay put for half an hour. I switched off the engine and the lights and sat in the dark Viva, staring across the car park at the Gaiety, the lights from the bar giving me a good view of both the phonebox and the pub itself.

The Gaiety, an ugly modern pub with all the ugly old charms of any pub which bordered both Harehills and Chapeltown. A restaurant that served no food and a hotel that had no beds, that was the Gaiety.

I lit a cigarette, opened the window a crack, and tilted my head back.

About four months ago, soon after I'd first come back North, I'd spent almost an entire day, and some of the next, getting pissed out of my skull in the Gaiety with George Greaves, Gaz from Sport, and Barry.

About four months ago, when being back North was still a novelty and slumming in the Gaiety was a right laugh and a bit of an eye-opener.

About four months ago, when Ronald Dunford, Clare Kemplay, and Barry Gannon were still alive.

That all-day session hadn't actually been much of a laugh, but it'd been a useful introduction for a new and very green North of England Crime Correspondent.

'This is Jack Whitehead Country,' George Greaves had whispered as we pulled back the double doors and walked into the Gaiety around eleven that morning.

After about five hours I had been willing to go home but the Gaiety didn't abide by local licensing laws and, despite having no food or beds or dancefloor, was able to sell alcohol from 11 a.m. to 3 a.m. by virtue of being either a restaurant or hotel or disco depending on which copper you talked to. And, unlike say the Queen's Hotel in the city centre, the Gaiety also offered its daytime regulars a lunchtime strip-show. And additionally, instead of an actual hot food menu, the Gaiety was also able to offer its patrons the unique opportunity to eat out any member of the lunchtime strip-show at very reasonable rates. It was a snack that Gaz from Sport had assured me was worth a fiver of anybody's money.

'He was Olympic Muff Diving Champion, our Gaz at Munich,' George Greaves had laughed.

'Not something the nig-nogs care for, mind,' added Gaz.

I'd first puked about six but had felt well enough to go on, staring at the pubes spinning in the broken toilet bowl.

The Gaiety's daytime and evening clientele were pretty much the same, with only the ratios changing. During the day there were more prostitutes and Paki taxi drivers, while the night saw an increase in labourers and businessmen. Pissed journalists, off-duty coppers, and sullen West Indians were constant, day and night, day in, day out.

'*This is Jack Whitehead Country.*'

The last thing I really remember about that day was puking some more in the car park, thinking this is Jack's Country not mine.

I emptied the Viva's ashtray out of the window as a slot machine in the Gaiety paid out over the cheers that greeted yet another spin on the jukebox for *The Israelites*. I wound the window back up and wondered how many times I must have heard that bloody record that day about four months ago. Didn't they ever get fucking tired of it?

At five to ten, as *Young, Gifted and Black* came on again, I got out of the Viva and Memory Lane and went over to wait by the phonebox.

At ten o'clock on the dot, I picked up the phone on the second ring. 'Hello?'

'Who's this?'

'Edward Dunford.'

'You alone?'

'Yeah.'

'You're driving a green Vauxhall Viva?'

'Yeah.'

'Go on to Harehills Lane, where it meets Chapeltown Road, and park outside the hospital.'

The line went dead again.

*

At ten-ten I was parked outside the Chapel Allerton Hospital, where Harehills Lane and Chapeltown Road met and became the more promising Harrogate Road.

At ten-eleven someone tried the passenger door and then tapped on the glass. I leant across the passenger seat and opened the door.

'Turn the car around and head back into Leeds,' said the Maroon Suit with orange hair, getting in. 'Anybody know you're here?'

'No,' I said, turning the car around, thinking Bad Fucking Bowie.

'What about your girlfriend?'

'What about her?'

'She know you're here?'

'No.'

The Maroon Suit sniffed hard, his orange hair turning this way and that. 'Turn right at the park.'

'Here?'

'Yeah. Follow the road down to the church.'

At the junction by the church the Maroon Suit sniffed hard again and said, 'Pull up here and wait ten minutes and then walk down Spencer Place. After about five minutes you'll come to Spencer Mount, it's the fifth or sixth on the left. Number 3 is on the right. Don't ring the bell, just come straight up to flat 5.'

I said, 'Flat 5, 3 Spencer Mount . . .' But the Maroon Suit and his orange hair were off and running.

At about ten-thirty I was walking along Spencer Place, thinking fuck him and this cloak and dagger shit. And fuck him again for making me walk down Spencer Place at ten-thirty like it was some kind of sodding test.

'Just looking are you, love?'

From ten until three, seven nights a week, Spencer Place was the busiest stretch of road in Yorkshire, bar the Manningham area of Bradford. And tonight, despite the cold, was no exception. Cars crawled up and down the road in both directions, brakelights shining red, looking like a Bank Holiday tailback.

'Like what you see, do you?'

The older women sat on low walls in front of unlit terraces

while the younger ones walked up and down, stamping their boots to keep the cold at bay.

'Excuse me Mr Officer . . .'

The only other men on the street were West Indians, hopping in and out of parked cars, trailing heavy smoke and music behind them, offering wares of their own and keeping an eye on their white girlfriends.

'You tight fucking bastard!'

The laughter followed me round the corner on to Spencer Mount. I crossed the road and went up three stone steps to the front door of number 3, above which a chipped Star of David had been painted on the grey glass.

From Yid Town to Pork City, in how many years?

I pushed open the door and went up the stairs.

I said, 'Nice neighbourhood.'

'Piss off,' hissed the Maroon Suit, holding open the front door to flat 5.

It was a one-room bedsit with too much furniture, big windows and the stink of too many Northern winters. Karen Carpenter stared down from every wall, but it was Ziggy playing guitar from inside a tiny Dancette. There were fairy lights but no tree.

The Maroon Suit cleared some clothes from one of the chairs and said, 'Please sit down Eddie.'

'I'm afraid you have the advantage,' I smiled.

'Barry James Anderson,' said Barry James Anderson proudly.

'Another Barry?' The armchair smelt stale.

'Yeah, but you can call this one BJ,' he giggled. 'Everybody does.'

I didn't bite. 'OK.'

'Yep, BJ's the name, bjs the game.' He stopped laughing and hurried over to an old wardrobe in the corner.

'How did you know Barry?' I said, wondering if Barry Gannon had been a puff.

'I saw him around, you know. Just got talking.'

'*Backdoor Barry. Fucking puff.*'

'Saw him around where?'

'Just around. Cup of tea?' He said, rooting around in the back of the wardrobe.

'No thanks.'

'Suit yourself.'

I lit a cigarette and picked up a dirty plate for an ashtray.

'Here,' said BJ, handing me a Hillards carrier bag from the back of the wardrobe. 'He wanted you to have this if anything happened to him.'

'If anything happened to him?' I repeated, opening the bag. It was stuffed full of cardboard folders and manila envelopes. 'What is it?'

'His life's work.'

I stubbed out my cigarette in dried tomato sauce. 'Why? I mean, what made him leave it here?'

'Say it: why me, you mean,' sniffed BJ. 'He came round here last night. Said he needed somewhere safe to keep all this. And, if anything happened to him, to give it to you.'

'Last night?'

BJ sat down on the bed and took off his jacket. 'Yeah.'

'I saw you last night, didn't I? In the Press Club?'

'Yeah, and you weren't very nice were you?' His shirt was covered in thousands of small stars.

'I was pissed.'

'Well, that makes it all right then,' he smirked.

I lit another cigarette and hated the sight of the little queer and his star shirt. 'What the fuck was your business with Barry?'

'I've seen things, you know?'

'I bet,' I said, glancing at my father's watch.

He jumped up from the bed. 'Listen, don't let me keep you.'

I stood up. 'I'm sorry. Sit down, please. I'm sorry.'

BJ sat back down, his nose still in the air. 'I know people.'

'I'm sure you do.'

He was on his feet again, stamping his feet. 'No, fuck off. Famous people.'

I stood up, my hands out. 'I know, I know . . .'

'Listen, I've sucked the cocks and licked the balls of some of the greatest men this country has.'

'Like who?'

'Oh no. You don't get it that easy.'

'All right, then. Why?'

'For money. What else is there? You think I like being me? This body? Look at me! This isn't me.' He was on his knees, screwing up his star shirt. 'I'm not a puff. I'm a girl in here,' he screamed, leaping to his feet and tearing down one of the Karen Carpenter pin-ups, screwing it up in my face. 'She knows what it's like. He knows,' he said, turning and kicking the stereo, sending Ziggy scratching to a halt.

Barry James Anderson fell to the floor by the record player and lay with his head buried, shaking. 'Barry knew.'

I sat back down and then stood back up again. I went over to the crumpled boy in his silver star shirt and maroon trousers and picked him up, gently putting him down on the bed.

'Barry knew,' he whimpered again.

I went over to the Dancette and put the needle on the record, but the song was depressing and jumped, so I turned off the music and sat back down in the stale armchair.

'Did you like Barry?' He'd dried his face and was sitting up, looking at me.

'Yeah, but I didn't really know him that well.'

BJ's eyes were filling up again. 'He liked you.'

'Why'd he think something was going to happen to him?'

'Come on!' BJ jumped up. 'Fuck. It was obvious.'

'Why was it obvious?'

'It couldn't go on. He had so many things on so many people.'

I leant forward. 'John Dawson?'

'John Dawson's just the tip of the fucking iceberg. Haven't you read this stuff?' He flicked his wrist at the carrier bag at my feet.

'Just what he gave the *Post*,' I lied.

He smiled. 'Well, all the cats are in that bag.'

I hated the little sod, his games, and his flat. 'Where did he go last night after here?'

'He said he was going to help you.'

'Me?'

'That's what he said. Something to do with that little girl in Morley, how he could tie it all together.'

I was on my feet. 'What do you mean? What about her?'

'That's all he said . . .'

Consumed by a vision of wings stitched into her back, of cricket ball tits on him, I flew across the room at Barry James Anderson, shouting, 'Think!'

'I don't know. He didn't say.'

I had him by the stars on his shirt, pressed into the bed. 'Did he say anything else about Clare?'

His breath was as stale as the room and in my face. 'Clare who?'

'The dead girl.'

'Just he was going out to Morley and it would help you.'

'How the fuck would that help me?'

'He didn't bloody say! How many more times?'

'Nothing else?'

'Nothing. Now fucking let go will you.'

I grabbed his mouth and squeezed hard. 'No. You tell me why Barry told you this,' I said, tightening my grip on his face as hard as I could before letting go of him.

'Maybe because my eyes are open. Because I see things and I remember.' His bottom lip was bleeding.

I looked down at the silver stars clasped in my other hand and let them fall. 'You know bugger all.'

'Believe what you want.'

I stood up and went over to the Hillards bag. 'I will.'

'You should get some sleep.'

I picked up the bag and walked over to the door. I opened the door and then turned back to the bedsit hell with one last question. 'Was he drunk?'

'No, but he'd been drinking.'

'A lot?'

'I could smell it on him.' Tears were running down his cheeks.

I put down the carrier bag. 'What do you think happened to him?'

'I think they killed him,' he sniffed.

'Who?'

'I don't know their names and I don't want to know.'

Haunted, *'There are Death Squads in every city, in every country.'*

I said, 'Who? Dawson? The police?'

'I don't know.'

'Why then?'

'Money, what else? To keep those cats in that bag of yours. To put them in the river.'

I stared across the room at a poster of Karen Carpenter hugging a giant Mickey Mouse.

I picked up the carrier bag. 'How can I reach you?'

Barry James Anderson smiled. '442189. Tell them Eddie called and I'll get the message.'

I wrote down the number. 'Thank you.'

'Mention it.'

Back down Spencer Place in a sprint, foot down into Leeds and on to Motorway One, hoping to fuck I never saw him again:

Planet of the Apes, Escape from the Dark, theories racing:

The rain on the windscreen, the moon stolen.

Cut to the chase:

I knew a man who knew a man.

'He could tie it all together . . .'

Angels as devils, devils as angels.

The bones of the thing:

ACT LIKE NOTHING'S WRONG.

I watched my mother sleeping in her chair and tried to tie it all together.

Not here.

Up the stairs, emptying carrier bags and envelopes, scattering files and photographs across my bed.

Not here.

I scooped the whole bloody lot into one big black bin-sack, stuffing my pockets with my father's pins and needles.

Not here.

Back down the stairs, a kiss upon my mother's brow, and out the door.

Not here.

Foot down, screaming through the Ossett dawn.

Not here.

Chapter 5

Dawn at the Redbeck Cafe and Motel, Tuesday 17 December 1974.

I'd driven all night and then come back here, as though it all came back here.

I paid two weeks up front and got what I paid for:

Room 27 was round the back, two bikers on one side and a woman and her four kids on the other. There was no phone, toilet, or TV. But two quid a night got me a view of the car park, a double bed, a wardrobe, a desk, a sink, and no questions.

I double-locked the door and drew the damp curtains. I stripped the bed and tacked the heaviest sheet over the curtains and then propped the mattress up against the sheet. I picked up a used johnny and stuffed it inside a half-eaten packet of crisps.

I went back out to the car, stopping for a piss in *those* toilets where I'd bought my ticket to this death trip.

I stood there pissing, not sure if it was Tuesday or Wednesday, knowing this was as close as I could get. I shook it off and kicked open the cubicle door, knowing there'd be nothing but a melting yellow turd and puffter graffiti.

I went round the front to the cafe and bought two large black coffees with loads of sugar in dirty styrofoam cups. I opened the boot of the Viva and took the black bin-sack and the black coffees back to Room 27.

I double-locked the door again, drank down one of the coffees, emptied the bin-sack over the wooden base of the bed and went to work.

Barry Gannon's files and envelopes were by name. I laid them out alphabetically on one half of the bed and then went through Hadden's thick manila envelope, stuffing the sheets of paper into Barry's relevant files.

Some names had titles, some ranks, most just plain mister. Some names I knew, some rang bells, most meant nothing.

On the other half of the bed, I spread out my files in three thin piles and one big one: Jeanette, Susan, Clare and, to the right, Graham Goldthorpe, Ratcatcher.

In the back of the wardrobe I found a roll of wallpaper. Taking a handful of my father's pins, I turned over the wallpaper and tacked it to the wall above the desk. With a big red felt-tip pen I divided the back of the paper into five big columns. At the top of each column, in red block capitals, I wrote five names: JEANETTE, SUSAN, CLARE, GRAHAM, and BARRY.

Next to the wallpaper chart I pinned a map of West Yorkshire from the Viva. With my red pen, I marked four red crosses and a red arrow straight out Rochdale way.

Drinking down the second cup of coffee, I steeled myself.

With trembling hands, I took an envelope from the top of Clare's pile. Asking for forgiveness, I ripped open the envelope and took out three large black and white photographs. My stomach hollow, my mouth full of pins, I walked back over to my wallpaper chart and carefully pinned the three photographs above three of the names.

I stood back, tears on my cheeks, and gazed upon my new wallpaper, upon skin so pale, hair so fair, and wings so white.

An angel in black and white.

Three hours later, my eyes red with tears from the things I'd read, I got up from the floor of Room 27.

Barry's story: 3 rich men: John Dawson, Donald Foster, and a third who Barry couldn't or wouldn't name.

My story: 3 dead girls: Jeanette, Susan, and Clare.

My story, his story – two stories: Same times, same places, different names, different faces.

Mystery, History:

One Link?

I had a small stack of coins on top of the payphone inside the lobby of the Redbeck.

'Sergeant Fraser please?'

The lobby was all yellows and browns and stank of smoke. Through the double glass doors I watched some kids playing pool and smoking.

'This is Sergeant Fraser.'

'It's Edward Dunford speaking. I've received some information about Sunday night, about Barry . . .'

'What kind of information?'

I cradled the phone between my chin and my neck and struck a match. 'It was an anonymous call to the effect that Mr Gannon had gone to Morley in connection with Clare Kemplay,' I said with a cigarette between my teeth.

'Anything else?'

'Not over the phone.' To the side of the phone, etched in biro, were the words *Young Cock* and six telephone numbers.

'We better meet before the inquest,' said Sergeant Fraser.

Outside it had started to rain again and the lorry drivers were all pulling coats over their heads as they ran for the cafe and the bogs.

I said, 'Where?'

'Angelo's Cafe in an hour? It's opposite Morley Town Hall.'

'OK. But I need a favour?' I looked for an ashtray but had to use the wall.

Fraser whispered down the line, 'What?'

The pips went and I put in another coin. 'I need the names and addresses of the workmen who found the body.'

'What body?'

'Clare Kemplay's.' I began to count the love-hearts scribbled here and there around the phone.

'I don't know . . .'

'Please,' I said.

Someone had written *4eva 2geva* inside one of the hearts in red.

Fraser said, 'Why me?'

'Because I think you're a decent bloke and I need a favour and don't know anybody else to ask.'

Silence, then, 'I'll see what I can do.'

'One hour then,' I said, hanging up.

I replaced the receiver, picked it up again, put in another coin, and dialled.

Des Shags Convicts Wives.

'Yeah?'

'Tell BJ, Eddie called and give him this number, 276578. Tell him to ask for Ronald Gannon, Room 27.'

Fuck You Wakey Ken.

I replaced the receiver, picked it up again, put in another coin, and dialled.

True Love Never Dies.

'Peter Taylor speaking?'

'Hello. Is Kathryn there please?'

'She's still asleep.'

I looked at my father's watch.

I said, 'When she wakes up, can you tell her Edward called.'

'All right,' said her father, like it was some fucking enormous favour.

'Bye.' I replaced the receiver, picked it up again, put in my last coin, and dialled.

An old woman came into the lobby from the cafe smelling of bacon.

'Ossett 256199.'

'It's me, Mum.'

'Are you all right, love? Where are you?'

One of the kids was chasing another around the pool table, brandishing a pool cue.

I said, 'I'm fine. I'm at work.'

The old woman had sat down in one of the brown lobby chairs opposite the payphone and was staring out at the lorries and the rain.

'I might have to go away for a couple of days.'

'Where?'

The kid with the pool cue had the other one pinned down on the baize.

'Down South,' I said.

'You'll phone, won't you?'

The old woman farted loudly and the kids in the pool room stopped fighting and came running out into the lobby.

'Of course . . .'

'I love you, Edward.'

The kids rolled up their sleeves, put their lips to their arms, and began blowing raspberries.

'Me too.'

The old woman was staring out at the lorries and the rain, the kids dancing round her.

I replaced the receiver.

4 LUV.

Angelo's Cafe, opposite Morley Town Hall, breakfast busy.

I was on my second cup of coffee, way past tired.

'Can I get you anything?' Sergeant Fraser was at the counter.

'Cup of coffee, please. Black, two sugars.'

I stared around the cafe at the wall of headlines guarding every breakfast:

£534 Million Trade Deficit, Gas Up 12%, IRA Xmas Truce, a picture of the new Dr Who, and Clare.

'Morning,' said Fraser, setting down a cup of coffee in front of me.

'Thanks.' I drained my cold cup and took a sip from the hot one.

'I spoke with the coroner first thing. He says they're going to have to adjourn.'

'They were pushing it a bit anyway.'

A waitress brought over a full breakfast and set it down in front of the Sergeant.

'Yeah, but what with Christmas and the family, it would've been nice.'

'Shit, yeah. The family.'

Fraser heaped half the plate on to his fork. 'Do you know them?'

'No.'

'Lovely people,' sighed Fraser, mopping up the juice of the eggs and the tomatoes with a piece of toast.

'Yeah?' I said and wondered how old Fraser was.

'They'll release the body though, so they'll be able to have the funeral.'

'Get it out the way.'

Fraser put down his knife and fork and pushed the spotless plate to one side. 'Thursday, I think they said.'

'Right. Thursday.' I couldn't remember if we'd cremated my father last Thursday or Friday.

Sergeant Fraser sat back in his chair. 'What about this anonymous call then?'

I leant forward, my voice low. 'Like I said. Middle of the bleeding night . . .'

'Come on Eddie?'

I looked up at Sergeant Fraser, his blond hair, watery blue eyes and puffy red face, the trace of a Scouse accent and the simple wedding ring. He looked like the boy I had sat next to in chemistry.

'Can I level with you?'

'I think you'd better,' said Fraser, offering me a cigarette.

'Barry had a source, you know.' I lit the cigarette.

'A grass, you mean?'

'A source.'

Fraser shrugged, 'Go on.'

'I got a call at the office last night. No name, just be at the Gaiety on Roundhay Road. You know it, yeah?'

'No,' laughed Fraser. 'Course I bloody do. How did you know this was straight up?'

'Barry had a lot of contacts. He knew a lot of people.'

'What time was this?'

'About ten. Anyway, I went along and met this lad . . .'

Fraser had his sleeves on the table, leaning forward, smiling. 'Who was he then?'

'Black lad, no name. Said he'd been with Barry on the Sunday night.'

'What did he look like?'

'Black, you know.' I stubbed out my cigarette and took another one from my own pack.

'Young? Old? Short? Tall?'

'Black. Curly hair, big nose, thick lips. What do you want me to say?'

Sergeant Fraser smiled. 'He say if Barry Gannon was drinking?'

'I asked him and he said Barry had had a few but he wasn't smashed or anything.'

'Where was this?'

I paused, thinking this was where I'd fuck up, then said, 'The Gaiety.'

'Be some witnesses then?' Fraser had taken out his notebook and was writing in it.

'Gaiety witnesses, yeah.'

'I don't suppose you tried to persuade our dark friend to relate any of this information to a member of his local constabulary?'

'No.'

'So then?'

'About eleven or so, he said Barry said he was going over to Morley. That it was something to do with the Clare Kemplay murder.'

Sergeant Fraser was staring over my shoulder at the rain and the Town Hall opposite. 'Like what?'

'He didn't know.'

'You believe him?'

'Why not?'

'Fuck off, he's having you on. Eleven o'clock on a Sunday night, after a skinful in the Gaiety?'

'That's what he said.'

'All right. What do you reckon Gannon knew that could have made him come all the way over here, at that time on a Sunday night?'

'I don't know. I'm just telling you what this lad told me.'

'And that's it?' Sergeant Fraser was laughing. 'Bollocks. You're supposed to be a journalist. You must have asked him more questions than that.'

I lit another bloody cigarette. 'Yeah. But I'm telling you, the lad knew fuck all.'

'All right, so what do you think Gannon found out?'

'I've told you, I don't know. But it does explain why he was in Morley.'

'Brass'll love this,' sighed Fraser.

A waitress came over and took away the cups and the plate. The man on the next table was listening to us, looking at a photofit of the Cambridge Rapist that could have been anyone.

I said, 'Did you get the names?'

Sergeant Fraser lit another cigarette and leant forward. 'This is between us?'

'Of course,' I said and took out a pen and a piece of paper from my jacket.

'Two builders, Terry Jones and James Ashworth. They're

working on the new houses behind Wakefield Prison. It's Foster's Construction, I think.'

'Foster's Construction,' I echoed, thinking Donald Foster, Barry Gannon, link.

'I don't have their addresses and I wouldn't give you them even if I did. So that's your lot.'

'Thank you. Just one more thing?'

Fraser stood up. 'What?'

'Who has access to the Clare Kemplay post-mortem report and photographs?'

Fraser sat back down. 'Why?'

'I'm just curious. I mean, can any copper working the case get to see it?'

'It's available, yeah.'

'Have you seen it?'

'I'm not on the case.'

'But you must have been part of the search party?'

Fraser looked at his watch. 'Yeah, but the Murder Room's out of Wakefield.'

'So you wouldn't know when it first became available?'

'Why?'

'I just want to know about the procedure. I'm just curious.'

Fraser stood back up. 'They're not good questions to be asking, Eddie.' Then he smiled and winked and said, 'I best be off. See you across the road.'

'Yeah,' I said.

Sergeant Fraser opened the cafe door and then turned back. 'Keep in touch, yeah?'

'Yeah. Of course.'

'And not a bloody word right?' He was half laughing.

'Not a word,' I muttered, folding up my piece of paper.

Gaz from Sport was coming up the Town Hall steps.

I was having a last cigarette, sat on the steps. 'What the fuck are you doing here?'

'That's right bloody charming that is,' said Gaz, giving me his toothless grin. 'I'm a witness I am.'

'Yeah?'

The grin was gone. 'Yeah, straight up. I was supposed to meet Baz on Sunday night but he didn't show up.'

'It's going to be adjourned, you know?'

'You're fucking joking? Why?'

'Police still don't know what he was doing on Sunday night.' I offered Gaz a cigarette and lit another one for myself.

Gaz solemnly took the cigarette and the light. 'Know he was fucking dead though, don't they?'

I nodded and said, 'Funeral's Thursday.'

'Fuck. That quick?'

'Yeah.'

Gaz sniffed hard and then spat on one of the stone steps. 'Seen the boss?'

'I haven't been inside yet.'

He stubbed out his cigarette and started up the steps. 'Best make a move.'

I said, 'I'm going to wait here. If they need me, they know where I am.'

'Don't blame you.'

'Listen,' I said, calling after him. 'You heard anything about Johnny Kelly?'

'Fuck all,' said Gaz. 'Some bloke in the Inns last night was saying Foster's had it with him this time though.'

'Foster?'

'Don Foster. Trinity Chairman.'

I stood up. 'Don Foster's the chairman of Wakefield Trinity?'

'Yeah. Where the fuck you been?'

'Waste of bloody time that was.' Thirty minutes later, Gaz from Sport was coming down the Town Hall steps with Bill Hadden.

'You can't rush these things Gareth,' Hadden was saying, looking odd without a desk.

I got up from my cold step to greet them. 'At least they can go ahead with the funeral.'

'Morning Edward,' said Hadden.

'Morning. Have you got a minute?'

'Family seemed to be taking it better than you'd think,' said Gaz, lowering his voice and glancing back up the steps.

I said, 'That's what I'd heard.'

'Very strong people. You want a word?' Hadden put his hand on my shoulder.

'I'll see everyone later,' said Gaz from Sport, down the steps two at a time, seizing his chance to dance.

'What about Cardiff City?' Hadden called after him.

'We'll murder them Boss!' Gaz shouted back.

Hadden was smiling. 'You can't buy that kind of enthusiasm.'

'No,' I said. 'That's true.'

'What was it then?' Hadden said, folding his arms against the cold.

'I thought I'd go and see the two men who found the body, tie it in with this psychic and a bit about the history of Devil's Ditch.' I said it much too quickly, like a man who'd had thirty minutes to think about it.

Hadden began stroking his beard, which was always bad news. 'Interesting. Very interesting.'

'You think so?'

'Mmm. Except the tone worries me a little.'

'The tone?'

'Mmm. This medium, this psychic, it's more of a background feature. Supplement stuff. But the men who found the body, I don't know . . .'

Right back in his face: 'But you said she knows the name of the killer. That's not background, that's Front Page.'

Hadden, not rising to the bait, said, 'You're going to talk to them today?'

'I thought I'd go over there now, seeing as I've got to go over to Wakefield anyhow.'

'All right,' said Hadden, walking off towards his Rover. 'Bring it all back to me by five and we'll go over it for tomorrow.'

'You got it,' I shouted, checking my father's watch.

A Leeds and Bradford A to Z open on my lap, my notes on the passenger seat beside me, I nosed through the back and side streets of Morley.

I turned on to Victoria Road and drove slowly along, pulling up just before the junction with Rooms Lane and Church Street.

Barry must have been coming the other way, heading towards the Wakefield Road or the M62. The lorry would have been here, at the traffic lights on Victoria Road, waiting to turn right up Rooms Lane.

I flicked back through my notebook, faster and faster, back to the very first page.

Bingo.

I started the car, pulling out to wait at the traffic lights.

To my left, on the other side of the crossroads, a black church and, next to it, Morley Grange Junior and Infants.

The lights changed, I was still reading.

'At the junction of Rooms Lane and Victoria Road, Clare said goodbye to her friends and was last seen walking down Victoria Road towards her home . . .'

Clare Kemplay.

Last seen.

Goodbye.

I drove across the junction, a Co-op lorry waiting to turn right up Rooms Lane.

Barry's lorry would have been here too, at the traffic lights on Victoria Road, waiting to turn right up Rooms Lane.

Barry Gannon.

Last seen.

Goodbye.

I crawled slowly along Victoria Road, car horns at my rear, Clare skipping along on the pavement beside me in her orange kagool and her red Wellington boots.

'Last seen walking down Victoria Road towards her home.'

The Sports Ground, Sandmead Close, Winterbourne Avenue.

Clare was standing at the corner of Winterbourne Avenue, waving.

I indicated left and turned on to Winterbourne Avenue.

It was a cul-de-sac of six older semi-detached and three new detached.

A policeman was standing in the rain outside number 3.

I reversed up the drive of one of the new detached houses to turn around.

I stared across the road at 3 Winterbourne Avenue.

Curtains drawn.

The Viva stalled.

A curtain twitched.

Mrs Kemplay, arms folded, in the window.

The policeman checked his watch.

I pulled away.

Foster's Construction.

The building site was behind Wakefield Prison, yards from Devil's Ditch.

Lunchtime on a wet Tuesday in December and the place was as quiet as the grave.

A low tune on the damp air, *Dreams Are Ten A Penny.*

I followed my ears.

'All right?' I said, pulling back the tarpaulin door of an unfinished house.

Four men chewing sandwiches, slurping tea from flasks.

'Help you?' said one.

'Lost are you?' said another.

I said, 'I'm actually looking for . . .'

'Never heard of them,' said one.

'Journalist are you?' said another.

'Shows does it?'

'Yeah,' they all said.

'Well, do you know where I can find Terry Jones and James Ashworth?'

A big man in a donkey jacket stood up, swallowing half a loaf of bread. 'I'm Terry Jones.'

I stuck out my hand. 'Eddie Dunford. *Yorkshire Post.* Can I have a word?'

He ignored my hand. 'Going to pay me are you?'

Everybody laughed into their tea.

'Well, we can certainly discuss it.'

'Well, you can certainly piss off if you don't,' said Terry Jones to more laughter.

'Seriously,' I protested.

Terry Jones sighed and shook his head.

'Got a right bloody nerve, some folk,' said one of the men.

'Least he's fucking local,' said another.

'Come on then,' yawned Terry Jones, before swilling out his mouth with the last of his tea.

'Make sure he bloody coughs up,' shouted another man as we went outside.

'Have you had a lot of papers here?' I asked, offering Terry Jones a cigarette.

'Lads said there was a photographer from *Sun*, but we were up Wood Street Nick.'

There was a thick drizzle in the air and I pointed to another half-built house. Terry Jones nodded and led the way.

'Police keep you long?'

'No, not really. Thing like this though, they're not going to take any bloody chances are they?'

'What about James Ashworth?' We were standing in the doorway, the rain just missing us.

'What about him?'

'They keep him a long time?'

'Same.'

'Is he about?'

'He's sick.'

'Yeah?'

'Something going around.'

'Yeah?'

'Yeah.' Terry Jones dropped his cigarette and ground it out with his boot and added, 'Gaffer's been off since Thursday, Jimmy yesterday and today, couple of other lads last week.'

I said, 'Who found her, you or Jimmy?'

'Jimmy.'

'Where was she?' I said, looking out across the mud and the piss.

Terry Jones hawked up a massive piece of phlegm and said, 'I'll show you.'

We walked in silence over the building site to the trough of wasteland that runs parallel to the Wakefield-Dewsbury Road. A ribbon of blue and white police tape was strung along the ridge of the ditch. Across the ditch, on the road side, two coppers were sat in a Panda car. One of them looked across at us and nodded at Terry Jones.

He waved back. 'How long do they keep this up?'

'No idea.'

'They had tents all over this until last night.'

I was staring down into Devil's Ditch, at the rusted prams and the bicycles, at the cookers and the fridges. Foliage and litter snaked through everything, pulling it down into its mouth, making it impossible to see the bottom.

'Did you see her?' I asked.

'Yes.'

'Fuck.'

'She was lying on top of a pram, about halfway down.'

'A pram?'

He was staring off at something far, far away. 'Police took it. She had, aw fuck . . .'

'I know.' I had my eyes closed.

'Police said we hadn't to tell anyone.'

'I know, I know.'

'But, fuck . . .' He was fighting with a lump in his throat, tears in his eyes.

I handed him another cigarette. 'I know. I saw the photographs from the post-mortem.'

He pointed with the unlit cigarette at a separately marked piece of ground. 'One of the wings was over there, near the top.'

'Fuck.'

'I wish to Christ I'd never seen her.'

I stared into Devil's Ditch, the photos on the wall at the Redbeck swimming through my mind.

'If only it hadn't been her,' he whispered.

'Where does Jimmy Ashworth live?'

Terry Jones looked at me. 'I don't think that's a right good idea.'

'Please?'

'He's taken it badly. He's only a lad.'

'It might help him to talk,' I said, looking at a dirty blue pram halfway down the slope.

'That's bollocks,' he sniffed.

'Please?'

'Fitzwilliam,' said Terry Jones and turned and walked away.

I ducked down under the blue police ribbon and, leaning into Devil's Ditch by the root of a dead tree, I plucked a white feather from a bush.

*

An hour to kill.

I drove up past the Queen Elizabeth Grammar School, parked, and jogged back into Wakefield through the rain, quickening my pace as I passed the school.

Fifty minutes to kill.

Being Tuesday, I walked round the second-hand market, smoking cigarettes and getting soaked to the skin, staring at the prams and the children's bicycles and the pickings from the house clearances of the dead.

The Indoor Market stank of wet clothes and there was still a book stall where Joe's Books had been.

I glanced at my father's watch, leafing through the pile of old superheroes.

Forty minutes to kill.

Every Saturday morning for three years, my father and I had got the 126 at half-past seven from Ossett bus station, my father reading the *Post*, talking about football or cricket, the empty shopping bags on his lap, as I dreamt of the pile of comics that was always my wage for helping Joe.

Every Saturday morning until that Saturday morning Old Joe hadn't opened up and I had stood there waiting, my father coming by with two bags of shopping, the cheese wrapped in paper on the top.

Thirty-five minutes to kill.

In the Acropolis at the top of Westgate, where I'd once fancied the waitress, I forced down a plate of Yorkshire Pudding and onion gravy and then puked it straight back up in the little toilet in the back, the toilet where I'd always fantasised I'd finally get to fuck that waitress called Jane.

Twenty-five minutes to kill.

Outside in the rain, I headed on up to the Bullring, past the Strafford Arms, *the hardest pub in the North*, past the hairdresser's where my sister had worked part-time and met Tony.

Twenty minutes to kill.

In Silvio's, my mother's favourite cafe and the place where I used to secretly meet Rachel Lyons after school, I ordered a chocolate eclair.

I took out my damp notebook and began to read through the scant notes I had on Mystic Mandy.

'The future, like the past, is written. It cannot be changed, but it can help to heal the wounds of the present.'

I sat in the window and stared out at Wakefield.

Futures past.

It was raining so hard now that the whole city looked under water. I wished to Christ it was, that the rain would drown the people and wash the place the fuck away.

I had killed all the time I had.

I drank down the cup of hot sweet tea, left the eclair, and headed back up to St Johns, a tea-leaf stuck to my lip and a feather in my pocket.

Blenheim Road was one of the most beautiful in Wakefield, with big strong trees and large houses set back in their own small grounds.

Number 28 was no exception, a rambling old house that had been subdivided into flats.

I walked across the drive, avoiding the holes full of puddles, and went inside. The windows in the hallway and on the stairs were stained glass and the whole place had the stink of an old church in winter.

Number 5 was on the first-floor landing, to the right.

I looked at my father's watch and rang the doorbell. The chimes sounded like *Tubular Bells* and I was thinking of *The Exorcist* when the door opened.

A middle-aged woman, fresh from the pages of *Yorkshire Life* in her country blouse and country skirt, held out her hand.

'Mandy Wymer,' she said and shook hands briefly.

'Edward Dunford. From the *Yorkshire Post*.'

'Please, come in.' She pressed herself into the wall as I passed, leaving the front door ajar as she followed me down the dim hall, hung with dim oils, into a big dim room with large windows blocked by larger trees. There was a litter tray in one corner and the whole room smelt of it.

'Please sit down,' said the lady, pointing to the far corner of a large sofa draped in a tie-dyed cloth.

The woman's conservative appearance jarred, both with the Oriental-cum-hippy decor and with her profession. It was a thought I obviously couldn't disguise.

'My ex-husband was Turkish,' she suddenly said.

'Ex?' I said, switching on the Philips Pocket Memo in my pocket.

'He went back to Istanbul.'

I couldn't resist. 'You didn't see it coming?'

'I'm a medium, Mr Dunford, not a fortune teller.'

I sat on the far end of the sofa, feeling like a twat, unable to think of anything to say.

Eventually I said, 'I'm not making a very good impression, am I?'

Miss Wymer rose quickly from her chair. 'Would you care for some tea?'

'That'd be nice, if it's no trouble?'

The woman almost ran from the room, stopping suddenly in the doorway as though she had walked into a plate of glass.

'You smell so strongly of bad memories,' she said quietly, her back to me.

'Pardon?'

'Of death.' She stood in the doorway, shaking and pale, her hand gripping the frame of the door.

I got up. 'Are you OK?'

'I think you'd better leave,' she whispered, slipping down the frame of the door and on to the floor.

'Miss Wymer . . .' I went across the room towards her.

'Please! No!'

I reached out, wanting to pick her up. 'Miss Wymer . . .'

'Don't touch me!'

I backed off, the woman curling into a tight ball.

'I'm sorry,' I said.

'It's so strong.' She was moaning, not speaking.

'What is?'

'It's all over you.'

'What is?' I shouted, angry, thinking of BJ and these days and nights spent in rented rooms with the mentally ill. 'What is, tell me?'

'Her death.'

The air was suddenly thick and murderous.

'What are you fucking talking about?' I was going towards her, the blood drumming in my ears.

'No!' She was screaming, sliding back on her arse up the hall, her arms and legs splayed, her country skirt riding up. 'God no!'

'Shut up! Shut up! Shut up!' I was screaming now, flying up the hall after her.

She scrambled to her feet, begging, 'Please, please, please, leave me alone.'

'Wait!'

She turned into a room and slammed the door on me, trapping one of the fingers of my left hand in the hinges for a second.

'You fucking bitch!' I shouted, kicking and punching the locked door. 'You crazy fucking bitch!'

I stopped, put my throbbing left fingers in my mouth and sucked.

The flat was silent.

I leant my head against the door and quietly said, 'Please, Miss Wymer . . .'

I could hear scared sobs from behind the door.

'Please, Miss Wymer. I need to talk to you.'

I heard the sound of furniture being moved, of chests of drawers and wardrobes being placed in front of the door.

'Miss Wymer?'

A faint voice came through the layers and layers of wood and doors, a child whispering to a friend beneath the covers.

'Tell them about the others . . .'

'Pardon?'

'Please tell them about the others.'

I was leaning against the door, my lips tasting the varnish. 'What others?'

'The others.'

'What fucking others?' I shouted, pulling and twisting at the handle.

'All the others under those beautiful new carpets.'

'Shut up!'

'Under the grass that grows between the cracks and the stones.'

'Shut up!' My fists into wood, my knuckles into blood.

'Tell them. Please tell them where they are.'

'Shut up! Fucking shut up!'

My head against the door, the tide of noise retreating, the flat silent and dim.

'Miss Wymer?' I whispered.

Silence, dim silence.

As I left the flat, licking and sucking my knuckles and fingers, I saw the door across the landing open slightly.

'Keep your fucking nose out!' I shouted, running down the stairs.

'Less you want it bloody cutting off!'

Ninety miles an hour, spooked.

Foot down on Motorway One, exorcising the Ghosts of Wakefield Past and Present.

Into the rearview mirror, a green Rover hugging my tail. Me paranoid, making it for an unmarked police car.

Eyes high into the sky, driving inside the fat belly of a whale, the sky the colour of its grey flesh, stark black trees its mighty bones, a damp prison.

Into the mirror, the Rover gaining.

Taking the Leeds exit at the charred remains of the gypsy camp, the black frames of the burnt-out caravans more bones, standing in some pagan circle to their dead.

Into the mirror, the green Rover heading North.

Underneath the station arches, parking the Viva, two black crows eating from black bin-bags, ripping through the wasted meat, their screams echoing into the dark in this, the Season of the Plague.

Ten minutes later I was at my desk.

I dialled Directory Enquiries, then James Ashworth, then BJ.

No answers, everybody Christmas shopping.

'You look terrible.' Stephanie, files in her arms, fat as fuck.

'I'm fine.'

Stephanie stood there, in front of my desk, waiting.

I stared at the only Christmas card on my desk, trying to switch off the visions of Jack Whitehead fucking her up trap two, getting a little hard myself.

'I spoke to Kathryn last night.'

'So?'

'Don't you bloody care?' She was already angry.

So was I. 'It's none of your business how I fucking feel.'

She didn't move, just kept standing there, shifting her weight from foot to foot, her eyes filling up.

I felt bad and so I said, 'I'm sorry Steph.'

'You're a pig. A fucking pig.'

'I'm sorry. How is she?'

She was nodding her fat face, agreeing with her own fat thoughts. 'It's not the first time is it?'

'What did Kathryn say?'

'There have been others haven't there?'

Others, always the bloody others.

'I know you, Eddie Dunford,' she went on, leaning forward across the desk, her arms like thighs. 'I know you.'

'Shut up,' I said quietly.

'How many others have there been, eh?'

'Keep your bloody nose out, you fat bitch.'

Applause and cheers rang out across the office, fists banging on desks, feet stamping.

I stared at Kathryn's Christmas card.

'You pig,' she spat.

I looked up from the card but she was gone, sobbing out the door.

Across the office George Greaves and Gaz raised their cigarettes in salute, giving me the thumbs up.

I held up my thumb, fresh blood on my knuckle.

It was five o'clock.

'I still need to talk to the other one, James Ashworth. He was the one who actually found the body.'

Hadden looked up from his pile of Christmas cards. He put one of the larger cards to the bottom of the pile and said, 'It's all a bit thin.'

'She was round the bloody twist.'

'Did you try and get a quote from the police.'

'No.'

'Maybe just as well,' he sighed, continuing to look through his cards.

I was tired beyond sleep, hungry beyond food, the room beyond hot and all too real.

Hadden was looking up from his cards at me.

'Anything new today?' I asked, my mouth suddenly full of bilious water.

'Nothing that's fit to print. Jack's off on one of his . . .'

I swallowed. 'One of his?'

'He's playing his cards close to his chest, shall we say.'

'I'm sure he's doing what's best.'

Hadden handed back the draft of my piece.

I opened the folder on my knee, putting away the one piece and taking out another. 'And then there's this?'

Hadden took the sheet from me and pushed his glasses up the bridge of his nose.

I stared out of the window behind him, the reflection of the yellow office lights on top of a dark wet Leeds.

'Mutilated swans, eh?'

'As I'm sure you know, there's been a spate of animal mutilations.'

Hadden sighed, his cheeks turning red. 'I'm not stupid. Jack showed me the post-mortem.'

I could hear people laughing in another part of the building.

'I'm sorry,' I said.

Hadden took off his glasses and rubbed at the bridge of his nose. 'You're trying too bloody hard.'

'I'm sorry,' I said again.

'You're like Barry. He was the same, always . . .'

'I wasn't going to mention the post-mortem or Clare.'

Hadden was on his feet, pacing. 'You can't just write things and then assume it's the bloody truth because you think it is.'

'I never do that.'

'I don't know,' he was talking to the night. 'It's like you're shooting at the whole bloody bush just on the off-chance there might be something in there worth killing.'

I said, 'I'm sorry you think that.'

'There's more than one way to skin a cat, you know.'

'I know.'

Hadden turned round. 'Arnold Fowler's worked for us for years.'

'I know.'

'You don't want to be going out there and frightening the poor bloke with your horror stories.'

'I wouldn't do that.'

Hadden sat back down and sighed loudly. 'Get some quotes. Give it a paternal tone and don't mention the bloody Clare Kemplay case.'

I stood up, the room suddenly going dark and then light again. 'Thank you.'

'We'll run it on Thursday. Straightforward abuse of animals.'

'Of course.' I opened the door for air, support, and an exit.

'Like the pit ponies.'

I ran for the bogs, my guts in my gob.

'Hello. Is Kathryn there please?'

'No.'

The office was quiet and I had almost finished what I had to do.

'Do you know when she'll be back?'

'No.'

I was drawing wings and roses upon my blotter. I put down my pen.

'Can you tell her Edward called?'

They hung up.

I scrawled *The Medium & The Message* across the top of the article in biro, then added a question mark and lit a cigarette.

After a few drags, I tore a sheet of paper from my notebook, stubbed out my cig, and wrote two lists. At the bottom of the page I wrote Dawson and underlined it.

I felt tired, hungry, and utterly lost.

I closed my eyes against the harsh bright office light and the white noise that filled my thoughts.

It took me a moment to pick out the sound of the phone.

'Edward Dunford speaking?'

'This is Paula Garland.'

I leant forward in my chair, my elbows on the desk supporting the weight of the phone and my head. 'Yes?'

'I heard you saw Mandy Wymer today.'

'Yeah, sort of. How did you know?'

'Our Paul said.'

'Right.' I'd no idea what to say next.

There was a long pause, then she said, 'I need to know what she said.'

I was upright in my chair, changing hands and wiping the sweat on my trouser leg.

'Mr Dunford?'

'Well, she didn't say very much.'

'Please, Mr Dunford. Anything at all?'

I had the phone cradled between my ear and my chin, looking at my father's watch and stuffing *The Medium & The Message* into an envelope.

I said, 'I can meet you in the Swan. About an hour?'

'Thank you.'

Down the corridor, into records.

Through the files, cross index, tear it down.

Looking at my father's watch, 8.05 p.m.

Back in time:

July 1969, the Moon Landings, small steps and giant leaps.

12 July 1969, Jeanette Garland, 8, missing.

13 July, *A Mother's Emotional Plea.*

14 July, Detective Superintendent Oldman appeals.

15 July, police retrace Jeanette's last small steps.

16 July, police widen search.

17 July, police baffled.

18 July, police call off search.

19 July, *Medium Contacts Police.*

Small Steps and Giant Leaps.

17 December 1974, a notebook full of scrawled quotes.

Looking at my father's watch, 8.30 p.m.

Out of time.

The Swan, Castleford.

I was at the bar, ordering a pint and a Scotch.

The place was Christmas busy with a works do, everybody chanting along to the jukebox.

A hand at my elbow.

'Is one of them for me?'

'Which one do you want?'

Mrs Paula Garland picked up the whisky and made her way through the crowd to the cigarette machine. She put her handbag and glass on top of the machine.

'Do you come here often, Mr Dunford?' she smiled.

'Edward, please.' I put my pint down on top of the machine. 'No, not often enough.'

She laughed and offered me a cigarette. 'First time?'

'Second,' I said, thinking of the last time.

She took a light from me. 'It's not usually this busy.'

'You come here often then?'

'Are you trying to pick me up, Mr Dunford?' She was laughing.

I blew smoke above her head and smiled.

'I used to come here a lot,' she said, the laughter suddenly gone.

I was unsure what to say and said, 'Seems like a nice local.'

'It was.' She picked up her drink.

I tried very hard not to stare but she was so pale against the red of her sweater, the rolls and folds of its neck making her whole head seem so very small and fragile.

And, as she drank the whisky, little spots of red appeared on her cheeks, making her look as though she'd been punched or beaten.

Paula Garland took another mouthful and drained her glass. 'About Sunday. I . . .'

'Forget it. I was right out of order. Another one?' I said, all a bit too quickly.

'I'm all right for now, ta.'

'Well, just say.'

Elton John took over from Gilbert O'Sullivan.

We both looked awkwardly around the pub, smiling at the party hats and the mistletoe.

Paula said, 'You saw Mandy Wymer then?'

I lit another cigarette, my stomach flipping. 'Yeah.'

'Why did you go?'

'She claimed she told the police where to find Clare Kemplay's body.'

'You don't believe her?'

'Two builders found the body.'

'What did she say?'

'I didn't really get a chance to ask her,' I said.

Paula Garland pulled hard on her cigarette and then said, 'Does she know who did it?'

'She claims to.'

'She didn't say?'

'No.'

She was playing with her empty glass, spinning it on top of the cigarette machine. 'Did she mention Jeanette?'

'I don't know.'

'You don't know?' There were tears in her eyes.

'She said something about "the others", that's all.'

'What? What did she say?'

I stared around the pub. We were almost whispering but it was the only sound I could hear, like the rest of the world had been switched off.

'She said I should "tell them about the others" and then she just rambled on about bloody carpets and the grass between the stones.'

Paula Garland had turned her back to me, her shoulders trembling.

I put my hand on her shoulder. 'I'm sorry.'

'No, I'm sorry Mr Dunford,' she said to the red velvet wallpaper. 'You've been very kind to come here, but I need to be alone now.'

Paula Garland picked up her bag and her cigarettes. When she turned around her face was streaked with faint black lines from her eyes to her lips.

I held up my palms, blocking her path. 'I don't think this is a good idea.'

'Please,' she insisted.

'At least let me give you a lift home.'

'No thank you.'

She pushed past me, out through the crowd and the door.

I drained my pint and picked up my cigs.

*

Brunt Street, the dark line of terraces facing the white-fronted semis, few lights on either side.

I parked on the semi side, at the opposite end to Number 11, and counted Christmas trees as I waited.

There was a tree but no lights in Number 11.

Nine trees and five minutes later, I heard her tall brown boots. I watched from low down in my seat as Paula Garland unlocked the red door and went inside.

No lights went on in Number 11.

I sat in the Viva just watching, wondering what I'd say if I dared to knock upon that red door.

Ten minutes later, a man in a cap with a dog came out of one of the semis and crossed the road. He turned and stared at my car as his dog took a shit on the terrace side of the street.

The lights in Number 11 had still not gone on.

I started the Viva.

My mouth greasy from a bad plate of Redbeck chips, I arranged a small stack of coins on top of the payphone and dialled.

'Yeah?'

'Did you tell BJ Eddie called?'

I could see the same kids playing pool through the double glass doors.

'He left a message. He'll call you back at twelve.'

I hung up.

I checked my father's watch, 11.35 p.m.

I picked up the receiver and dialled again.

On the third ring, I hung up.

Fuck her.

I sat down to wait in the brown lobby chair where the woman had farted this morning, the click of the pool balls and the curses of the kids keeping me awake.

Twelve on the dot I was out of my chair and on top of the phone before any of the kids had a chance.

'Yeah?'

BJ said, 'Ronald Gannon?'

'It's me, Eddie. You got my message?'

'Yeah.'

'I need your help and I want to help you.'

'You didn't seem so sure last night.'

'I'm sorry.'

'So you should be. Have you got a pen?'

'Yeah,' I said, scrambling through my pockets.

'You might want to speak to Marjorie Dawson. She's in the Hartley Nursing Home in Hemsworth and she's been there since Sunday, since she saw Barry.'

'How the fuck did you find that out?'

'I know people.'

'I want to know who told you.'

'I want never gets.'

'Fuck off, BJ. I have to know.'

'I can't tell you.'

'Fuck.'

'I can tell you this though: I saw Jack Whitehead coming out of the Gaiety and he looked smashed and mad. You should be careful my dear.'

'You know Jack?'

'We go way, way back.'

'Thank you.'

'Mention it,' he laughed and hung up.

I awoke three times from the same dream on the floor of Room 27.

Each time thinking, I'm safe now, I'm safe now, go back to sleep.

Each time the same dream: Paula Garland on Brunt Street, clutching a red cardigan tight around her, screaming ten years of noise into my face.

Each time a big black crow came out of a sky a thousand shades of grey and clawed through her dirty blonde hair.

Each time chasing her down the street, after her eyes.

Each time frozen, waking cold on the floor.

Each time the moonlight seeping into the room, shadows making the photos on the wall come to life.

The last time, the windows all running with blood.

Chapter 6

Wednesday 18 December 1974.

7 a.m. and out the room, thank fuck.

A cup of tea and a slice of buttered toast in the Redbeck Cafe.

Truck drivers held up front pages:

Wilson Denies Stonehouse Spying, Man Killed as Three Bombs Explode, Petrol Up to 74p.

Johnny Kelly on the back pages, going National:

League's Lord Lucan? Where's Our Likely Lad?

Two policemen came in, hats off, sitting down at a window table.

My heart stopped, flopping across the scratches in my notebook:

Arnold Fowler, Marjorie Dawson, and *James Ashworth.*

Three dates.

Back in the Redbeck lobby, a fresh stack of change.

'Arnold Fowler speaking.'

'This is Edward Dunford from the *Post*. I'm sorry to disturb you, but I'm doing a piece on the attacks on the swans up in Bretton Park.'

'I see.'

'I was hoping we'd be able to get together.'

'When?'

'Sometime this morning? I know it's a bit short notice.'

'I'm actually up at Bretton this morning. I'm doing a Nature Walk with Horbury Juniors, but it doesn't start till half-ten.'

'I can be up there for half-past nine.'

'I'll meet you in the Main Hall.'

'Thank you.'

'Bye.'

Bright brittle winter sunshine pierced the windscreen on the drive over to Bretton, the heater turning as loud as the radio:

The IRA and Stonehouse, the race to be the Christmas

Number One, Clare Kemplay dying all over again on the National Stage.

I checked the rearview mirror.

One hand on the tuner, I went local:

Clare still breathing on Radio Leeds, phone-ins demanding that something be done about this kind of thing and what kind of animal would do such a thing and, anyroad, hanging's too good for the likes of thems that do this kind of thing.

The police suddenly quiet, no leads, no press conference.

Me thinking, the calm before the fucking shit-storm.

'Nice day for it,' I said, all smiles.

'For a change,' said Arnold Fowler, sixty-five and clothes to match.

The Main Hall was large and cold, the walls plastered with children's drawings and paintings of birds and trees.

High above, a huge papier-mâché swan hung from the roof beams.

The hall stank like another church in winter and I was thinking of Mandy Wymer.

'I knew your father,' said Arnold Fowler, leading me into a small kitchen with two chairs and a pale blue Formica-topped table.

'Really?'

'Oh aye. Fine tailor.' He unbuttoned his tweed jacket to show me a label I'd seen every day of my life: *Ronald Dunford, Tailor.*

'Small world,' I said.

'Aye. Though not like it used to be.'

'He'd be very flattered.'

'I don't reckon so. Not if I remember Ronald Dunford.'

'You're right there,' I smiled, thinking it had only been a week.

Arnold Fowler said, 'I was very sorry to hear of his passing.'

'Thank you.'

'How's your mother?'

'You know, bearing up. She's very strong.'

'Aye. Yorkshire lass through and through.'

I said, 'You know, you came to Holy Trinity when I was there.'

'I'm not surprised. I reckon I've been to every school in the West Riding at some time or other. Did you enjoy it?'

'Yeah. I can remember it well, but I couldn't draw to save me life.'

Arnold Fowler smiled. 'You never joined my Nature Club then?'

'No, sorry. I was Boy's Brigade.'

'For the football?'

'Yeah.' I laughed for the first time in a long time.

'We still lose out to this day.' He handed me a mug of tea. 'Help yourself to sugar.'

I heaped in two big spoonfuls and stirred them for a long time.

When I looked up, Arnold Fowler was staring at me.

'What's with Bill Hadden's sudden interest in the swans then?'

'It's not Mr Hadden. I did a piece on the injuries to those ponies over Netherton way and then I heard about the swans.'

'How did you hear about them?'

'Just talk at the *Post*. Barry Gannon, he . . .'

Arnold Fowler was shaking his head. 'Terrible, terrible business. I know his father too. Know him very well.'

'Really?' I asked, playing it typecast, playing it dumb.

'Aye. Such a shame. Very talented young man, Barry.'

I took a scalding mouthful of sweet tea and then said, 'I don't know any of the details.'

'I'm sorry?'

'About the swans.'

'I see.'

I took out my notebook. 'How many of these attacks have there been?'

'Two this year.'

'When were they?'

'One was in August sometime. Other was just over a week ago.'

'You said this year?'

'Aye. There are always attacks.'

'Really?'

'Aye. Sickening it is.'

'The same kind?'

'No, no. These ones this year, they were just plain barbaric.'

'What do you mean?'

'Tortured, they were.'

'Tortured?'

'They hacked the bloody wings off. Swans were alive and all.'

My mouth was bone-dry as I spoke. 'And usually?'

'Crossbows, air rifles, pub darts.'

'What about the police? You always report them?'

'Aye. Of course.'

'And what did they say?'

'Last week?'

'Yeah,' I nodded.

'Nothing. I mean, what can they say?' Arnold Fowler was suddenly fidgeting, playing with the sugar spoon.

'The police haven't been back to see you at all since last week then?'

Arnold Fowler looked out of the kitchen window, across the lake.

'Mr Fowler?'

'What kind of story are you writing Mr Dunford?'

'A true one.'

'Well, I've been asked to keep my true stories to myself.'

'What do you mean?'

'There are things I've been asked to keep to myself.' He looked at me as though I was dumb.

I picked up my mug and drained the tea.

'Have you got time to show me where you found them?' I asked.

'Aye.'

We stood up and walked out through the Main Hall, under the swan.

At the big door, I asked him, 'Did Clare Kemplay ever come here?'

Arnold Fowler walked over to a pencil drawing curling on the wall above a heavy painted radiator. It was a picture of two swans kissing on the lake.

He smoothed down one of the corners. 'What a bloody world we live in.'

I opened the door to the hollow sunshine and went outside.

We walked down the hill from the Main Hall towards the bridge that crossed Swan Lake.

On the other side of the lake the clouds were moving quickly across the sun, making shadows along the foot of the Moors, the purples and browns like some bruised face.

I was thinking of Paula Garland.

On the bridge, Arnold Fowler stopped.

'The last one looked like it had just been tossed over the side here, back into the lake.'

'Where did they cut the wings off?'

'I don't know. To tell the truth, no-one's really looked either.'

'And the other one, the one in August?'

'Hanging by her neck from that tree.' He pointed to a large oak on the other side of the lake. 'They'd crucified her first, then cut off the wings.'

'You're joking?'

'No, I'm not joking at all.'

'And no-one saw anything?'

'No.'

'Who found them?'

'The one on the oak was some kids, the last one was one of the park-keepers.'

'And the police haven't done anything?'

'Mr Dunford, we've made a world where crucifying a swan is seen as a prank, not a crime.'

We walked back up the hill in silence.

In the car park a coach was unloading a class of children, pushing and pulling at each other's coats as they got off.

I unlocked the car door.

Arnold Fowler held out his hand. 'Take care, Mr Dunford.'

'And you,' I said, shaking his hand. 'It was nice to see you again.'

'Aye. I'm sorry it was under such circumstances.'

'I know.'

'And good luck,' said Arnold Fowler, walking away towards the children.

'Thank you.'

I parked in an empty pub car park, somewhere between Bretton and Netherton.

The public phonebox had all its glass and most of its red paint missing, and the wind blew through me as I dialled.

'Morley Police Station.'

'Sergeant Fraser, please.'

'May I have your name please, sir?'

'Edward Dunford.'

I waited, counting the cars going past, picturing fat fingers over the mouthpiece, shouts across Morley Police Station.

'Sergeant Fraser speaking.'

'Hello. This is Edward Dunford.'

'I thought you were down South?'

'Why'd you think that?'

'Your mother.'

'Shit.' Counting cars, counting lies. 'You've been trying to contact me then?'

'Well, there was the small matter of our conversation yesterday. My superiors are quite keen that I should get a formal statement from you.'

'I'm sorry.'

'So what did you want?'

'Another favour?'

'You're bloody joking aren't you?'

'I'll trade.'

'What? You been listening to the jungle drums again?'

'Did you question Marjorie Dawson about last Sunday?'

'No.'

'Why not?'

'Because she's down South somewhere, visiting her dying mother.'

'I don't think so.'

'Where is she then, Sherlock?'

'Near.'

'Don't be a twat, Dunford.'

'I said, I'll trade.'

'Like fuck you will.' He was whispering down the line,

hissing. 'You'll tell me where she is or I'll have you for obstruction.'

'Come on. I only want to know what they have on some dead swans up at Bretton Park.'

'You on bloody drugs? What dead swans?'

'Last week some swans had their wings cut off up at Bretton. I just want to know what the police think, that's all.'

Fraser was breathing heavily. 'Cut off?'

'Yeah, cut off.' He's heard the rumours, I thought.

Fraser said, 'They find them?'

'What?'

'The wings.'

'You know they fucking did.'

Silence, then, 'All right.'

'All right what?'

'All right, I'll see what I can find out.'

'Thanks.'

'Now where the fuck is Marjorie Dawson?'

'The Hartley Nursing Home, Hemsworth.'

'And how the bloody hell did you find that out?'

'Jungle drums.'

I left the phone dangling.

Me, foot down.

Sergeant Fraser, size tens running through the station.

Me, ten minutes from the Hartley Nursing Home.

Sergeant Fraser, buttoning his jacket, grabbing his hat.

Me, the window open a crack, a cigarette lit, Radio 3 and Vivaldi on loud.

Sergeant Fraser sat outside the Chief's office, looking at the cheap watch his wife bought him last Christmas.

Me, smiling, at least one whole hour ahead.

Fresh flowers in my hand, I rang the doorbell of the Hartley Nursing Home.

I had never taken flowers to St James.

Never taken my father a single stem.

The building, looking like an old stately home or a hotel, cast a cold dark shadow over its untended grounds. Two old women stared at me through the bay window of a conservatory. One of the women was massaging her left tit, squeezing the nipple between her fingers.

I wondered when my mother had stopped taking flowers for my father.

A red-faced middle-aged woman in a white coat opened the door.

'Can I help you?'

'I do hope so. I'm here to see my Aunty Marjorie. Mrs Marjorie Dawson?'

'Really? I see. Please come this way,' said the lady, holding the door open for me.

I couldn't remember the last time I had visited my father, whether it had been the Monday or the Tuesday.

'How is she?'

'Well, we've had to give her something for her nerves. Just to quieten her down.' She led me into a large hall dominated by a larger staircase.

I said, 'I'm sorry to hear that.'

'Well, I heard she was in a bit of a state when they brought her back.'

Back, I thought, biting my tongue.

'When did you last see your Aunt, Mr . . .?'

'Dunston. Eric Dunston,' I said, extending my hand with a smile.

'Mrs White,' said Mrs White, taking my hand. 'The Hartleys are away this week.'

'Pleased to meet you,' I said, genuinely thankful not to be meeting the Hartleys.

'She's upstairs. Room 102. Private room of course.'

My father had ended up in a private room, the flowers all gone, a pile of bones inside a brown hide bag.

Mrs White, in her tight white coat, led the way up the stairs.

The heating was on full and there was the low hum of a television or radio. The smell of institution cooking followed us up the stairs, like it had tailed me all the way from the St James Hospital, Leeds.

At the top of the stairs we walked down a sweating corridor filled with big iron radiators and came to room 102.

My heart beating loud and fast, I said, 'It's OK. I've kept you long enough, Mrs White.'

'Oh, don't be daft,' smiled Mrs White, knocking on the door and opening it. 'It's no trouble.'

It was a beautiful room, drenched in winter sunlight and filled with flowers, Radio 2 quietly playing something light.

Mrs Marjorie Dawson was lying with her eyes closed atop two full pillows, the collar of her dressing gown poking out from under all the bedding. A faint film of sweat covered her face and flattened her perm, actually making her appear younger than she probably was.

She looked like my mother.

I stared at the bottles of Lucozade and Robinson's Barley Water, glimpsing my father's gaunt face in the glass.

Mrs White went to the pillows, gently touching Mrs Dawson on the arm.

'Marjorie, dear. You have a visitor.'

Mrs Dawson slowly opened her eyes and looked about the room.

'Would you like some tea bringing?' Mrs White asked me as she primped the flowers on the bedside table.

'No, thank you,' I said, my eyes on Mrs Dawson.

Mrs White seized my flowers and went over to the sink in the corner. 'Well then, I'll just put these in some water for you and then I'll be out of your way.'

'Thanks,' I said, thinking fuck.

Mrs Dawson was staring straight at me, through me.

Mrs White finished filling the vase full of water.

'It's Eric, dear. Your nephew,' she said, turning to me and whispering, 'Don't worry. It sometimes takes her a little while to come round. She was the same with your uncle and his friends last night.'

Mrs White put the vase of fresh flowers on the bedside table. 'Well, that's me finished. I'll be in the conservatory if you need anything. Bye-bye for now,' she smiled, giving me a wink as she closed the door.

The room was suddenly unbearably full of Radio 2.

Unbearably hot.

My father gone.

I walked over to the window. The catch had been painted over. I ran a finger along the paintwork.

'It's locked.'

I turned around. Mrs Dawson was sitting upright in her bed.

'I see,' I said.

I stood there by the window, my whole body wet beneath my clothes.

Mrs Dawson reached over to the bedside table and switched off the radio.

'Who are you?'

'Edward Dunford.'

'And why are you here, Mr Edward Dunford?'

'I'm a journalist.'

'So you've been telling dear Mrs White more lies?'

'Privilege of the profession.'

'How did you know I was here?'

'I received an anonymous tip.'

'I suppose I should feel flattered, to be the subject of an anonymous tip,' said Mrs Dawson, pushing her hair back behind her ears. 'It sounds so very glamorous, don't you think?'

'Like a racehorse,' I said, thinking of BJ.

Mrs Marjorie Dawson smiled and said, 'So why are you interested in an old nag like me, Mr Edward Dunford?'

'My colleague, Barry Gannon, came to see you last Sunday. Do you remember?'

'I remember.'

'You said his life was in danger.'

'Did I really? I say so many things.' Mrs Dawson leant over and smelt the flowers I had brought her.

'He was killed on Sunday night.'

Mrs Dawson looked up from the flowers, her eyes wet and fading.

'And you came to tell me this?'

'You didn't know?'

'Who can tell what I'm supposed to know these days?'

I looked out across the grounds at the bare trees, their cold shadows waning with the sunshine.

'Why did you tell him his life was in danger?'

'He was asking reckless things about reckless men.'

'What kind of things? About your husband?'

Mrs Dawson smiled sadly. 'Mr Dunford, my husband may be many things but reckless isn't one of them.'

'What did you talk about then?'

'Mutual friends, architecture, sport, that kind of thing.' A tear slid down her cheek on to her neck.

'Sport?'

'Rugby League, would you believe?'

'What about it?'

'Well, I'm not a fan so it was all a bit one-sided.'

'Donald Foster's a fan, isn't he?'

'Really? I thought it was the wife.' Another tear.

'His wife?'

'Really, Mr Dunford, here we go again. Reckless talk costs lives.'

I turned back to the window.

A blue and white police car was coming up the gravel drive.

'Shit.'

Fraser?

I looked at my father's watch.

It had been just over forty minutes since I'd phoned.

Not Fraser?

I walked over to the door.

'You're leaving so soon?'

'I'm afraid the police are here. They may want to talk to you about Barry Gannon.'

'Not again?' sighed Mrs Dawson.

'Again? What do you mean again?'

There was a stampede of boots and shouts up the stairs.

'I really think you should be going,' said Mrs Dawson.

The door burst open.

'Yep, I really think you should be going,' said the first policeman through the door.

The one with the beard.

Not Fraser.

Fuck Fraser.

'I thought we'd told you about bothering people who don't want bothering,' said the other, shorter officer.

There were just the two of them, but the room felt as though it was full of men in black uniforms, with iron-shod boots and truncheons in their hands.

The short one stepped towards me.

'Here comes a copper to chop off your head.'

A sharp pain from a kick to my ankle brought me falling to my knees.

I sprawled across the carpet, my eyes blinking wet with burning red tears, trying to stand.

A pair of white tights walked towards me.

'You lying bastard,' hissed Mrs White.

A big pair of feet led her away.

'You're dead,' whispered the bearded officer, seizing me by my hair and dragging me from the room.

I looked back at the bed, my scalp red raw.

Mrs Dawson was lying on her side, her back to the door, the radio on loud.

The door shut.

The room was gone.

Big monkey hands pinched me hard under the armpits, the smaller claws still at the roots of my hair.

I saw a huge radiator, the paint flaking in strips.

Fuck, white warm wool into black yellow pain.

I was at the top of the stairs, my shoes struggling to stay on my feet.

Then I was holding on to the banister halfway down.

Fuck, I'd lost the breath from my chest and my ribs.

And then I was at the foot of the stairs, trying to stand, one hand on the bottom step, one upon my chest.

Fuck, my scalp red yellow black pain.

Then all the heat was gone and there was only cold air and bits of the gravel drive in my palms.

Fuck, my back.

And then we were all running together down the drive.

Fuck, my head into the green Viva door.

Then they were touching my cock, their hands in my pockets, making me giggle and squirm.

Fuck, big leather hands squeezing my face into yellow red pain.

And then they were opening the door of my car, holding my hand out.

Fuck, fuck, fuck.

Then black.

Yellow light.

Who will love our Little Red Eddie?

Yellow light again.

'Oh, thank heavens for that.'

My mother's pink face, shaking from side to side.

'What happened love?'

Two tall black figures behind her, like huge crows.

'Eddie, love?'

A yellow room full of blacks and blues.

'You're in Pinderfields Casualty,' said a man's deep voice from the black beyond.

There was something at the end of my arm.

'Can you feel anything?'

A big fat bandaged hand at the end of my arm.

'Careful, love,' said my mother, a gentle brown hand upon my cheek.

Yellow light, black flashes.

'They know who I am! They know where we live!'

'Best leave him for now,' said another man.

Black flash.

'I'm sorry, Mum.'

'Don't be worrying about me, love.'

A taxi, Paki radio talk and the scent of pines.

I stared down at my white right hand.

'What time is it?'

'Just gone three.'

'Wednesday?'

'Yes, love. Wednesday.'

Out the window, Wakefield city centre slugging past.

'What happened Mum?'

'I don't know love.'

'Who called you?'

'Called me? It was me that found you.'

'Where?'

My mother, her face to the window, sniffing.

'In the drive.'

'What happened to the car?'

'I found you in the car. You were on the back seat.'

'Mum . . .'

'Covered in blood.'

'Mum . . .'

'Just lying there.'

'Please . . .'

'I thought you were bloody dead.' She was crying.

I stared down at my white right hand, the stink of the bandages stronger than the cab.

'What about the police?'

'The ambulance driver called them. He took one look at you and reported it.'

My mother put her hand on my good arm, eye to eye:

'Who did this to you love?'

My cold right hand throbbed to the pulse beneath the bandages.

'I don't know.'

Back home, Wesley Street, Ossett.

The taxi door slammed shut behind me.

I jumped.

There were brown smears on the Viva's passenger door.

My mother was coming up the drive behind me, closing her bag.

I put my left hand into my right pocket.

'What are you doing?'

'I've got to go.'

'Don't be daft, lad.'

'Mum, please.'

'You're not fit.'

'Mum, stop it.'

'No, you stop it. Don't do this to me.'

She made a grab for the car keys.

'Mum!'

'I hate you for this, Edward.'

I reversed out the drive, tears and black flashes.
My mother, standing in the drive, watching me go.

The one-armed driver.
Red light, green light, amber light, red.
Crying in the Redbeck car park.
Black pain, white pain, yellow pain, more.

Room 27, untouched.
One hand cupping cold water over my head.
A face in the mirror running brown with old blood.
Room 27, all blood.

Twenty minutes later, on the slow road to Fitzwilliam.
Driving with one hand on the rearview mirror, eating the lid off a bottle of paracetamol, gobbling six to null the pain.
Fitzwilliam looming, a dirty brown mining town.
My fat white right hand upon the steering wheel, left hand through my pockets. My one good hand and my teeth unfolding a torn-out page from the Redbeck's phone book:
Ashworth, D., 69 Newstead View, Fitzwilliam.
Circled and underlined.
FUCK THE IRA was sprayed on the iron bridge into town.
'Aye-up lads. Where's Newstead View?'
Three teenage boys in big green trousers, sharing a cigarette, spitting big pink-streaked chunks of phlegm at a bus shelter window.
They said, 'You what?'
'Newstead View?'
'Right by offy. Then left.'
'Ta very much.'
'I should think so.'
I struggled to wind up my window and stalled as I drove off, the three big green trousers waving me off with a big pink shower and two forked fingers all round.
Under my bandages, four fingers smashed into one.
Right at the off-licence, then left on to Newstead View.
I pulled over and switched off the engine.
Newstead View was a single line of terraces looking out on

to dirty moorland. Ponies grazed between rusting tractors and piles of scrap metal. A pack of dogs chased a plastic shopping bag up and down the road. Somewhere babies were crying.

I felt around inside my jacket pockets.

I took out my pen, my stomach empty, my eyes filling.

I stared at the white right hand that wouldn't close, at the white right hand that wouldn't write.

The pen rolled slowly off the bandages and on to the floor of the car.

69 Newstead View, a neat garden and flaking window frames.

TV lights on.

Knock, knock.

I switched on the Philips Pocket Memo in my right jacket pocket with my left hand.

'Hello. My name is Edward Dunford.'

'Yes?' said a prematurely grey woman through bucked teeth and an Irish accent.

'Is your James home?'

Hands stuffed deep into a blue housecoat, she said, 'You're the one from the *Post* aren't you?'

'Yes, I am.'

'The one that's been talking to Terry Jones?'

'Yes.'

'What do you want with our Jimmy?'

'Just a quick chat, that's all.'

'He had enough of a chat with the police. He doesn't need to keep going over it. Specially with likes of . . .'

I reached out to steady myself, grabbing at the frame of the front door.

'You been in some kind of accident have you?'

'Yeah.'

She sighed and mumbled, 'You'd better come in and sit yourself down. You don't look right clever.'

Mrs Ashworth shooed me into the front room and a chair too close to the fire.

'Jimmy! There's that gentleman from the *Post* here to see you.'

My left cheek already burning, I heard two loud thumps from the room up above.

Mrs Ashworth switched off the TV, plunging the room into an orange darkness. 'You should have been here earlier.'

'Why?'

'Well I didn't see it myself like, but they said the place was swarming with police.'

'When?'

'About five this morning.'

'Where?' I asked, staring through the gloom at a school photo on top of the TV, a long-haired youth smirking back at me, the knot in his tie as big as his face.

'Here. This street.'

'Five o'clock this morning?'

'Yeah, five. No-one knows what it were about, but everyone reckons it were . . .'

'Shut up Mam!'

Jimmy Ashworth was standing in the doorway in an old school shirt and purple tracksuit bottoms.

'Ah, you're up. Cup of tea?' said his mother.

I said, 'Please.'

'Yeah,' said the youth.

Mrs Ashworth walked out of the room half backwards, muttering.

The boy sat down on the floor, his back against the sofa, flicking the lank strands of hair from his eyes.

'Jimmy Ashworth?'

He nodded. 'You're bloke what spoke to Terry?'

'Yeah, that's me.'

'Terry said there might be some brass for us?'

'Could be.' I was desperate to change seats.

Jimmy Ashworth reached up behind him to a packet of cigarettes on the arm of the sofa. The packet fell on to the carpet and he took out a cigarette.

I sat forward and said quietly, 'You want to tell me what happened?'

'What happened to your hand?' said Jimmy, lighting up.

'I got it caught in a car door. What about your eye?'

'Shows does it?'

'Only when you spark up. Coppers give you it?'

'Maybe.'

'Give you a hard time, did they?'

'Could say that.'

'So get some brass out of it. Tell us what happened?'

Jimmy Ashworth pulled hard on his cigarette and then exhaled slowly into the orange glow of the fire.

'We were waiting for Gaffer, but he never come and it was raining so we were just arsing about, you know, drinking tea and stuff. I went over to Ditch to have a waz and that's when I saw her.'

'Where was she?'

'In Ditch, near top. It were like she'd rolled down or something. Then I saw them, them . . .'

The kettle in the kitchen began to whistle.

'Wings?'

'You know then?'

'Yeah.'

'Terry tell you?'

'Yeah.'

Jimmy Ashworth brushed at the hair in his face, singeing it slightly with the end of his cig. 'Shit.'

The smell of burnt hair filled the room.

Jimmy Ashworth looked at me. 'They was all caught up.'

'What did you do?' I said, turning as far as I could from the fire.

'Nothing. I just fucking froze. I couldn't believe it was her. She looked so different, so white.'

Mrs Ashworth came back in with a teatray and set it down. 'They were always saying what a lovely little thing she was,' she whispered.

My whole right arm felt like the blood had stopped moving in it. 'And you were alone?' I asked.

'Yeah.'

The hand throbbed again, the bandage sweating and itching. 'What about Terry Jones?'

'What about him?'

'Thanks,' I said, taking a cup from Mrs Ashworth. 'When did Terry see her?'

'Well I went back to tell lads didn't I?'

'When was this?'

'How do you mean?'

'Well you just said you froze, so I was wondering how long you were standing there before you told the others?'

'I don't fucking know.'

'Jimmy, please. Not in this house,' his mother said quietly.

'But he's same as bleeding coppers. I don't know how long it was.'

'I'm sorry Jimmy,' I said, putting down the cup of tea on top of the fireplace so I could scratch at my bandage.

'I went back to shed and I was hoping Gaffer'd be there, but . . .'

'Mr Foster?'

'Nah, nah. Mr Foster's Boss. Gaffer is Mr Marsh.'

'George Marsh. Very nice man,' said Mrs Ashworth.

Jimmy Ashworth looked at his mother and sighed and said, 'Anyroad, Gaffer weren't there, just Terry.'

'What about the others?'

'They'd pissed off in van somewhere.'

'So you told Terry Jones and he went back over to Devil's Ditch with you?'

'No, no. I went and telephoned police. Once were enough for me.'

'So Terry went over there to have a look while you telephoned the police?'

'Yeah.'

'By himself?'

'By his sen, that's what I said.'

'And?'

Jimmy Ashworth looked off into the orange glow. 'And police came and took us up Wood Street Nick.'

'They thought he'd done it, you know.' Mrs Ashworth was dabbing at her eyes.

'Mum shut up!'

'What about Terry Jones?' I said, my hand throbbing hard then stopping numb, sensing something missing.

'He's no good that one.'

'Mum, will you bloody shut up!'

I was hot, numb, and tired.

I said, 'The police questioned him?'

'Yeah.'

I was sweating and itching and desperate to get the fuck out of this oven.

'But they didn't think he'd done it, did they?'

'I don't know. Ask them.'

'Why did they think you did it, Jimmy?'

'Like I said, ask them.'

I stood up. 'You're a smart lad, Jimmy.'

He looked up, surprised. 'How's that?'

'Keeping it shut.'

'He's a good boy, Mr Dunford. He didn't do nothing,' Mrs Ashworth said, standing up.

'Thanks for letting me come in, Mrs Ashworth.'

'What are you going to write about him?' She was standing in the doorway, hands deep in her blue pockets.

'Nothing.'

'Nothing?' said Jimmy Ashworth, on his bare feet.

'Nothing,' I said, holding up my fat white right hand.

I drove slowly back through the black to the Redbeck, gobbling pills and scattering more on the floor, lorry lights and Christmas trees, like ghosts from the gloom.

I had tears on my cheeks and not from the pain.

'What a bloody world we live in.'

Children were slaughtered and no-one gave a fuck. King Herod Lives.

In the bright yellow lobby, I took another stack of coins and dialled Wesley Street, letting it ring for five minutes.

'I hate you for this, Edward!'

I thought about phoning my sister's house, but I changed my mind.

I went and bought an *Evening Post* and drank a cup of coffee in the Redbeck's cafe.

The paper was full of price rises and the IRA. There was a small piece about the Clare Kemplay inquiry, bland statements from Detective Superintendent Noble, tucked inside page 2 with no byline.

What the fuck was Jack doing?

'I saw Jack Whitehead coming out of the Gaiety and he looked smashed and mad.'

The back pages were full of Leeds United, football giving Rugby League the boot.

No Johnny Kelly, no Wakefield Trinity, just St Helens 7 points clear.

'Really? I thought it was the wife.'

I was making circles with a dried coffee spoon:

Missing girl: Clare Kemplay –

Clare Kemplay's body found by James Ashworth –

James Ashworth, employed by Foster's Construction –

Foster's Construction, owned by Donald Foster –

Donald Foster, Chairman of Wakefield Trinity Rugby League Club –

Wakefield Trinity's star player, Johnny Kelly –

Johnny Kelly, brother of Paula Garland –

Paula Garland, mother of Jeanette Garland –

Jeanette Garland: Missing girl.

'Everything's linked. Show me two things that aren't connected.'

Barry Gannon, like he was sitting right there, across the table:

'What's your plan then?'

Back in the bright yellow lobby, just gone six, I ripped through the phone book.

'It's Edward Dunford.'

'Yes?'

'I need to see you.'

'You'd better come in.'

Mrs Paula Garland, standing in the doorway of Number 11, Brunt Street, Castleford.

'Thank you.'

I stepped inside another warm terraced room, *Coronation Street* just starting, my right hand in my pocket.

A short fat red-haired woman came out of the kitchen. 'Hello, Mr Dunford.'

'This is Scotch Clare, lives two down. She's just going, aren't you?'

'Aye. Pleased to meet you,' said the woman, squeezing my left hand.

'You're not going on my account, I hope?' I lied, by trade.

'Ooh, he's got some manners has this one, eh?' laughed Scotch Clare, walking over to the bright red door.

Paula Garland was still holding open the door. 'I'll see you tomorrow, love.'

'Aye. Nice to meet you Mr Dunford. Maybe we'll see you again for a wee Christmas drink, eh?'

'Eddie, please. That'd be nice,' I smiled.

'See you then, Eddie. Merry Christmas,' grinned Clare.

Paula Garland walked a little way out into the street with Clare. 'See you then,' she said outside, giggling.

I stood for a moment alone in the front room, staring at the photograph on top of the TV.

Paula Garland came back in and closed the red door. 'Sorry about that.'

'No, it's me that should be sorry, just phoning up . . .'

'Don't be daft. Sit down will you.'

'Thanks,' I said and sat down on the off-white leather sofa.

She started to say, 'About last night, I . . .'

I put up my hands. 'Forget it.'

'What's happened to your hand?' Paula Garland had her own hand to her mouth, staring at the greying lump of bandages on the end of my arm.

'Someone slammed my car door on it.'

'You're joking?'

'No.'

'Who?'

'Two policemen.'

'You're joking?'

'No.'

'Why?'

I looked up and tried to smile. 'I thought you might be able to tell me.'

'Me?'

She had a piece of red cotton thread hanging from her brown

flared skirt and I wanted to stop what I had started and tell her about the piece of red cotton thread.

But I said, 'The same two coppers warned me off after I was here on Sunday.'

'Sunday?'

'The first time I came here.'

'I never said anything to the police.'

'Who did you tell?'

'Just our Paul.'

'Who else?'

'No-one.'

'Please tell me?'

Paula Garland was standing in the middle of the furniture, surrounded by trophies and photographs and Christmas cards, pulling her yellow and green and brown striped cardigan tight around her.

'Please, Mrs Garland . . .'

'Paula,' she whispered.

I just wanted to stop, to reach over, to pick off the piece of red cotton thread and hold her as tight as life itself.

But I said, 'Paula please, I need to know.'

She sighed and sat down in the off-white leather armchair opposite me. 'After you went, I was upset and . . .'

'Please?'

'Well, the Fosters came over . . .'

'Donald Foster?'

'And his wife.'

'Why did they come here?'

Paula Garland's blue eyes flashed cold. 'They're friends, you know.'

'I'm sorry. I didn't mean it like that.'

She sighed, 'They came to see if I'd heard from Johnny.'

'When was this?'

'About ten or fifteen minutes after you'd gone. I was still crying and . . .'

'I'm sorry.'

'It wasn't just you. They'd been phoning all weekend, wanting to speak to Johnny.'

'Who had?'

'The papers. Your mates.' She was talking to the floor.

'And you told Foster about me?'

'I didn't tell him your name.'

'What did you tell him?'

'Just that some fucking journalist had been round asking about Jeanette.' Paula Garland looked up, staring at my right hand.

'Tell me about him,' I said, my dead hand waking again.

'Who?'

The pain was growing, throbbing. 'Donald Foster.'

Paula Garland, beautiful blonde hair tied back, said, 'What about him?'

'Everything.'

Paula Garland swallowed. 'He's rich and he likes Johnny.'

'And?'

Paula Garland, her eyes blinking fast, whispered, 'And he was very kind to us when Jeanette went missing.'

My mouth dry, my hand on fire, staring at the piece of red cotton thread, I said, 'And?'

'And he's a bastard if you cross him.'

I held up my white right hand. 'You think he'd do something like this?'

'No.'

'No?'

'I don't know.'

'You don't know?'

'No I don't know, because I don't know why he'd do it.'

'Because of what I know.'

'What do you mean, what you know?'

'Because I know everything's connected and he's the link.'

'Link to what? What are you talking about?' Paula Garland was scratching at her forearms.

'Donald Foster knows you and Johnny, and Clare Kemplay's body was found on one of his building sites in Wakefield.'

'That's it?'

'He's the link between Jeanette and Clare.'

Paula Garland was white and shaking, tearing at the skin on her arms. 'You think Donald Foster killed that little girl and took my Jeanette from me?'

'I'm not saying that, but he knows.'

'Knows what?'

I was on my feet, my bandages flailing, shouting, 'There's a man out there and he's taking and raping and murdering little girls and he'll take and rape and murder again and nobody is going to stop him because nobody really fucking cares.'

'I care.'

'I know you care, but they don't. They just care about their little lies and their money.'

Paula Garland flew from the chair, kissing my mouth, kissing my eyes, kissing my ears, holding me tight, saying over and over, 'Thank you, thank you, thank you.'

My left hand clutched at the bones in her spine, my right hand dangling numb, pawing at her skirt, the piece of red cotton thread catching on my bandage.

'Not here,' said Paula and gently picked up my white right hand, leading me up the steep, steep stairs.

There were three doors at the top of the stairs, two closed and a bathroom door ajar. Two tacked on plastic door plates: *Mummy & Daddy's Room* and *Jeanette's Room.*

We fell through the *Mummy & Daddy* door, Paula kissing me harder and harder, talking faster and faster:

'You care and you believe. You don't know how much that means to me. It's been so long since someone cared.'

We were on the bed, the light from the landing making warm shadows of the wardrobe and the dressing table.

'You know how many times I still wake up and think, I must make Jeanette's breakfast, I must wake her up?'

I was on top, kissing back, the sound of shoes hitting the bedroom floor.

'I just want to be able to sleep and wake up like everybody else.'

She sat up and took off her yellow and green and brown striped cardigan. I tried to lean on my right hand, pulling at the little flower buttons of her blouse with my left.

'It used to be so important to me, you know, that nobody ever forgot her, that nobody ever spoke about her like she was dead or in the past.'

My left hand was pulling down the zip of her skirt, her own hand on my fly.

'We weren't happy, you know, Geoff and me. But after we had Jeanette, it was like it was all worth it.'

My mouth tasted of salt water, her tears and words a hard and ceaseless rain.

'Even then though, even when she was just a baby, I'd lie awake at night and wonder what I'd do if anything happened to her, seeing her dead; lying awake, seeing her dead.'

She was squeezing my cock too tight, my hand inside her knickers.

'Usually hit by a car or a lorry, just lying there in the street in her little red coat.'

I was kissing her tits, moving across her stomach, running from her words and her kisses, down to her cunt.

'And sometimes I'd see her strangled, raped and murdered, and I'd run to her room and I'd wake her up and I'd hug her and hug her and hug her.'

She was running her fingers through my hair, picking scabs loose, my blood beneath her nails.

'And then when she never came home, everything I'd imagined, all those terrible things, it had all come true.'

My hand was burning, her voice white noise.

'It had all come true.'

Me, cock hard and fast inside her dead room.

Her, cries and whispers in the dark.

'We bury our dead alive, don't we?'

I was pulling at her nipple.

'Under stones, under grass.'

Biting at the lobe of her ear.

'We hear them everyday.'

Sucking her lower lip.

'They talk to us.'

Squeezing her hip bones.

'They're asking us why, why, why?'

Me, faster and faster.

'I hear her everyday.'

Faster.

'Asking me why?'

Faster.

'Why?'

Dry sore skin on dry sore skin.

'Why?'

I was thinking of Mary Goldthorpe, of her silk knickers and her stockings.

'She knocks on this door and she wants to know why?'

Faster.

'She wants to know why?'

My dry edges against her dry edges.

'I can hear her saying, why Mummy?'

I was thinking of Mandy Wymer, her country skirt riding up.

'Why?'

Fast.

Dry.

Thinking of the wrong Garland.

Spent.

'I can't be alone again.'

My cock dry and sore, I was listening to her talking through the dark.

'They took her from me. Then Geoff, he . . .'

My eyes open, thinking of double-barrelled shotguns, of Geoff Garland and Graham Goldthorpe, of bloody patterns.

'He was a coward.'

Passing headlights drew shadows across the ceiling and I wondered if Geoff had blown his brains out in this house, in this room, or someplace else.

She was saying, 'The ring always felt loose anyway.'

I was lying in a widow and a mother's bed, thinking of Kathryn Taylor and screwing up my eyes so it was like I wasn't really here.

'And now Johnny.'

I'd counted only two bedrooms and a bathroom. I wondered where Paula Garland's brother slept, if Johnny slept in Jeanette's room.

'I can't live like this any more.'

I was gently stroking my own right arm, her pillow whispers lapping me up, on the verges of sleep.

It was the night before Christmas. There was a new cabin made of logs in the middle of a dark wood, candles burning yellow in the windows. I was walking through the wood, light snow underfoot, heading home. On the cabin porch I stamped my boots loose of snow and opened the heavy wooden door. A fire was burning in the hearth and the room was filled with the smell of good cooking. Under a perfect Christmas tree, there were boxes of beautifully wrapped presents. I went into the bedroom and saw her. She was lying under a home-made quilt, her golden hair splayed across the gingham pillows, her eyes closed. I sat down on the edge of the bed, unbuttoning my clothes. I slid quietly under the quilt, nuzzling up to her. She was cold and she was wet. I felt for her arms and legs. I sat up, ripping back the quilt and blankets, everything red. Only her head and her chest, open at the seams, her arms and legs lost. I fell through the blankets, her heart dropping to the floor with a dull thud. I picked it up with a bandaged hand, dust and feathers stuck in the blood. I pressed the dirty heart against her breast, stroking her golden locks. The hair came loose in my hand, sliding from her scalp, leaving me lying on a bed all covered in feathers and blood, the night before Christmas, someone knocking at the door.

'What was that?' I was wide awake.

Paula Garland was getting out of bed. 'It's the phone.'

She picked up her yellow and green and brown cardigan, putting it on as she went downstairs with her arse showing, the colours doing nothing for her.

I lay on the bed, listening to the scratchings of mice or birds in the roof.

After two or three minutes I sat up in the bed, got up and dressed, and went downstairs.

Mrs Paula Garland was rocking back and forth in the off-white leather armchair, clutching Jeanette's school photograph.

'What is it? What's happened?'

'It was our Paul . . .'

'What? What's wrong?' I was thinking shit, shit, shit; visions of cars crashed and windscreens bloodied.

'The police . . .'

I was on my knees, shaking her. 'What?'

'They've got him.'

'Who? Paul?'

'Some kid from Fitzwilliam.'
'What?'
'They're saying he did it.'
'Did what?'
'They're saying he killed Clare Kemplay and . . .'
'What?'
'He says he's done others.'
Everything seemed suddenly red, blood-blind.
She was saying, 'He says he killed Jeanette.'
'Jeanette?'
Her mouth and eyes were open, no sound, no tears.
I ran up the stairs, my hand on fire.
Back down the stairs, my shoes in one hand.
'Where are you going?'
'The office.'
'Please don't go.'
'I must.'
'I can't be alone.'
'I've got to go.'
'Come back.'
'Of course.'
'Cross your heart and hope to die?'
'Cross my heart and hope to die.'

10 p.m. Wednesday 18 December 1974.
The motorway, slick, black, and wet.
One arm on the wheel, heavy on the pedal, ice-wind
screaming through the Viva, thinking Jimmy James Ashworth.
'They thought he'd done it, you know.'
I checked my rearview mirror, the motorway empty but for
lorries and lovers and Jimmy James Ashworth.
'Mum shut up!'
Exiting at the gypsy camp, black on black hiding the damage,
shaking the blood warm in my right hand, thinking Jimmy
James Ashworth.
'Why did they think you did it, Jimmy?'
Through the Christmas lights of Leeds City Centre, writing
copy in my head, thinking Jimmy James Ashworth.
'Ask them.'

The *Yorkshire Post* building, yellow lights on ten floors. I parked underneath, grinning and thinking, Jimmy James Ashworth.

'You're a smart lad, Jimmy.'

A large Christmas tree in the foyer, double glass doors sprayed white with Season's Greetings. I pressed the lift button, thinking Jimmy James Ashworth.

'Keeping it shut.'

The lift doors opened. I stepped inside and pressed the 10 button, my heart beating, thinking Jimmy James Ashworth.

'He's a good boy, Mr Dunford. He didn't do nothing.'

The lift doors opened on the tenth floor, the office alive, the hum everywhere. The look on every face, shouting out, WE GOT HIM!

I clutched the Philips Pocket Memo in my left hand, thinking Jimmy James Ashworth, thanking Jimmy James Ashworth.

'What are you going to write about him?'

Thinking Scoop.

No knock, into Hadden's office.

The room, eye-of-the-hurricane still.

Jack Whitehead looking up, two days beard and eyes as big as dinner plates.

'Edward . . .' Hadden, glasses halfway down his nose.

'I interviewed him this afternoon. I fucking interviewed him!'

Hadden winced. 'Who?'

'No you didn't,' grinned back Jack, the stink of drink in the air.

'I sat in his front room and he practically told me everything.'

'Really?' Jack, mock-quizzical.

'Yeah, really.'

'Who are we talking about, Scoop?'

'James Ashworth.'

Jack Whitehead looked at Bill Hadden, smiling.

'Sit down,' said Hadden, pointing at the seat next to Jack.

'What is it?'

'Edward, they didn't arrest any James Ashworth,' he said as kindly as he could.

Jack Whitehead pretended to look at some notes, arching an

eyebrow even higher, unable to resist saying, 'Not unless he also goes by the name of Michael John Myshkin.'

'Who?'

'Michael John Myshkin,' repeated Hadden.

'Parents are Polacks. Can't speak a word of English,' laughed Jack, like it was funny.

'That's lucky,' I said.

'Here Scoop. Have a read.' Jack Whitehead tossed the morning first edition at me. It bounced off me and on to the floor. I leant forward to pick it up.

'What on earth happened to your hand?' said Hadden.

'I got it trapped in a door.'

'Trust it's not going to hamper your style, eh Scoop?'

I flapped around with the paper in my left hand.

'Need a hand?' laughed Jack.

'No.'

'Front Page,' he smiled.

CAUGHT screamed the headline.

Clare: Murder Squad Arrest Local Man, teased the subheading.

BY JACK WHITEHEAD, CRIME REPORTER OF THE YEAR, boasted the byline.

I read on:

Early yesterday morning police arrested a Fitzwilliam man in connection with the murder of ten-year-old Clare Kemplay.

According to a police source, exclusive to this newspaper, the man has confessed to the murder and has been formally charged. He will be remanded in custody at Wakefield Magistrates Court later this morning.

The police source further revealed that the man has also confessed to a number of other murders and formal charges are expected shortly.

Senior Detectives from around the country are due to arrive in Wakefield throughout the day to question the man about other similar unsolved cases.

I let the paper fall to the floor.

'I was right.'

Jack said, 'You think so?'

I turned to Hadden. 'You know I was. I said they were connected.'

'Which ones are they talking about Jack?' asked Hadden.

'Jeanette Garland and Susan Ridyard,' I said, tears in my eyes.

'For starters,' said Jack.

'I fucking told you.'

'Language, Edward,' muttered Hadden.

I said, 'I sat in this office, I sat in Oldman's office, and I told you both.'

But I knew it was over.

I sat there at the end of it all with Hadden and Jack Whitehead, my hand frozen with pain. I looked from one to the other, Jack grinning, Hadden fiddling with his glasses. The room, the outer office, the streets beyond, all suddenly silent. For one moment I wondered if it was snowing outside.

For just one moment, and then it started again:

'Have you got an address?' I asked Hadden.

'Jack?'

'54 Newstead View.'

'Newstead View! That's the same fucking street.'

'What?' Hadden, drained of patience.

'James Ashworth, the lad who found her body, he lives on the same bloody street as this bloke.'

'So?' smiled Jack.

'Fuck off, Jack!'

'Please watch your language in my office.'

Jack Whitehead had his arms up in mock surrender.

I saw red, red, and only red, my head alive with pain. 'They live on the same bloody street, in the same town, ten miles from where the body was found.'

'Coincidence,' said Jack.

'You reckon?'

'I reckon.'

I sat back, my right hand heavy with still blood, feeling the same heaviness creep over everything, like it was snowing here in this room, here in my brain.

Jack Whitehead said, 'He coughed for them. What more do you want?'

'The fucking truth.'

Jack was laughing, really laughing, big fat belly laughs.

We were pushing Hadden too far.

Quietly, I said, 'What did they get him on?'

Hadden sighed, 'Faulty brakelights.'

'You're joking?'

Jack had stopped laughing. 'Wouldn't pull over. Panda car gives chase. They haul him in, out of the blue he coughs for all this.'

'What kind of car was it?'

'Transit van,' said Jack, avoiding my eyes.

'What colour?'

'White,' smiled Jack, offering me a cigarette.

I took the cigarette, thinking of Mrs Ridyard and her posters, sitting in her neat front room with its spoiled view.

'How old is he?'

Jack lit his cigarette and said, 'Twenty-two.'

'Twenty-two? That'd make him only sixteen or seventeen in '69.'

'So?'

'Come on, Jack?'

'What's he do?' Hadden asked Jack, but looking at me.

'Works for a photo lab. Develops photos.'

My head awash, swimming with school girl photos.

Jack said, 'It feels wrong doesn't it, Scoop?'

'No,' I whispered.

'You don't want it to be him, I know.'

'No.'

Jack leant forward in his chair. 'I was the same. All that hard work, all those hunches, and it just doesn't sit right.'

'No,' I muttered, adrift in a white transit van plastered with photographs of the smiling, fair-haired, little dead.

'It's a bitter pill, but they got him.'

'Yeah.'

'You get used to it,' winked Jack as he stood up unsteadily. 'I'll see you both tomorrow.'

Hadden said, 'Yeah, thanks Jack.'

'Big day, eh?' said Jack, closing the door behind him.

'Yeah,' I said blankly.

The room was quiet and still smelt of Jack and drink.

After a few seconds, I said, 'What happens now?'

'I want you to do the background on this Myshkin feller. The whole thing's technically sub-judice, but if he's confessed and on remand we'll be all right.'

'When are you going to print his name?'

'Tomorrow.'

'Who's covering the remand hearing?'

'Jack'll do that and the press conference.'

'He's going to do both?'

'Well, you can go but, what with the funeral and everything, I thought . . .'

'Funeral? What funeral?'

Hadden looked at me over the top of his glasses. 'It's Barry's funeral tomorrow.'

I was staring at a Christmas card on his desk, a picture of a warm and glowing cottage in the middle of a snow-covered wood. 'Shit, I'd forgotten,' I whispered.

'I think it's best Jack stays on it tomorrow.'

'What time's the funeral?'

'Eleven. Dewsbury Crematorium.'

I stood up, all my limbs weak with the weight of dead blood. I walked across the seabed to the door.

Hadden looked up from his forest of cards and quietly said, 'Why were you so sure it was James Ashworth?'

'I wasn't,' I said and closed the door on my way out.

Paul Kelly was sitting on the edge of my desk.

'Our Paula's been ringing you.'

'Yeah?'

'What's going on Eddie?'

'Nothing.'

'Nothing?'

'She called me. Said you'd told her about me seeing that Mandy Wymer woman.'

'Leave her be, Eddie.'

Two hours straight shit-work, one-handed typing making it four. I transcribed my Ridyard notes for Jack Whitehead's big story, glossing over my meetings with Mrs Paula Garland:

Jack – Mrs Garland is reluctant to talk about the disappearance of her daughter. Her cousin is Paul Kelly, an employee of this paper, and he has asked that we respect her wish to be left alone.

I picked up the receiver and dialled.

On the second ring, 'Hello, Edward?'

'Yeah.'

'Where are you?'

'At work.'

'When are you coming back?'

'I've been warned off again.'

'Who by?'

'Your Paul.'

'I'm sorry. He means well.'

'I know, but he's right.'

'Edward, I . . .'

'I'll ring you tomorrow.'

'Are you going to court?'

Alone in the office, I said, 'Yeah.'

'It's him, isn't it?'

'Yeah, it looks that way.'

'Please come over.'

'I can't.'

'Please?'

'I'll ring tomorrow, I promise. I've got to go.'

The line went dead and my stomach knotted.

I had my head in my good and bad hands, the stink of hospitals and her on them both.

I lay in the dark on the floor of Room 27, thinking of women.

The lorries in the car park came and went, their lights making shadows dance like skeletons across the room.

I lay on my stomach, my back to the wall, eyes closed and hands over my ears, thinking of girls.

Outside in the night, a car door slammed.

I jumped up, out of my skin, screaming.

Chapter 7

6 a.m.

Thursday 19 December 1974.

My mother was sat in her rocking chair in the back room, staring out at the garden in the grey morning sleet.

I handed her a cup of tea and said, 'I've come for my black suit.'

'There's a clean shirt on your bed,' she said, still looking out of the window, not touching the tea.

'Thanks,' I said.

'What the fuck happened to your hand?' said Gilman from the *Manchester Evening News*.

'I got it caught,' I smiled, taking my seat down the front.

'Not the only one, eh?' winked Tom from Bradford.

West Yorkshire Metropolitan Police HQ, Wood Street, Wakefield.

'Aye, and how's that bird?' laughed Gilman.

'Shut it,' I whispered, red-faced, checking my father's watch, 8.30.

'Someone died?' said New Face, sitting down behind three black suits.

'Yeah,' I said and didn't turn round.

'Shit, sorry,' he mumbled.

'Southern wanker,' muttered Gilman.

I looked back at all the TV lights. 'Fuck, it's hot.'

'Which way you come in?' asked Tom from Bradford.

New Face said, 'The front.'

'Many folk outside?'

'Fucking hundreds.'

'Shit.'

'Got a name?' whispered Gilman.

'Yeah,' I smiled.

'Address?' said Gilman, loud and proud.

'Yeah,' we all said together.

'Fuck.'

'Morning ladies,' said Jack Whitehead, sitting down directly behind me, kneading my shoulders hard.

'Morning Jack,' said Tom from Bradford.

'Keeping your hand in, Scoop?' he laughed.

'Just in case you miss anything, Jack.'

'Now, now, girls,' winked Gilman.

The side door opened.

Three big smiles in three big lounge suits.

Chief Constable Ronald Angus, Detective Chief Superintendent George Oldman, and Detective Superintendent Peter Noble.

Three fat cats who had got their cream.

A bang and a whistle as the microphones went on.

Chief Constable Angus picked up a piece of white A4 paper and grinned broadly.

'Gentlemen, good morning. A man was arrested early yesterday morning on the Doncaster Road, Wakefield, following a brief police chase. Sergeant Bob Craven and PC Bob Douglas had signalled to the driver of a white Ford transit van to pull over in connection with a faulty brakelight. When the driver of the van refused, the officers gave chase and eventually forced the vehicle off the road.'

Chief Constable Angus, wavy hair like a grey walnut whip, paused, still beaming, like he was expecting applause.

'The man was brought here to Wood Street, where he was questioned. During the course of a preliminary interview, the man indicated he had information about more serious matters. Detective Superintendent Noble then proceeded to interview the man in relation to the abduction and murder of Clare Kemplay. At eight o'clock yesterday evening, the man confessed. He was then formally charged and will appear in court before Wakefield Magistrates later this morning.'

Angus sat back with the look of a man stuffed full of Christmas Pudding.

The room erupted in a firestorm of questions and names.

The three men bit their tongues and broadened those grins.

I stared into Oldman's black eyes.

'You think you're the only cunt putting that together?'

Oldman's eyes on mine.

'*My senile bloody mother could.*'

The Detective Chief Superintendent looked at his Chief Constable and exchanged a nod and a wink.

Oldman raised his hands. 'Gentlemen, gentlemen. Yes, the man in custody is also being questioned about other similar offences. However, at the present time, that is all the information I'm able to give you. But, on behalf of the Chief Constable, Detective Superintendent Noble, and all the men who have been involved in this investigation, I would like to publicly thank Sergeant Craven and PC Douglas. They are outstanding officers, who have our heartfelt thanks.'

Again, the room was ablaze with names, dates, and questions.

Jeanette '69 and Susan '72, unanswered.

The three men and their grins stood up.

'Thank you, gents,' shouted Noble, holding the side door open for his superiors.

'Fuck off!' I shouted in my black suit, clean shirt, and grey bandages.

HANG THE BASTARD,
  HANG THE BASTARD,
  HANG THE BASTARD NOW!
Wood Street, Wakefield's Trinity of Government:
The Nick, the Court, and the Town Hall.
Just gone nine and mob deep.
COWARD, COWARD, MYSHKIN IS A COWARD!
Two thousand housewives and their unemployed sons.
Gilman, Tom, and me, in the thick of the thick.
Two thousand hoarse raw throats and their sons.
A suedehead with his Mam, a *Daily Mirror*, and a home-made noose.
Proof enough.
COWARD, COWARD, MYSHKIN IS A COWARD!
Ugly hands pulling, grabbing, and pushing us;
This way and that way and that way and this.
Suddenly pinched, getting my collar felt by the long arm of the law.
Sergeant Fraser to the rescue.

STRING HIM UP!
STRING HIM UP!
STRING THE BLOODY BASTARD UP!

Behind the marble walls and the thick oak doors of Wakefield Magistrates Court there lay a brief kind of calm, but not for me.

'I need to talk to you,' I whispered, spinning round and straightening my tie.

'Too fucking right,' hissed Fraser. 'But not here and not now.'

The size tens tapped off down the corridor.

I pushed through the door into Court Number Two, packed tight and quiet.

Every seat taken, standing room only.

No families, only the gentlemen of the press.

Jack Whitehead down the front, leaning over the wooden railing, laughing with an usher.

I stared up at the stained-glass windows with their scenes of hills and sheep, mills and Jesus, the light outside so dull that the glass just reflected back the strips of electric lights that buzzed so loudly overhead.

Jack Whitehead turned round, narrowed his eyes, and saluted me.

Low beneath the marble and the oak, the muffled chants of the crowd outside seemed to bleed in under all our whispers, their screams marking out time on some ancient galley.

'It's fucking mental out there,' panted Gilman.

'At least we got in,' I said, leaning against the back wall.

'Aye. Fuck knows what happened to Tom and Jack.'

I pointed to the front of the public gallery. 'Jack's down there.'

'How the fuck he get there so fast?'

'There must be some underground tunnel or something linking here and the Nick.'

'Aye. And Jack'll have a bloody key,' snorted Gilman.

'That's our Jack.'

I turned suddenly towards the stained-glass windows as a black shape rose on the outside and then fell away like some giant bird.

'What the fuck was that?'

'A placard or something. Natives are getting restless.'

'Not the only ones.'

And then there he was, right on cue.

A dock full of plainclothes staring out at the court, one of them handcuffed to him.

Michael John Myshkin stood at the front of the dock in a dirty pair of blue overalls and a black donkey jacket, fat as fuck with a head too big.

I swallowed hard, my stomach churning with rising bile.

Michael John Myshkin blinked and blew a bubble of spit with his lips.

I reached for my pen, pain shooting from my nail to my shoulder, and had to lean back against the wall.

Michael John Myshkin, looking older than twenty-two, grinned at us with the smile of a boy half his age.

The Court Clerk stood up in the pit below, coughed once and said, 'Are you Michael John Myshkin of 54 Newstead View, Fitzwilliam?'

'Yes,' said Michael John Myshkin, looking round at one of the detectives in the dock.

'You are accused that on or between the twelfth and fourteenth of December you did murder Clare Kemplay against the peace of Our Sovereign Lady the Queen. Further, you are charged that at Wakefield on the eighteenth of December you did drive without due care and attention.'

Michael John Myshkin, Frankenstein's Monster in manacles, rested his one free hand on the front of the dock and sighed.

The Clerk of the Court nodded at another man sat opposite.

The man stood up and announced, 'William Bamforth, County prosecuting solicitor. For the record, Mr Myshkin has no legal representation at present. On behalf of the West Yorkshire Metropolitan Police, I am asking that Mr Myshkin be remanded in custody for a further eight days so that he might continue to be questioned about offences of a similar nature to that with which he has already been charged. I would also like to remind the people in court and particularly the members of the press that this case remains sub-judice. Thank you.'

The Clerk stood up again. 'Mr Myshkin, do you have any

objection to the prosecuting solicitor's request that you be held in custody for a further eight days?'

Michael John Myshkin looked up and shook his head. 'No.'

'Do you wish reporting restrictions be lifted?'

Michael John Myshkin looked at one of the detectives.

The detective shook his head ever so slightly and Michael John Myshkin whispered, 'No.'

'Michael John Myshkin, you will be remanded in custody for eight days. Reporting restrictions remain.'

The detective turned, pulling Myshkin behind him.

The whole of the public gallery craned forward.

Michael John Myshkin stopped at the top of the stairs, turned to look back at the court, then almost slipped and had to be steadied by one of the officers.

The last we saw of him was a big hand disappearing down the steps into the belly of the court, waving bye-bye.

That was the hand that took life, I thought.

And then the murdering bastard was gone.

'What do you think?'

I said, 'He looks the part.'

'Aye. He'll do,' winked Gilman.

It was going up to eleven when the Viva, followed by Gilman's car, turned into Dewsbury Crematorium.

The sleeting rain had eased to a cold drizzle but the wind was as raw as it had been last week, and there was no fucking way I could light a cigarette with one hand in bandages.

'Later,' muttered Sergeant Fraser at the door.

Gilman looked at me but said nowt.

Inside, the crematorium was packed silent.

One family, plus press.

We took a pew at the back of the chapel, straightening ties and wetting down hair, nodding at half the newspaper offices of the North of England.

Jack fucking Whitehead down the front, leaning over his pew, chatting with Hadden, his wife, and the Gannons.

I stared up at another stained-glass wall of hills and sheep, mills and Jesus, praying that Barry got a better one than my father had.

Jack Whitehead turned, narrowed his eyes, and waved my way.

The wind whistled round the building outside, like the cries of the sea and her gulls, and I sat and wondered whether birds could talk or not.

'Wish they'd bloody get on with it,' whispered Gilman.

'Where's Jack?' asked Tom from Bradford.

'Down there,' I smiled.

'Fuck me. Not another bloody tunnel?' laughed Gilman.

'Mind your language,' whispered Tom.

Gilman studied his prayer book. 'Shit, sorry.'

I turned suddenly towards the stained-glass window as Kathryn Taylor, all in black, walked down the aisle past the glass, arm in arm with Fat Steph and Gaz from Sport.

Gilman gave me a hard nudge and a wink. 'You lucky barstool.'

'Fuck off,' I hissed, red-faced, watching the knuckles on my one good hand turn from red to white as they gripped the wooden pew.

Suddenly the organist hit all the bloody keys at once.

Everybody stood up.

And there he was.

I stared at the coffin at the front of the room, unable to remember if my father's had been a paler or darker wood than Barry's.

I looked down at the prayer book on the ground, thinking of Kathryn.

I looked up, wondering where she was sitting.

A fat man in a brown cashmere coat was staring at me across the aisle.

We both turned and looked down at the floor.

'Where have you been?'

'Manchester,' said Kathryn Taylor.

We were outside the crematorium, standing on the slope between the door and the cars, the wind and the rain colder than ever. Black suits and coats were filing out, trying to light cigarettes, put up umbrellas, and shake hands.

'What were you doing in Manchester?' I asked, knowing full bloody well what she was doing in Manchester.

'I don't want to talk about it,' she said, walking away towards Fat Steph's car.

'I'm sorry.'

Kathryn Taylor kept walking.

'Can I phone you tonight?'

Stephanie opened the passenger door and Kathryn bent down and picked up something from the seat.

She turned round and hurled a book at me, screaming, 'Here, you forgot this the last time you fucked me!'

A Guide to the Canals of the North flew across the crematorium drive, scattering schoolgirl photographs in its wake.

'Fuck,' I spat, scrambling to pick up the photos.

Fat Steph's small white car reversed out of the crematorium car park.

'Plenty more fish in the sea.'

I looked up from the ground. Sergeant Fraser handed me a picture of a smiling blonde ten-year-old.

'Fuck off,' I said.

'There's no need for that.'

I snatched the photo from him. 'No need for what?'

Hadden, Jack Whitehead, Gilman, Gaz, and Tom were all milling about up by the doorway, watching us.

Fraser said, 'I'm sorry about your hand.'

'You're sorry? You fucking set me up.'

'I don't know what the fuck you're talking about.'

'Bet you fucking don't.'

'Listen,' said Fraser. 'We need to talk.'

'I've got nothing to say to you.'

He pushed a scrap of paper into my top pocket. 'Call me tonight.'

I walked away towards my car.

'I'm sorry,' shouted Fraser against the wind.

'Piss off,' I said, taking my keys out.

Next to the Viva, two big men were stood talking by a deep red Jaguar. I unlocked my door, took the keys out, then opened it, all with my left hand. I leant inside the car, dumped the fucking book and the photos on the back seat, and put the keys in the ignition.

'Mr Dunford?' said the fat man in the brown cashmere coat, across the roof of the Viva.

'Yeah?'

'Fancy a spot of lunch?'

'What?'

The fat man smiled, rubbing his leather-gloved hands together. 'I'll treat you to lunch.'

'Why would you want to do that?'

'I want to talk to you.'

'What about?'

'Let's just say, you won't regret it.'

I looked back up the hill to the crematorium doorway.

Bill Hadden and Jack Whitehead were talking to Sergeant Fraser.

'All right,' I said, thinking fuck a Press Club wake.

'Do you know Karachi Social Club on Bradford Road?'

'No.'

'It's next to Variety Club, just before you come into Batley.'

'Right.'

'Ten minutes?' said the fat man.

'I'll just follow you.'

'Champion.'

Paki Town, the only colour left.

Black bricks and saris, brown boys playing cricket in the cold.

The Mosque and the Mill, make it Yorkshire 1974:

The Curry and the Cap.

Having lost the Jag at the last set of traffic lights, I pulled into the unsurfaced car park next to the Batley Variety Club and parked beside the deep red car.

Shirley Bassey was playing the Christmas Show next door and I could hear her band rehearsing as I picked my way through the dirty puddles, full of cigarette ends and crisp packets, to the strains of *Goldfinger*.

The Karachi Social Club was a detached three-storey building that had once been something to do with the rag trade.

I walked up the three stone steps to the restaurant, switched on the Philips Pocket Memo, and opened the door.

Inside, the Karachi Social Club was a cavernous red room with heavy floral wallpaper and the piped sounds of the East.

A tall Pakistani in a spotless white tunic showed me to the only table with customers.

The two fat men were sitting side by side, facing the door, two pairs of leather gloves before them.

The older man, the one who had invited me to lunch, stood up with an outstretched hand and said, 'Derek Box'.

I shook hands across the table with my left hand and sat down looking at the younger man with the well-boxed face.

'This is Paul. He helps me,' said Derek Box.

Paul nodded but said nowt.

The waiter brought over a silver tray with thin popadums and pickles.

'We'll all have the special, Sammy,' said Derek Box, breaking a popadum.

'Very good, Mr Box.'

Box smiled at me. 'Hope you like your curry hot.'

'I've only had it once before,' I said.

'Well, you're in for a right bloody treat then.'

I stared around the huge dim room with its heavy white tablecloths and thick silver cutlery.

'Here,' said Derek Box, spooning some pickles and yoghurt on to a popadum. 'Pile a load of this on.'

I did as I was told.

'You know why I like this place?'

'No?' I said, wishing I hadn't.

'Because it's private. Just wogs and us.'

I picked up my sagging popadum in my left hand and shoved it into my mouth.

'That's the way I like things,' said Box. 'Private.'

The waiter returned with three pints of bitter.

'And the fucking grub's not bad either, eh Sammy?' laughed Box.

'Thank you very much Mr Box,' said the waiter.

Paul smiled.

Derek Box raised his pint glass and said, 'Cheers.'

Paul and I joined him and then drank.

I took out my cigarettes. Paul held out a heavy Ronson lighter for me.

'This is nice, eh?' said Derek Box.

I smiled. 'Very civilised.'

'Aye. Not like that kind of shit there,' said Box, pointing at my grey bandaged hand on the white tablecloth.

I looked down at my hand and then back at Box.

He said, 'I was a great admirer of your colleague's work, Mr Dunford.'

'You knew him well?'

'Oh aye. We had a very special relationship.'

'Yeah?' I said, picking up my pint.

'Mmm. Mutually beneficial it was.'

'In what way?'

'Well, I'm in the fortunate position to be able to occasionally pass on information that comes my way.'

'What kind of information?'

Derek Box put down his pint and stared at me.

'I'm no grass, Mr Dunford.'

'I know.'

'I'm no angel either, but I am a businessman.'

I took a big gob full of beer and then quietly I asked him, 'What kind of businessman?'

He smiled. 'Motor cars, though I have ambitions towards the building trade, I make no bones about it.'

'What kind of ambitions?'

'Thwarted ones,' laughed Derek Box. 'At moment.'

'So how did you and Barry . . .'

'As I say, I'm no angel and I've never pretended otherwise. However, there are men in this country, in this county, who have a bit too much of the pie for my liking.'

'The construction pie?'

'Aye.'

'So you were giving Barry information about certain people and their activities in the building world?'

'Aye. Barry showed a particular interest in, as you say, the activities of certain gentlemen.'

The waiter returned with three plates of yellow rice and three bowls of deep red sauce. He laid a dish and a plate in front of each of us.

Paul picked up his bowl and upended it over the plate of rice, mixing it all in together.

The waiter said, 'Would you like nans, Mr Box?'

'Aye, Sammy. And another round.'

'Very good, Mr Box.'

I took the spoon from my curry bowl and let a small amount slide on to the rice.

'Get stuck in, lad. We don't stand on ceremony here.'

I took a forkful of curry and rice, felt the fire in my mouth, and drained my pint.

After a minute, I said, 'Yeah, that's all right that is.'

'All right? It's fucking delicious is what it is,' laughed Box with an open red mouth.

Paul nodded, breaking into a matching curry grin.

I took another forkful of curry and rice, watching the two fat men edging nearer to their plates with every mouthful.

I remembered Derek Box, or at least I remembered the stories people used to tell about Derek Box and his brothers.

I took a mouthful of yellow rice, looking over to the kitchen door for the next pint.

I remembered the stories of the Box Brothers practising their high-speed getaways down Field Lane, how kids would come down and watch them on a Sunday morning, how Derek was always the driver and Raymond and Eric were always the ones jumping in and out of the cars as they sped up and down Church Street.

The waiter returned with another silver tray of beer and three flat nan breads.

I remembered the Box Brothers getting sent down for robbing the Edinburgh Mail Train, how they claimed they'd been fitted up, how Eric had died inside just weeks before their release, how Raymond had moved to Canada or Australia, and how Derek had tried to enlist for Vietnam.

Derek and Paul were ripping their nans apart and wiping their bowls clean.

'Here,' said Derek Box, tossing me half a nan.

Having finished, he smiled, lit a cigar, and edged his chair back from the table. He took a big pull off his cigar, examined the end, exhaled and said, 'Were you an admirer of Barry's work?'

'Mm, yeah.'

'Such a waste.'

'Yeah,' I said, the lights catching the beads of sweat in Derek Box's fair hairline.

'Seems a pity to let it go unfinished, so much of it unpublished, don't you think?'

'Yeah. I mean, I don't know . . .'

Paul held out the Ronson for me.

I inhaled deeply and tried to flex the grip of my right hand. It hurt like fuck.

'If you don't mind me asking, what are you working on at the moment, Mr Dunford?'

'The Clare Kemplay murder.'

'Appalling,' sighed Derek Box. 'Bloody appalling. There aren't words. And?'

'That's about it.'

'Really? Then you're not continuing your late friend's crusade?'

'What makes you ask that?'

'I was led to believe you were in receipt of the great man's files.'

'Who told you that?'

'I'm not a grass, Mr Dunford.'

'I know, I'm not saying you are.'

'I hear things and I know people who hear things.'

I looked down at a forkful of rice lying cold upon my plate. 'Who?'

'Do you ever drink in the Strafford Arms?'

'In Wakefield?'

'Aye,' smiled Box.

'No. I can't say that I do.'

'Well, maybe you should. See, upstairs is a private club, bit like your own Press Club. A place where a businessman such as myself and an officer of the law can get together in a less formal setting. Let our hair down, so to speak.'

I suddenly saw myself on the back seat of my own car, the

black upholstery wet with blood, a tall man with a beard driving and humming along to Rod Stewart.

'You all right?' said Derek Box.

I shook my head. 'I'm not interested.'

'You will be,' winked Box, his eyes small and lashless, straight from the Deep.

'I don't think so.'

'Give it to him, Paul.'

Paul reached down under the table and brought out a thin manila envelope, tossing it across the dirty plates and empty pints.

'Open it,' Box dared me.

I picked up the manila envelope and stuck my left hand inside, feeling the familiar sheen of glossy enlargements.

I looked across the white tablecloth at Derek Box and Paul, visions of little girls wearing black and white wings stitched into skin swimming through the lunchtime bitter.

'Take a fucking look.'

I held the envelope down with my grey bandages and slowly removed the photographs with my left. I pushed back the plates and the bowls and laid out the three enlarged black and white photographs.

Two men naked.

Derek Box was grinning, a slash for a smile.

'I hear you're a bit of a cunt man, Mr Dunford. So I apologise for the vile content of these snaps.'

I moved each picture apart.

Barry James Anderson, sucking the cock and licking the balls of an old man.

I said, 'Who is it?'

'Well, how the mighty have fallen,' sighed Derek Box.

'They're not very clear.'

'I think you'll find they're clear enough to Councillor and former Alderman William Shaw, brother of the more famous Robert Shaw, should you ever wish to present him with a couple of snaps for his family album.'

The old body came into focus, the flabby belly and the skinny ribs, the white hairs and the moles.

'Bill Shaw?'

'I'm afraid so,' smiled Box.

Christ.

William Shaw, Chairman of the new Wakefield Metropolitan District Council and the West Yorkshire Police Authority, a former regional organiser of the Transport and General Workers' Union, representing that union on the National Executive Committee of the Labour Party.

I stared at the swollen testicles, the silhouettes of the knotted veins in his cock, the grey pubic hairs.

William Shaw, brother of the more famous Robert.

Robert Shaw, the Home Office Minister of State and the man widely tipped Most Likely to Succeed.

Councillor Shaw, the Man Most Likely to Suck.

Fuck.

Councillor Shaw as Barry's Third Man?

Dawsongate.

I said, 'Barry knew?'

'Aye. But he lacked the tools, so to speak.'

'You want me to blackmail Shaw with these?'

'Blackmail's not the word I had in mind.'

'What word had you in mind?'

'Persuade.'

'Persuade him to do what?'

'Persuade the Councillor that he should bare his soul of all his public wrongdoings, safe in the knowledge that his private life shall remain exactly that.'

'Why?'

'The Great British Public get the kind of truth they deserve.'

'And?'

'And we,' winked Box. 'We get what we want.'

'No.'

'Then you're not the man I thought you were.'

I looked down at the black and white photographs lying on the white tablecloth.

'And what kind of man was that?' I asked.

'A brave one.'

'You call these brave?' I said, pushing the photographs away with my grey right hand.

'In these times, yes I do.'

I took a cigarette from my pack and Paul reached across the table with the Ronson.

I said, 'He's not married is he?'

'Makes no odds,' smiled Box.

The waiter came back carrying an empty tray. 'Ice-cream, Mr Box?'

Box waved his cigar in my direction. 'Just one for my friend here.'

'Very good, Mr Box.' The waiter began piling the dirty plates and glasses on to the silver tray, leaving only the ashtray and the three photographs.

Derek Box ground out his cigar in the ashtray and leant across the table.

'This country's at war, Mr Dunford. The government and the unions, the Left and the Right, the rich and the poor. Then you got your Paddys, your wogs, your niggers, the puffs and the perverts, even the bloody women; they're all out for what they can get. Soon there'll be nowt left for the working white man.'

'And that's you?'

Derek Box stood up. 'To the victor, the spoils.'

The waiter returned with a silver bowl of ice-cream.

Paul helped Derek Box into his cashmere coat.

'Tomorrow lunchtime, upstairs in Strafford Arms.'

He squeezed my shoulder tightly as he went out.

I stared down at the ice-cream in front of me, sitting in the middle of the black and white photographs.

'Enjoy your ice-cream,' shouted Derek Box from the door.

I stared at the cocks and the balls, at the hands and the tongues, the spit and the spunk.

I pushed the ice-cream away.

A one-coin call at the top of Hanging Heaton, the stink of curry on the receiver.

No answer.

Out the door, a fart in my stride.

The one-armed driver on the road to Fitzwilliam, the radio on low:

Michael John Myshkin leading on the local two o'clock, the IRA Christmas ceasefire on the national.

I glanced at the envelope on the passenger seat and pulled over.

Two minutes later and the one-armed driver was back on the road, the manila sins of Councillor William Shaw hidden beneath the passenger seat.

I checked the rearview mirror.

Almost dark and not yet three.

Newstead View revisited.

Back amongst the ponies and the dogs, the rust and plaggy bags.

I drove slowly along the dark street.

TV lights on in Number 69.

I parked in front of what was left of 54.

The pack had been to the terrace, feasting and fighting, leaving three black eyes where the windows had been.

Hang the Pervert and *LUFC* were written in dripping white paint above the front window.

A brown front door lay amongst a forest of chopped and charred sticks of furniture, kicked and severed in the middle of a tiny lawn strewn with a family's tat.

Two dogs chased their arses in and out of the Myshkin family's home.

I picked my way up the garden path, over the headless lamps and slashed cushions, nervously past a dog wrestling with a giant stuffed panda, and through the splintered doorway.

There was the smell of smoke and the sound of running water.

A metal dustbin sat on a sea of broken glass in the centre of a wrecked front room. There was no television or stereo, just the spaces where they'd been and a plastic Christmas tree bent in two. No presents or cards.

I stepped over a pile of human shit on the bottom step and went up the sodden stairs.

All the taps in the bathroom were on full, the bath overflowing.

The toilet and the sink had both been kicked in and shattered, flooding the blue carpet. There was runny yellow diarrhoea down the outside of the bath and *NF* sprayed in red above it.

I turned off the taps and pushed up the sleeve of my left arm with my bandages. I stuck my left hand into the ice-cold brown water and felt for the plug. My hand brushed against something solid at the bottom of the bath.

There was something in the bath.

My one good hand froze, then quickly I pulled the plug and my hand straight out together.

I stood staring at the draining water, drying my hand on my trousers, a dark shape forming beneath the shitty brown water.

I stuck both hands under my armpits and screwed up my eyes.

There was a blue leather Slazenger sports bag in the bottom of the bath.

It was zipped up and on its side.

Fuck it, leave it, you don't want to know.

Mouth dry, I crouched down and flicked the bag upright.

The bag felt heavy.

The last of the water ran down the plughole, leaving just a shit-stained sludge, a nail brush, and the blue leather Slazenger bag.

Fuck it, leave it, you don't want to know.

I used the bandaged hand to steady the bag and began to unzip it with my left.

The zip jammed.

Fuck it.

It jammed again.

Leave it.

The fresh stench of shit.

You don't want to know.

Fur, I could see fur.

A fat dead tabby cat.

A twisted spine and an open mouth.

A blue collar and a name tag I wouldn't touch.

Memories of pet funerals, Archie and Socks buried back in the Wesley Street garden.

Fuck it, leave it, but you bloody asked.

Out on the landing, two more doors.

The bigger bedroom, the one on the left with the two twin beds, stank of piss and old smoke. The mattresses had been pulled off and the clothes piled on them. There were scorch marks up the wall.

Again sprayed in red, *Wogs Out, Fuck the Provos*.

I walked across the landing to another cheap plastic plate that said, *Michael's Room*.

Michael John Myshkin's room was no bigger than a cell.

The single bed had been tipped on its side, the curtains pulled from their rail, the window cracked by the falling wardrobe. Posters torn from the walls, having taken strips of the magnolia wallpaper with them as they went, lay on a floor strewn with American and English comics, sketch pads and crayons.

I picked up a copy of *The Hulk*. The pages were wet and reeked of piss. I let it fall and used my foot to sift through the piles of comics and pieces of paper.

Beneath a book about Kung-Fu, a sketch book looked intact. I bent down and flicked it open.

A full page cover of a comic stared back up at me. It had been hand-drawn in felt-tip pen and crayon:

Rat Man, Prince or Pest?

By Michael J. Myshkin.

In a childish hand, a giant rat with human hands and feet was sitting on a throne in a crown, surrounded by hundreds of smaller rats.

Rat Man was grinning, saying, '*Men are not our judges. We judge men!*'

Above the Rat Man logo, in biro, was written:

Issue 4, 5p, MJM Comics.

I turned to the first page.

In six panels, the Rat People asked Rat Man, their Prince, to go above ground and save the earth from the humans.

On page two, Rat Man was above ground being chased by soldiers.

By page three, Rat Man had escaped.

He'd sprouted wings.

Fucking swan's wings.

I stuffed the sketch pad comic inside my jacket and closed the door on Michael's Room.

I walked down the stairs, banging and children's voices coming from the front door.

A ten-year-old boy in a green sweater with three yellow stars was stood on a dining room chair, balanced on the front step, hammering a nail into the frame above the door.

His three friends were egging him on, one of them holding a washing-line noose in his dirty little hands.

'What you doing?' said one of the boys as I came down the stairs.

'Yeah, who are you?' said another.

I looked pissed off and official and said, 'What are you doing?'

'Nothing,' said the boy with the hammer, jumping from the chair.

The boy with the noose said, 'You police?'

'No.'

'We can do what we want then,' said the boy with the hammer.

I took out some coins and said, 'Where's his family?'

'Pissed off,' said one.

'Not coming back and all, if they know what's good for them,' said the boy with the hammer.

I shook the coins and said, 'Father's a cripple?'

'Yeah,' they laughed, making spastic wheezing noises.

'What about his Mam?'

'She's a fucking evil witch, she is,' said the boy with the washing-line.

'She work?'

'She's a cleaner at school.'

'Which one?'

'Fitz Junior on main road.'

I moved the chair out of the doorway and walked down the path, looking at the dark quiet terraces on either side.

'You going to give us some brass?' the youngest boy shouted after me.

'No.'

The boy with the hammer put the chair back, took the line

from his friend, stood on the chair, and hung the noose from the nail.

'What's that for?' I asked, unlocking the Viva.

'Perverts,' shouted one of the boys.

'Here,' laughed the boy with the hammer, standing on the chair. 'You best not be one.'

'There's a dead cat upstairs in the bath,' I said as I got into the car.

'We know,' giggled the youngest boy. 'We fucking killed it, didn't we?'

1, 2, 3, 4, 5, 6, 7, all good children go to heaven.

I sat in my car across the road from Fitzwilliam Junior and Infants.

It was going up to five and the school lights were still on, illuminating walls of Christmas drawings and paintings inside.

There were children playing soccer in the dark playground, chasing after a cheap orange ball in a pack of baggy trousers and dark wool sweaters with those big yellow stars.

I sat freezing in the Viva, my bandages stuffed up into my armpit, thinking of the Holocaust and wondering if Michael John Myshkin had gone to this school.

After ten minutes or so, some of the lights went out and three fat white women came out of the building with a thin man in blue overalls. The women waved goodbye to the man as he walked over to the children and tried to take their ball from them. The women were laughing as they left the school gates.

I got out of the car and jogged across the road after the women.

'Excuse me, ladies?'

The three fat women turned round and stopped.

'Mrs Myshkin?'

'You're joking?' spat the largest woman.

'Press are you, love?' smirked the oldest.

I smiled and said, '*Yorkshire Post.*'

'Bit late aren't you?' said the largest.

'I heard she worked here?'

'Until yesterday, aye,' said the oldest.

'Where'd she go?' I asked the woman with the steel-rimmed spectacles who hadn't said anything.

'Don't look at me. I'm new,' she said.

The oldest woman said, 'Our Kevin says one of your lot is putting them up in some posh hotel over in Scarborough.'

'That's not right,' said the new one.

I stood there, thinking fuck, fuck, fuck.

There were shouts from the playground and a charge of monkey boots.

'They're going to put that bloody window through,' sighed the largest woman.

I said, 'You two worked with Mrs Myshkin, yeah?'

'For more than five years, aye,' said the oldest.

'What's she like then?'

'Had a hard life, she has.'

'How do you mean?'

'Well he's on Sick because of dust . . .'

'The husband was a miner?'

'Aye. Worked with our Pat,' said the largest.

'What about Michael?'

The women looked at each other, grimacing.

'He's not all there,' whispered the new woman.

'How do you mean?'

'Bit slow, I heard.'

'Does he have any mates?'

'Mates?' said two of the women together.

'He plays with some of the young ones on his street, like,' said the oldest woman, shuddering. 'But they're not mates.'

'Ugh, makes you feel sick, doesn't it?' said the new woman.

'There must be someone?'

'Don't pall around with anyone much, not that I know.'

The other two women both nodded their heads.

'What about people from work?'

The fattest woman shook her head, saying, 'Doesn't work round here, does he? Castleford way?'

'Aye. Our Kevin said he's at some photographer's.'

'Mucky books, I heard,' said the new one.

'You're having me on?' said the oldest woman.

'What I heard.'

The man in the blue overalls was stood back at the school gates, a padlock and a chain in his hands, shouting at the children.

'Bloody kids these days,' said the largest woman.

'Bloody nuisance they are.'

I said, 'Thanks for your time, ladies.'

'You're welcome, love,' smiled the older one.

'Anytime,' said the largest lady.

The women giggled as they walked away, the new one turning round to wave at me.

'Merry Christmas,' she called.

'Merry Christmas.'

I took out a cigarette and fumbled in my pockets for some matches, finding Paul's heavy Ronson lighter.

I weighed the lighter in my left hand and then lit the cigarette, trying to remember when I'd picked it up.

The pack of children ran past me on the pavement, kicking their cheap orange football and swearing at the caretaker.

I walked back to the padlocked school gates.

The caretaker in the blue overalls was walking across the playground, back to the main building.

'Excuse me,' I shouted over the top of the red painted gates.

The man kept walking.

'Excuse me!'

At the door to the school the man turned round and looked straight at me.

I cupped my hands. 'Excuse me. Can I have a word?'

The man turned away, unlocked the door, and went inside the black building.

I leant my forehead against the gate.

Someone had tattooed *Fuck* out of the red paint.

Into the night, wheels spinning.

Farewell Fitzwilliam, where the night comes early and nowt feels right, where the kids kill cats and the men kill kids.

I was heading back to the Redbeck, turning left on to the A655, when the lorry came screaming out of the night, slamming its brakes on hard.

I braked, horns blaring, skidding to a stop, the lorry inches from my door.

I stared into the rearview mirror, heart pounding, headlights dancing.

A big bearded man in big black boots jumped down from his cab and walked towards the car. He was carrying a big black fucking bat.

I turned the ignition, slamming my foot down on to the accelerator, thinking Barry, Barry, Barry.

The Golden Fleece, Sandal, just gone six on Thursday 19 December 1974, the longest day in a week of long days.

A pint on the bar, a whisky in my belly, a coin in the box.

'Gaz? It's Eddie.'

'Where the fuck you sneak off to?'

'Didn't fancy Press Club, you know.'

'You missed a right bloody show.'

'Yeah?'

'Yeah, Jack totally fucking lost it, crying . . .'

'Listen, do you know Donald Foster's address?'

'What the fuck do you want that for?'

'It's important, Gaz.'

'This to do with Paul Kelly and their Paula?'

'No. Look, I know it's Sandal . . .'

'Yeah, Wood Lane.'

'What number?'

'They don't have fucking numbers on Wood Lane. It's called Trinity Towers or something.'

'Cheers, Gaz.'

'Yeah? Just don't fucking mention my name.'

'I won't,' I said, hanging up and wondering if he was fucking Kathryn.

Another coin, another call.

'I need to speak to BJ.'

A voice on the other end, mumbling from the other end of the world.

'When will you see him? It's important.'

A sigh from the ends of the earth.

'Tell him, Eddie called and it's urgent.'

I went back to the bar and picked up my pint.

'That your bag over there?' said the landlord, nodding at a Hillards plastic bag under the phone.

'Yeah, thanks,' I said and drained my pint.

'Don't be leaving bloody plastic bags lying around, not in pubs.'

'Sorry,' I said, walking back over to the phone, thinking fuck off.

'There's me thinking it could be a bomb or anything.'

'Yeah, sorry,' I muttered as I picked up Michael John Myshkin's sketch book and the photos of Councillor William Shaw and Barry James Anderson, thinking it is a bomb you stupid fucking cunt.

I parked up on the pavement outside Trinity View, Wood Lane, Sandal.

I stuffed the plastic bag back under the driver's seat with *A Guide to the Canals of the North*, stubbed out my cigarette, took two painkillers, and got out.

The lane was quiet and dark.

I walked up the long drive towards Trinity View, triggering floodlights as I went. There was a Rover in the drive and lights on upstairs in the house. I wondered if it had been designed by John Dawson.

I pressed the doorbell and listened to the chimes cascade through the house.

'Yes? Who is it?' said a woman from behind the artificially aged door.

'The *Yorkshire Post*.'

There was a pause and then a lock turned and the door opened.

'What do you want?'

The woman was in her early forties with dark expensively permed hair, wearing black trousers, a matching silk blouse, and a surgical collar.

I held up my bandaged right hand and said, 'Looks like we've both been in the wars.'

'I asked you what you wanted.'

Mr Long Shot Kick de Bucket said, 'It's about Johnny Kelly.'

'What about him?' said Mrs Patricia Foster, much too quickly.

'I was hoping either you or your husband might have some information about him.'

'Why would we know anything about him?' said Mrs Foster, one hand on the door, one hand on her collar.

'Well, he does play for your husband's club and . . .'

'It's not my husband's club. He's only the Chairman.'

'I'm sorry. You've not heard from him then?'

'No.'

'And you've no idea where he might be?'

'No. Look, Mr . . .?'

'Gannon.'

'Gannon?' said Mrs Patricia Foster slowly, her dark eyes and tall nose like an eagle's looking down on me.

I swallowed and said, 'Would it be possible to come inside and have a word with your husband?'

'No. He's not home and I have nothing else to say to you,' Mrs Foster said, closing the door.

I tried to stop the door shutting in my face. 'What do you think's happened to him, Mrs Foster?'

'I'm going to call the police, Mr Gannon, and then I'm going to call my very good friend Bill Hadden, your boss,' she said from behind the door as the lock turned.

'And don't forget to call your husband,' I shouted and then turned and ran down the floodlit drive, thinking a plague on both your houses.

Edward Dunford, North of England Crime Correspondent, in a phonebox on the Barnsley Road, beating the ground to startle the snakes.

Here goes nothing:

'Wakefield Town Hall, please?'

'361234.'

I looked at my father's watch, thinking 50/50.

'Councillor Shaw, please?'

'I'm afraid Councillor Shaw's in a meeting.'

'It's a family emergency.'

'Can I have your name, please?'

'I'm a friend of the family. It's an emergency.'

I looked across the road at the warm front rooms with their yellow lights and Christmas trees.

A different voice said, 'Councillor Shaw's up at County Hall. The number is 361236.'

'Thanks.'

'Nothing serious, I hope?'

I hung up, picked up, and dialled again.

'Councillor Shaw, please?'

'I'm sorry, the Councillor's in a meeting.'

'I know. It's a family emergency. I was given this number by his office.'

In one of the upstairs windows across the road, a child was staring out at me from a dark room. Downstairs a man and a woman were watching the TV with the lights off.

'Councillor Shaw speaking.'

'You don't know me Mr Shaw, but it's very important we meet.'

'Who is this?' a voice said, nervous and angry.

'We need to talk, sir.'

'Why would I want to talk to you? Who are you?'

'I believe someone is about to attempt to blackmail you.'

'Who?' the voice pleaded, afraid.

'We need to meet, Mr Shaw.'

'How?'

'You know how.'

'No I don't.' The voice, shaking.

'You have an appendix scar and you like to have it kissed better by a mutual friend with orange hair.'

'What do you want?'

'What kind of car have you got?'

'A Rover. Why?'

'What colour?'

'Maroon, purple.'

'Be in the long-stay car park at Westgate Station at nine o'clock tomorrow morning. Alone.'

'I can't.'

'You'll find a way.'

I hung up, my heart beating ninety miles an hour.

I looked up at the window across the road but the child had gone.

Edward Dunford, North of England Crime Correspondent, bringing a plague to all their houses, bar one.

'Where've you been?'

'All over.'

'Did you see him?'

'Can I come in?'

Mrs Paula Garland held open the red front door, wrapping her arms tight around herself.

A cigarette was burning in a heavy glass ashtray and *Top of the Pops* was on low on the TV.

'What did he look like?'

'Shut the door, love. It's cold.'

Paula Garland closed the red front door and stood staring at me.

On the TV, Paul Da Vinci was singing *Your Baby Ain't Your Baby Anymore*.

A tear dripped from her left eye on to her milk-white cheek.

'She's dead then.'

I walked over to her and put my arms around her, feeling for her spine beneath the thin red cardigan.

I had my back to the TV and I could hear applause and then the opening to *Father Christmas Do Not Touch Me*.

Paula lifted her head up and I kissed the corner of her eye, tasting the salt from her damp stained skin.

She was smiling at the TV.

I turned to one side and watched as Pan's People, dressed as Sexy Santas, cavorted around the Goodies, their hair alight with tinsel and trimmings.

I lifted Paula up, moving her small stockinged feet on to the tops of my shoes, and we began to dance, banging the backs of our legs into the furniture until she was laughing and crying and holding me tight.

I woke with a start on her bed.

Downstairs, the room was quiet and smelt of old smoke.

I didn't switch on a light, but sat down on the sofa in my underpants and vest and picked up the phone.

'Is BJ there? It's Eddie,' I whispered.

The ticking of the clock filled the room.

'What luck. It's been too long,' whispered back BJ down the line.

'You know Derek Box?'

'Unfortunately that's a pleasure I've yet to have.'

'Well he knows you and he knew Barry.'

'It's a small world.'

'Yeah, and not a pretty one. He gave me some photos.'

'That's nice.'

'Don't piss around BJ. They're photos of you sucking the cock of Councillor William Shaw.'

Silence. Just *Aladdin Sane* on high at the other end of the world.

I said, 'Councillor Shaw is Barry's Third Man, yeah?'

'Give the boy a prize.'

'Fuck off.'

The light went on.

Paula Garland was standing at the bottom of the stairs, her red cardigan barely covering her.

I smiled and mouthed apologies, the phone wet in my hand.

'What are you going to do?' said BJ down the line.

'I'm going to ask Councillor Shaw the questions Barry never got to ask.'

BJ whispered, 'Don't get involved in this.'

I was staring at Paula as I said, 'Don't get involved? I'm already involved. You're one of the fucking bastards who got me involved.'

'You're not involved with Derek Box, neither was Barry.'

'Not according to Derek Box.'

'This is between him and Donald Foster. It's their fucking war, leave them to it.'

'You've changed your tune. What are you saying?'

Paula Garland was staring at me, pulling down the bottom of her cardigan.

I raised my eyes in apology.

'Fuck Derek Box. Burn the photos or keep them for yourself. Maybe you'll find another use for them,' giggled BJ.

'Fuck off. This is serious.'

'Of course it's fucking serious, Eddie. What did you think it was? Barry's fucking dead and I couldn't even go to his funeral cos I'm too fucking frightened.'

'You're a lying little prick,' I hissed and hung up.

Paula Garland was still staring at me.

Me, the circles in my head.

'Eddie?'

I stood up, the leather sofa stinging the backs of my bare legs.

'Who was that?'

'No-one,' I said, pushing past her up the stairs.

'You can't keep doing this to me,' she shouted after me.

I went into the bedroom and took a painkiller from my jacket pocket.

'You can't keep cutting me out like this,' she said, coming up the stairs.

I picked up my trousers and put them on.

Paula Garland was standing in the bedroom doorway. 'It's my little girl that's dead, my husband that killed himself, my brother that's gone.'

I was struggling with the buttons of my shirt.

'You chose to get involved with this whole fucking bloody mess,' she whispered, tears falling on to the bedroom carpet.

My shirt buttons still undone, I put on my jacket.

'No-one made you.'

I pushed a dirty grey bandaged fist into her face and said, 'What about this? What do you think this is?'

'The best thing that ever happened to you.'

'You shouldn't have said that.'

'Why? What you going to do?'

We were stood in the doorway at the top of the stairs, surrounded by silence and night, staring at each other.

'But you don't care, do you Eddie?'

'Fuck off,' I cursed, down the stairs and out the door.

'You don't really fucking care, do you?'

Chapter 8

Hate Week.

Dawn on Friday 20 December 1974.

Awake on the floor of Room 27, covered in the ripped-up snow of a hundred sheets of red penned lists.

Lists, I'd been writing lists since I'd left Paula's.

A big fat red felt-tip pen in my left hand, circles in my head, scrawling illegible lists across the backs of sheets of wallpaper.

Lists of names.

Lists of dates.

Lists of places.

Lists of girls.

Lists of boys.

Lists of the corrupt, the corrupted, and the corruptible.

Lists of the police.

Lists of the witnesses.

Lists of the families.

Lists of the missing.

Lists of the accused.

Lists of the dead.

I was drowning in lists, drowning in information.

About to write a list of journalists, but tearing the whole fucking lot into confetti, cutting my left hand and numbing my right.

DON'T TELL ME I DON'T FUCKING CARE.

On my back, thinking of lists of the women I'd fucked.

Dawn on Friday 20 December 1974.

Hate Week.

Bringing the pain.

9 a.m. in the long-stay car park, Westgate Station, Wakefield.

I sat frozen in the Viva, watching a dark purple Rover 2000 pull into the car park, a single black and white photograph in a manila envelope beside me.

The Rover parked in the furthest space from the entrance.

I sat and let him wait through the radio news, through the

IRA ceasefire, through Michael John Myshkin's continuing efforts to help the police with their enquiries, through sightings of Mr John Stonehouse MP in Cuba, and through Reggie Bosanquet's failing marriage.

No-one moved inside the Rover.

I lit another fucking cigarette and, just to show him who was the fucking boss, I sat through Petula's *Little Drummer Boy*.

The Rover's engine started up.

I stuffed the photograph inside my jacket pocket, pressed record on the Philips Pocket Memo, and opened the door.

The Rover's engine went dead as I approached through the grey light.

I tapped on the glass of the passenger door and opened it.

I glanced at the empty back seat and got in, shutting the door.

'Just look straight ahead, Councillor.'

The car was warm and expensive and smelt of dogs.

'What do you want?' William Shaw sounded neither angry nor afraid, just resigned.

I was staring straight ahead too, trying not to look at the thin grey figure of respectability, his driving gloves limply clutching the steering wheel of a parked car.

'I asked you what you want,' he said, glancing at me.

'Keep looking straight ahead, Councillor,' I said, taking the creased photograph out of my pocket and putting it on the dashboard in front of him.

With one glove Councillor William Shaw picked up the photograph of BJ sucking his cock.

'I'm sorry, it's a bit bent,' I smiled.

Shaw tossed the photograph on to the floor by my feet. 'This doesn't prove anything.'

'Who says I'm trying to prove anything?' I said and picked up the photograph.

'It could be anyone.'

'It could be. But it's not, is it?'

'So what do you want?'

I leant forward and pushed in the cigarette lighter below the car radio.

'That man in the photograph, how many times have you met him?'

'Why? Why do you want to know that?'

'How many times?' I repeated.

Shaw tightened his gloves around the steering wheel. 'Three or four times.'

The lighter popped out and Shaw flinched.

'Ten times. Maybe more.'

I put a cigarette to my lips and lit it, thanking God again for helping out a one-armed man.

'How did you meet him?'

The Councillor closed his eyes and said, 'He introduced himself.'

'Where? When?'

'At some bar in London.'

'London?'

'Some Local Government conference in August.'

They set you up, I was thinking, they fucking set you up Councillor.

'And then you met him again up here?'

Councillor William Shaw nodded.

'And he's been blackmailing you?'

Another nod.

'How much?'

'Who are you?'

I stared out across the long-stay car park, the station announcements echoing over the empty cars.

'How much have you given him?'

'A couple of thousand.'

'What did he say?'

Shaw sighed, 'He said it was for an operation.'

I stubbed out the cigarette. 'Did he mention anyone else?'

'He said there were men who wanted to hurt me and he could protect me.'

I looked at the black dashboard, afraid to look at Shaw again.

'Who?'

'No names.'

'He say why they wanted to hurt you?'

'He didn't have to.'

'Tell me.'

The Councillor let go of the steering wheel, looking round. 'First you tell me who the bloody hell you are.'

I turned quickly, pushing the photograph hard into his face, forcing his right cheek against the glass of the driver's door.

I didn't let go, pressing the photograph harder into his face, whispering into the Councillor's ear, 'I'm a man who can hurt you very fucking quickly and very fucking now, if you don't stop whining and start answering my fucking questions.'

Councillor William Shaw was banging his hands against the tops of his thighs in surrender.

'Now you tell me, you fucking puff.'

I let the photograph fall and sat back.

Shaw leant forward over the steering wheel, rubbing both sides of his face between his gloves, tears and veins in his eyes.

After almost a minute, he said, 'What do you want to know?'

Far away on the other side of the car park I could see a small local train crawl into Westgate Station, dumping its tiny passengers on the cold platform.

I closed my eyes and said, 'I need to know why they want to blackmail you.'

'You know,' sniffed Shaw, sitting back in his seat.

I turned sharply, slapping him once across the cheek. 'Just fucking say it!'

'Because of the deals I've done. Because of the people I've done deals with. Because of the fucking money.'

'The money,' I laughed. 'Always the money.'

'They want in. Do you want figures, dates?' Shaw was hysterical, shielding his face.

'I don't give a fuck about your shitty little backhanders, about your weak fucking cement and all your dodgy fucking deals, but I want to hear you say it.'

'Say what? What do you want me to say?'

'Names. Just say their fucking names!'

'Foster, Donald Richard Foster. Is that who want?'

'Go on.'

'John Dawson.'

'That's it?'

'Of them that matter.'

'And who wants in?'

Ever so slowly and quietly Shaw said, 'You're a bloody journalist aren't you?'

A feeling, a gut feeling.

'Have you ever met a man called Barry Gannon?'

'No,' screamed Shaw, banging his forehead down into the steering wheel.

'You're a fucking liar. When was it?'

Shaw lay against the steering wheel, shaking.

Suddenly sirens wailed through Wakefield.

I froze, my belly and balls tight.

The sirens faded.

'I didn't know he was a journalist,' whispered Shaw.

I swallowed and said, 'When?'

'Just twice.'

'When?'

'Last month sometime and then a week ago, last Friday.'

'And you told Foster?'

'I had to. It couldn't go on, it just couldn't.'

'What did he say?'

Shaw looked up, the whites of his eyes red. 'Who?'

'Foster.'

'He said he'd deal with it.'

I stared out across the car park at the London train arriving, thinking of seaview flats and Southern girls.

'He's dead.'

'I know,' whispered Shaw. 'What are you going to do?'

I picked a dog hair off my tongue and opened the passenger door.

The Councillor had the photograph in his hands, holding it out towards me.

'Keep it, it's you,' I said, getting out.

'He looks so white,' said William Shaw, alone in his expensive motor, staring at the photograph.

'What did you say?'

Shaw reached over to close the door. 'Nothing.'

I leant back into the car, holding the door open, shouting, 'Just tell me what you fucking said.'

'I said he looks so different that's all, paler.'

I slammed the door on him, tearing across the car park, thinking Jimmy James fucking Ashworth.

Ninety miles an hour.

One hand in the glove compartment, a bandage on the wheel, sifting through the pills and the maps, the rags and the fags.

The Sweet on the radio.

Nervous darts into the rearview mirror.

Finding the micro-cassette, yanking the Philips Pocket Memo out of my jacket, ripping one tape out, ramming another in.

Rewind.

Pressing play:

'It were like she'd rolled down or something.'

Forward.

Play:

'I couldn't believe it was her.'

Listen.

'She looked so different, so white.'

Stop.

Fitzwilliam.

69 Newstead View, TV lights on.

Ninety miles an hour, up the garden path.

Knock, knock, knock, knock.

'What do you want?' said Mrs Ashworth, trying to close the door on me.

A foot in the door, pushing it back.

'Here, you can't just come barging into people's houses.'

'Where is he?' I said, knocking past her into one of her saggy tits.

'He's not here, is he. Here, come back!'

Up the stairs, banging open doors.

'I'm calling the police,' shouted Mrs Ashworth from the foot of the stairs.

'You do that, love,' I said, looking at an unmade bed and a Leeds United poster, smelling winter damp and teenage wank.

'I'm warning you,' she shouted.

'Where is he?' I said as I came back down the stairs.

'He's at work, isn't he.'

'Wakefield?'

'I don't know. He never says.'

I looked at my father's watch. 'What time did he set off?'

'Van came at quarter to seven, same as always.'

'He's mates with Michael Myshkin, isn't he?'

Mrs Ashworth held the door open, her lips pursed.

'Mrs Ashworth, I know they're friends.'

'Jimmy always felt bloody sorry for him. He's like that, it's his character.'

'Very touching, I'm sure,' I said, walking out the door.

'It doesn't mean anything,' shouted Mrs Ashworth from the front step.

At the bottom of the path, I opened the garden gate and stared up the road at the burnt-out Number 54. 'I hope your neighbours agree.'

'You're always making something out of nothing, you people,' she screamed after me, slamming the front door shut.

Flat out down the Barnsley Road into Wakefield, glances in the rearview mirror.

Radio on.

Jimmy Young and the Archbishop of Canterbury debating *Anal Rape* and *The Exorcist* with the housebound of Britain.

'*They should ban them both. Disgusting, that's what they are.*'

Through the Christmas lights and the first spits of rain, up past the County and Town Halls.

'*Exorcism, as practised by the Church of England, is a deeply religious rite and not something to be entered into lightly. This film creates a totally false impression of exorcism.*'

I parked opposite Lumbs Dairy by the Drury Lane Library, the rain coming down cold, grey, and heavy.

'*If you take the guilt out of sex, you take guilt away from society and I do not think society could function without guilt.*'

Radio off.

I sat in the car smoking, watching the empty milk floats return home.

Just gone eleven-thirty.

I jogged down past the prison and on to the building site, the Foster's Construction sign rattling under the rain.

I pushed open the tarpaulin door of an unfinished house, the radio playing *Tubular Bells*.

Three big men, stinking and smoking.

'Fuck, not you again,' said one big man with a sandwich in his mouth and flask of tea in his hand.

I said, 'I'm looking for Jimmy Ashworth.'

'He's not here, is he,' said another big man with the back of his NCB donkey jacket to me.

'What about Terry Jones?'

'He's not here either,' said the donkey jacket to the grins of the other two men.

'Do you know where they are?'

'No,' said the sandwich man.

'What about your Gaffer, is he about?'

'Just not your lucky day is it.'

'Thanks,' I said, thinking choke on it you thick fucking twat.

'Don't mention it,' sandwich man smiled as I went back out.

I turned up the collar of my jacket and stuck my hands and bandages deep into my pockets. Down there, with Paul's Ronson lighter and the odd pennies, I found a feather in my pocket.

I walked through the piles of cheap bricks and the half-built houses towards Devil's Ditch, thinking of that last school photograph of Clare, with her nervous pretty smile, stuck on to the black and white shots on my Redbeck walls.

I looked up, the feather in my fingers.

Jimmy Ashworth was stumbling and running across the wasteland towards me, big red spots of blood dropping from his nose and his scalp on to his skinny white chest.

'What the fuck's going on?' I shouted.

He slowed to a walk as he drew near me, pretending like nothing was up.

'What happened to you?'

'Just piss off, will you.'

In the distance, Terry Jones was coming up behind Jimmy from Devil's Ditch.

I grabbed Jimmy's arm. 'What did he say to you?'

He tried to twist free, screaming, 'Get off me!'

I grabbed the other arm of his jacket. 'You'd seen her before, hadn't you?'

'Fuck off!'

Terry Jones had broken into a jog, waving at us.

'You told Michael Myshkin about her, didn't you?'

'Fuck off,' shouted Jimmy, twisting out of his jacket and shirt, breaking into a run.

I span round, rugby tackling him into the mud.

He fell into the mud beneath me.

I had him pinned down, shouting, 'Where had you fucking seen her?'

'Fuck off!' Jimmy Ashworth was screaming, looking up past me into a big grey sky that was pissing down all over his muddy, bloody face.

'Tell me where you'd fucking seen her.'

'No.'

I slapped my bandaged hand across his face, pain shooting up my arm into my heart, yelling, 'Tell me!'

'Get the fuck off him,' said Terry Jones, pulling me backwards by the collar of my jacket

'Fuck off,' I said, my arms flailing and lashing out at Terry Jones.

Jimmy Ashworth, breaking free from my legs, got to his feet and ran bare-chested towards the houses, the rain, the mud, and the blood running down his naked back.

'Jimmy!' I shouted, wrestling with Terry Jones.

'Leave it fucking be,' hissed Jones.

Over by the houses, the three big men had come out and were laughing at Jimmy as he sprinted past them.

'He'd fucking seen her before.'

'Leave it!'

Jimmy Ashworth kept on running.

The three big men stopped laughing and started walking over towards me and Terry Jones.

He released me, whispering, 'You best piss off.'

'I'm going to fucking have you, Jones.'

Terry Jones picked up Jimmy Ashworth's shirt and jacket. 'Then you're wasting your time.'

'Yeah?'

'Yeah,' he smiled sadly.

I turned and walked away towards Devil's Ditch, wiping the mud from my hands on to my trousers.

I heard a shout and looked round to see Terry Jones, his arms up, shepherding the three big men back towards the half-built houses.

There was no sign of Jimmy Ashworth.

I stood on the lip of the Ditch, looking down at the rusted prams and bicycles, the cookers and the fridges, thinking all of modern life is here and so was Clare Kemplay, aged ten.

My fingers black with dirt, I took the small white feather from my pocket.

At Devil's Ditch, I looked up into the big black sky and put the small white feather to my pale pink lips thinking, if only it hadn't been her.

The Strafford Arms, the Bullring, Wakefield.

The dead centre of Wakefield, the Friday before Christmas.

Mud Man, up the stairs and through the door.

Members only.

'It's all right Grace, he's with me,' said Box to the woman behind the bar.

Derek Box and Paul at the bar, whiskys and cigars in their hands.

There was Elvis on the jukebox.

Just Derek, Paul, Grace, Elvis, and me.

Box got up from his stool and walked across the room to a table in the window.

'You look like shit. What the fuck happened to you?'

I sat down opposite Box, my back to Paul and the door, looking out on a wet Wakefield.

'I went down Devil's Ditch.'

'I thought they'd got someone for that?'

'So did I.'

'Some things are best left,' said Derek Box, examining the end of his cigar.

'Like Councillor Shaw?'

Box relit his cigar. 'Did you see him?'

'Yeah.'

Paul put a whisky and a pint in front of me.

I tipped the whisky into my pint.

'And?'

'And he's probably talking to Donald Foster as we speak.'

'Good.'

'Good? Foster had Barry fucking killed.'

'Probably.'

'Probably?'

'Barry got ambitious.'

'What are you talking about?'

'You know what I'm talking about. Barry had his own agenda.'

'So what? Foster must be fucking insane. We can't just let it go. We've got to do something about it.'

'He's not insane,' said Box. 'Just motivated.'

'You know him well or something?'

'We were in Kenya together.'

'Business?'

'Her Majesty's business. We did our National fucking Service in the Highlands, protecting fat cunts like I am now, fighting the fucking Mau Maus.'

'Fuck.'

'Yeah. They'd come down from the hills like a tribe of bloody Red Indians, raping the women, cutting the cocks off the men, stringing them upon fence posts.'

'You're joking?'

'Do I look like I'm joking?'

'No.'

'We weren't angels, Mr Dunford. I was with Don Foster when we ambushed a fucking War Party. We shot them in the knees with .303s so we could have some fun.'

'Fuck.'

'Foster took his time. He taped the screams, the dogs barking, claimed it helped him sleep.'

I picked up Paul's lighter from the table and lit a cigarette.

Paul brought over two more whiskys.

'It was war, Mr Dunford. Just like now.'

I picked up my glass.

Box was sweating as he drank, his eyes off deep in the dark.

'A year ago they were going to bring back rationing. Now we got inflation at fucking 25 per cent.'

I took a mouthful of whisky, drunk, scared, and bored. 'What does that have to do with Don Foster or Barry?'

Box lit another cigar and sighed. 'The trouble with your generation is that you know nowt. Why do you think the man with the boat beat the man with the pipe in '70?'

'Wilson was complacent.'

'Complacent my arse,' laughed Box.

'Go on then, you tell me.'

'Because likes of Cecil King, Norman Collins, Lord Renwick, Shawcross, Paul Chambers at ICI, Lockwood at EMI and McFadden at Shell, and others like them, they sat down and said enough was bloody enough.'

'So?'

'So these men have power; the power to build or break men.'

'What's that got to do with Foster?'

'You're not fucking listening to me! I'll spell it out in your talk.'

'Please . . .'

'Power's like glue. It sticks men like us together, keeps everything in place.'

'You and Foster are . . .'

'We're peas in a pod, me and him. We like to fuck and make a buck and we're not right choosey how we do either. But he's got too big for his fucking boots and now he's cutting me out and it pisses me off.'

'So you use me and Barry to blackmail his mates?'

'We had a deal, me and Foster and another man. That other man is dead. They waited until he came back from Australia and took him as he came out of his mother's flat in Blackpool. They bound his arms behind him with a towel and then wrapped him in twenty foot of tape from his shoulders to his hips. Then they stuffed him into the boot of his car and drove him on to Moors. When it was dawn, three men held him upright and a fourth thrust a knife into his heart five times.'

I was looking down into my whisky glass, the room slightly spinning.

'That was my brother they killed. He'd been back home one fucking day.'

'I'm sorry.'

'At the funeral, there was a card. No name, just said, *Three can keep a secret, if two are dead.*'

'I don't want any part of this,' I said quietly.

Box nodded once at Paul sat over by the bar and said loudly, 'It seems like we overestimated you, Mr Dunford.'

'I'm just a journalist.'

Paul came up behind me, a heavy hand on my shoulder.

'Then you'll do as you're told, Mr Dunford, and you'll get your story. Leave the rest to us.'

I said again, 'I don't want to be part of this.'

Box cracked his knuckles and smiled. 'Tough shit. You are a part of it.'

Paul picked me up by my collar.

'Now piss off!'

Mud Man on the run.

Back down Westgate.

Fuck, fuck, fuck.

Barry and Clare.

Little dead Clare Kemplay, kissed this boy and made him cry.

Clare and Barry.

Dirty Barry, when he'd been good he'd been very, very good, when he'd been bad he'd been very, very bad.

A policeman stood in a doorway, keeping out of the rain. Me, the urge to fall to my knees at his feet, praying he was a good man, and tell him the whole fucking sad story, to come in out of the rain.

But tell him what?

Tell him I was in over my head, covered in mud and drunk as fuck.

Mud Man, straight into Leeds, dirt cracking as I drove.

Mud Man, straight into the office bogs, caked in shit.

A clean face and one clean hand, a dirty suit and a black bandage, sitting down behind my desk at 3 p.m. on Friday 20 December 1974.

'Nice suit, Eddie lad.'

'Fuck off, George.'

'Merry Christmas to you too.'

Messages and cards littered the desk; Sergeant Fraser calling twice that morning, Bill Hadden requesting my presence at my earliest convenience.

I slumped back in my chair, George Greaves farting to the applause of the few back from lunch.

I smiled and picked up the cards; three from Down South, plus one with my name and office punched into plastic Dymo tape and stuck to the envelope.

On the other side of the office, Gaz was taking bets on the Newcastle–Leeds game.

I opened the envelope and pulled out the card with my teeth and my left hand.

'Do you want in, Eddie?' shouted Gaz.

On the front of the card was a cabin made of logs in the middle of a snow-covered forest.

'Ten bob on Lorimer,' I said, opening the card.

'Jack's got him.'

Inside the card, over the Christmas message, were stuck two more strips of Dymo tape.

Quietly I said, 'I'll have Yorath then.'

Punched into the top plastic strip was: KNOCK ON THE DOOR OF . . .

'You what?'

Punched into the bottom plastic strip was: FLAT 405, CITY HEIGHTS.

'Yorath,' I said, staring at the card.

'Anyone I know?'

I looked up.

Jack Whitehead said, 'I just hope it's from a woman.'

'What do you mean?'

'I heard you were hanging around with young boys,' smiled Jack.

I put the card inside my jacket pocket. 'Yeah?'

'Yeah. With orange hair.'

'Who'd you hear that from then, Jack?'

'A little bird.'

'You stink of drink.'

'So do you.'

'It's Christmas.'

'Not for much longer,' grinned Jack. 'Boss wants to see you.'

'I know,' I said, not moving.

'He asked me to come and find you, make sure you didn't get lost again.'

'Going to hold my hand?'

'You're not my type.'

'Bollocks.'

'Fuck off, Jack. Listen.'

I pressed play again:

'*I couldn't believe it was her. She looked so different, so white.*'

'Bollocks,' said Jack again. 'He's talking about the photographs in the papers, on TV.'

'I don't think so.'

'Her face was everywhere.'

'Ashworth knows more than that.'

'Myshkin fucking confessed.'

'That means fuck all and you know it.'

Bill Hadden sat behind his desk, his glasses halfway down his nose, stroking his beard and saying nowt.

'You should see all the shit they took from the little pervert's room.'

'Like what?'

'Photos of little girls, boxes of them.'

I looked at Hadden and said, 'Myshkin didn't do it.'

He said slowly, 'But why make a scapegoat of him?'

'Why do you think? Tradition.'

'Thirty years,' said Jack. 'Thirty years and I know firemen never lie and coppers often do. But not this time.'

'They know he didn't do it and you know he didn't.'

'He did it. He coughed.'

'So fucking what?'

'You ever heard the word forensic?'

'That's bullshit. They've got nothing.'

'Gentlemen, gentlemen,' said Hadden, leaning forward in his chair. 'It seems like we've had this conversation before.'

'Exactly,' muttered Jack.

'No, before I believed Myshkin did it, but . . .'

Hadden raised his hands. 'Edward, please.'

'Sorry,' I said, staring at the cards on his desk.

He said, 'When are they going to remand him again?'

'First thing Monday,' said Jack.

'More charges?'

'He's already coughed to Jeanette Garland and that Rochdale lass . . .'

'Susan Ridyard,' I said.

'But I've heard there's more in offing.'

I said, 'He said owt about where the bodies are?'

'Your back garden, Scoop.'

'Right then,' said Hadden, being Dad. 'Edward, you have that background piece on Myshkin ready for Monday. Jack, you do the remand.'

'Will do, Chief,' said Jack, getting up.

'Nice piece on those two coppers,' nodded Hadden, ever the proud father.

'Thanks. Nice blokes, I've known them a while,' said Jack at the door.

Hadden said, 'See you tomorrow night, Jack.'

'Yep. See you Scoop,' laughed Jack as he left.

'Bye.' I was on my feet, still looking at the cards on Hadden's desk.

'Sit down for a moment, will you,' said Hadden, standing up.

I sat back down.

'Edward, I want you to take the rest of the month off.'

'What?'

Hadden had his back to me, staring out at the dark sky.

'I don't understand,' I said, understanding him exactly, focusing on one small card tucked in amongst the rest.

'I don't want you coming into the office like this.'

'Like what?'

'Like this,' he said, turning and pointing at me.

'I was on a building site this morning, getting the story.'

'What story?'

'Clare Kemplay.'

'It's over.'

I stared at the desk, at that one card, at another cabin made of logs in the middle of another snow-covered forest.

'Take the rest of the month off. Get that hand seen to,' said Hadden, sitting back down.

I stood up. 'You still want that Myshkin piece?'

'Yeah, of course. Type it up and give it to Jack.'

I opened the door, last ditch, thinking fuck 'em all:

'Do you know the Fosters?'

Hadden didn't look up from his desk.

'Councillor William Shaw?'

He looked up. 'I'm sorry, Edward. Really I am.'

'Don't be. You're right,' I said. 'I need help.'

At my desk for the last time, thinking take it fucking national, sweeping the whole bloody table-top into a dirty old Co-op carrier bag, not giving a fuck who knew I was gone.

Jack fucking Whitehead slapped an *Evening News* on to the empty desk, beaming, 'Something to remember us by.'

I looked up at Jack, counting backwards.

The office silent, all eyes on me.

Jack Whitehead right back in my face, not blinking.

I looked down at the folded paper, the banner headline:

WE SALUTE YOU.

'Turn it over.'

A telephone was ringing on the other side of the office, no-one answering it.

I turned over the bottom half of the paper to a photograph of two uniformed coppers shaking hands with Chief Constable Angus.

Two uniformed coppers, naked:

A tall one with a beard, a short one without.

I stared down at the paper, at the photograph, at the words beneath the photograph:

Chief Constable Angus congratulates Sergeant Bob Craven and PC Bob Douglas on a job well done.

'They are outstanding police officers who have our heartfelt thanks.'

I picked up the paper and folded it in two, stuffing it into the carrier bag, winking, 'Thanks, Jack.'

Jack Whitehead said nothing.

I gathered up the carrier bag and walked across the silent office.

George Greaves was looking out the window, Gaz from Sport was staring at the end of his pencil.

The telephone began to ring on my desk.

Jack Whitehead picked it up.

At the door, Fat Steph, with an armful of files, smiled and said, 'I'm sorry, love.'

'It's Sergeant Fraser,' shouted Jack from my desk.

'Tell him to fuck off. I've been sacked.'

'He's been sacked,' said Jack, hanging up.

One two three four, down the stairs and through the door:

The Press Club, members only, going up to five.

At the bar, a member for now, a Scotch in one hand, the phone in the other.

'Hello. Is Kathryn there please?'

Yesterday Once More on the jukebox, my money.

'Do you know when she'll be back?'

Fuck The Carpenters, my eyes stinging from my own smoke.

'Can you tell her Edward Dunford called?'

I hung up, downed the Scotch, lit another cigarette.

'Same again please, love.'

'And one for me, Bet.'

I looked round.

Jack fucking Whitehead taking the next stool.

'You fucking fancy me or something?'

'No.'

'Then what the fuck do you want?'

'We should talk.'

'Why?'

The barmaid set two Scotches in front of us.

'Someone's setting you up.'

'Yeah? Big fucking news, Jack.'

He offered me a cigarette. 'Who is it then, Scoop?'

'How about we start with your mates, the Two Bobbies?'

Jack lit a cigarette for himself and whispered, 'How's that?'

I swung my right hand round, waving the bandages in his

face, toppling forward and shouting, 'How's that? What the fuck do you think this is?'

Jack moved out of the way, catching my bandages in his own hand.

'They did that?' he said, pushing me back into my seat, eyes on the black wad at the end of my arm.

'Yeah, in between burning down gypsy camps, stealing post-mortem photos, and beating confessions out of the retarded.'

'What are you talking about?'

'Just the new West Yorkshire Metropolitan Police going about their business, supported by the good old *Yorkshire Post*, the copper's friend.'

'You've fucking lost it.'

I downed the Scotch. 'So everyone keeps saying.'

'Fucking listen to them then.'

'Piss off, Jack.'

'Eddie?'

'What?'

'Think of your mother.'

'What the fuck does that mean?'

'Hasn't she been through enough? It's barely been a week since you buried your father.'

I leant over and poked two fingers into his bony chest. 'Don't you ever fucking bring my family into this.'

I stood up and took out my car keys.

'You're not fit to drive.'

'You're not fit to write, but you do.'

He was stood up, holding me by the arms. 'You're being set up, just like Barry was.'

'Fucking let go.'

'Derek Box is as bad as it fucking gets.'

'Let go.'

He sat back down. 'Don't say you weren't warned.'

'Piss off,' I hissed, climbing the stairs, hating his lying guts and the stinking world in which he dwelt.

The M1 southbound out of Leeds, seven o'clock busy, the rain beginning to sleet in my headlights.

Always on My Mind on the radio.

In the fast lane, glances in the rearview mirror, glances to the left, the gypsy camp gone.

Flicking through the radio stations, avoiding the news.

Suddenly the Castleford turn-off came out of the dark like a lorry, its lights on full.

I swerved across three lanes, horns screaming at me, the trapped faces of angry ghosts in their cars cursing me.

Inches from death, thinking bring it on.

Bring it on.

Bring it on.

Knock on the door of . . .

'You're drunk.'

'I just want to talk,' I said on the step of Number 11, waiting for that big red door in my face.

'You'd better come in.'

The fat Scottish woman from two down was sat on the sofa in front of *Opportunity Knocks*, staring at me.

'He's had a few,' said Paula, closing the door.

'There's nothing wrong with that,' laughed the Scottish woman.

'I'm sorry,' I said and sat down on the sofa next to her.

Paula said, 'I'll make a cup of tea.'

'Thanks.'

'Do you want another, Clare?'

'No, I'll get off,' she said, following Paula into the kitchen.

I sat on the sofa in front of the TV, listening to whispers from the next room, watching a young girl tapdance into the hearts and homes of millions. Just above her, on top of the TV, Jeanette smiled her handicapped grin across the room at me.

'See you later, Eddie,' said Scotch Clare at the door.

I thought about getting up, but stayed put and mumbled, 'Yeah, goodnight.'

'Aye. Be nice,' she said as she closed the big red door behind her.

There was applause on the screen.

Paula handed me a mug of tea. 'Here you go.'

I said, 'I'm sorry about this. And last night.'

She sat down next to me on the sofa. 'Forget it.'

'Always turning up like this and then all that shit I said last night, I didn't mean any of it.'

'It's all right, forget it. You don't have to say anything.'

Some robot aliens were eating instant mashed potato on the TV.

'I do care.'

'I know.'

I wanted to ask about Johnny but I put down the tea and leant over, bringing her face closer to my own with my left hand.

'How's your hand?' she whispered.

'It's fine,' I said, kissing her lips, her chin, and her cheeks.

'You don't have to do this,' she said.

'I want to.'

'Why?'

A monkey in a flat cap was drinking a cup of tea on TV.

'Because I love you.'

'Please don't say it if you don't mean it.'

'I mean it.'

'So say it again.'

'I love you.'

Paula pushed me away and took my hand, switching off the TV and leading me up the steep, steep stairs.

Mummy and Daddy's Room, the bedroom so cold I could see my breath.

Paula sat down on the bed and began to undo her blouse, her bare skin all covered in goose-bumps.

I pushed her back on to the eiderdown, kicking off my shoes with two loud thuds.

She squirmed beneath me, trying to wriggle free of her trousers.

I pushed up her blouse and black bra and began sucking at her pale brown nipples, biting her ever so slightly.

She was pulling off my jacket and pushing down my trousers.

'You're filthy,' she giggled.

'Thanks,' I smiled, feeling the laughter in her belly.

'I love you,' she said and pulled her hands through my hair, pushing my head gently down.

I went where I was told, tugging down the zip of her trousers and pulling off her pale blue cotton knickers with them.

Paula Garland pushed my head into her cunt, wrapping her legs across my back.

My chin became wet, stinging as it dried.

She pushed me back.

I went.

'I love you,' she said.

'I love you,' I mumbled, a face full of cunt.

She pulled me back up, over her tits.

I kissed her as I went, hitting her lips with the taste of herself.

Her tongue on mine, both tasting of cunt.

I pulled myself up, pain in my arm, and pushed her over on to her belly.

Paula lay on the eiderdown, her face in the pillow, wearing only her bra.

I looked down at my cock.

Paula raised her arse slightly and then back down.

I pushed her hair up and kissed her neck and the backs of her ears, working myself between her legs.

She raised her arse again, juices and sweat making it wet.

I sat back and began rubbing my cock on the lips of her cunt, bandages in her hair, my left palm flat on the small of her back.

She raised her arse higher, backing her cunt on to my cock.

My cock touched her arse.

She reached her hand round to my cock, guiding it away from her arse and into her cunt.

Inside and out, inside and out.

Paula, opening and closing her fist on the bed.

Inside and out, inside and out.

Paula, face down, fists closed.

I slipped out hard.

Paula, fists open, sighing.

My cock touched her arse.

Paula, trying to look round.

A bandaged hand on the back of her neck.

Paula, a hand flailing after my cock.

My cock on the edge of her arsehole.

Paula, shouting into the pillow.

In tight.

Paula Garland, screaming and screaming into the pillow.

A bandaged hand pinning down her face, another round her belly.

Paula Garland, trying to break free from my cock.

Me, fucking her hard up the arse.

Paula, limp and shaking with tears.

Inside and out, inside and out.

Paula, blood on her arse.

Inside and out, inside and out, blood on my cock.

Paula Garland, crying.

Coming and coming and coming again.

Paula, calling out for Jeanette.

Me, coming again.

Dead dogs and monsters and rats with little wings.

There was someone walking around in my head, shining a torch and wearing big boots.

She was outside in the street, pulling a red cardigan tight around herself, and smiling at me.

Suddenly a big black bird swooped down from the sky and into her hair, chasing her down the street, taking out huge clumps of blonde hair all bloody at the roots.

She was lying in the road with her pale blue cotton knickers showing, like a dead dog hit by a lorry.

I awoke and went back to sleep, thinking I'm safe now, I'm safe now, go back to sleep.

Dead dogs and monsters and rats with little wings.

There was someone walking around in my head, shining a torch and wearing big boots.

I was sitting in a wooden cabin gazing at a Christmas tree, the smell of good cooking filling the house.

I took a big box, gift-wrapped in newspaper, from under the tree and pulled the red ribbon loose.

Carefully I opened the paper so I might read it later.

I stared at the small wooden box on my knee, resting on the newspaper and the red length of ribbon.

I closed my eyes and opened the box, the dull thud of my heart filling the house.

'What is it?' she said, coming up behind me and touching my shoulder.

I covered the box with my bandaged hand, burying my head in her red gingham folds.

She took the box from my hands and looked inside.

The box fell to the floor, the house full of good cooking, the thud of my heart, and her bloody screams.

I watched as it slid out of the box and across the floor, writing spidery messages with its bloody cord as it went.

'Get rid of it,' she screamed. 'Get rid of it now!'

It flipped on to its back and smiled at me.

I awoke and went back to sleep, thinking I'm safe now, I'm safe now, go back to sleep.

Dead dogs and monsters and rats with little wings.

There was someone walking around in my head, shining a torch and wearing big boots.

I was awake, lying underground on a door, freezing.

Above me, I could hear the muffled sounds of a television, *Opportunity Knocks.*

I stared up into the dark, tiny specks of light coming closer.

Above me, I could hear the muffled sounds of a telephone ringing and wings beating.

I saw through the dark, rats with little wings that looked more like squirrels with their furry faces and kind words.

Above me, I could hear the muffled sounds of a record playing, *The Little Drummer Boy.*

The rats were at my ear, whispering harsh words, calling me names, breaking my bones worse than any sticks or stones.

Beside me, the muffled sounds of children crying.

I jumped up to put on the light but it was already on.

I was awake, lying on the carpet, freezing.

Chapter 9

'What the fuck is this?'

A newspaper full across the face woke me.

Saturday 21 December 1974.

'You tell me you love me, tell me you care, and then you fuck me up the arse and write this shit.'

I sat up in the bed, rubbing the side of my face with a bandaged hand.

Yeah, Saturday 21 December 1974.

Mrs Paula Garland, in blue flared jeans and a red wool sweater, stood over the bed.

The *Yorkshire Post* headline stared up from the eiderdown: *11 DAY IRA XMAS TRUCE.*

'What?'

'Don't give me that, you lying piece of shit.'

'I don't know what you're talking about.'

She picked up the paper, opened it, and started to read:

A Mother's Plea by Edward Dunford.

Mrs Paula Garland, sister of the Rugby League star Johnny Kelly, wept as she told of her life since the disappearance of her daughter, Jeanette, just over five years ago.

'I've lost everything since that day,' said Mrs Garland, referring to her husband Geoff's suicide in 1971, following the fruitless police investigation into the whereabouts of their missing daughter.

'I just want it all to end,' wept Mrs Garland. 'And maybe now it can.'

Paula stopped reading. 'Do you want me to go on?'

I sat on the edge of the bed, a sheet around my balls, staring at a patch of bright white sunlight on the thin flowered carpet.

'I didn't write that.'

'By Edward Dunford.'

'I didn't write it.'

The arrest of a Fitzwilliam man in connection with the disappearance and murder of Clare Kemplay has brought a tragic hope of sorts to Mrs Garland.

'I never thought I'd say it but, after all this time, I just want to

know what happened,' cried Mrs Garland. 'And if that means knowing the worst, I'll just have to try and live with it.'

'I didn't write it.'

'By Edward Dunford,' she repeated.

'I didn't write it.'

'You liar!' screamed Paula Garland, grabbing me by the hair and dragging me off the bed.

I fell naked on to the thin flowered carpet, repeating, 'I didn't write it.'

'Get out!'

'Please, Paula,' I said, reaching for my trousers.

She pushed me over as I tried to stand, screaming and screaming, 'Get out! Get out!'

'Fuck off, Paula, and listen to me.'

'No!' she screamed again, taking a piece out of my ear with her nails.

'Fuck off,' I shouted and pushed her away, gathering up my clothes.

She collapsed into a corner by the wardrobe, curling into a ball and sobbing, 'I fucking hate you.'

I put on my trousers and shirt, blood dripping from my ear, and picked up my jacket.

'I never want to see you again,' she whispered.

'Don't worry, you won't have to,' I spat back, down the stairs and out the door.

Bitch.

The clock in the car coming up to nine, bright white winter light half blinding me as I drove.

Fucking bitch.

The A655 morning clear, flat brown fields as far as the eye could see.

Bloody fucking bitch.

The radio on, Lulu's *Little Drummer Boy*, the back seat full of carrier bags.

Stupid bloody fucking bitch.

Pips on the hour, my ear still smarting, here comes the news: *'West Yorkshire Police have launched a murder investigation fol-*

*lowing the discovery of a woman's body in a flat in the St John's part
of the city, yesterday.'*

The blood dead in my arms, cold.

'The woman has been named as 36-year-old Mandy Denizili.'

Flesh strangling bone, off the road and on to the verge.

*'Mrs Denizili worked as a medium under her maiden name of
Wymer and became nationally known after helping the police with a
number of investigations. Most recently, Mrs Denizili claimed to have
led police to the body of murdered schoolgirl Clare Kemplay. This was
a claim strongly denied by Detective Superintendent Peter Noble, the
man leading that investigation.'*

My forehead on the steering wheel, hands over my mouth.

*'While police are at present releasing few details about the actual
crime itself, it is believed to have been particularly brutal.'*

Struggling with the door and the bandage, bile down the
armrest and on to the grass.

*'The police are appealing for anyone who knew Mrs Denizili to
please contact them as a matter of urgency.'*

Crazy bloody fucking bitch.

Out of the car and on to my knees, the bile trailing down
my chin and into the dirt.

Bloody fucking bitch.

Spitting bile and phlegm, that scream in my ears as she'd
slid back on her arse up the hall, those arms and legs splayed,
that country skirt riding up.

Fucking bitch.

Gravel in my palms, soil on my forehead, staring at the grass
in the cracks in the road.

Bitch.

From the pages of *Yorkshire Life*.

Thirty minutes later, my face black with dirt and my hands
stained with grass, I was stood in the lobby of the Redbeck
Motel, a bandage round the phone.

'Sergeant Fraser, please.'

The yellows, the browns, the stink of smoke – it almost felt
like home or much the same.

'Sergeant Fraser speaking.'

Thinking of crows perched on telephone wires, I swallowed and said, 'This is Edward Dunford.'

Silence, only the hum of the line waiting for words.

The click of pool balls from behind the glass doors, wondering what day of the week it was, wondering if it was a school day, thinking of the crows on the telephone wires and wondering what Fraser was thinking.

'You're fucked, Dunford,' said Fraser.

'I need to see you.'

'Fuck off. You've got to turn yourself in.'

'What?'

'You heard. You're wanted for questioning.'

'In connection to what?'

'In connection to the murder of Mandy Wymer.'

'Fuck off.'

'Where are you?'

'Listen . . .'

'No, you fucking listen. I've been trying to speak to you for two fucking days . . .'

'Listen, please . . .'

Silence again, just the hum of the line waiting for his words or mine.

The click of pool balls from behind the glass doors, wondering if it was always the same game, wondering if they even bothered to keep score, thinking of the crows on the wire again and wondering if Fraser was tracing this call.

'Go on,' said Fraser.

'I'll give you names and dates, all the information I have about Barry Gannon and all the stuff he found out.'

'Go on.'

'But I need to know everything you've heard about what's going on with Michael Myshkin, what he's saying about Jeanette Garland and Susan Ridyard. And I want his confession.'

'Go on.'

'I'll meet you at twelve noon. I'll give you all I've got, you give me what you've got. And I want your word you won't try and bring me in.'

'Go on.'

'If you arrest me, I'll drop you right in it.'

'Go on.'

'Give me till midnight, then I'll come in.'

Silence, only the hum waiting for the word.

The click of pool balls from behind the glass doors, wondering where the farting old woman was, wondering if she had died in her room and nobody had found her, thinking of the crows on the wire and wondering if Fraser had set me up at the Hartley Nursing Home.

'Where?' whispered Sergeant Fraser.

'There's a disused petrol station at the junction of the A655 and the B6134 going out to Featherstone.'

'Twelve?'

'Noon.'

The line dead, the hum gone, feeling much the same.

The click of pool balls from behind the glass doors.

On the floor of Room 27, emptying my pockets and bags, staring at the tiny cassettes marked BOX and SHAW, pressing play:

'I'm no angel either, but I am a businessman.'

Transcribing my words and theirs in my own injured hand.

'Persuade the Councillor that he should bare his soul of all his public wrongdoings.'

Putting a photograph to one side.

'Tomorrow lunchtime, upstairs in the Strafford Arms.'

Changing cassettes, pressing play:

'Because of the fucking money.'

Printing in capitals.

'Foster, Donald Richard Foster. Is that who you want?'

Listening to lies.

'I didn't know he was a journalist.'

Turning over the tape.

'All of the others under those beautiful new carpets.'

Rewind.

'Don't touch me!'

Pressing record to erase.

'You smell so strongly of bad memories.'

On the floor of Room 27, stuffing a manila envelope full of Barry's bits and the things he'd found, licking it locked and scrawling Fraser's name across the front.

'*You didn't see it coming?*'

At the door of my Redbeck room, swallowing a pill and lighting a cigarette, a manila envelope in my hand and a Christmas card in my pocket.

'*I'm a medium Mr Dunford, not a fortune teller.*'

One door left.

Noon.

Saturday 21 December 1974.

Between a lorry and a bus, driving past the disused Shell petrol station at the junction of the A655 and the B6134.

A mustard-yellow Maxi sat on the forecourt, Sergeant Fraser leaning against the bonnet.

I drove on for a hundred yards and pulled in, wound down my window, turned round, pressed record on the Philips Pocket Memo, and drove back.

Pulling up beside the Maxi, I said, 'Get in.'

Sergeant Fraser, a raincoat over his uniform, walked round the back of the Viva and got in.

I pulled out of the forecourt and turned left up the B6134 to Featherstone.

Sergeant Fraser, arms folded, stared straight ahead.

For one moment, I felt like I'd stepped into an alternate world straight out of Dr fucking Who, where I was the cop and Fraser was not, where I was good and he was not.

'Where are we going?' said Fraser.

'We're here.' I pulled into a lay-by just past a red caravan selling teas and pies.

Turning off the engine, I said, 'You want anything?'

'No, you're all right.'

'Am I? You know Sergeant Craven and his mate?'

'Yeah. Everyone knows them.'

'You know them well?'

'By reputation.'

I stared out of the brown mud-stained window, over the low brown hedges dividing the flat brown fields with their lone brown trees.

'Why?' said Fraser.

I took a photograph of Clare Kemplay out of my pocket, one

of her lying on a hospital slab, a swan's wing stitched into her back.

I handed the photo to Fraser. 'I think either Craven or his partner gave me this.'

'Fuck. Why?'

'They're setting me up.'

'Why?'

I pointed to the carrier bag at Fraser's feet. 'It's all in there.'

'Yeah?'

'Yeah. Transcripts, documents, photographs. Everything you need.'

'Transcripts?'

'I've got the original tapes and I'll hand them over when you decide you need them. Don't worry, it's all there.'

'It better be,' said Fraser, peering into the bag.

I took two pieces of paper from inside my jacket and gave one of them to Fraser. 'Knock on this door.'

'Flat 5, 3 Spencer Mount, Chapeltown,' read Fraser.

I put the other piece back in my pocket. 'Yeah.'

'Who lives here?'

'Barry James Anderson; he's an acquaintance of Barry Gannon's and the star of some of the snaps and tapes you'll find in the bag.'

'Why are you giving me him?'

I stared out towards the ends of the flat brown fields, at blue skies turning white.

'I've got nothing else left to give.'

Fraser put the piece of paper inside his pocket, taking out a notebook.

'What have you got for me?'

'Not so bloody much,' said Fraser, opening the notebook.

'His confession?'

'Not verbatim.'

'Details?'

'There aren't any.'

'What's he said about Jeanette Garland?'

'He's copped for it. That's it.'

'Susan Ridyard?'

'Same.'

'Fuck.'

'Yeah,' said Sergeant Fraser.

'You think he did them?'

'He's the one confessing.'

'He say where he did all these things?'

'His Underground Kingdom.'

'He's not all there.'

'Who is?' sighed Fraser.

In the green car, by the brown field, under the white sky, I said, 'Is that it?'

Sergeant Fraser looked down at the notebook in his hands and said, 'Mandy Wymer.'

'Fuck.'

'Neighbour found her yesterday about 9 a.m. She had been raped, scalped, and hung with wire from a light fitting.'

'Scalped?'

'Like Indians do.'

'Fuck.'

'They're keeping that from your lot,' smiled Fraser.

'Scalped,' I whispered.

'Cats had had a go too. Real horror show stuff.'

'Fuck.'

'Your ex-boss turned you in,' said Fraser and closed the notebook.

'They think I fucking did it?'

'No.'

'Why not?'

'You're a journalist.'

'So?'

'So they think you might know who did it.'

'Why me?'

'Because you must have been one of the last fucking people to see her alive, that's why.'

'Fuck.'

'She mention her husband?'

'She didn't say anything.'

Sergeant Fraser flicked open the notebook again. 'Neighbours have told us that Miss Wymer was involved in some kind of argument on Tuesday afternoon. According to your former employer, that must have been either just before or just after she saw you.'

'I don't know anything about that.'

Sergeant Fraser looked me in the eye and closed his notebook again.

He said, 'I think you're lying.'

'Why would I?'

'I don't know, force of habit?'

I turned and looked out over the dead brown hedge at the dead brown field with its dead brown tree.

'What did she say about Clare Kemplay?' said Fraser quietly.

'Nothing much.'

'Like what?'

'You think there's a link?'

'Obviously.'

'How?' I said, my dry mouth cracking, my wet heart thumping.

'Fuck, how do you think they're linked? She was working the cases.'

'Noble and his lot are denying it.'

'So what? We all know she was.'

'And?'

'And then there's always you.'

'Me? What about me?'

'The missing link.'

'And that makes it all somehow connected?'

'You tell me?'

I said, 'You should've been a bloody journalist.'

'You too,' hissed Fraser.

'Fuck off,' I said, starting the car.

'Everything's connected,' said Sergeant Fraser.

I checked the rearview mirror twice and pulled out.

At the junction of the B6134 and the A655, Fraser said, 'Midnight?'

I nodded and pulled up alongside the Maxi on the forecourt of the empty garage.

'Make it Morley,' said Sergeant Fraser, picking up the carrier bag as he got out.

'Yeah. Why not?'

One card left to play, I checked the rearview mirror as I pulled away.

City Heights, Leeds.

I locked the car under white skies going grey with their threats of rain and never snow, thinking it must be all right round here in the summer.

Clean sixties high-rise: flaking yellow and sky-blue paint-work, railings beginning to rust.

Climbing the stairs to the fourth floor, the slap of a ball against a wall, children's shrieks upon the wind, I was thinking of The Beatles and their album covers, of cleanliness, of Godliness, and children.

On the fourth floor, I walked along the open passageway, past steamed-up kitchen windows and muffled radios, until I came to the yellow door marked 405.

I knocked on the door of Flat 405, City Heights, Leeds, and waited.

After a moment, I pressed the doorbell too.

Nothing.

I bent down and lifted up the metal flap of the letterbox.

Warmth watered my eyes and I could hear the sounds of horse racing on a TV.

'Excuse me!' I yelled into the letterbox.

The racing died.

'Excuse me!'

Eyeball back to the letterbox; I spy a pair of white towelling socks, coming this way.

'I know you're in there,' I said, standing up.

'What do you want?' said a man's voice.

'I just want a word.'

'What about?'

Playing the last card in my last hand, I said to the door, 'Your sister.'

A key turned and the yellow door opened.

'What about her?' said Johnny Kelly.

'Snap,' I said, holding up my bandaged right hand.

Johnny Kelly, blue jeans and sweater, a broken wrist and beaten Irish face, said again, 'What about her?'

'You should get in touch with her. She's worried about you.'

'And who the fuck are you?'

'Edward Dunford.'

'Do I know you?'

'No.'

'How'd you know I was here?'

I took the Christmas card from my pocket and handed it to him. 'Merry Christmas.'

'Stupid bitch,' said Kelly, opening it and staring at the two plastic strips of Dymo tape.

'Can I come in?'

Johnny Kelly turned back into the flat and I followed him down a narrow hall, past a bathroom and a bedroom, and into the living room.

Kelly sat down in a vinyl armchair, clutching his wrist.

I sat on the matching settee facing a colour TV full of horses silently jumping fences, my back to another winter afternoon in Leeds.

Above the gas fire a Polynesian girl was smiling in various shades of orange and brown, a flower in her hair, and I was thinking of brown-haired gypsy girls and roses where roses were never meant to go.

The half-time scores were coming up under the horses: Leeds were losing at Newcastle.

'Paula all right is she?'

'What do you think?' I said, nodding at the open paper on the Formica coffee table.

Johnny Kelly leant forward, peering at the print. 'You're from the fucking papers, aren't you?'

'I know your Paul.'

'It were you who fucking wrote that shit, weren't it?' said Kelly, leaning back.

'I didn't write that.'

'But you're from the fucking *Post*?'

'Not now, no.'

'Fuck,' said Kelly, shaking his head.

'Listen, I'm not going to say anything.'

'Right,' smiled Kelly.

'Just tell us what happened and I promise I'll say nothing.'

Johnny Kelly stood up. 'You're a fucking journalist.'

'Not any more.'

'I don't fucking believe you,' said Kelly.

'All right, say I am. I could just write any old shit anyway.'

'Usually do.'

'Right, so just talk to me.'

Johnny Kelly was behind me, looking out of the huge cold window at the huge cold city.

'If you're not a journalist any more, why you here?'

'I'm here to try and help Paula.'

Johnny Kelly sat back down in the vinyl armchair, rubbing his wrist, and smiled. 'Not another.'

The room was darkening, the gas fire brightening.

I said, 'How'd it happen?'

'Car accident.'

'Yeah?'

'Yeah,' said Kelly.

'You were driving?'

'She was.'

'Who?'

'Who do you think?'

'Mrs Patricia Foster?'

'Bingo.'

'What happened?'

'We'd been away and were on our way back . . .'

'When was this?'

'Last Friday night.'

'Go on,' I said, thinking of pens and paper, cassettes and tapes.

'We'd stopped off for a few coming back and so she said she'd better drive last bit because I'd had more than her like. Anyway, we were coming down the Dewsbury Road and, I don't know, we were mucking around I suppose, and next news some bloke just steps out into the road and, bang, we hit him.'

'Where?'

'Legs, chest, I don't know.'

'No, no. Where on Dewsbury Road?'

'As you come into Wakey, near Prison.'

'Near them new houses Foster's building?'

'Yeah. Suppose so,' smiled Johnny Kelly.

Thinking everything's connected, thinking there's no such thing as chance, there is a plan, and so there is a god, I swallowed and said, 'You know they found Clare Kemplay near there?'

'Yeah?'

'Yeah.'

Kelly was looking beyond me. 'I didn't know that.'

'What happened then?'

'I reckon we only glanced him like, but it was dead icy so the car started to spin and she lost control.'

I sat there in my polyester clothes, on the vinyl settee, staring at the Formica tabletop, in the concrete flat, thinking of the rubber and the metal, the leather and the glass.

The blood.

'We must have hit the curb and then a lamppost or something.'

'What about the man you hit?'

'I don't know. As I say, I reckon we only clipped him like.'

'Did you look?' I asked, offering him a cigarette.

'Did we fuck,' said Kelly, taking a light.

'Then what?'

'I got her out, checked she was all right. Her neck was not too clever, but there was nothing broke. Just whiplash. We got back in and I drove her home.'

'The car was all right then?'

'No, but it went like.'

'What did Foster say?'

Kelly stubbed out his cigarette. 'I didn't bloody wait to find out.'

'And you came here?'

'I needed to get out of the road for a bit. Keep me head down.'

'He knows you're here?'

'Course he bloody does,' said Kelly, touching his face. He picked up a white card from the Formica table and tossed it across to me. 'Bastard even sent me an invite to his fucking Christmas party.'

'How did he find you?' I said, squinting at the card in the dark.

'It's one of his places, isn't it?'

'So why hang around?'

'Cause at the end of the fucking day, he can't say so bloody much can he.'

I had the feeling that I'd just forgotten something very fucking bad. 'I'm not with you?'

'Well he's been shagging me fucking sister every Sunday since I was seventeen.'

Thinking, that wasn't it.

'Not that I'm complaining.'

I looked up.

Johnny Kelly looked down.

I had remembered that very fucking bad thing.

The room was dark, the gas fire bright.

'Don't look so fucking shocked pal. You're not the first who's tried to help her and you won't be last.'

I stood up, the blood in my legs cold and wet.

'You off to the party, are you?' grinned Kelly, nodding at the invitation in my hands.

I turned and walked down the narrow hall, thinking fuck them all.

'Don't forget to wish them a merry bloody Christmas from Johnny Kelly, will you?'

Thinking fuck her.

Hello love.

Cash and carrying it.

Ten seconds later, parked outside some Paki shop, the last of my cash in bottles and bags on the floor of the car, radio rocking to a Harrods bomb, a cigarette in the ashtray, another in my hand, pulling pills out of the glove compartment.

Drunk and driving.

Ninety miles an hour, necking Scotchmen, upping downers and downing uppers, scattering Southern girls and seaview flats, ploughing through the Kathryns and the Karens and all the ones that went before, chasing tail-lights and little girls, scrambling love under my wheels, turning it over in the tread of my tyres.

Fuhrer of a bunker of my own design, screaming, I'VE NEVER DONE BAD THINGS.

Motorway One, foot down and taking it bad, sucking the night and its bombs and their shells through the vents in my car and the teeth in my mouth, trying and crying and dying for one more kiss, for the way she talks and the way she walks, offering up prayers without deals, love without schemes, begging her to live again, live again, HERE FOR ME NOW.

Tears soft and cock hard, screaming across six lanes of shit, I'VE NEVER DONE ONE SINGLE FUCKING GOOD THING.

Radio 2 suddenly silent, white motorway lines turning gold, men dressed in rags, men dressed in crowns, some men with wings, others without, braking hard to swerve around a crib of wood and straw.

On the hard shoulder, hazard lights on.

Bye-bye love.

11 Brunt Street, all in black.

Brakes to wake the dead, out the green Viva and kicking the fuck out of the red door.

11 Brunt Street, the back way.

Round the houses, over the wall, a dustbin lid through the kitchen window, taking out shards of glass with my jacket as in I went.

Honey, I'm home.

11 Brunt Street, quiet as the grave.

Inside, thinking, when I get home to you, I'm going to show you what I can do, taking a knife from the kitchen drawer (where I knew it would be).

Is this what you wanted?

Up the steep, steep stairs, into Mummy and Daddy's room, tearing up the eiderdown, ripping out the drawers, tipping shit this way and that, make-up and cheap knickers, tampons and fake pearls, seeing Geoff swallowing the shotgun, thinking NO FUCKING WONDER, your daughter dead, your wife a whore who fucks her brother's boss and more, spinning a chair into the mirror, BECAUSE THERE COULD BE NO LUCK WORSE THAN THIS FUCKING LUCK.

Giving you all you ever wanted.

I walked across the landing and opened the door to Jeanette's room.

So quiet and so cold, the room felt like a church. I sat down upon the little pink bedspread next to her congregation of teddys and dolls and, dropping my head into my hands, I let the knife fall to the floor, the blood on my hands and the tears on my face freezing before they could both join the knife.

For the first time, my prayers were not for me but for everyone else, that all of those things in all of my notebooks, on all of those tapes, in all of those envelopes and bags in my room, that none of them were true, that the dead were alive and the lost were found, and that all of those lives could be lived anew. And then I prayed for my mother and sister, for my uncles and aunts, for the friends I'd had, both good and bad, and last for my father wherever he was, Amen.

I sat for a while with my head down, clasping my hands together, listening to the sounds of the house and my heart, picking the one from the other.

After a time, I rose from Jeanette's bed and, closing the door on the room, I went back into Mummy and Daddy's room and the damage I'd done. I picked up the eiderdown and put back the drawers, gathering up her make-up and her underwear, her tampons and her jewellery, sweeping up the mirror's shards with my shoe and righting the chair.

I went back down the stairs and into the kitchen, picking up the bin lid and closing all the cupboards and the doors, thanking Christ no-one had called the fucking cops. I put the kettle on, let it boil, and brewed a milky mug with five large sugars. I took the tea into the front room, stuck the telly on, and watched white ambulances tear across the black wet night, ferrying the bombed and blown this way and that as a bloody Santa and a senior policeman both wondered what kind of person could do such a thing and so near to Christmas.

I lit a cigarette, watching the football scores and cursing Leeds United, wondering which game would be on *Match of the Day* and who'd be the guests on *Parkinson*.

There was a tap on the front window, then a knock on the door, and I suddenly froze, remembering where I was and what I'd done.

'Who is it?' I said, stood up in the middle of the room.

'It's Clare. Who's that?'

'Clare?' I turned the latch and opened the door, my heart beating ninety miles an hour.

'Ah, it's you Eddie.'

A heart dead in its tracks. 'Yeah.'

Scotch Clare said, 'Paula in, is she?'

'No.'

'Oh, right. Saw the light and I thought she must be back. Sorry,' smiled Scotch Clare, squinting into the light.

'No she's not back yet, sorry.'

'Never mind. I'll see her tomorrow.'

'Yeah. I'll tell her.'

'Are you OK, love?'

'Fine.'

'OK. See you then.'

'Night,' I said, my breathing coming fast and shallow as I shut the door.

Scotch Clare said something I didn't catch and then her footsteps went away, back down the street.

I sat back down on the sofa and stared at the school photograph of Jeanette on top of the TV. There were two cards beside her, one of a cabin made of logs in the middle of a snow-covered forest, the other plain white.

I took Johnny Kelly's plain white invitation from Donald Foster out of my pocket and walked over to the TV.

I switched off Max Wall and Emerson Fittipaldi and went back out into the silent night.

Snap.

Back to the big houses.

Wood Lane, Sandal, Wakefield.

The lane was strung with parked cars. I picked my way through the Jags and the Rovers, the Mercs and the BMWs.

Trinity View, all floodlit and party decked.

A huge Christmas tree stood on the front lawn, dripping in white lights and tinsel.

I walked up the drive towards the party, following the competing strains of Johnny Mathis and Rod Stewart.

The front door was open this time and I stood for a moment in the doorway, watching women in long dresses carrying paper plates of food from one room to the next and forming queues up the stairs for the bathroom, while men in velvet tuxedos stood around with tumblers of Scotch and fat cigars.

Through the door to the left I could see Mrs Patricia Foster, minus collar, refilling the glasses of a group of big men with red faces.

I walked into the room and said, 'I'm looking for Paula.'

The room went dead.

Mrs Foster opened her mouth but didn't speak, her eagle eyes darting about the room.

'Do you want to step outside, son?' said a voice behind me.

I turned round into Don Foster's smiling face.

'I'm looking for Paula?'

'I heard. Let's go outside and talk about it.'

Two big men with moustaches stood behind Foster, the three of them all in tuxedos and bow ties, frills down the fronts of their shirts.

'I'm here for Paula.'

'You weren't invited. Let's go.'

'Merry bloody Christmas from Johnny Kelly,' I said, flicking Kelly's invitation at Foster.

Foster glanced at his wife and then turned slightly to one of the men and muttered, 'Outside.'

One of the men stepped towards me. I raised my hands in surrender and walked towards the door.

Turning round at the door, I said, 'Thanks for the Christmas card, Pat.'

I watched the woman swallow and look at the carpet.

One of the men gently pushed me forward into the hall.

'Is everything all right, Don?' asked a man with grey curly hair and a fist full of Scotch.

'Yeah. This gentleman was just leaving,' said Foster.

The man tilted his head my way. 'Do I know you?'

'Probably,' I said. 'I used to work for that bloke over there with the beard.'

Chief Constable Ronald Angus turned and looked into the other room, where Bill Hadden was stood talking with his back to the door.

'Really? How interesting,' said Chief Constable Angus, taking another mouthful of whisky and rejoining the party.

Donald Foster was holding open the door for me and I got another gentle push in the back.

There was laughter coming from an upstairs room; a woman's laugh.

I walked out of the house, the two men at my side, Foster behind me. I thought about sprinting across the lawn, making a dash for the Golden Fleece, wondering if they'd try and stop me in front of the party, knowing they would.

'Where are we going?'

'Just keep walking,' said one of the men, the one wearing a claret shirt.

We were at the top of the drive and I could see a man coming up from the gate towards us, half running, half walking.

'Shit,' said Don Foster.

We all stopped.

The two men looked at Foster, waiting for an order.

'It never bloody rains,' muttered Foster.

Councillor Shaw was out of breath, shouting, 'Don!'

Foster walked a little way down to meet him, arms open, palms up, 'Bill, nice to see you.'

'You shot my dog! You shot my bloody dog.'

Shaw was shaking his head, crying, trying to push Foster away.

Foster took him in a big bear hug, hushing him.

'You shot my dog!' screamed Shaw, breaking free.

Foster pulled him back into his arms, burying the man's head inside his velvet tux.

Behind us on the steps to the door, Mrs Foster and a few guests stood shivering.

'What's going on, love?' she said, her teeth and glass chattering.

'Nothing. Everyone go back and have a good time.'

They all stood there on the steps, frozen.

'Go on. It's bloody Christmas!' shouted Foster, Santa fucking Claus himself.

'Who wants to dance with me?' laughed Pat Foster, shaking her skinny tits and turning everyone back inside.

Dancing Machine thumped through the door, the fun and games resumed.

Shaw stood there, sobbing into Foster's black velvet jacket.

Foster whispering, 'This isn't the time, Bill.'

'What about him?' said the man in the claret shirt.

'Just get him out of here.'

The other man in the red shirt took my elbow and started to lead me down the drive.

Foster didn't look up, whispering into Shaw's ear, 'This is special, special for John.'

We walked past them, down the drive.

'You drive here did you?'

'Yeah.'

'Pass us your keys,' said Claret.

I did as I was told.

'That yours?' said Red pointing at the Viva, up on the pavement.

'Yeah.'

The men smiled at each other.

Claret opened the passenger door and lifted up the seat. 'Get in the back.'

I got in the back with Red.

Claret got in behind the wheel and started the engine. 'Where to?'

'New houses.'

I was sat in the back wondering why I hadn't even bothered to try and get away, thinking maybe it wouldn't be as bad as all that and how it couldn't be any worse than the beating I'd taken at the Nursing Home, when Red hit me so fucking hard my head cracked the plastic side window.

'Shut the bloody fuck up,' he laughed, grabbing me by the hair and forcing my head down between my knees.

'If he were a nig-nog, he'd make you suck his cock,' shouted Claret from the front.

'Let's have some fucking music,' said Red, still holding my head down.

Rebel Rebel filled the car.

'Turn it up,' shouted Red, lifting me back up by the hair, whispering, 'Fucking puff.'

'Is he bleeding?' shouted Claret over the music.

'Not enough.'

He pushed me back towards the window, gripped me by the throat with his left hand, sat back a little way and rabbit-punched me on the bridge of my nose, sending hot blood across the car.

'That's better,' he said and gently laid my head against the cracked glass.

I looked out at the centre of Wakefield on the Saturday before Christmas, 1974, the warm blood trickling from my nose to my lips and down on to my chin, thinking it's quiet for a Saturday night.

'Is he out?' said Claret.

'Yep,' said Red.

Bowie gave way to Lulu or Petula or Sandy or Cilla, *The Little Drummer Boy* washing over me, as Christmas lights became prison lights and the car bumped over the waste ground of Foster's Construction.

'Here?'

'Why not.'

The car stopped, the Little Drummer Boy gone.

Claret got out and held up the driver's seat as Red tipped me out on to the ground.

'He's fucking gone, Mick.'

'Aye. Sorry, like.'

I lay face down between them, playing dead.

'What we supposed to do? Just leave him?'

'Fuck no.'

'What then?'

'Have some fun.'

'Not tonight Mick, I can't be arsed with it.'

'Just a bit, eh?'

They took an arm each and dragged me across the ground, bringing my trousers down to my knees.

'In here?'

'Aye.'

They pulled me through the tarpaulin and across the wooden floor of a half-built house, splinters and nails ripping through my knees.

They sat me on a chair and bound my hands behind my back, pulling off my trousers over my shoes.

'Go bring car over here and put lights on.'

'Someone'll see us.'

'Like who?'

I heard one of them go out and the other one come in close. He put his hand down inside my underpants.

'I hear you like a bit of cunt,' Red said, squeezing my balls.

I heard the engine of the car and the room was suddenly filled with white light and *Kung-Fu Fighting*.

'Let's get it over with,' said Claret.

'Joe Bugner!' said a punch to the gut.

'Coon Conteh!' said another.

'George fucking Foreman,' said one across the jaw.

'The Ali Shuffle,' a pause, me waiting, then one from the left, one from the right.

'Bruce fucking Lee!'

I went flying back on the chair on to the ground, my chest fucked.

'Fucking puff,' said Claret, bending down and spitting into my face.

'We should fucking bury the cunt.'

Claret was laughing, 'Best not mess with George's foundations.'

'I hate these fucking brainy bastards.'

'Leave him. Let's go.'

'That it?'

'Fuck it, let's just get back.'

'Take his car?'

'Get a taxi on Westgate.'

'Fucking hell.'

A kick in the back of the head.

A foot upon my right hand.

Lights out.

The cold woke me.

Everything was pitch-black with purple borders.

I kicked the chair away and pulled my hands out of the binding.

I sat up in my underpants on the wooden floor, my head loose, my body raw.

I reached across the floor and pulled my trousers to me. They were wet and stank of another man's piss.

I put them on over my shoes.

Slowly, I stood up.

I fell back down once and then walked out of the half-built house.

The car was sitting in the dark, doors shut.

I tried both doors.

Locked.

I picked up a broken brick, walked round to the passenger window and put the brick through it.

I put my hand inside and pulled up the lock.

I opened the door, picked up the brick and battered in the lock on the glove compartment.

I pulled out map books and damp cloths and a spare key.

I went round to the driver's side, opened the door and got in.

I sat in the car, staring at the dark empty houses, remembering the best game I'd been to with my father.

Huddersfield were playing Everton. Town got a free kick on the edge of the Everton area. Vic Metcalfe steps up, bends the ball round the wall, Jimmy Glazzard heads it in. Goal. Referee disallows it, forget why, says take it again. Metcalfe steps up again, bends the ball round the wall, Glazzard heads it in. Goal, the whole crowd in fucking stitches.

8 fucking 2.

'Press'll have a field day. Bloody bury them,' laughed my father.

I started the engine and drove back to Ossett.

*

In the drive at Wesley Street, I looked at my father's watch.

It was fucking gone.

Must have been about three or so.

Fuck, I thought as I opened the back door. There was a light on in the back room.

Fuck, I ought to at least say hello. Get it over with.

She was in her rocking chair, dressed but asleep.

I closed the door and went up the stairs, one at a time.

I lay on the bed in my piss-stinking clothes, looking at the poster of Peter Lorimer in the dark, thinking it would've broken my Dad's heart.

Ninety miles an hour.

Part 3
We are the dead

Chapter 10

Sunday 22 December 1974.

At five in the morning, ten policemen led by Detective Superintendent Noble broke down the door of my mother's house with sledgehammers, slapped her across the face when she came out into the hall and pushed her back inside the room, ran up the stairs with shotguns, dragged me from my bed, pulling my hair out in clumps, kicked me down the stairs, punching me as I landed, and dragged me out the door and across the tarmac and into the back of a black van.

They slammed the doors and drove away.

In the back of the van they beat me unconscious, then slapped me across the face and urinated on me until I came round.

When the van stopped, Detective Superintendent Noble opened the back door and pulled me out by my hair, spinning me across the rear car park of Wakefield Police Station, Wood Street.

Two uniformed officers then pulled me by my feet up the stone steps and inside the Police Station, where the corridors were all lined with black bodies, punching and kicking and spitting on me as they dragged me by my heels again and again, up and down, up and down, the yellow corridors.

They took photographs, stripped me, cut the bandage off my right hand, took more photographs, and fingerprinted me.

A Paki doctor shone a torch into my eye, wiped a spatula round my mouth, and scraped under my nails.

They took me naked into a ten by six interrogation room with white lights and no windows, sat me down behind a table and handcuffed my hands behind my back.

Then they left me alone.

Sometime later they opened the door and threw a bucket of piss and shit across my face.

Then they left me alone again.

Sometime later they opened the door and hosed me down with ice water until I fell over on the chair.

Then they left me alone, lying on the floor, handcuffed to the chair.

I could hear screams from another room.

The screaming went on for what seemed like an hour, and then stopped.

Silence.

I lay on the floor and listened to the humming of the lights.

Sometime later the door opened and two big men in good suits came in carrying chairs.

They unlocked the handcuffs and picked up the chair.

One of the men had sideburns and a moustache and was about forty. The other man had fine sandy hair and his breath smelt of puke.

Sandy said: 'Sit down and put your palms flat upon the desk.'

I sat down and did as I was told.

Sandy tossed the handcuffs to Moustache and sat down opposite me.

Moustache walked around the room behind me, playing with the handcuffs.

I looked down at my right hand, flat upon the table, four fingers made one, a hundred shades of yellow and red.

Moustache sat down and stared at me, putting the handcuffs on his fist like a knuckle-duster.

Suddenly he jumped up and brought the handcuffed fist down on top of my right hand.

I screamed.

'Put your hands back.'

I put them on the table.

'Flat.'

I tried to lay them down flat.

'Nasty.'

'You should get that seen to.'

Moustache was sitting down opposite me, smiling.

Sandy got up and went out of the room.

Moustache said nothing, just smiled.

My right hand throbbed blood and pus.

Sandy came back with a blanket and put it over my shoulders.

He sat down and took out a pack of JPS, offering one to Moustache.

Moustache took out a lighter and lit both their cigarettes.

They sat back and blew smoke at me.

My hands began to twitch.

Moustache leant forward and dangled the cigarette over my right hand, rolling it between two fingers.

I pulled my hand back a bit.

Suddenly he leant forward and grabbed my right wrist with one hand, grinding the cigarette into the back of my hand with the other.

I screamed.

He let go of my wrist and sat back.

'Put your hands back.'

I put them on the table.

My burnt skin stank.

'Another?' said Sandy.

'Don't mind if I do,' he said, taking another JPS.

He lit the cigarette and stared at me.

He leant forward and began to dangle the cigarette over my hand.

I stood up, 'What do you want?'

'Sit down.'

'Tell me what you want!'

'Sit down.'

I sat down.

They stood up.

'Stand up.'

I stood up.

'Eyes front.'

I could hear a dog barking.

I flinched.

'Don't move.'

They moved the chairs and tables to the wall and left the room.

I stood in the centre of the room, staring at the white wall, not moving.

I could hear screams and the dog barking in another room.

The screaming and the barking went on for what seemed like an hour, and then stopped.

Silence.

I stood in the centre of the room, wanting a piss, listening to the humming of the lights.

Sometime later the door opened and two big men in good suits came in.

One of the men had grey greased-back hair and was about fifty. The other man was younger with brown hair and an orange tie.

They both smelt of drink.

Grey and Brown walked around me in silence.

Then Grey and Brown brought the chairs and table back to the centre of the room.

Grey put a chair behind me.

'Sit down.'

I sat down.

Grey picked up the blanket from the floor and put it over my shoulders.

'Put your palms flat on the desk,' said Brown, lighting a cigarette.

'Please tell me what you want.'

'Put your palms flat.'

I did as I was told.

Brown sat down opposite me, while Grey walked around the room.

Brown laid a pistol on the table between us and smiled.

Grey stopped walking around and stood behind me.

'Eyes front.'

Suddenly Brown jumped up and pinned down my wrists, as Grey grabbed the blanket and twisted it around my face.

I fell forward off the chair, coughing and choking, unable to breathe.

They continued to hold down my wrists, continued to twist the blanket around my face.

I knelt on the floor, coughing and choking, unable to breathe.

Suddenly Brown let go of my wrists and I spun round in the blanket into a wall.

Crack.

Grey threw off the blanket and picked me up by the hair, standing me against the wall.

'Turn round and eyes front.'

I turned round.

Brown had the pistol in his right hand and Grey had some bullets and was throwing them up and catching them.

'Boss says it's all right to shoot him.'

Brown held the pistol with both hands at arm's length, pointing at my head.

I closed my eyes.

There was a click and nothing happened.

'Fuck.'

Brown turned away, fiddling with the pistol.

There was piss running down my leg.

'I've fixed it. It'll be all right this time.'

Brown pointed the pistol again.

I closed my eyes.

There was a loud bang.

I thought I was dead.

I opened my eyes and saw the pistol.

There were shreds of black material coming out of the barrel, floating down to the floor.

Brown and Grey were laughing.

'What do you want?'

Grey stepped forward and kicked me in the balls.

I fell to the floor.

'What do you want?'

'Stand up.'

I stood up.

'On your toes.'

'Please tell me?'

Grey stepped forward again and kicked me in the balls. I fell to the floor.

Brown walked over, kicked me in the chest, and then handcuffed my hands behind my back, pushing my face towards the floor.

'You don't like dogs, do you Eddie?'

I swallowed.

'What do you want?'

The door opened and a uniformed policeman came in with an Alsatian on a lead.

Grey pulled my face up by my hair.

The dog was staring at me, panting, its tongue out.

'Get him, get him.'

The dog started growling and barking and straining on its leash.

Grey pushed my head forward.

'He's starving.'

'He's not the only one.'

'Careful.'

The dog was getting nearer.

I struggled, crying, trying to get loose.

Grey pushed me in closer.

The dog was a foot away.

I could see its gums, see its teeth, smell its breath, feel its breath.

The dog was growling and barking and straining on its leash.

Shit fell from my arse.

Spit from its gums hit my face.

Everything was going black.

'Tell me what I've done.'

'Again.'

The dog was inches away.

I closed my eyes.

'Tell me what I've done.'

'Again.'

'Tell me what I've done.'

'Good boy.'

Everything was black and the dog was gone.

I opened my eyes.

Detective Superintendent Noble was sitting across the table opposite.

I was naked, shivering, sitting in my own shit.

Detective Superintendent Noble lit a cigarette.

I flinched.

'Why?'

Tears welled in my eyes.

'Why'd you do it?'
'I'm sorry.'
'That's good.'
Detective Superintendent Noble gave me his cigarette.
I took it.
He lit another.
'Just tell me why?'
'I don't know.'
'Shall I help you?'
'Yes.'
'Yes what?'
'Yes, sir.'
'You fancied her, right?'
'Yes, sir.'
'Fancied her loads, didn't you?'
'Yes, sir.'
'But she wouldn't give you any, would she?'
'No, sir.'
'What wouldn't she give you?'
'She wouldn't give me any.'
'She didn't want any, did she?'
'No, sir.'
'But you took some anyway, didn't you?'
'Yes, sir.'
'What did you take?'
'I took some anyway.'
'Took her in the cunt, didn't you?'
'Yes, sir.'
'Took her in the mouth, didn't you?'
'Yes, sir.'
'Took her up the arse, didn't you?'
'Yes, sir.'
'What did you do?'
'I took her in the cunt.'
'And?'
'I took her in the mouth.'
'And?'
'I took her up the arse.'
'You didn't care, did you?'

'No, sir.'
'She wouldn't shut up though, would she?'
'No, sir.'
'Then what?'
'She wouldn't shut up.'
'Said she was going to tell the police, didn't she?'
'Yes, sir.'
'What did she say?'
'Said she was going to tell the police.'
'We couldn't have that could we?'
'No, sir.'
'So you had to shut her up, didn't you?'
'Yes, sir.'
'Strangled her, didn't you?'
'Yes, sir.'
'What did you do?'
'I strangled her.'
'But she was still looking at you, wasn't she?'
'Yes, sir.'
'So you cut off her hair, didn't you?'
'Yes, sir.'
'What did you do?'
'I cut off her hair.'
'Why?'
'I cut off her hair.'
Detective Superintendent Noble took the cigarette from me.
'Because she was still looking at you, wasn't she?'
'Yes, sir.'
'So what did you do?'
'I cut off her hair.'
'Why?'
'Because she was still looking at me.'
'Good boy.'
Detective Superintendent Noble stubbed out the cigarette on the floor.
He lit another cigarette and passed it to me.
I took it.
'You fancied her, didn't you?'
'Yes, sir.'

'But she wouldn't give you any, would she?'

'No, sir.'

'So what did you do?'

'I took some anyway.'

'What did you do?'

'I took her in the cunt.'

'And?'

'I took her in the mouth.'

'And?'

'I took her up the arse.'

'Then what?'

'She wouldn't shut up.'

'What did she say?'

'Said she was going to tell the police.'

'What did you do?'

'I strangled her.'

'Then what did you do?'

'I cut off her hair.'

'Why?'

'She was still looking at me.'

'Just like the other one?'

'Yes, sir.'

'Like what?'

'Like the other one.'

'You want to make a confession, don't you?'

'Yes, sir.'

'What do you want to make?'

'I want to make a confession.'

'Good boy.'

Detective Superintendent Noble stood up.

Then he left me alone.

Sometime later a policeman opened the door and took me down the yellow corridor to a room with a shower and a toilet.

The policeman gave me some soap and ran some hot water in the shower.

I stood in the warm shower and washed myself all over.

Then shit started falling down my legs again.

The policeman didn't say anything.

He gave me another bar of soap and ran some more hot water.

I stood in the shower and washed myself all over again.

The policeman gave me a towel.

I dried myself.

Then the policeman gave me a pair of blue overalls.

I put them on.

Then the policeman took me back down the yellow corridor to a ten by six interrogation room, with four chairs and a table.

'Sit down.'

I did as I was told.

Then the policeman left me alone.

Sometime later the door opened and three big men in good suits came in: Detective Chief Superintendent Oldman, Detective Superintendent Noble, and the man with sandy hair.

They all sat down opposite me.

Detective Chief Superintendent Oldman sat back in his chair with his arms folded.

Detective Superintendent Noble placed two cardboard folders on the desk and began flicking through papers and big black and white photographs.

Sandy had a pad of A4 paper open on his knee.

'You want to make a confession, do you?' said Detective Chief Superintendent Oldman.

'Yes, sir.'

'Go on then.'

Silence.

I sat on the chair, listening to the humming of the lights.

'You fancied her, didn't you?' said Detective Superintendent Noble, passing a photograph to his boss.

'Yes, sir.'

'What?'

'I fancied her.'

Sandy began writing.

Detective Chief Superintendent Oldman was looking at the photograph and smiling.

'Go on,' he said.

'She wouldn't give me any.'

Detective Chief Superintendent Oldman looked up at me.

'So?' said Detective Superintendent Noble.

'I took some anyway.'

'What did you do?' asked Oldman.

'I took her in the cunt.'

'And?' said Noble, passing another photograph to Oldman.

'I took her in the mouth.'

'And?'

'I took her up the arse.'

'Then what happened?'

'She wouldn't shut up.'

'What was she saying?'

'Said she was going to tell the police.'

'So what did you do?'

Noble passed another photograph to Oldman.

'I strangled her.'

'Then what did you do?'

'I cut off her hair.'

Detective Chief Superintendent Oldman looked up from the last photograph and said, 'Why'd you do that?'

'She wouldn't stop looking at me.'

'Same as the other one?' said Detective Superintendent Noble, opening the second cardboard folder and passing more photographs to Oldman.

'Just like the other one,' I said.

Detective Chief Superintendent Oldman flicked through the photographs and then handed them back to Noble.

Oldman sat back in his chair, arms folded, and nodded at Sandy.

Sandy looked down at the pad and began to read:

'I fancied her but she wouldn't give me any, so I took some anyway. I took her in the cunt and in the mouth and up the arse. Then she wouldn't shut up. She said she was going to tell the police, so I strangled her. Then I cut off her hair because she wouldn't stop looking at me. Just like the other one.'

Detective Chief Superintendent Oldman stood up and said, 'Edward Leslie Dunford, you are charged first that on or about Tuesday 17 December 1974, you did rape and then murder Mrs Mandy Denizili of Flat 5, 28 Blenheim Road, Wakefield. Second, you are charged that on or about Saturday 21 December 1974, you did rape and then murder Mrs Paula Garland of 11 Brunt Street, Castleford.'

Silence.

Detective Superintendent Noble and Sandy stood up.

The three men left the room and I think I began to cry.

Sometime later a policeman opened the door and took me down the yellow corridor.

Through the open door to another room I saw Scotch Clare from two doors down.

She looked up at me, her mouth open.

The policeman took me down another yellow corridor to a stone cell.

Above the door was a noose.

'Inside.'

I did as I was told.

On the floor of the cell was a paper cup filled with tea and a paper plate with a quarter of a pork pie on it.

He shut the door.

Everything was black.

I sat down on the floor, kicking over the tea.

I found the pork pie and began to nibble at it.

I closed my eyes.

Sometime later two policemen opened the door and threw a bundle of clothes and a pair of shoes into the cell.

'Put these on.'

I did as I was told.

They were my own clothes and shoes, smelling of piss and covered in mud.

'Hands behind your back.'

I did as I was told.

One of the policemen came into the cell and put a pair of handcuffs on me.

'Hood him.'

The policeman put a blanket over my head.

'Move.'

The policeman pushed me in the back.

I began to walk.

I was suddenly gripped under each arm and led along. Through the blanket I could see only yellow.

'Let me at him. I haven't fucking touched him yet.'

'Get him out of here.'

Then I hit some doors with my head and I was outside.

I fell over.

They picked me up.

I thought I was inside a van.

I heard doors slam and an engine start.

I was still under the blanket but in the back of a van with maybe two or three other men.

'Fucking bastard.'

'Don't be going to sleep under there.'

I was punched in the head.

'Don't worry, I'll make bloody sure of that.'

'Fucking bastard.'

Another punch.

'Keep your fucking head up.'

'Fucking bastard.'

I could smell cigarette smoke.

'He fucking coughed, I don't believe it.'

'I know, fucking bastard.'

I was kicked on the shin.

'We should stretch his fucking balls.'

'Fucking rapist bastard.'

I froze.

'Do what we did to that other one.'

'Aye, fucking bastards the pair of them.'

The back of my head hit the side of the van.

'Fucking bastard!'

'What about here?'

I heard banging inside the van.

'Take the fucking bastard's hood off.'

'Here?'

The van suddenly seemed colder.

They took off the blanket.

I was alone with Moustache, Grey, and Brown.

The doors to the back of the van were open.

It looked like dawn outside.

'Uncuff the fucking bastard.'

Moustache pulled me forward by the hair and took the hand-cuffs off.

I could see flat brown fields flying past.

'Kneel him over here,' said Brown.

Moustache and Grey pulled me to the doors of the van, kneeling me down with my back to the open brown fields.

Brown crouched down in front of me.

'This is it.'

He took out a revolver.

'Open your mouth.'

I saw Paula lying naked face down on her bed, her cunt and arse bleeding, her hair all gone.

'Open your mouth!'

I opened my mouth.

He shoved the muzzle into my mouth.

'I'm going to blow your fucking head off.'

I closed my eyes.

There was a click.

I opened my eyes.

He took the gun out of my mouth.

'There's something fucking up with this one,' he laughed.

'Lucky fucking bastard,' said Moustache.

'Get it done,' said Grey.

'I'll try again.'

I could feel the air, the cold, the fields behind me.

'Open your mouth.'

I saw Paula lying naked face down on her bed, her cunt and arse bleeding, her hair all gone.

I opened my mouth.

Brown shoved the muzzle back into my mouth.

I closed my eyes.

There was a click.

'Fucking bastard must have a charmed life.'

I opened my eyes.

He took the gun out of my mouth.

'Third time lucky, eh?'

'Fuck that,' said Moustache, grabbing the revolver and pushing Brown away.

He had the gun by the muzzle, raising it over his head.

I saw Paula lying naked face down on her bed, her cunt and arse bleeding, her hair all gone.

He brought the gun down upon my head:

'THIS IS THE NORTH. WE DO WHAT WE WANT!'

I fell backwards seeing Paula lying naked on the road, her cunt and arse bleeding, her hair all gone.

Chapter 11

We were jumping into a river holding hands.

The water was cold.

I let go of her hand.

I opened my eyes.

It felt like a morning.

I was lying at the side of a road in the rain and Paula was dead.

I sat up, my head splitting, my body numb.

A man was getting out of a car further up the road.

I looked out across empty brown fields and tried to stand.

The man came running towards me.

'I almost bloody killed you!'

'Where am I?'

'What the hell happened to you?'

A woman was standing by the passenger door of the car, looking down the road at us.

'I was in an accident. Where am I?'

'Doncaster Road. Do you want us to call an ambulance or something?'

'No.'

'The police?'

'No.'

'You don't look so good.'

'Could you give me a lift?'

The man looked back at the woman standing by the car. 'Where to?'

'Do you know the Redbeck Cafe, on the way into Wakefield?'

'Yeah,' he said, looking from me to the car and back again. 'OK.'

'Thanks.'

We walked slowly back down the road to the car.

I got in the back.

The woman was sitting in the front, looking straight ahead. She had blonde hair the same shade as Paula's, only longer.

'He's been in an accident. We're going to drop him down the road,' said the man to the woman, starting the engine.

The clock in the front said six.

'Excuse me,' I said. 'What day is it?'

'Monday,' said the woman, not turning round.

I stared out at the empty brown fields.

Monday 23 December 1974.

'So tomorrow's Christmas Eve then?'

'Yes,' she said.

The man was looking at me in his rearview mirror.

I turned back to the empty brown fields.

'This OK?' asked the man, pulling over by the Redbeck.

'Yeah. Thanks.'

'You sure you don't want a doctor or anything?'

'I'm sure, thanks,' I said, getting out.

'Bye then,' said the man.

'Bye and thanks very much,' I said, shutting the door.

The woman was still looking straight ahead as they drove away.

I walked across the car park, through the holes filled with muddy rain water and lorry oil, round the back to the motel rooms.

The door to Room 27 was open a crack.

I stood before the door listening.

Silence.

I pushed open the door.

Sergeant Fraser, in uniform, was asleep on a blanket of papers and folders, tapes and photographs.

I closed the door.

He opened his eyes, looked up, then stood up.

'Fuck,' he said, looking at his watch.

'Yeah.'

He stared at me.

'Fuck.'

'Yeah.'

He went over to the sink and began to run some water.

'You'd better sit down,' he said, leaving the sink to tip over the base of the bed.

I walked across the papers and the files, the photos and the maps, and sat down on the bare base of the bed.

'What are you doing here?'

'I'm going to be suspended.'

'What the fuck did you do?'

'Know you.'

'So?'

'So I don't want to be suspended.'

I could hear the rain coming down hard outside, lorries reversing and parking, their drivers running for cover.

'How did you find this place?'

'I'm a policeman.'

'Really?' I said, holding my head.

'Yeah, really,' said Sergeant Fraser, taking off his jacket and rolling up his sleeves.

'Have you been here before?'

'No. Why?'

'No reason,' I said.

Fraser soaked the only towel in the sink, wrung it out, and tossed it across to me.

I put it to my face, ran it through my hair.

It came away the colour of rust.

'I didn't do it.'

'I didn't ask.'

Fraser picked up a grey bedsheet and began tearing off strips.

'Why'd they let me go?'

'I don't know.'

The room was going black, Fraser's shirt grey.

I stood up.

'Sit down.'

'It was Foster, wasn't it?'

'Sit down.'

'It was Don Foster, I fucking know it.'

'Eddie . . .'

'They fucking know it, don't they?'

'Why Foster?'

I picked up a fistful of foolscap. 'Because he's the link in all this shit.'

'You think Foster killed Clare Kemplay?'

'Yeah.'

'Why?'

'Why not?'

'Bollocks. And Jeanette Garland and Susan Ridyard?'

'Yeah.'

'And Mandy Wymer and Paula Garland?'

'Yeah.'

'So why stop there? What about Sandra Rivett? Maybe it wasn't Lucan after all, maybe it was Don Foster. And what about the bomb in Birmingham?'

'Fuck off. She's dead. They're all dead.'

'No but why? Why Don Foster? You haven't given me a single fucking reason.'

I sat back down on the bed with my head in my hands, the room black, nothing making sense.

Fraser handed me two strips of grey bedsheet.

I wrapped the strips around my right hand and pulled tight.

'They were lovers.'

'So?'

'I have to see him,' I said.

'You're going to accuse him?'

'There are things I need to ask him. Things only he knows.'

Fraser picked up his jacket. 'I'll drive you.'

'You'll be suspended.'

'I told you, I'm going to be suspended anyway.'

'Just give me the keys.'

'Why should I?'

'Because you're all I've got.'

'Then you're fucked.'

'Yeah. So let's leave it at me.'

He looked like he was going to puke, but tossed me his keys.

'Thanks.'

'Don't mention it.'

I went over to the sink and rinsed the old blood off my face.

'Did you see BJ?' I asked.

'No.'

'You didn't go to the flat?'

'I went to the flat.'

'And?'

'And he's either done a runner or been nicked. Fuck knows which.'

I heard dogs barking and men screaming.

'I should phone my mother,' I said.

Sergeant Fraser looked up. 'What?'

I was standing at the door, his keys in my hand. 'Which one is it?'

'The yellow Maxi,' he said.

I opened the door. 'Bye then.'

'Bye.'

'Thanks,' I said, like I'd never see him ever again.

I closed the door to Room 27 and walked across the car park to his dirty yellow Maxi, parked between two Findus lorries.

I pulled out of the Redbeck and switched on the radio: the IRA had blown up Harrods, Mr Heath had missed a bomb by minutes, Aston Martin was going bust, Lucan had been spotted in Rhodesia, and there was a new Mastermind.

It was going up to eight as I parked beside the high walls of Trinity View.

I got out of the car and walked up to the gates.

They were open, the white lights on the tree still on.

I looked up the drive, across the lawn.

'Fuck!' I shouted aloud, running up the drive.

Halfway up, a Rover had hit the back of a Jaguar.

I cut across the grass, slipping in the cold dew.

Mrs Foster, in a fur coat, was bent over something on the lawn by the front door.

She was screaming.

I made a grab for her, my arms around her.

She lashed out in every direction with every available limb as I tried to push her back, back towards the house, back from whatever was on the lawn.

And then I got a look at him, a good look:

Fat and white, trussed with a length of black flex that ran round his neck and bound his hands behind him, in a pair of soiled white underpants, his hair all gone, his scalp red raw.

'No, no, no,' Mrs Foster was screaming.

Her husband's eyes were wide open.

Mrs Foster, the fur coat streaked black with rain, made another rush for the body.

I blocked her hard, still staring down at Donald Foster, at the white flabby legs running in mud, at the knees smeared in blood, at the triangular burns on his back, at the tender head.

'Get inside,' I shouted, holding her tight, pushing her back through the front door.

'No, cover him.'

'Mrs Foster, please . . .'

'Please cover him!' she cried, thrashing out of her coat.

We were inside the house at the foot of the staircase.

I pushed her down on to the bottom stair.

'Wait here.'

I took the fur coat and walked back outside.

I draped the damp coat over Donald Foster.

I went back inside.

Mrs Foster was still sat on the bottom step.

I poured two glasses of Scotch from a crystal decanter in the living room.

'Where were you?' I handed her a large glass.

'With Johnny.'

'Where's Johnny now?'

'I don't know.'

'Who did this?'

She looked up. 'I don't know.'

'Johnny?'

'God no.'

'So who did?'

'I told you, I don't know.'

'Who did you hit that night on the Dewsbury Road?'

'What?'

'Who did you hit on the Dewsbury Road?'

'Why?'

'Tell me.'

'You tell me why, why does it matter now?'

Falling, grasping, clutching. Like the dead were living and the living dead, saying: 'Because I think whoever it was you hit, I think they killed Clare Kemplay, and whoever killed Clare, they killed Susan Ridyard, and whoever that was, they killed Jeanette Garland.'

'Jeanette Garland?'

'Yeah.'

Her eagle eyes had suddenly flown and I was staring into big black panda eyes, full of tears and secrets, secrets she couldn't keep.

I pointed outside. 'Was it him?'

'No, god no.'

'So who was it?'

'I don't know.' Her mouth and hands were trembling.

'You know.'

The glass was loose in her hands, tipping whisky over her dress and the stairs. 'I don't know.'

'Yes you do,' I hissed and looked back at the body, framed in the doorway with that huge fucking Christmas tree.

I clenched my fist as best I could and turned back round, bringing up my arm.

'Tell me!'

'Don't fucking touch her!'

Johnny Kelly was standing at the top of the stairs, covered in blood and mud, a hammer in his good hand.

Patricia Foster, miles from home, didn't even glance round.

I edged back into the doorway. 'You killed him?'

'He killed our Paula and Jeanie.'

Wishing he was right, knowing he was wrong, telling him, 'No he didn't.'

'The fuck you know about it?' Kelly stepped down on to the stairs.

'Did you kill him?'

He was coming down the stairs, staring straight at me, tears in his eyes and on his cheeks, a hammer in his hand.

I took another step back, seeing way too fucking much in those tears.

'I know you didn't do it.'

He kept coming, the tears too.

'Johnny, I know you've done some bad things, some terrible things, but I know you didn't do this.'

He stopped at the foot of the stairs, the hammer an inch from Mrs Foster's hair.

I walked towards him.

He dropped the hammer.

I went over and picked it up, wiping it with a dirty grey handkerchief like all the bad guys and dirty cops on *Kojak.*

Kelly was staring down at her hair.

I dropped the hammer.

He started stroking her hair, pulling it rougher and rougher, someone else's blood tangling and knotting the curls.

She didn't flinch.

I pulled him away.

I didn't want to know any more; I wanted to buy some drugs, buy some drink, and get the fuck out of there.

He looked me in the eye and said, 'You should get out of here.'

But I couldn't. 'You too,' I said.

'They'll kill you.'

'Johnny,' I said, taking him by the shoulder. 'Who was it you hit on the Dewsbury Road?'

'They'll kill you. You'll be next.'

'Who was it?' I pushed him back against the wall.

He said nothing.

'You know who did it don't you, you know who killed Jeanette and the other two?'

He pointed outside. 'Him.'

I hit Kelly hard, a shot of sheer pain shooting stars to my eyes.

The star of Rugby League fell back on to the shagpile. 'Fuck.'

'No. You fuck off.' I was bending over him, champing to crack open his skull and scoop out all his dirty little fucking secrets.

He lay on the floor at her feet, looking up like he was ten bloody years old, Mrs Foster rocking back and forth like it was all on someone else's TV.

'Tell me!'

'It was him,' he whimpered.

'You're a fucking liar.' I reached behind me, grabbing the hammer.

Kelly slid out from between my legs, crawling through a patch of whisky towards the front door.

'You fucking wish it was him.'

'No.'

I grabbed him by his collar, twisting his face back round into mine. 'You want it to be him. Want it to be that easy.'

'It was him, it was him.'

'It wasn't, you know it wasn't.'

'No.'

'You want your bloody vengeance, then tell me who the fuck it was that night.'

'No, no, no.'

'You're not going to do anything about it, so fucking tell me or I'll smash your fucking skull in.'

He was pushing my face away with his hands. 'It's over.'

'You want it to be him so it's over. But you know it's not over,' I screamed, smashing the hammer into the side of the stairs.

She was sobbing.

He was sobbing.

I was sobbing.

'It'll never be over until you tell me who you fucking hit.'

'No!'

'It's not over.'

'No!'

'It's not over.'

'No!'

'It's not over, Johnny.'

He was coughing tears and bile. 'It is.'

'Tell me, you piece of shit.'

'I can't.'

I saw the moon in the day, the sun in the night, me fucking her, her fucking him, Jeanette's face on every body.

I had him by the throat and hair, the hammer in my bandaged hand. 'You fucked your sister.'

'No.'

'You were Jeanette's fucking father, weren't you?'

'No!'

'You were her father.'

His lips were moving, bubbles of bloody spit bursting on them.

I leant close into his face.

Behind me, she said, 'George Marsh.'

I span round, reaching out and pulling her into us. 'Say again.'

'George Marsh,' she whispered.

'What about him?'

'On the Dewsbury Road. It was George Marsh.'

'George Marsh?'

'One of Donny's foremen.'

'*Under those beautiful new carpets, between the cracks and the stones.*'

'Where is he?'

'I don't know.'

I let go of them and stood up, the hall suddenly much bigger and lighter.

I closed my eyes.

I heard the hammer drop, Kelly's teeth chattering, and then everything was small and dark again.

I went over to the phone and took out the telephone directory. I went to the Ms and the Marshes and found the G. Marshes. There was one in Netherton at 16 Maple Well Drive. The telephone number was 3657. I closed the directory.

I picked up a soft floral phonebook and turned to the Ms.

In fountain pen, *George 3657.*

Bingo.

I closed the book.

Johnny Kelly had his head in his hands.

Mrs Foster was staring up at me.

'*Under those beautiful new houses, between the cracks and the stones.*'

'How long did you know?'

The eagle eyes were back. 'I didn't,' she said.

'Liar.'

Mrs Patricia Foster swallowed, 'What about us?'

'What about you?'

'What are you going to do with us?'

'Pray God forgives the fucking lot of you.'

I walked towards the front door and Donald Foster's body.

'Where are you going?'

'To finish it.'

Johnny Kelly looked up, bloody fingerprints on his face. 'You're too late.'

I left the door open.

'Under those beautiful new carpets, between the cracks and the stones.'

I drove Fraser's Maxi back into Wakefield and out through Horbury, the rain beginning to sleet.

I sang along to Christmas songs on Radio 2 and changed to Radio 3 to avoid the News at Ten, listening to England lose the Ashes down under instead, shouting out my own news at ten:

Don Foster dead.

Two fucking killers, maybe three.

Me next?

Counting the killers.

Pushing the Maxi out Netherton way, the sleet now suddenly rain again.

Counting the dead.

Tasting gun metal, smelling my own shit.

Dogs barking, men screaming.

Paula dead.

There were things I had to do, things I must finish.

'Under those beautiful new carpets, between the cracks and the stones.'

I asked in Netherton Post Office and an old woman who didn't work there told me where Maple Well Drive was.

Number 16 was a bungalow like the rest of the street, much like Enid Sheard's, much like the Goldthorpe's. A neat little garden with a low hedge and a bird table.

Whatever George Marsh had done, it hadn't been here.

I opened the little black metal gate and walked up the path. I could see TV pictures through the nets.

I knocked on the glass door, the air making me gyp.

A chubby woman with grey permed hair and a tea-towel opened the door.

'Mrs Marsh?'

'Yes?'

'Mrs George Marsh?'

'Yes?'

I pushed the door hard back into her face.

'What the bloody hell?' She fell back on her arse into the house.

I barged in over the Wellington boots and the gardening shoes. 'Where is he?'

She had the tea-towel over her face.

'Where is he?'

'I haven't seen him.' She was trying to stand.

I slapped her hard across her face.

She fell back down.

'Where is he?'

'I haven't seen him.'

The hard-faced bitch was wide-eyed, thinking about some tears.

I raised my hand again. 'Where?'

'What did he do?' There was a gash above her eye and her lower lip was already swelling.

'You know.'

She smiled, a pinched little fucking smile.

'Tell me where.'

She lay there on top of the shoes and the umbrellas looking straight back up into my face, her dirty mouth in a half-open smile like we were thinking about having a fuck.

'Where?'

'The shed, up on the allotments.'

I knew then what I would find.

'Where is it?'

She was still smiling. She knew what I would find.

'Where?'

She raised up the tea-towel. 'I can't . . .'

'Show me,' I hissed, grabbing her by the arm.

'No!'

I pulled her up on her feet.

'No!'

I swung the door back.

'No!'

I dragged her down the path, her scalp red raw beneath her tight grey perm.

'No!'

'Which way?' I said at the gate.

'No, no, no.'

'Which fucking way?' I tightened my grip.

She spun round, looking back and beyond the bungalow.

I pushed her through the gate and marched her round the back of Maple Well Drive.

There was an empty brown field behind the bungalows, rising steeply up into the dirty white sky. There was a gate in a wall and a tractor path and, where the field met the sky, I could see a row of black sheds.

'No!'

I pulled her off the road and pushed her up against the dry stone wall.

'No, no, no.'

'Shut your bloody mouth you fucking bitch.' I gripped her mouth in my left hand, making a fish head of her face.

She was shaking but there were no tears.

'Is he up there?'

She looked straight at me, then nodded once.

'If he isn't, or if he hears us coming, I'm going to fucking do you, you understand?'

She was looking straight at me, again she nodded just once.

I let go of her mouth, make-up and lipstick on my fingers.

She stood against the stone wall, not moving.

I took her by the arm and pushed her through the gate.

She stared up at the black line of sheds.

'Move,' I said, shoving her in the back.

We started up the tractor path, its trenches full of black water, the air stinking of animal shit.

She stumbled, she fell, she got back up.

I looked back down at Netherton, the same as Ossett, the same as anywhere.

I saw its bungalows and terraces, its shops and its garage.

She stumbled, she fell, she got back up.

I saw it all.

I saw a white van bumping up this path, throwing its little cargo around in the back.

I saw a white van bumping back down, its little cargo silent and still.

I saw Mrs Marsh at her kitchen sink, that fucking tea-towel in her hand, watching that van coming and going.

She stumbled, she fell, she got back up.

We were almost at the top of the hill, almost at the sheds. They looked like a stone-age village, built from the mud.

'Which one's his?'

She pointed to the end one, at a patchwork of tarpaulin and fertiliser sacks, corrugated iron and house bricks.

I went ahead, dragging her along behind me.

'This one,' I whispered, pointing at a black wooden door with a cement sack for a window.

She nodded.

'Open it.'

She pulled back the door.

I shoved her inside.

There was a work-bench and tools, bags of fertiliser and cement stacked up, plant pots and feed trays. Empty plastic sacks covered the floor.

It stank of the earth.

'Where is he?'

Mrs Marsh was giggling, the tea-towel up over her nose and mouth.

I spun round and punched her hard through the tea-towel.

She shrieked and howled and fell to her knees.

I grabbed some grey perm and dragged her over to the work-bench, forcing her cheek into the wood.

'Ah, ha-ha-ha. Ah, ha-ha-ha.'

She was laughing and screaming, her whole body shaking, one hand flailing through the plastic sacks upon the floor, the other squeezing her skirt up into her cunt.

I picked up some kind of chisel or wallpaper scraper.

'Where is he?'

'Mmm, ha-ha-ha. Mmm, ha-ha-ha.'

Her screams were a hum, her giggles rationed.

'Where is he?' I put the chisel to her flabby throat.

'Ah, ha-ha-ha. Ah, ha-ha-ha.'

Again she began to kick out, thrashing through the plastic sacks with her knees and feet.

I looked down through the sacks and the bags and saw a piece of thick muddy rope.

I let go of her face and pushed her away.

I kicked away the sacks and found a manhole cover threaded through like a giant metal button with the dirty black rope.

I coiled the rope around my good and bad hands and pulled up the manhole cover, swinging it to the side.

Mrs Marsh was sat on her arse giggling under the bench, drumming her heels in hysterics.

I peered into the hole, into a narrow stone shaft with a metal ladder leading down into a faint light some fifty odd feet below.

It was some kind of drainage or ventilation shaft to a mine.

'He down there?'

She drummed her feet up and down faster and faster, blood still running down from her nose into her mouth, suddenly spreading her legs and rubbing the tea-towel over the top of her tan tights and ruby red knickers.

I reached under the bench and dragged her out by her ankles. I pulled her over on to her stomach and sat astride her arse.

'Ah, ha-ha-ha. Ah, ha-ha-ha.'

I reached up and took some rope from the bench. I hooked it round her neck and then ran it down round her wrists, finally knotting it twice round the leg of the bench.

Mrs Marsh had pissed herself.

I looked back down the shaft, turned round and put one foot into the dark.

I eased myself down into the shaft, the metal ladder cold and wet, the brick walls slippery against my sides.

Down I went, ten feet down.

I could hear the faint sound of running water beneath Mrs Marsh's shrieks and screams.

Down I went, twenty feet down.

A circle of grey light and madness above.

Down I went, thirty feet down, the laughter and the cries dying with the descent.

I could sense water below, picturing mine shafts sunk with black water and open-mouthed bodies.

Down I went towards the light, not looking up, certain only that I was just going down.

Suddenly one of the sides to the shaft was gone and I was there in the light.

I twisted round, looking into the yellow mouth of a horizontal passage leading off to my right.

I went a little way further down and then turned, putting my elbows on to the mouth of the hole.

I pulled myself up into the light and crawled on to the shelf. The light was bright, the tunnel narrow and stretching off.

Unable to stand, I forced my belly and elbows across the rough bricks, along the passage towards the source of the light.

I was sweating and tired and dying to stand.

I kept on crawling, thinking of feet and then miles, all distance lost.

Suddenly the ceiling went up and I got to my knees, shuffling along, thinking of mountains of dirt piled on top of my head, until my knees and shins were raw and rebelled.

I could hear things moving in the dim light, mice or rats, children's feet.

I put out my hand into the shale and the slime and brought back a shoe; a child's sandal.

I lay on the bricks in the dust and the dirt and fought back the tears, stuck with the shoe, unable to throw it, unable to leave it.

I stood in a stoop and began to move again, banging my back on girders and beams, making a yard here, a foot there.

And then the air changed and the sound of water was gone and I could smell death and hear her moaning.

The ceiling went up again and there were more wooden beams to bang my head on and then I turned a corner at an old fall of rock and there I was.

I stood upright in the mouth of a big tunnel in the glare of ten Davy lamps, panting and sweating and thirsty as fuck, trying to take it all in.

Santa's bloody grotto.

I dropped the shoe, tears streaking through my dirty face.

The tunnel had been bricked up about fifteen feet ahead, the bricks painted blue with white clouds, the floor covered in sacking and white feathers.

Against the two side walls were ten or so thin mirrors all lined up in a row.

Christmas tree angels and fairies and stars hung from the beams, all shining in the glow of the lamps.

There were boxes and there were bags, there were clothes and there were tools.

There were cameras and there were lights, there were tape recorders and there were tapes.

And, beneath the blue wall at the end of the room, lying under some bloody sacking, there was George Marsh.

On a bed of dead red roses.

I walked across the blanket of feathers towards him.

He turned into the light, his eyes holes, his mouth open, his face a mask of red and black blood.

Marsh opened and closed his mouth, bubbles of blood bursting and popping, the howl of a dying dog coming up from within the pit of his belly.

I bent down and looked into the holes from where his eyes had once seen, into the mouth from where his tongue had once spoken, and spat a little piece of me.

I stood up and pulled back the sacking.

George Marsh was naked and dying.

His torso was purple, green, and black, smeared with shit, mud, and blood, burnt.

His cock and balls were gone, flaps of loose skin and pooled blood.

He was twitching and reached up to me, his little finger and thumb all he had left.

I stood up, kicking the blanket back at him.

He lay there with his head raised, praying for an end, the low moan of a man calling for death filling the cavern.

I went to the bags and to the boxes, tipping them over, spilling out clothes and tinsel, baubles and knives, paper crowns and giant needles, looking for books, looking for words.

I found pictures.

Boxes of them.

Schoolgirl photographs, head-shots of wide white smiles and big blue eyes, yellow hair and pink skin.

And then I saw it all again.

Black and white shots of Jeanette and Susan, dirty knees pulled up in corners, tiny hands across shut eyes, big white flashes filling up the room.

The adult smiles and the child's eyes, dirty knees in angel suits, tiny hands across bloody holes, big white laughs filling up the room.

I saw a man in a paper crown and nothing else, fucking little girls underground.

I saw his wife stitching angel suits, kissing them better.

I saw a halfwit Polack boy, stealing photos and developing more.

I saw men building houses, watching little girls playing out across the road, taking their photos and making their notes, building new houses next to the old.

And then I was staring down at George Marsh again, the Gaffer, dying in agony on his bed of dead red roses.

'*George Marsh. Very nice man.*'

But it wasn't enough.

I saw Johnny Kelly, a hammer in his hand, a job half done.

It still wasn't enough.

I saw a man wrapped in paper and plans, consumed by dark visions of angels, drawing houses made out of swans, pleading for silence.

And it still wasn't enough.

I saw the same man crouched down on his arches in a dim corner, screaming do this for me George, because I WANT MORE AND I WANT IT NOW.

I saw John Dawson.

And it was too much, much too much.

I fled from the room back down the tunnel, stooping then crawling, listening for water and the shaft to the shed, his screams filling the dark, their screams my head:

'*There was a lovely view before they put them new houses up.*'

I came to the ladder and pulled myself up, scraping my back on the lip to the light.

Up I went, up.

I got to the top and hauled myself back into the shed.

She was still there, trussed on her belly and tied to the bench.

I lay on the plastic sacks, panting and sweating and running on fear.

She smiled at me, drool down her chin, piss on her tights.

I grabbed a knife from the bench and cut through the ropes.

I pushed her over to the shaft and pulled her head back by her perm, the knife at her throat.

'You're going back down there.'

I turned her around and kicked her legs into the void.

'You can climb or fall. I don't give a fuck.'

She put a foot upon a rung and began to climb down, her eyes on mine.

'Until death do you part,' I spat after her.

Her eyes shone up from the dark, not blinking.

I turned round, picked up the thick black rope, and swung the manhole cover back over the hole.

I grabbed a bag of cement and hauled it over on to the manhole, and then another, and another, and another.

Then I took bags of fertiliser and put them on top of the bags of cement.

I sat on the bags and felt my legs and feet go cold.

I got up and picked a padlock and a key off the work-bench.

I got up and went out of the shed. I closed the door and locked it with the padlock.

I ran down the field, throwing the key off into the mud.

The door to Number 16 was still ajar, *Crown Court* on the TV.

I went inside and took a shit.

I turned off the TV.

I sat on their sofa and thought about Paula.

Then I went through their rooms and all of their drawers.

I found a shotgun in the wardrobe and boxes of shells. I wrapped it in a bin bag and went out to the car. I put the shotgun and the shells in the boot of the Maxi.

I went back to the bungalow and had a last look around, then I locked the door and went down the path.

I stood by the wall and looked up at the black row of sheds, the rain on my face, me covered in mud.

I got in the car and drove away.

4 LUV.
All for love.

Shangrila, raindrops falling from its gutters, crouched alone against the worn grey sky.

I parked behind another dirty hedge on another empty road and walked up another sad drive.

It was sleeting and I wondered again if it made a blind bit of difference to the giant orange fish in the pond and I knew George Marsh was suffering and that Don Foster must have suffered too and I didn't know how that made me feel.

I wanted to go and see those big bright fish, but I kept on walking.

There were no cars in the drive, just two wet pints of milk sitting on the doorstep in a wire-frame basket.

I felt sick and scared.

I looked down.

I had a shotgun in my arms.

I pressed the doorbell and listened to the chimes echo through Shangrila, thinking of George Marsh's bloody cock and Don Foster's bloody knees.

There was no answer.

I pressed the doorbell again and started knocking with the butt of the gun.

Still no answer.

I tried the door.

It was open.

I went inside.

'Hello?'

The house was cold and almost quiet.

I stood in the hallway and said again, 'Hello?'

There was a low hissing noise followed by a repeated dull click.

I turned left into a large white living room.

Above an unused fireplace there was an enlarged black and white photograph of a swan taking off from a lake.

She wasn't alone:

On every table, on every shelf, on every windowsill, wooden swans, glass swans, and china swans.

Swans in flight, swans asleep, and two giant swans kissing, their necks and bills forming a big love-heart.

Two swans swimming.

Bingo.

Even down to the matchboxes above the empty fireplace.

I stood staring at the swans, listening to the hissing and the clicking.

The room was freezing.

I walked over to a big wooden box, leaving muddy footprints on the cream carpet. I put down the shotgun and lifted up the lid of the box and picked the needle off the record. It was Mahler.

Songs for Dead Children.

I turned around suddenly, looking out across the lawn, thinking I could hear a car coming up the drive.

It was just the wind.

I went over to the window and stood looking down at the hedge.

There was something down there, something in the garden.

For a moment, I thought I could see a brown-haired gypsy girl sitting under the hedge, barefoot with twigs in her hair.

I closed my eyes, opened them, and she was gone.

I could hear a faint drumming sound.

I stepped back on to a deep cream rug, kicking a glass that was already lying on its side in a damp stain. I picked it up and placed it on a swan coaster on a glass coffee table, next to a newspaper.

It was today's newspaper, my newspaper.

Two huge headlines, two days before Christmas:

RL STAR'S SISTER MURDERED.

COUNCILLOR RESIGNS.

Two faces, two sets of dark newsprint eyes staring up at me.

Two stories, by Jack fucking Whitehead and George Greaves.

I picked up the paper, sat down on a big cream sofa, and read the news:

The body of Mrs Paula Garland was found by police at her Castleford home early Sunday morning, after neighbours reported hearing screams.

Mrs Garland, thirty-two, was the sister of Wakefield Trinity forward Johnny Kelly. In 1969, Mrs Garland's daughter Jeanette, aged eight, disappeared on her way home from school and, despite a massive police hunt, has never been found. Two years later, in 1971, Mrs Garland's husband Geoff committed suicide.

Police sources told this correspondent that they are treating Mrs Garland's death as murder and a number of people are believed to be helping police with their enquiries. A news conference has been scheduled for early Monday morning.

Johnny Kelly, twenty-eight, was unavailable for comment.

The dark newsprint eyes, Paula not smiling, looking already dead.

William Shaw, the Labour leader and Chairman of the new Wakefield Metropolitan District Council, resigned on Sunday in a move that shocked the city.

In a brief statement, Shaw, fifty-eight, cited increasing ill-health as the reason behind his decision.

Shaw, the older brother of the Home Office Minister of State Robert Shaw, entered Labour politics through the Transport and General Workers' Union. He rose to be a regional organiser and represented the T.G.W.U. on the National Executive Committee of the Labour Party.

A former Alderman and active for many years in West Riding politics, Shaw was, however, a leading advocate of Local Government reform and had been a member of the Redcliffe–Maud Committee.

Shaw's election as Chairman of the first Wakefield Metropolitan District Council had been widely welcomed as ensuring a smooth transition during the changeover from the old West Riding.

Local Government sources, last night, expressed consternation and dismay at the timing of Mr Shaw's resignation.

Mr Shaw is also Acting Chairman of the West Yorkshire Police Authority and it is unclear as to whether he will continue.

Home Office Minister of State Robert Shaw was unavailable for comment on his brother's resignation. Mr Shaw himself is believed to be staying with friends in France.

Two more dark newsprint eyes, Shaw not smiling, looking already dead.

Oh fucking boy.

'The Great British Public get the kind of truth they deserve.'

And I'd got mine.

I put down the paper and closed my eyes.

I saw them at their typewriters, Jack and George, stinking of Scotch, knowing their secrets, telling their lies.

I saw Hadden, reading their lies, knowing their secrets, pouring their Scotch.

I wanted to sleep for a thousand years, to wake up when their like were gone, when I didn't have their dirty black ink on my fingers, in my blood.

But the fucking house wouldn't let me be, the typewriter keys mixing with that faint drumming noise, chattering in my ears, deafening my skull and bones.

I opened my eyes. On the sofa next to me were huge rolled-up papers, architect's plans.

I laid one out across the glass coffee table, over Paula and Shaw.

It was for a shopping centre, The Swan Centre.

To be built at the Hunslet and Beeston exit of the M1.

I closed my eyes again, my little gypsy girl standing in her ring of fire.

'Because of the fucking money.'

The Swan Centre:

Shaw, Dawson, Foster.

The Box Brothers wanting in.

Foster fucking with the Boxes.

Shaw and Dawson putting their various pleasures before business.

Foster as Ringmaster, trying to keep the fucking circus on the road.

Everybody out of their league, their tree, whatever.

Everybody fucked.

'Because of the fucking money.'

I stood up and walked out of the living room, into a cold and light expensive kitchen.

A tap was running into an empty stainless steel sink. I turned it off.

I could still hear the drumming.

There was a door to the back garden and another to the garage.

The drumming was coming from behind the second door.

I tried to open the door but it wouldn't.

From under the door I saw four slight trickles of water.

I tried the door again and it still wouldn't open.

I flew out the back door and ran round to the front of the house.

There were no windows built into the garage.

I tried to open the double garage doors but they wouldn't.

I went back inside through the front door.

A ring of keys was hanging by another from inside the keyhole.

I took the keys back into the kitchen and the drumming.

I tried the biggest, the smallest, and another.

The lock turned.

I opened the door and swallowed exhaust fumes.

Fuck.

A Jaguar, engine running, sat alone in the dark on the far side of the double garage.

Fuck.

I grabbed a kitchen chair and wedged the door open, kicking away a pile of damp tea-towels.

I ran across the garage, the light from the kitchen shining on two people in the front seat and a hosepipe running from the exhaust into a back window.

The car radio was on loud, Elton belting out *Goodbye Yellow Brick Road*.

I ripped the hose and more wet towels out of the exhaust pipe and tried the driver's door.

Locked.

I ran round to the passenger door, opened it and caught a lung full of carbon monoxide and Mrs Marjorie Dawson, still looking like my mother, a bloody crimson freezer bag wrapped round her head, as she fell into my knees.

I tried to push her back upright, leaning across the body to turn off the ignition.

John Dawson was slumped against the steering wheel, another freezer bag over his head, his hands bound before him.

'Here we go again. Reckless talk costs lives.'

They were both blue and dead.

Fuck.

I switched off the ignition and Elton and sat back on the garage floor, bringing Mrs Dawson with me, her head in the bag in my lap, the two of us staring up at her husband.

The architect.

John Dawson, at last and too late, a face in a plastic freezer bag.

John bloody Dawson, ever the ghost and now for real, a ghost in a plastic freezer bag.

John fucking Dawson, just his works remaining, looming and haunting, leaving me as robbed and fucked as the rest of them; robbed of the chance to ever know and fucked of the hope it might bring, sat there before him with his wife in my arms, desperate to raise the dead for just one second, desperate to raise the dead for just one word.

Silence.

I raised Mrs Dawson as gently as I could back into the Jaguar, propping her up against her husband, their freezer bag heads slumped together in more, more, fucking silence.

Fuck.

'Reckless talk costs lives.'

I took out my dirty grey handkerchief and started the dusting.

Five minutes later I closed the door to the kitchen and went back into the house.

I sat down on the sofa next to their plans, their schemes, their fucked-up dreams, and thought of my own, the shotgun in my lap.

The house was quiet.

Silent.

I stood up and walked out of the front door of Shangrila.

I drove back to the Redbeck, the radio off, the wipers squeaking like rats in the dark.

I parked in a puddle and took the black bin-bag from the boot. I limped across the car park, every limb stiff from my time underground.

I opened the door and went in out of the rain.

Room 27 was cold and no home, Sergeant Fraser long gone.

I sat on the floor with the lights off, listening to the lorries come and go, thinking of Paula and barefoot dances to *Top of the Pops* just days ago, from another age.

I thought of BJ and Jimmy Ashworth, of teenage boys crouched in the giant wardrobes of damp rooms.

I thought of the Myshkins and the Marshes, the Dawsons and the Shaws, the Fosters and the Boxes, of their lives and of their crimes.

Then I thought of men underground, of the children they stole, and of the mothers they left.

And, when I could cry no more, I thought of my own mother and I stood up.

The yellows of the lobby were brighter than ever, the stink stronger.

I picked up the receiver, dialled, and put the coin to the slot.
'Hello?'

I dropped the coin in the box. 'It's me.'

'What do you want?'

Through the double glass doors, the pool room was dead.

'To say I'm sorry.'

'What did they do to you?'

I looked round at the brown lobby chairs, looking for the old woman.

'Nothing.'

'One of them slapped me, you know.'

I could feel my eyes stinging.

'In my own house, Edward!'

'I'm sorry.'

She was crying. I could hear my sister's voice in the background. She was shouting at my mother. I stared at the names and the promises, the threats and the numbers, scribbled by the payphone.

'Please come home.'

'I can't.'

'Edward!'

'I'm really sorry, Mum.'

'Please!'

'I love you.'

I hung up.

I picked the receiver up again, tried to dial Kathryn's number, couldn't remember it, hung up again, and ran back through the rain to Room 27.

The sky above was big and blue without a cloud.

She was outside in the street, pulling a red cardigan tight around her, smiling.

Her hair was blonde and blowing in the breeze.

She reached out towards me, putting her arms around my neck and shoulders.

'I'm no angel,' she whispered into my hair.

We kissed, her tongue hard against mine.

I moved my hands down her back, crushing our bodies closer together.

The wind whipped my face with her hair.

She broke off our kiss as I came.

I woke on the floor with come in my pants.

Down to my underpants at the sink of my Redbeck room, luke-warm grey water slopping down my chest and on to the floor, wanting to go home but not wishing to be anyone's son, photo-graphs of daughters smiling in the mirror.

Crosslegged on the floor of my Redbeck room, unravelling the black bandages around my hand, stopping just short of the mess and the flesh, ripping another sheet with my teeth and binding my hand with the strips, worse wounds grinning from the wall above.

Back in my muddy clothes at the door of my Redbeck room, swallowing pills and lighting cigarettes, wanting to sleep but not wishing to dream, thinking this'll be the day that I die, pictures of Paula waving bye-bye.

Chapter 12

1 a.m.

Rock On.

Tuesday 24 December 1974.

Christmas bloody Eve.

Sleigh bells ring, are you listening?

I drove down the Barnsley Road into Wakefield, homes switching off their Christmas lights, *The Good Old Days* finished.

I had the shotgun in the boot of the car.

I crossed the Calder, went up past the market, and into the Bullring, the Cathedral trapped in the black sky up above.

Everything was dead.

I parked outside a shoe shop.

I opened the boot.

I took the shotgun out of the black bin-bag.

I loaded the gun in the boot of the car.

I put some more shells in my pocket.

I took the shotgun out of the boot.

I closed the boot of the car.

I walked across the Bullring.

On the first floor of the Strafford the lights were on, downstairs everything dark.

I opened the door and went up the stairs one at a time.

They were at the bar, whiskys and cigars all round:

Derek Box and Paul, Sergeant Craven and PC Douglas.

Rock 'n' Roll Part 2 was on the jukebox.

Barry James Anderson, his face black and blue, dancing alone in the corner.

I had a hand on the barrel, a finger on the trigger.

They looked up.

'Fucking hell,' said Paul.

'Drop the gun,' said one of the coppers.

Derek Box smiled, 'Evening, Eddie.'

I told him what he already knew. 'You killed Mandy Wymer?'

Box turned and took a big pull on a fat cigar. 'Is that right?'

'And Donald Foster?'

'So?'

'I want to know why.'

'Ever the journalist. Take a wild bloody guess, Scoop.'

'Over a fucking shopping centre?'

'Yeah, over a fucking shopping centre.'

'What the fuck did Mandy Wymer have to do with a shopping centre?'

'You want me to spell it out?'

'Yeah, spell it out.'

'No architect, no shopping centre.'

'So she knew?'

He was laughing, 'Fuck knows.'

I saw little dead girls and brand new shopping schemes, scalped dead women and the rain off your head.

I said, 'You enjoyed it.'

'I told you from the start, we'd all get what we wanted.'

'Which was?'

'Revenge and money, the perfect combination.'

'I didn't want revenge.'

'You wanted fame,' hissed Box. 'It's the same.'

There were tears running down my face, on to my lips.

'And Paula? What was that?'

Box took another big pull on his fat cigar. 'Like I said, I'm no angel . . .'

I shot him in the chest.

He fell back into Paul, air hissing out of him.

Rock 'n' Roll.

I reloaded.

I fired again and hit Paul in his side, knocking him over.

Rock 'n' Roll.

The two policemen stood there staring.

I reloaded and fired.

I hit the short one in the shoulder.

I started to reload but the tall one with the beard stepped forward.

I turned the shotgun round and swung the handle into the side of his face.

He stood there looking at me, his head to one side, a little bit of blood dripping from his ear on to his jacket.

Rock 'n' Roll.

The room was filled with smoke and the strong smell of the shotgun.

The woman behind the bar was screaming and there was blood on her blouse.

A man at a table by the window had his mouth open and his hands up.

The tall policeman was still standing, eyes blank, the short one crawling towards the toilets.

Paul was lying on his back looking up at the ceiling, opening and closing his eyes.

Derek Box was dead.

BJ had stopped dancing.

I pointed the gun at him, chest high.

I said, 'Why me?'

'You came so highly recommended.'

I dropped the gun and went back down the stairs.

I drove back to Ossett.

I parked Fraser's Maxi in a supermarket car park and walked back to Wesley Street.

The Viva was alone in the drive, my mother's house all dark and asleep beside it.

I got into the car and switched on the engine and the radio.

I lit my last cigarette and said my little prayers:

Clare, here's one for you.

Susan, here's one for you.

Jeanette, here's one for you.

Paula, they're all for you.

And the unborn.

I sat there, singing along to *The Little Drummer Boy*, with those far-off days, those days of grace, coming down.

Waiting for the blue lights.

Ninety miles an hour.

Also by David Peace and published by Serpent's Tail

Nineteen Seventy Seven

1977 – the year of punk; the year of the Yorkshire Ripper and the Silver Jubilee

No more heroes in 1977, just an urban wasteland where bad men do bad things and get way with them again and again and again.

If you thought fiction couldn't get darker than David Peace's extraordinary debut, *Nineteen Seventy Four*, then think again. *Nineteen Seventy Seven*, the second part of his Yorkshire Quartet, is one long noir nightmare. Its heroes – the half-way decent copper Bob Fraser and the burnt-out feral hack Jack Whitehead – would be considered villains in most people's books. Fraser and Whitehead have one thing in common though, they're both desperate men dangerously in love with Chapeltown whores. And as the summer moves remorselessly towards the bonfires of Jubilee Night, the killings accelerate and it seems as if Fraser and Whitehead are the only men who suspect or care that there may be more than one killer at large.

Out of the horror of true crime David Peace has fashioned a work of terrible beauty. Like James Ellroy before him, David Peace tells us the true and fearsome secret history of our times.